the ABCs of Spellcraft

the ABCs of Spellcraft

COLLECTION
VOLUME 3

JORDAN CASTILLO PRICE

First published in the United States in 2021 by JCP Books
www.JCPBooks.com

ISBN 978-1-944779-24-5

First Edition

Also available in audiobook

DEDICATION

To my family.

CONTENTS

PRESENT TENSE

DIXON

1

Winter. It's the time of year when frost etches pretty pictures on your windows and the world outside is nestled in a soft white blanket. A time when you get to snuggle up in your mismatched mittens, and no one comments on how many hot chocolates you've had—if you don't start acting too hyper, anyhow.

I've always had a fondness for winter.

And since there was snow on the ground and a nip in the air back when I first met Yuri, now I love it even more.

December is also traditionally a lucrative time for my people. While it's widely known that Spellcraft has no business in politics or religion, nowadays Christmas is pretty secular. And who wouldn't want to impress their special someone with a bespoke piece of Crafting?

My family had been working hard these past few weeks, and if my dad had his druthers, Practical Penn would be open on Christmas Eve to snag those last-minute shoppers. But our official Seer had negotiated Christmas Eve as one of his annual days off, and we didn't dare break his contract by letting Yuri fill his shoes. Or wield his paintbrush, since shoes don't really have anything to do with Spellcraft. And Rufus Clahd has unusually small feet.

Speaking of feet—there was still a bit of snow clinging to my shoes. I stomped it off on the welcome mat in my parents' vestibule, then hung up my winter coat on the nearby coat tree. It was actually more like an alien life form than a tree, with a giant ball of winter coats up top that took up half the room. I'm not sure it was even possible to dig down to the innermost layers anymore. But if you did, you'd probably find something so old it had come back in style again. Maybe more than once.

My mother hustled in as I was draping my coat over the top of the coat-ball. Once my hands were free, she enveloped me in a big, squishy hug, and greeted me with, "Where's Yuri?"

I adored the way she loved him as much as I did. "Picking up dinner."

"That's generous of him—but he really didn't need to. We've got plenty of leftovers in the fridge."

"What can I say? He insisted." I steered Mom into the living room where my dad was clicking through channels from his favorite recliner. I gave him a kiss on the top of the head, then said, "You guys've both been working so hard lately, might as well let us pamper you."

Mom settled into her chair with considerable arranging and re-arranging of her bulk—not unlike the way my cockatoo friend, Meringue, fastidiously fluffs her feathers as she's settling onto her perch. "Just so it's understood this isn't a Christmas present."

"Don't worry, Mom, it's not. He just wanted to do something nice."

"Yuri might be a Seer, but he wasn't raised in the Craft."

"Trust me—I'm awesome at explaining our traditions. And Yuri knows. No gifts."

Mom was skeptical. "Because there's nothing less meaningful than being trapped into an endless cycle of reciprocal obligation with the people you're supposed to love."

"That's just what I said." Actually, it was more like, *Spellcrafters don't do Christmas presents*. Same difference. "I think Yuri actually seemed pretty relieved."

Dad paused in his channel-changing, looked at my mom and said, "Speaking of traditions, you told Dixon about the Magi...right?"

Normally, I would've presumed this was some kind of setup for a cheesy joke—except that my mother stopped rearranging herself and said, "I thought *you* did."

"Magi?" I said. "As in the story about the guy who sold his pocket watch and the girl who cut off her hair?"

"As in the three wise men," my mother said testily.

"That sounds kind of...biblical." I could've sworn my mother thought the Bible was full of baloney. Speaking of which, I hoped Yuri remembered to grab us a nice relish tray, since I was feeling a mite peckish.

"I'm sure it's all just superstition," Dad said.

Mom gave him her patented single-squinty-eyeball look. "And since when does superstition stop a Spellcrafter from doing something? Everyone knows superstition is just the poor cousin of luck. The way my parents explained it to me, the Magi were the first Seer and Scrivener."

I supposed legends had to start somewhere. "But aren't there supposed to be three Magi?"

"The third guy was their customer," Mom said. Huh, lucky him. I wonder if they Crafted a way for his camel to go faster...or at least not spit so much. "The Magi didn't turn up for every single one of their messiah's birthdays bearing gifts...just the first one. And so, it's Scrivener tradition to surprise your partner with a small gift on your first Christmas together."

"In fact," my father said, "it's bad luck if you don't."

"And you're just telling me this now?"

Mom looked somewhat chagrined. "We meant to say something. You know how crazy it's been at the shop."

"And now I've got nothing for Yuri!" I scrambled to recall if I'd seen any stores open on our way over, but all I could think of was the car wash with the big inflatable noodle-guy flailing around in the parking lot. Was a premium car wash a good gift? Maybe for some people. But if I ran the pickup truck through the high-powered water jets, I'd likely blast off the rust that was holding on the fender. "It's too late to shop online, and all the local stores are closed."

"How about the gas station?" Mom suggested. "The one by the highway to Strangeberg is open twenty-four-seven."

Dad set down the remote, pried himself from the recliner and dusted his hands together. "Before Dixon tries to figure out how to make an air freshener and a bag of pork rinds look festive, I suggest he take a gander at The Stash."

The Stash was Dad's collection of assorted useable objects that just needed a little TLC to bring them back to their former glory. In theory, it was a great resource for someone looking to spend a lazy Sunday afternoon tinkering at the workbench. But in reality, my father just can't stand seeing anything of potential value being thrown away...and he likes gathering things a lot more than he likes fixing them. I wasn't quite sure how much longer I could count on the supermarket keeping Yuri busy—but since those places are more cutthroat on Christmas Eve than a roller derby, I hoped I could head down to the basement and find some random item that would pass for a thoughtful gift.

Unfortunately, the current state of The Stash was less than encouraging. You've seen organizing shows where a stack of plastic bins makes a roomful of stuff miraculously fit onto a closet shelf? This wasn't like that. At *all*. Cheap plastic storage containers teetered in tall stacks, and because they were all from some no-name bargain bin, most of them were cracked or warped, and none of them quite fit together.

Still, an invitation from my father to go through The Stash was not to be taken lightly. With Mom always hinting that she'd take great pleasure in throwing it all away, over the years he'd grown protective. But as I rifled through bin after cracked plastic bin, I wasn't so sure there was anything there worth protecting. Jewelry—not even the good stuff, with its faux gemstones and plastic pearls scattered like ball bearings in the bottoms of the containers. Weird kitchen gadgets you might buy on TV when insomnia struck.

Kitschy little statuettes that needed a touch-up to their paint job. And while I did know my way around a paintbrush—I've always been fond of flourishing—I strongly suspected Yuri was the wrong audience for the big-eyed baby statuettes and chubby-cheeked cherubs. He's none too keen on looking at an inanimate object only to find it looking back.

"Aha!" my father said. "This looks promising."

Too bad that exclamation could only work so many times. And since I couldn't really see Yuri being particularly enthused over a broken foot massager or a promotional backscratcher, it took me a moment to realize precisely what had been plucked from the teetering stack. "Dad...is that what I think it is?"

"No clue. I'm still trying to get the top open."

"That box you're holding...it's my favorite box!"

Dad looked skeptical. "It's just your average cardboard box, Dixon."

"You say *average* like it's a bad thing—but just look at it. Not too big, not too small, not too flimsy, and not too thick. In short, it's an absolutely perfect box. I thought it was long gone, smashed flat in some far distant recycling bin. But here it is!" I took it from his unresisting hands with a happy sigh. "In all its boxy glory."

"And even better, if you look inside, you might find something for Yuri."

After a few tries, the old cellophane tape yielded to my thumbnail, and with great eagerness, I pulled open the flap. And inside was....

Another box.

Not a cardboard box, but a wooden box. A fancy wooden box—very sturdy. Very solid. And very elaborate. My breath caught as I held it up to the fluorescent light and said, "What's this?"

"Dunno. Open it and see."

When I popped the seal, a smell wafted out that was mostly dust, but something else, too. Oranges. Cloves. And beneath it all...cedar. I opened the lid to a bunch of wood shavings. "I hope there wasn't originally a hamster in here."

"Potpourri," my father said decisively. "All the rage in the eighties. You'd be hard-pressed to find a bathroom without it."

I gave the box a dubious shake. The smell of mingled spices tickled my senses.

Dad said, "That lid's awfully plain, though, don't you think? Maybe you're holding it upside down."

I flipped it over and discovered he was right. The actual lid was very decorative. Unfortunately, there was a word etched within the carvings. A very unfortunate word.

Poopourri.

My heart sank. "Well, that's a shame. I was just thinking Yuri would actually like this. But he's never once laughed at an American pun. Not in my presence, at least."

"Maybe he's just never found the right one." Dad eyed the lettering. "Though as jokes go, this one's not so hot. But take a look at the etching. It's pretty shallow. You could add some flourishes with a wood burner and turn the word into a decorative design."

I'd only ever seen my father use the wood burning tool to singe our name onto our patio furniture in case any of our neighbors ever decided to appropriate it—which they never did—but it seemed straightforward enough. I'm no artist. Not like Yuri, with his ability to evoke a morning mist with a swipe of a half-cleaned brush or a distant horizon with a single horizontal stroke. But all Scriveners receive extensive calligraphy training, so decorative elements like cartouches and ornaments were certainly in my calligraphic vocabulary. As I considered the shape and position of the current lettering, the bowls and stems of the letters shifted in my mind's eye to become the twigs and fruits of an elaborate bouquet of holly. Seasonal, yet secular.

In other words, perfect!

YURI

2

Offering to procure dinner might have seemed altruistic on my part, but in actuality, I was leery of my ability to consume something called "pigs in a blanket." I see eye to eye with Florica Penn on many things. Her cooking is not one of them.

Braving Bay Mart on Christmas Eve, however...I was beginning to rethink that strategy.

Pinyin Bay's only supermarket sprawled at the back half of a parking lot that was never more than a quarter of the way full. But on this night, I had to park at the farthest end—and wait for someone else to finally leave, too. Calling the inside of the store chaos would be generous. More like pandemonium. Beleaguered parents scolded their children. Children threw tantrums in the aisles. And a pair of old women were having a tug-of-war over the last honey glazed ham. I managed to grab one of the cooked chickens, though I may have accidentally stomped on the foot of an obnoxious businessman to do it. Since he was braying on at the top of his lungs about a trip to Tahiti on his Bluetooth earpiece, I felt it was a stomp well-deserved.

But I could hardly show up with just a single chicken.

Normally, there were dozens of options in the deli case, both hot and cold. True, most of them contained mayonnaise—but in Dixon's family, that was considered a food group. Tonight, the line at the counter was at least a dozen people deep, and all the bins looked perilously empty.

The whole store, it seemed, was picked over. In Russia, I wouldn't have given it a second thought.

The fact that I even noticed goes to show how easy it is to be spoiled by such plenty.

I was about to admit defeat, despite the fact that not only would I be inconveniencing Dixon's mother, but would also be forced to eat one of her "specialities," when I noticed there were a few trays left toward the top of the refrigerated shelves, where most people could not reach. The first tray, cheese logs rolled in nuts, had obviously been dropped face-down, then haphazardly mashed back together through the plastic. The next was a bizarre attempt at Christmas festivity—a liverwurst Santa with sauerkraut beard—and that sauerkraut was now leaking through the plastic. There was one more tray. I expected there to be something horribly wrong with it, but the sausage was normal sausage, the cheese was normal cheese, and there was enough to feed even Dixon's father, who can consume an impressive amount of processed meat in one sitting.

Florica met me at the front door and held the tray as I hung up my coat. "Would you look at the size of that cold cut platter! Johnny will be raving about it till New Year's."

Some part of me must have been expecting criticism...but I was slowly getting used to the family's praise. Once I allowed Dixon's mother to hug me, I craned my head around the corner to greet his father and found the recliner empty. "Where is Johnny?"

Florica cut her eyes to the cellar door. "Down at the workbench with Dixon—you know how men and their toys are."

I doubted she was referring to the sorts of toys in the X-rated videos Dixon introduced me to. Good thing I did not easily blush.

She caught me by the sleeve and dragged me through the dining room, pausing only for us to relieve ourselves of the platter. "While they're both busy, come do me a favor."

She seemed so secretive about it, I half-expected her to ask me for a Seen. Magical paintings were my only currency, my main advantage. And yet, when anyone in the Penn family asked—as, occasionally, they did—it surprised me that I always felt eager to help them. Perhaps because they'd been so eager to embrace me as one of their own...and not just because I was a Seer.

I was reaching for my travel paintbox when Florica surprised me by thrusting a jar of pickles at me, whispering, "Open this."

I did.

She took the pickles, then handed me a small bottle of maraschino cherries. "Now this."

I dreaded to think what the two of them would taste like together. "You really don't need to go through any trouble—there's a pie at the bottom of the bag."

She placed her finger to her lips. "This isn't for tonight—I'm planning for the week ahead. Johnny is always complaining about how hard it is to open a jar these days. He's got all kinds of theories—like the canning equipment being on the fritz—and I'd just for once like to have our afternoon pickles and old-fashioneds in peace." She took the cherries and pressed a jar of tomato sauce into my hand. "Let's keep this between you and me."

"Fine."

She cut her eyes toward the basement. "And...since we're already in collusion...I should probably mention that a token Christmas present would not go amiss with my son."

"But Dixon told me Spellcrafters did not celebrate the holiday!"

"As a religious event, no. I don't know how it is in Russia, but around here? Christmas is mostly secular. After all, you don't see reindeer in the Bible, do you?" Florica frowned in thought. "Actually, can't say I've ever read it, so maybe you do. Most parents go through all kinds of rigmarole to make their kids think Santa Claus is real—but Dixon was always convinced we were lying about Santa being nothing more than some Handless marketing racket.

Not that I'm saying he still believes in Santa—I should hope he's figured it out by now. The point is, it wouldn't hurt to give him a little something to commemorate your first Christmas together."

Dinner was tense. I racked my brain trying to think of somewhere I could find a gift on such short notice. And while Johnny enthused over the deli platter and Florica picked the chicken clean, I could not shake the feeling that something unspoken was simmering just below the surface. Especially when we said our goodbyes, and Dixon hoisted a medium sized box onto his hip.

It was not unusual to leave his parents' house with an armful of *something*. In fact, I often suspected they used our visits as an excuse to unload a few things and carve out a bit of space in their overcrowded home. But the fact that Dixon had not remarked on it in any way? He remarks on everything...so of course, I was suspicious.

I put the key in the ignition, but did not turn it. Instead, I cut my eyes to the box and said, "What is it?"

"This?" Dixon laughed wanly. "It's just, ah...towels."

"Bath...towels?"

"Shop towels." He patted the box as if to reassure himself of its squareness. "So we don't need to get our bath towels dirty. We've got so many projects going on up in the attic, no doubt something at some point will need drying off. And no one likes a gritty bath towel."

True. And perhaps he was nervous because he had a particular home improvement project in mind—yet another one he presumed I would object to. (It wasn't so much that I disliked the idea of an indoor swimming pool, just that I doubted the house's ability to support the weight.) But when I swerved around a pothole, something shifted in his box. Something which let out a definite clunk. I cut my eyes to Dixon and he gave me a forced smile.

The American saying, pick your battles, is one which I seldom need to use with Dixon. He is cheerful. He is agreeable. And he can change his mind faster than a street in Scrivener Village changes direction. But as long as he was not bringing home yet another small animal—a toad, a snail, a hermit crab—it mattered little to me what he was protecting.

Plus, he might actually be telling the truth. In which case, I was glad whatever was thumping around was a shop towel, and not a bath towel. Though now that I thought about it, too bad it wasn't a bath towel. Because once Dixon got himself ensconced in the tub, with bubbles and candles and a good book—or even a passable one—he'd be occupied for the rest of the night. Enough time for me to find a store which was still open...and which sold something that would pass for a gift.

The bath plan did have merit. If I encouraged him to listen to some "relaxing" music (and if I turned that music up loud enough) he wouldn't even know I'd slipped away. The trick to manipulating Dixon was to not seem overly eager. It also helped that he was somehow still so enamored of my accent, he took everything I said at face value. Still, he was raised by a family with a very broad definition of the word *truth*, so I found myself rehearsing the suggestion, *How about a nice bath?* all the way home, as I trailed him across the sidewalk and up the stairs.

With my hand on the light fixture, I was just about to speak when a different light flared to life: the refrigerator light.

Aside from our bedroom and bathroom, the rest of the attic we call home is wide open, with sloped ceilings, a brick chimney, and at the far end, a large louvered window. The kitchen was more like the suggestion of a kitchen, with a salvaged sink, two dorm fridges stacked on top of one another, and a massive old microwave that turned everything to leather. Dixon was silhouetted by the light of the top fridge as he pulled out the half-gallon of milk. He unscrewed the top, met my eye, then tipped it back.

Straight from the carton, he drank. And drank.

And drank.

He drank until the plastic carton flexed empty and his eyes watered. And once he'd drained the milk dry, he smacked the empty container down on our folding card table, swiped the back of his hand across his mouth, gasped thickly, and said, "Well. That hit the spot."

I blinked stupidly. Dixon never drinks milk...not unless it is mixed with bright pink strawberry syrup, anyhow. And that concoction is mostly syrup. "You were craving...milk?"

"Yep. Sure was." He swallowed at nothing a few more times as if to hold back a belch, then gave the empty carton a shake. "Oh no. Did I drink all of it—every last drop? How can that be? And now you have no milk for your morning coffee. I'll have to go get you some more."

"Now?"

"Better now than tomorrow—Christmas morning. You know how crabby the Handless can be about working on Christmas."

Obviously, Dixon was up to something...though this is usually a pretty good bet. But if he was providing me with a good excuse to go find him a gift, I would not squander the chance. "I will go. I am very, ah, *picky* about my milk. You stay here. In case...Meringue needs you."

DIXON

3

We both cut our eyes to the cockatoo. She was already asleep with her head tucked under her wing, though at the sound of her name, she ruffled ever so slightly. Yuri turned around and headed back out the door before I could ask what on earth Meringue might need.

Perfect.

I'd known full well that Yuri would never let me venture off to the store after dark. He was convinced I had lousy night vision, and I didn't have the heart to tell him that the time I sideswiped that dumpster, I was just busy admiring the new billboard out by the strip mall—the one with the cute dancing hedgehogs. And who could blame me? They truly are adorable, one in a pearl necklace and the other in a bow tie and top hat. I wonder what kind of music they're dancing to? Those music notes floating around in the air were no help. If the mandatory recorder recital at my third grade holiday pageant taught me anything, it's that a note's position on a staff is what means something...though what that something was, I'd never quite grasped. Only that I always missed the F# in Silent Night.

I blinked. How long had I been humming that darn earworm? Long enough to wake up Meringue, who always loved to join in whenever she heard someone singing, albeit never with the same song. Her enthusiasm totally made up for her lack of musical ability.

While Meringue croaked out the theme to the channel eight weather report, I plugged in the wood burner to warm up. Good thing I was quick with my flourishing. I wasn't sure where Yuri would be likely to find milk on Christmas Eve, but Pinyin Bay is hardly a sprawling metropolis. There were several gas stations or convenience stores within ten minutes of the attic we called home, so I'd better get burning, quick.

It was hard to think of a less appealing neologism than "poopourri," but by sketching additional circles around the letter o's and p's, I could definitely camouflage the word. The other letters became vegetation, and the angularity in the letter r's worked perfectly for stylized, pointy holly leaves.

As Meringue embarked on her fifth round of the weather intro—or maybe her sixth—I began to wonder if maybe I should pick something less seasonal for my design. Yuri had actually been relieved, back when I told him Scriveners weren't big on Christmas. What if holly brought up painful memories?

I, on the other hand, primarily associated Christmas with a sense of longing. My cousin Sabina always got gifts, while I got stale Christmas cookies on sale...*after* New Year's. My parents were adamant about not falling victim to the holiday commercialism and hype. But Sabina's mom was originally Handless—at least until Sabina was born, which made things official—and Uncle Fonzo was never one to turn down an opportunity to get a present.

According to Sabina, I had nothing to be jealous about. She claimed most of the boxes under the green plastic tree contained clothes. And her parents were obligated to keep her from running around naked, so essentially, they were just boxing up something they would have given her anyway and acting like they were doing her a favor.

Even so. I'd envied the idea of decorating a tree, then waking up and finding presents underneath it Christmas morning. "Maybe Yuri and I can institute our own holiday," I told Meringue. "Something kind of pagany-nondenominational, like Yule. Actually, that's probably a real holiday to someone somewhere, but you get the gist."

In reply, she whistled the first three notes of Jingle Bells...I think. Since they're the same note, it's hard to tell.

As I imagined what sorts of activities our bespoke holiday might entail, like gifts and food and plenty of snuggling in front of a video of a fireplace, my pencil swirled and swooped around my design as I sketched on the lid. It wasn't exactly like Scribing—after all, there were no words—but my hand had taken on a life of its own and created something delightful.

I glanced up at the clock. Yuri'd been gone nearly twenty minutes. But the wood burner was nice and hot, and it scorched through the cedar like nobody's business. Whorls and loops, scallops and circles. My design pulled together in an image that was both spontaneous and intricate—beautifully balanced, with zero remaining traces of *poopourri*.

There'd be just enough time to burn a cone of incense to cover up the cozy smell of smoldering cedar. We don't generally like a smoky attic...but when Uncle Fonzo has a hankering for liver and onions and the cooking smells waft up through the stairwell, scented candles don't quite cut it. "I know it was here somewhere." I rifled through the odds-and-ends cabinet. "Unless we used the last one...."

I was head and shoulders inside the cabinet when Meringue shrilled her imitation of the smoke detector. It wasn't a very good imitation—you can totally tell it's a bird—but it's darn near as loud. While her mimicry left something to be desired, it was interesting how she'd picked up on my desire to light incense. Then again, ever since she'd gifted me with her quill, the two of us shared a tangible bond. Maybe that's why all her singing and squawking never bothers me. Even the smoke detector routine.

Which suddenly became twice as loud, when the actual smoke detector joined in.

I spun around to find something to knock out the batteries—bonking my head on the cabinet door in the process—and was baffled to find that although the cooling wood burner was nowhere near it, the poopourri box was smoking. And not just tiny little wisps and tendrils from the wood burner, either. Smoke billowed from the seam of the lid. Thick, dark smoke.

Luckily for us, we inherited a few aquatic tanks from Precious Greetings, and we keep a full bucket of tap water beside the sink so the chlorine can evaporate before we top everything off. I grabbed the bucket and flung the water toward the smoking cedar box. It struck with a giant hiss, knocking the box right off the table—and knocking Meringue off her nearby perch on the back of the chair. She fluttered up into the rafters, muttering, "Dirty Scrivener."

I grabbed a tea towel and rounded the table, swatting at a final few stubborn smoldering bits of poopourri. "Of all the luck!" Distraught, I picked up the steaming box, expecting it to be a hunk of smoking charcoal. But weirdly enough, the box didn't look too bad.

It was the contents that had caught fire, not the box itself! The fragrance oils and resins must've been phenomenally flammable, not to mention the dried flower petals and orange peels. The box might have survived intact (a bit blackened inside), but the innards were smoldering ash that disintegrated the moment they were hit by the towel. As far as I could figure, some tiny ventilation holes in the cover must've allowed the wood burner to touch the highly volatile plant matter, and thanks to the smell of the tool on the cedar, I didn't notice...not until it was *way* too late.

"What am I gonna do?" I asked Meringue. "Yuri will be back any minute. There's gotta be something around here that'll pass for potpourri." Meringue answered with another smoke alarm chirp—probably because I was really warming to my new idea. "Maybe Sticky the stick insect won't mind me borrowing some of his wood chips. And if I toss them with a little aftershave and a bag or two of chamomile tea, I bet they'll seem pretty darn potpourri-ish."

Before I went through the trouble of assembling the filling, I gave the cedar box a good once-over to make sure it was still holding together. Luckily, the inside had faired pretty well. Once I wiped out the soot, you'd hardly know that mere moments ago it was on fire. Unfortunately, when I'd doused the flames, I'd made a pretty big mess of the room. I triaged the disaster, then tossed out the burnt remains, cracked the window to let the smoke out, and scrambled to swab up all the water. It was such a wreck, I was sure Yuri would walk in on me any second. But the longer I worked, the more it seemed as if I might get everything set to rights before he came home.

No clue why it might take him so long to find milk, but I wasn't about to look a gift delay in the mouth.

Instead of just hiding the evidence of the fire, I was able to blow out all the smoke and really clean up the kitchen. Though Yuri is a minimalist, he's not exactly a neatnik. And while I might envision living in a trendy apartment plucked right from the pages of a home decorating magazine, in reality, I tend to get distracted and leave half-done projects gathering dust on most horizontal surfaces. Mopping up all that water forced me to admit that I had no intention of finishing the used jigsaw puzzle, the dusty string-art, or misshapen crocheted potholder. So, into the trash they went.

By the time I was done wiping things down and mopping things up, I'd really spruced up the place. I was admiring my work when I heard the rattle of Yuri's truck pulling up outside.

All that remained of my escapade in wood burning was the cardboard box I'd rescued from my parents' basement—my favorite box, which fortunately made it through the ordeal unscathed. Or so I thought. When I picked it up to move it out of sight, the bottom disintegrated.

My heart broke a little as shop towels dropped to my shoes. I told myself to stop being ridiculous. It was silly to be so attached to a box, even one that was the perfect size and shape. Not too big. Not too small. Not too flimsy and not too thick. Surely I could find another one just as good. I was wondering exactly where one might trace a cardboard box's origins when my gaze fell on another box—the cedar potpourri holder in the middle of the card table. And as Yuri's quiet footfalls approached from the stairwell, I realized with sudden dismay that I'd been so focused on cleaning up the fire...I'd forgotten to replace the potpourri.

YURI 4

Since drinking milk anytime after lunch has been digested has the potential to put Dixon in a coma, with any luck, he'd have fallen asleep the moment I walked out the door. That's what I was hoping, anyhow, when I realized how difficult it was to find a fitting gift for my *vozljublennyj* on Christmas Eve. Frankly, I couldn't find anything I'd even give to an acquaintance, let alone my beloved. Cheap baseball hats. Tacky bumper stickers. Shot glasses printed with lewd slogans. It seemed I would have no luck shopping at gas stations...but nothing else was open.

I was staring at an automotive display considering how much damage Dixon might do with a tire pressure gauge when the gas station door whisked open with a whirl of snow. A Handless man strode in carrying a very festive looking gift. A pair of ruddy, whining children trailed him, one on either side, a boy and a girl. The boy whined, "I don't wa-a-ant a Game Buddy, I want a Tech Box. Nobody thinks Game Buddies are cool. Except Adeline."

"Nuh-uh!" Adeline whined even louder. "If Aiden gets a Tech Box, then I want a Tech Box."

Aiden said, "The only reason we're getting Game Buddies at all is because they don't make your stupid horse game for the Tech Box."

Adeline drew such a deep breath, she bypassed red and turned a shade of mottled violet. "Joyful Pony Farm is *not* stupid! *You're* stupid!"

"And you're stupid times two!"

"*You're* stupid times two...plus infinity!" Adeline declared.

Aiden grinned triumphantly. "I know you are, but what am I?"

A high-pitched whine escaped Adeline as tears sprang to her eyes and wobbled on her lower lashes. Were American children really that sensitive? Probably. Or maybe they were just strung out on sugar. And it didn't help that the dynamic between these two played out as though it had been developing for years.

The father's response had been building up, as well. Probably for just as long. "If you two spoiled brats don't shut up, then once we bring Uncle Bob his present, Christmas is cancelled—and neither of you gets a Tech Tock or a Bling Buddy or whatever the heck it was you wanted."

Aiden and Adeline stopped squabbling, and immediately shifted from enemies to allies. "Nuh-uh!" Adeline said.

Her brother added, "You don't have the guts to tear down the tree and take back all our presents."

Never would I have dreamed of taunting my own father in such a way. Not only would he have done as he threatened, but he would have swatted me with the dismantled tree to put me in my place. This was a different country—and a different generation—so the man who'd sired Adeline and Aiden was unlikely to get away with the same type of parenting my father doled out. No matter how sorely he might wish to put his foot down.

Though maybe I could use his frustration to my advantage.

The children deployed to grab handfuls of overpriced candy from the shelves, fighting now about whether caramel was better than nougat. I took their father aside and said, "Are you prepared to listen to them arguing all night?"

"What choice have I got? If I ditch 'em on the side of the road, the missus is bound to notice."

"Abandoning them might feel good now," I agreed, "but you'd pay for it later. But what if you could prove to them you were dead serious about cancelling Christmas?"

"How do I manage that? Their mother is bonkers about Christmas, so she'd never go for it. And besides, all the presents are wrapped and waiting to go under the tree once the little darlings are asleep."

I cut my eyes to the box. "All but this one. What's inside?"

The man's brow furrowed. "I dunno, my wife does all the shopping. Some Christmasy thing for her brother. We're just on our way to drop it off."

"Sell it to me. You can replace it with a gift card when you pay for your gas and the children will be none the wiser."

It was a harebrained idea...which didn't stop the man from palming the twenty-dollar bill I slipped him. And the look on the kids' faces when he shoved the gift into my arms and announced that Christmas was officially off? No doubt it would be one of his fondest holiday memories for years to come.

I hurried back home. As I pulled up to the curb, I was startled by a rap on the window—Dixon's cousin Sabina. She crammed her hand back into her pocket and huddled in her winter coat with her shoulders up around her ears. My driver side window was temperamental to open—sometimes it rolled back up, sometimes not—so I opened the door instead. "Sabinochka—how long have you been outside? Are you locked out?"

"No, I can get in, all right. After I sacrificed my door-opening Spellcraft, I figured I needed a new contingency plan. So I strung a spare key on a necklace and I've been wearing it ever since." She shivered. "I'm just waiting for the house to air out."

That didn't sound good. I motioned for her to join me in the truck, and she hopped in gratefully. "Did your father make liver and onions again?"

"Even worse. He used Christmas Eve as an excuse to smoke a big, nasty cigar in the house."

"Is this...an American tradition?"

"That's the thing about adopting a Handless holiday. You can get away with doing basically anything and claiming it's a unique spin on a time-honored tradition. And I dunno why, but this year, it's extra smoky."

She gave her shirt a sniff, shuddered, and only then noticed my gift. "What's that?"

I would have thought it was evident. "A present."

"For who? Everyone you know is a Scrivener."

"Florica told me it would make Dixon happy."

"True, he's never one to turn down a present. What is it?"

"I'm not sure," I admitted. "But I suppose I had better find out." By the dull glow of the dome light, I unwrapped the gift, taking care to keep the tape and paper intact. And inside the box was...a cookie jar.

A Santa Claus cookie jar.

While I had no great desire to endure the cookie jar staring at me, at least it would reside in the kitchenette, not the bedroom. Unless Dixon got some truly creative ideas for bedroom antics.

"Oh no!" Sabina cried.

Had she read my mind? "What is it?"

"You can't give this to Dixon—Santa totally freaks him out."

Dixon's cousin is a self-assured girl, and I admire her vehemence. But that does not mean she has always got her facts straight. "But his mother made it sound like was a big fan of Santa Claus."

"He was! Until the time we snuck off together to see Santa for ourselves. Aunt Florica and Uncle Johnny had always been so strict about their no-Christmas rule that Dixon must've been at least eleven or twelve—way too big to believe in Santa—but old enough to take the bus to the Christmas parade on Main Street. If it were anywhere else, word would've gotten back to our folks about us wandering around out there on our own. But there wasn't a Scrivener in sight, so no one said a word. Once the official tree was lit and a bunch of showoffs sang some carols, we got in line with all the Handless kids to sit on Santa's lap to tell him what we wanted."

"When Dixon was *twelve*?"

"That's right! He was the tallest kid in line. I told him Santa wasn't real—and so did the girl in front of him, and the kid in front of her. I thought we had him convinced...until he climbed up on that darn lap, and Santa took one look at him and said, 'Dixon Penn? Do your parents know you're here?'"

"So, he knew the man."

"Sure, we both did. Ladin Silver was always coming around on poker nights...and apparently other nights too, when my dad wasn't home. But I was too young to understand what *that* meant. Anyway, the thought that Santa Claus knew exactly who he was startled Dixon so badly, he was off like a shot. He vaulted over a pile of Christmas presents—they were really just empty boxes wrapped up in paper, so they scattered like snowflakes—and he took off into the crowd. It took me nearly an hour to find him again. Especially with all the weird Handless and their, 'little girl, where are your parents?' Honestly, you think they'd never seen an unattended child before."

She took the cookie jar from my unresisting hands.

I sighed. "And now I have nothing."

"But that's better than giving Dixon something that reminds him of his humiliation at the hands of a freaky Santa! Listen, Yuri. Before my cousin met you, he was in this weird, in-between place. His living arrangements were temporary. His job was temporary. He didn't even know he could Scribe! And then you came into his life, and he's happier than I've ever seen him."

Had I come into Dixon's life, or had he come into mine? I supposed an argument could be made either way. I still recall seeing him march through the doors of Precious Greetings, bright-eyed and full of hope. And yet, after all we'd been through together, he had ended up in the city of his birth, in the home of his family, doing the very task he had trained his whole life to do. And I was the one who had somehow found myself in the middle of it all.

"Look at it this way," Sabina said. "If Dixon did get you a gift, just act really surprised and appreciative and let him bask in the gift-giving glory. That's what presents are supposed to be about anyhow, right? Not getting stuff...but giving it."

Well, when she put it that way....

"I'll get rid of Santa." She hopped out of the truck and tucked the cookie jar under her arm like a football. "You go upstairs and slip into bed, and when Dixon rolls out his Christmas present tomorrow morning, just act really surprised."

Acting surprised would hardly be difficult. I had always thought myself wary of surprises. Too tough, too brittle. But Dixon was constantly surprising me...and (surprisingly enough) I'd actually grown to enjoy it.

I crept up the stairwell, lost in the improbability of Dixon and me finding one another...and wondering exactly how many cigars Fonzo had smoked. It was late—and Dixon had drunk a significant amount of milk—so I must have presumed he would be asleep. When I found him there, standing in our kitchenette with a look on his face I couldn't quite find the words to describe, I was surprised. And he hadn't even given me a gift yet.

"Yuri. You're home."

As he said the words, a cuckoo clock on the far wall struck midnight. I'd plucked out the noisemaking parts months ago, but the fake bird still made twelve small clicks when it popped from its lair, while Meringue roused herself for a single, sleepy, "Cuckoo."

Dixon glanced at the clock and said, "Merry Christmas." The words were soft, with an edge that skirted on poignance. Hopefully he wasn't having any Santa Claus flashbacks. He cut his eyes to the box I hadn't realized I was still carrying, and said, "Say, Yuri, is that a whole box of milk?"

"It is nothing." Wait. This was what Americans said all the time to convey a false modesty. "Really—nothing. It is empty."

He didn't seem to believe me, even when he came forward, took it from my hands, and tested its weight for himself. He had that same bright-eyed look about him I'd first seen at Precious Greetings—a look which never gets old. Enthusiasm and optimism, eagerness and wonder.

"Dixon—"

He opened the top, peered inside, proved to himself it was

empty...and said, “What a great box.”

“What?”

“Not too big. Not too small. Lightweight, but sturdy. And look, there’s a little origami-type catch on the top flap to keep it shut. It’s just like my mom always says: *Stop complaining, you big baby. Your luck is bound to turn around if you just give it half a chance.*” He sighed happily. “I just managed to annihilate my old favorite box—and before you know it, an even better box shows up!”

Normally, I would presume he was trying to spare my feelings—but if ever there was a man who would take pleasure in something as simple as a cardboard box, it was Dixon. Relief washed over me, and my knees went rubbery as the day caught up with me. I had been so carried away about this whole gift exchange that I lost sight of what I knew to be true. Somehow, I managed to make Dixon Penn happy. And somehow, against all odds, I had found happiness in him.

I sank gratefully into a kitchen chair, and only then did I get a good look around me and realize how clean and spacious everything looked. While I scoured Pinyin Bay for a gift, Dixon had not been sleeping a milk-induced sleep, but instead, he’d tidied up the flat...and burned incense, too. Or maybe made himself a few slices of toast. Or maybe Fonzo’s cigars truly were as pervasive as Sabina mentioned. No doubt the smell of char would dissipate soon enough. But what interested me the most, in the center of the cleared kitchen table, was a beautifully crafted wooden case.

Dixon became flustered as he noticed me noticing it. “Ignore that, Yuri. It’s nothing.”

I presume he meant American-nothing. I pulled the case toward me and admired the design scorched into the top, drew off my gloves, and ran my fingertip along the texture. “This reminds me of your calligraphy.”

“Oh. Right. Makes a lot of sense, since that *is* my original design—and nothing more. You know how I love to keep up with my calligraphy. I was just practicing my cartouches. Late at night. With a wood burner. On a cedar box that was most definitely empty...a box I did *not* set on fire. You can have it, if you like—though if you'd rather just toss it out when trash day rolls around, I'll understand."

I opened the cedar box, drew my travel paint set from my pocket, and placed it inside. "It's a perfect fit." I met his eyes and tried to convey the words, *just like us*...because some things are simply too sentimental to utter aloud. Dixon's eyes brightened as he smiled a tentative smile—he knew me well enough by now that I didn't need to spell it out. His smile broadened as he leaned over, looped his arms around my neck, and drew me into a tender, slightly smoky kiss.

"Dumb hack," Meringue murmured from her perch in the rafters, then tucked her head beneath her wing and settled in for a long winter's nap.

BROWNIE POINTS

DIXON

1

My mother always says, show me a person who doesn't like free stuff, and I'll show you a big, fat liar. Me, personally? I love a good freebie. Absolutely *adore* them. And so the annual Shop the Bay trade show was my favorite event of the year.

Shop the Bay was not a public event. It was only open to retail stores looking for wholesale goods. But Practical Penn was a retail store...technically. Maybe my office in the back of the shop was more of a repository for loud amphibians, and maybe the last work Yuri did was change a lightbulb no one else could reach, but Yuri and I were Practical Penn employees.

Technically.

And that was good enough for me.

The Bayside Convention Center stretched out before us like a glimmering sea of possibility. While it's true that the giveaways were all printed with some random business logo, most of the time you could scrape it off...or at least put a sticker over it. There were key fobs. There were water bottles. There were squishy little foam balls that purportedly provide some sort of stress relief. But best of all...there were pens.

You might think that a guy who's trained his whole life to wield a specialized writing implement—a magical hand-cut quill—would turn his nose up at a cheap, disposable pen. But I love making marks on paper, whether or not those marks harness the power of Spellcraft. And it's always fun to put a new pen through its paces and really see what it can do. I'd managed to gather up every pen in sight, from felt tip to ballpoint.

Yuri, meanwhile, appeared to be in the market for things like emery boards and back-scratchers and dinky little magnetic calendars with dates so small you could barely see them. Yuri has the predilections of someone at least two and a half times his age. Whether this was the result of growing up in Russia or his natural bent of personality, I couldn't say. I just knew it was adorable.

We'd drifted apart—me to a table with pens that had multicolored ink, Yuri to a podiatrist's booth. It was getting late. My pockets bristled with so many pens that my pants gave off a plasticky brreeeet with every step I took, and we'd still need to figure out what to do for dinner. Yes, there was some take-and-bake pizza left in the fridge. But after a couple of days, those slices are more like a doorstop than a dinner. Speaking of which....

"Say, Yuri." I sidled up to him so I didn't have to shout over the crowd and pitched my voice flirtily. "Is that a doorstop in your pocket, or are you just happy to see me?"

He blinked. "It is promotional doorstop."

Such a cutie.

I was about to nudge Yuri toward the parking lot when he suddenly stiffened. Not in a doorstop kind of way, either. More like a predator with something vulnerable and tasty in its sights. I tried to follow his gaze as best I could, but saw nothing but the backs of a bunch of heads. I went up on tiptoe and still saw nothing. I was about to give up and ask, when the crowd parted and it hit me: the alluring smell of chocolate.

I don't have a major sweet tooth—not like Yuri—but the smell was so enticing, so *good*, I half-expected it to turn into a cartoon hand beckoning us forward. We weren't the only ones to notice.

While Shop the Bay was thinning out and some of the vendors were even starting to pack up for the day, the crowd around Bruno's Brownies was more of a mob scene.

But crowds have a way of making room for Yuri. Often punctuated by the sort of "oof" sound you'd make when an elbow connected with your ribs.

As we elbowed our way toward the front, I found a big brute of guy hacking a sheet of brownies into cubes and dealing them onto tiny paper plates. He wore an apron embroidered with the name *Bruno*—a normal-sized apron, I presume, but on his burly frame it looked more like a front-facing thong. Not only did he have the physique of a grizzly prepping for hibernation, but he was just as hirsute. I come from a long line of hairy guys—though I'm told I'm more of an otter than a bear cub—and even I was impressed by Bruno's follicles. Chest hair bulged from the neck of his shirt. His forearm hair was more of a pelt. His beard was thick enough to merit its own hairnet. But despite all his fur, the thing that struck me the most about Bruno was his eyes. Small and sweet, blinking as though he'd just woken up from a long winter's nap...and completely overwhelmed by the bloodthirsty mob demanding his treats.

"One per customer," the frazzled baker entreated, though if anyone heeded his pleas, it was only because they were shoved out of the way before they could help themselves to seconds.

As fast as Bruno could put those brownie samples out, they disappeared. And when a voice over the loudspeakers announced that Shop the Bay would be closing in ten minutes, the mob grew even more frantic.

At his side, a tiny woman whose name tag read *Bernadette* was doling out the paper plates as fast as he could fill them. Her chef coat was two sizes too big, and her blondish hair was in a sloppy ponytail on top of her head, though maybe it had started the day more contained and just ended up looking messy. Despite the fact that she came off like a kid playing dress-up, she had the cheerful confidence of an adult as she worked the crowd. "Bruno's brownies are made only from the finest ingredients, from fair-trade chocolate, to organic flour, to locally sourced cream, butter and honey. Your customers will really taste the difference!"

Maybe so...if you could manage to get your hands on one.

The brownies were going alarmingly fast, and the people within reach of Yuri's elbows were falling like bowling pins. But when a girl of about seven or eight popped up in front of him, Yuri somehow stayed his elbow mid-jab. The kid was clearly into the color pink. Little pink T-shirt. Little pink baseball cap. Little pink jeans with a glitzy silver belt. And a little pink tongue that poked out at Yuri as she snatched up the last brownie and darted away, blowing raspberries. "Better luck next time, Chubby!"

"You're better off without the brownies, if you ask me," declared a desperate voice from over my shoulder. "Sweets are terrible for your blood sugar and your teeth."

I turned and found a tall beanpole of a guy watching the crowd cruise past his stall. His shop was Herb's Herbs and Veggies, according to the big, pumpkin-shaped sign. Why was it that only the second H was silent? Unless Yuri was pronouncing the word...but he'd picked up a lot of his pronunciation from British TV. Anyway, Herb still had plenty of samples to give away—but no takers. And now that he'd caught my eye, he seemed really invested in engaging my attention.

Herb was a middle-aged guy with a long, wispy ponytail and a tie-dyed shirt. But he wasn't one of those relaxed hippies you see sprawled in the corner of a coffee shop nursing a single soy latte. He was the sort who'd earnestly thrust a clipboard in your face to get you to sign a petition for some cause or another.

And in this case, the cause was produce.

"Most people know tomatoes are actually a fruit," he informed me, "but did you know their classification as a vegetable was for taxation purposes? As if something as glorious as a plant can be governed!"

"Er...can't say that I did."

"Did you know that in the seventeenth century, carrots were

originally purple, but were bred to be orange?"

"Oh. How about that?"

"And did you know the apples you buy in the supermarket can be as much as a year old?"

Don't get me wrong—I love it when someone's passionate about advocating for their cause. I've just never found vegetables particularly appealing unless they were covered in a bright orange blanket of cheese.

"Fascinating..." I started edging away. "But, wow, would you look at the time?"

The thing about tall people is that they take really big strides on their long, gangly legs, and before I could blend back into the brownie hubbub, Herb was shoving a little paper cup into my hand. A cup filled with something that looked suspiciously like wood chips.

"Herb's herbs and veggies are grown right here in Pinyin Bay, not shipped from halfway across the world. I use a special, year-round hydroponic growing system I developed myself. And they're preserved using time-tested, all-natural methods like brine and fermentation and sunshine. Don't settle for anything less!"

"Indeed I won't," I assured him brightly, then dodged around a chubby guy with brownie residue clinging to the corners of his mouth, and finally made my getaway.

The mob was only just starting to thin, but Yuri's shaved head is easy to spot. I checked in with him to see if the brownie folks had put out more product while I was being waylaid by Herb but, unfortunately, Bruno and his bubbly assistant were packing up shop with no more brownie samples to be had. It looked like we were out of luck—at least until I noticed a smug-looking guy threading through the crowd in the opposite direction, holding not one tiny paper plate aloft, but two.

No fair!

Instinctively, I called out, "Say, is that the Pinyin Bay Perch?" When Two-Brownie Guy paused to look, I made a grab. Thanks to my otter-like reflexes, I came away with half of his ill-gotten gains...and left a cup of dried veggie chips in its place.

The brownie was halfway to my mouth when I turned back and saw Yuri gazing forlornly at the now-empty brownie table. As good as the goodie might smell (and it smelled *really* good) I could hardly keep it for myself. Shielding my prize with my body, I sidled up to Yuri, jostled him playfully with my shoulder, and said, "Gee, what a shame we didn't find this booth sooner. And now the samples are all gone." I waggled my eyebrows at him and whipped out the brownie cube with a flourish. "All except...this one!"

It was a big one, too.

Yuri's expression transformed from disappointment to glee—well, as close to glee as Yuri gets, but by now I can read him pretty darn well. He snatched the brownie from my hand as if it might disappear, and shoved it in his mouth. But just as he was about to bite down, he said, "Should we split it?" That's what I understood through the brownie and the sexy Russian accent, anyhow.

I patted Yuri on his bulging bicep. That handsome hunk of man-meat has had a hard life. He's guarded and suspicious and even a tad bit pessimistic, and I think that's what makes it especially satisfying to see him really enjoy himself. Even outside the bedroom. "You eat the whole thing, Yuri. I'm sure it can't be any sweeter than watching you enjoy it."

That declaration brought a blush to Yuri's cheeks...but he wasn't too embarrassed to scarf down the entire brownie in two bites.

Satisfied, I turned to the table. There was nothing left but a few crumbs, a scattering of paper plates...and a business card.

Bruno's Brownerie
Bruno Baer, Proprietor
Wholesale Orders Only

I tucked the card into my pocket, wheels turning. "My parents' shop might not be in food service, but the strip mall is zoned for restaurants—Practical Penn even shares an entire wall with the pizza place—so technically, we should be able to place a wholesale order. How many brownies do you suppose that would entail? A gross? Isn't that a funny unit of measurement, considering that those brownies are anything *but* gross? I wonder how it came to be that the word for 'twelve dozen' and 'completely disgusting' is the same—probably a major case of buyer's remorse was at the root of it. And how confusing is it for you when English words have two entirely different meanings?"

"Everything about your language is confusing," Yuri said, though the words weren't as harsh as they might have been, given that they were thick with brownie. His cheeks went an even brighter red.

I could count the number of times I've made Yuri blush on one hand and still have enough fingers leftover for tiddlywinks, so I really did my best not to stare, so as not to make him feel too self-conscious. And yet, the sight of him looking all flushed sent my thoughts spiraling down a much more lascivious route. I gave his massive arm another firm pat, then went up on tiptoe and purred in his ear, "Homophones might be confusing, but I know a vocabulary that the two of us speak loud and clear." I took Yuri's face in both hands (with the intent of adding the word "naked" to avoid any potential ambiguity) when I realized his cheeks were unnaturally hot to the touch.

And even as I watched, the blush resolved itself into two clusters of bright red spots.

YURI

2

My main objective was to get home—as soon as possible. If something was seriously wrong, I had no desire to flaunt my weakness in public for all to see. We retreated to the truck. Cheeks burning, I struggled to make my way out of the expo parking lot without flattening another attendee.

"Have you had measles?" Dixon asked eagerly from the passenger seat. "Mumps? Rubella? Whooping cough?"

"These are the sicknesses of children."

"How about the heartbreak of psoriasis?"

"It is nothing. I just need to wash my face." I said this with more conviction than I actually felt.

Dixon consulted his phone.

I said, "Those medical websites give you nightmares."

Too late. He had already found one. "Nope, not psoriasis—yikes, these photos are really graphic...ooh, I know, maybe it's shingles! And how about that, yet another word with multiple meanings. Though according to this medical blog, as diseases go, it's pretty darned painful. I'm guessing it's preferable to keep your shingles up on the roof where they belong."

Dixon had called out the names of a half dozen more potential ailments, from vitiligo to leprosy, by the time we pulled up in front of the house. It was cool outside, early Spring with a nip in the air, but still, my cheeks were blazing. Even I could not be sure if this was entirely caused by some mysterious malady, or my embarrassment over catching it.

I cut the engine, stormed out of the truck and headed for the stairwell to our attic flat. Dixon trotted along behind me with one eye on his phone. "Have you traveled to the Congo recently? I suppose I would have noticed. How about Wyoming?"

I had been by his side for more than a year now, never farther than the corner store, and we both knew it. Still, Dixon could not help but give voice to every stray thought which crossed his mind. Picking up speed, I strode up the stairs, through the flat, and into the bathroom—where I closed the door behind me. Firmly.

Dixon was still talking. "It says here that people with certain genetic predispositions are especially susceptible to *tree man syndrome*...though there's no actual tree bark involved, but warts. Is there a history of anything like that in the Volnikov family?"

Ignoring him, I turned on the shaving light and peered into the mirror. My cheeks were just as red as they felt. But not in a rosy, healthful sort of way. Instead, they were livid and blotchy.

"Of course, there's always the chance that you were subjected to a strange chemical of some sort. Maybe it's something to do with your paint set. Have you tinkered with any new pigments lately? Manufacturers are always cutting corners and you never know what they'll grind up next. Say, did you know that purple dye was originally made from ground up snails? And insects can carry all kinds of strange parasites."

I ran the water, hoping to drown out Dixon's "helpful" trivia. I did splash my face, first with warm water, then with cool. But neither did any good.

"And, of course, we can't rule out hypnotic influence. Because if a well-placed command can make a person cluck like a chicken, who's to say it can't make them blush like a baboon's, bu-uh...well,

I kind of doubt it was hypnosis, but still, you never know. I'd be happy to try my hand at re-hypnotizing you, though I can't promise I won't make a few sexy suggestions—"

The doorknob jiggled, and the lock was flimsy at best. Because the bathroom walls were a do-it-yourself job, the door was not quite square and plumb, and tended to stick shut at certain inopportune moments, and pop open at others. Dixon and I had become proficient in pretending we saw nothing embarrassing in those moments. But right now, I had no desire to endure his unwanted assistance. Not until I had some idea what was going on, myself.

Luckily, there was a promotional doorstop in my pocket. Little did I realize when I picked it up it would come in handy so soon. I jammed it under the door and turned back to the mirror. My skin felt tight, as if I'd fallen asleep in the sun—or come too close to the charcoal grill. It was a disturbing sensation. A combination of sensitivity, itchiness...even pain.

Through the door, Dixon said, "Maybe we should ask Uncle Fonzo's lady friend."

Last summer, Dixon's uncle nearly lost a hand to a particularly insidious curse. Obviously, he could never disclose to a Handless what had actually happened. But Fonzo had a way of landing on his feet. He'd somehow wound up with a doctor credulous enough to believe his patched-together explanation of how he'd broken his finger—possibly because he couched his story in a ridiculous amount of flattery and flirtation. Not only did he heal well enough to hold his quill again, but he'd ended up on extremely *friendly* terms with Dr. Glenda Slaughter.

It galled me to ask anyone for favors. Even Dixon's family... despite the fact that he insisted none of them were keeping score. But Fonzo Penn had nearly lost a limb to his own poor judgment, and since I'd played a part in breaking the curse, I couldn't help but think he owed me.

Not that I was keeping score either.

Not exactly.

But I *would* concede to have him call his "lady friend" and see what she had to say.

Dixon happily relayed the request, while I lingered where I was until I heard the downstairs doorbell ring—not the doorbell itself, but our cockatoo's echo of the sound. Meringue has very sharp hearing, and she insists on repeating every bell, buzzer or chime.

When I finally tried to emerge from the bathroom, Dixon was standing directly outside the door with a long purple scarf in his hands. "Just in case you wanted to wrap up. I thought you might be feeling a tad bit self-conscious. Not that you have any reason to be. A sudden and startling medical condition is nothing to be ashamed of—"

"I'm fine," I snapped, and squeezed past while he made no effort whatsoever to make room for me. Once I muscled by, he followed me step for step, as if the friction of my passing had created an electromagnetic pull that dragged him along behind.

I made my way downstairs to the sound of Dixon listing all the reasons a person might have to be legitimately embarrassed, from belching in public to "butt-dialing," and stepped into the living room of Fonzo Penn and his daughter, Sabina.

If these two shared a philosophy about their home decor, it could be summarized as, *Still good!* All of their furniture had been in the family as long as I'd been alive. Many of the pieces had seen prior owners—usually several. And all of them were either faded, sagging, or missing important parts such as tops, bottoms or legs. A Spellcrafter and his money are not easily parted, and so they made do. Sheets were thrown over the worn upholstery, tables were leveled with discarded magazines, and the spring-laden "davenport" was approached with the caution it deserved.

Currently, the davenport was occupied by Sabina, sprawled there in ripped jeans, tattered T-shirt and worn combat boots, with her body expertly fitted around the most obtrusive lumps and jabs as she scrolled around her phone. A few weeks ago, she'd dyed the tips of her bleach-blonde hair acid green, but the color had faded to a gentle pastel and the black roots were coming in.

Fonzo was dressed in a shirt that still had most of its buttons. His dark hair was slicked back from his high widow's peak. He reeked of aftershave that was nearly pleasant, and his salt-and-pepper stubble was already coming back in. And standing in the circle of his arms was the inimitable Dr. Slaughter.

While Fonzo did enjoy a certain status as the Hand of the Penn family, this status carried no weight whatsoever among the Handless. No one quite understood how he'd managed to get so lucky as to land himself an emergency room doctor—especially one like Glenda. She was a dozen years younger than him, fit and attractive, and she earned more money than the entire Penn family combined.

It would be highly illegal, not to mention unethical, for Fonzo to have ensnared her with a bit of Spellcraft. Not that I would put it past him. But I did know for a fact that when the two of them met, he was unable to hold a pen.

Glenda had long, wavy hair, ash blonde, with a tendency toward corkscrew curls—which she ironed flat more often than not. But she was fresh from the hospital tonight in her navy scrubs and sensible shoes, and springy blonde tendrils had worked themselves free from her polka dot scrunchie.

Someone had apparently filled the doctor in on my "condition," as her gaze went immediately to me. She made a pouty face and said, "Who's got a boo-boo?"

Did I mention her most loyal patients were children?

I have never been comfortable in the face of sympathy. Already, the urge to retreat upstairs was overwhelming. But Dixon had planted himself firmly in the doorway behind me, and Glenda was descending on me with great purpose. "Don't worry, this isn't gonna hurt. I promise, I'll only look with my eyes."

"I am not worried," I said, affronted.

Glenda pulled a red lollipop from her pocket and waved it under my nose. "Then have a seat. And once we're done, someone gets a cherry sucker!"

I rolled my eyes as Sabina moved her feet to make room for

me beside her. With seemingly the whole room waiting for me to assume the position, I sat. Once Glenda took my temperature and my pulse, she slipped on a pair of glasses with magnifying lenses that made her eyes look comically large, then pulled out a penlight.

It was uncomfortable to endure all the scrutiny. Both from Glenda, with her bright light and cartoonish eyes, and from the Penn family with their unabashed curiosity. One may gain much support from being part of such a close-knit clan...but it comes with a cost: privacy.

I forced myself not to squirm.

"That's definitely quite an owie," she said.

I narrowed my eyes. "Is that your clinical assessment?"

"Things like this are usually diet-related. Think about anything you've eaten lately that's out of the ordinary."

I had grazed through many samples at Shop the Bay. But so had Dixon. Everything but the brownie. But I refused to believe I'd suddenly developed an allergy to such things. Allergies were afflictions of the weak. Perhaps the brownies were tainted. "Are you gonna prescribe a salve?" Dixon asked. "Or maybe a lotion? A balm? Ooh, I know, how about an unguent?"

Glenda said, "When you've known as many pharmaceutical reps as I have, you wouldn't be so quick to dash off a prescription. So many unwanted side effects! You're better off going with a natural approach." My doubt must have shown in my expression, because she added, "Not only is my remedy safer—it's a lot cheaper, too."

"Cheap is good," Fonzo said.

Glenda grabbed a purse from the sideboard and started rummaging through it. "In fact, I've got what you need right here. Lucky for you I was too busy sewing back in a severed tongue to eat lunch!" With a flourish, she pulled out....

A carton of plain yogurt.

"That's it?" I said. "Eat yogurt?"

"No, silly. Put it on your rash."

"You're joking."

"I can help you apply it," Dixon said flirtatiously. "Maybe it'll even be fun."

Glenda said, "Yogurt has natural anti-yeast properties. It's packed with probiotics."

Did we have any proof that Glenda was an actual doctor? Maybe she was just some middle-aged woman Fonzo picked up at the pancake house who happened to be wearing scrubs. The quickest thing to do would be to agree with her, then go to the pharmacy, buy all the various creams and lotions, and bathe in them until something made the redness go away.

Glenda shoved the yogurt into my hand.

"And the candy?" I prompted.

"Actually, you'll need to lay off the sweets until your rash calms down. There's nothing candida likes more than sugar, and it wouldn't hurt you to lose a few pounds. Besides, I'm sure you're plenty sweet as it is! Don't worry—I've got something even better for you than a sucker." She dug a small green marker from her pocket—a marker clearly made for a child—then handed it to me with a big smile. "For being such a fantastic patient!"

Patient? I felt anything but.

Glenda did not notice. "And don't worry if you make an oopsie. It washes right out. Plus, it smells like green apple—though I wouldn't suck on it if I were you. It's non-toxic...but even so, I'm told these things don't taste nearly as good as they smell."

While Fonzo lured Glenda into the kitchen with promises of vegetarian take-and-bake pizza, Dixon and Sabina whispered together at the opposite end of the davenport. I presumed they were making fun of me—or perhaps scheming to part me from my green marker—so I was surprised to find the two of them looking uncharacteristically serious.

Sabina craned her neck to ensure her father and Glenda were out of earshot, then crooked a finger in my direction. "C'mere, Yuri, lemme get a closer look."

She put her phone in flashlight mode and held it up to my face.

Once I was through seeing spots, I noted that both she and her cousin seemed alarmingly concerned. “What is it?” I asked.

Dixon double-checked that Glenda would not overhear him, lowered his voice dramatically, and said, “There’s a glimmer and a shimmer where there shouldn’t be, Yuri. It’s not yeasties causing your rash—it’s Spellcraft!”

DIXON

3

We hurried upstairs to our apartment—Yuri, Sabina and I—to try and figure out what to do. If Yuri's rosy-cheeked affliction was a result of Spellcraft, you'd think we would be uniquely qualified to Craft it away. But Spellcraft has a funny way of manifesting in the human body, and results can be unpredictable at best. Legally speaking, Spellcraft shops will get in a lot of trouble for dispensing anything that even remotely smacks of medical treatment. And clinically speaking, Spellcraft cures have proven to be about as effective as a placebo.

Those of us in the Craft don't take much stock in the evaluations of the Handless, though, so it's not uncommon for us to Craft our own home remedies. But in this instance? With a malady caused by Spellcraft to begin with? Anything we Crafted would be just as likely to "set" the spell as to cure it. Our only hope was to sniff out the original spell and Uncraft it.

"We'll need to retrace our steps," I said.

Sabina asked, "Where's the yogurt?"

I pulled out a sheet of paper to start a list, and wrote *Our Steps* across the top with only a moderate amount of flourishing. "Okay.

What's the last thing we did before the flushing started?"

Yuri was too distracted to answer, with Sabina circling him like a persistent gnat while he shielded the yogurt from her as best he could. "Come on, Yuri," she taunted. "Doctor's orders."

"Yuri?" I prompted. "Our steps?"

Sabina made a fruitless grab at the yogurt—which also contained no fruit, being as it was plain. And who the heck eats plain yogurt straight from the carton, anyway?

Sabina dodged around Yuri and made another grab, but came away empty-handed. She might be quick, but Yuri had a much longer reach. "Sabinochka...."

"What, are you *afraid* of a little yogurt?"

She just wanted to see Yuri with yogurt on his face (and we all knew it) so I took pity on him and did my best to bring us all back to the topic at hand. "Working backward, the last place we came into contact with when the spots showed up was the parking lot. So, think back. It was a little congested getting out of the lot. Did you make any Russian gestures you shouldn't have at an out-of-town Spellcrafter?"

Yuri held the yogurt aloft like a burly, shaven-headed Statue of Liberty and said, "It wasn't the parking lot—it was the brownie."

He seemed awfully sure about that—and, thinking it all through, it did make a certain amount of sense, since he'd had a brownie, I hadn't, he broke out, and I didn't. So much for my list. But who says you can't have a list of one? I wrote the word *brownie* nice and big, and underlined it with an ornate swoop.

"Lots of people ate those brownies," I said. "But Dr. Slaughter didn't mention her ER experiencing a big rash of rashes. Then again, Spellcrafters seem more sensitive to Craft-related things than Handless...and any other Scriveners who might've been at the expo aren't very likely to consult a Handless doctor."

As I puzzled things through, Yuri set the yogurt on the highest kitchen shelf. Out of Sabina's reach...but not Meringue's. The cockatoo fluttered down from the attic beams to pick at the foil top of the yogurt. But since she doesn't have fingers or hands, she's not what you'd call coordinated, and pretty soon the yogurt was face-down on the card table. Yuri gave an exasperated sniff, grabbed a sponge, and started cleaning it up with a great deal of excess force. Sabina watched wistfully as the yogurt went down the drain, muttering, "You could have at least given it a try."

But I was still looking at my list, and making an effort to sort out what it might mean. "So, was someone tinkering with the brownies to make them taste better? They were awfully popular."

Yuri gave the sponge a final wring, then nudged Meringue off the dish drainer and onto his finger while the bird chuckled to herself. He said, "Why would they go through the trouble and expense? Would it not be much cheaper to use good quality ingredients?"

True. Craftings didn't come cheap. I stroked my chin thoughtfully. "Maybe they wanted an extra boost for the expo."

"Or..." Sabina said dramatically, "maybe it was sabotage."

As soon as my cousin uttered the word *sabotage*, I knew exactly who was to blame!

Bright and early the next morning, the three of us set off on a reconnaissance mission to Herb's Herbs and Veggies. Technically, I should have been working on a Recrafting project, but as a freelancer, it was my prerogative to put off the boring jobs and focus on the fun tasks. At least until my clients started threatening to stop payment on their checks. And technically, Sabina was supposed to be at work too, minding the shop at Practical Penn. But those were the perks of working in a family business—no one was particularly surprised at a random and vaguely explained absence.

"You're looking awfully eager," my cousin said as we piled into the truck. "There must be a disguise involved."

Another thing about family. They tend know you awfully darn well. "I can't just go in bare-faced. Back at the expo, I talked to Herb for a pretty long stretch—or maybe he talked to me—whichever was the case, he'd recognize me in a heartbeat." I plucked my latest disguise from my pocket and gave it a good shake.

"Is that a wig?" Sabina asked.

"Even better." I looped the elastic around my ears and pulled it into place. "It's a prosthetic beard."

Sabina frowned. "Looks more like a merkin."

"What is merkin?" Yuri asked.

"Never mind," I said. "I'll have you know, Sabina, that this fine example of facial hair augmentation had nothing but enthusiastic five-star online reviews." Maybe they were worded like they'd been generated by a bot with a tenuous grasp on the language, but they were glowing, nonetheless.

My cousin gave the beard the hairy eyeball. "If you wanted a full beard, all you had to do was skip shaving for a few days."

"We don't have a few days." I gesticulated toward Yuri. "Just look at how red he is."

"Should've put that yogurt on it," Sabina said, while Yuri ignored both of us, or at least pretended to. But that only made it easier for Sabina to scrutinize him. "Wow, you're more flushed than the toilet at a laxative factory."

When she tried to prod his affliction, Yuri broke down and batted her finger away. "Leave it alone."

Not only were Yuri's cheeks bright and livid, but they were starting to swell. I didn't suppose he'd take kindly to being told he looked adorable with chipmunk cheeks, though I'll admit, it was very tempting.

"Stop staring," Yuri said testily.

I dutifully aimed my gaze at the road ahead...though my peripheral vision is surprisingly well-developed, and Yuri's cheeks were vivid enough to monitor even while pretending to keep my attention front and center for the remainder of the drive.

Not only was the Herb's Herbs booth situated just across the aisle from Bruno's Brownies back at the expo, but their shops were right next door to one another. In fact, you could sprint from one place to the other without even getting winded. I said, "No wonder Herb wants to sabotage his neighbor. Who would buy his dusty old kale chips when they could get chocolate chip brownies instead?"

Yuri was too busy scrutinizing his cheeks in the rearview to remark on my astute observation. Over the course of our short drive, his condition had become exponentially worse.

He did allow Sabina to touch it—gently, with the backs of her fingers. "Wow, you're burning up. I'll bet that means we're getting close to the Crafting!"

I said, "Maybe we can use Yuri's cheeks as a Geiger counter."

Yuri reached across Sabina and made a gesture. "Give me the beard."

I smoothed it down possessively. "But Herb will recognize me without it."

"What difference does that make? Give. It. To. Me."

There was no arguing with Yuri when he had his mind set on something—not to mention the fact that I was putty in his hands when he got all commanding—so I dutifully unlooped my ears and handed over my disguise. Which, now that I saw it on Yuri, did make me wonder if it was actually designed to be worn on the face.

We piled out of the truck and approached the store. Herb's Herbs and Veggies was a small clapboard storefront tacked onto a flat, industrial cinderblock building. For a store that sold the food group people only ate out of duty and shame, it was doing pretty brisk business. The shop was filled with herbs and spices, chips and chutneys, pickles and preserves. Several customers roamed the store looking puzzled and somewhat lost, and the till was unmanned. A door to the back gaped open behind the counter, and it was helpfully marked *Grow Room - Staff Only*. There was a bunch of clamor and commotion going on behind it. "Just a second," Herb called out frantically. "Be right out...just as soon as I—"

He was cut off by a crash and a clatter.

What luck! I've always found that the best way to shoehorn your way into a restricted area is to be helpful—even if it means getting shooed out the door five minutes later when it's discovered you have no skills whatsoever. With the confidence of someone who knew exactly what he was doing, I pushed through the staff-only door and said, "How can I...help?"

The door let into a massive room thick with greenery and buzzing with fluorescent lights...but hands down, the most fascinating thing about the place was that it was raining inside. That seemed like a pretty cool trick—until I deduced that the downpour was not intentional. A skeleton of clear tubing surrounded us, and that tubing was filled with plants suspended in water. Said water was currently spraying in a dozen different directions, turning the grow room into something more like a car wash. Herb was there—tall and lanky in his tie-dyed shirt—trying to stop the biggest leaks. Not very successfully at that. Water jetted out from between his fingers, and every time he grabbed a leak, another popped up somewhere else.

"By the potting bench," Herb called out. "Grab the duct tape."

If anyone knows his way around a roll of duct tape, it's Yuri. His truck is practically made of the stuff. He grabbed that tape in no time flat and yanked out a strip as long as his arm with a loud, tape-y squall. And, as always, he attempted to tear the tape off the roll cleanly by nicking the edge with his teeth. The way duct tape tears, so perfectly perpendicular, is such a profoundly satisfying thing that a person can't help but do it with great enthusiasm. Even Yuri (who, as a rule, is cautious about showing his enthusiastic side).

Unfortunately, in addition to being flexible, durable, and satisfying to tear, duct tape can also be pretty darned sticky. So when Yuri bit into the tape, the sticky side grabbed onto the prosthetic beard. Before Yuri even realized his face had been denuded, Herb had grabbed the tape from his grasp and wound it around the leaky seam.

On the plus side, the beard really seemed to help plug the gap... even if it was somewhat startling.

"Where'd that merkin come from?" Herb demanded.

I didn't bother to correct him, so as not to draw attention to Yuri's already-inflamed cheeks. "Never mind that. What happened to your sprinkler?"

"This is no sprinkler! My hydroponic system is going haywire."

The world can be incredibly random—and no doubt there were dozens of potential sources of malfunction besides Spellcraft. But despite the fact that I couldn't see the telltale magical shimmer through all the water spraying left and right, I had a gut feeling that the impromptu shower and Yuri's rash were somehow related.

Giving the trapped beard a wide berth, Sabina and I taped up Herb's pipes just as fast as Yuri could rip off tape strips. Within a few minutes, we'd contained the pluming plumbing to a few stubborn drips.

Herb swabbed his face with a bandanna and gave me the once-over. "Do I know you?"

"Dixon Penn. We met back at the expo. What's going on?"

"No idea! My system's been water-tight since I installed it a year ago. And now this?"

"When it rains, it pours," I couldn't help but observe. "Who's to say what caused it? I'm sure it could be any number of perfectly logical things. But right now, you've got a lot of eager customers in the shop."

"Those aren't customers, they're here for a pickup. A really *important* pickup. Parties for Smarties—have you heard of it? Awesome charity. They encourage the poorest kids in Pinyin Bay to stay in school by sponsoring all their big events. I've committed major guacamole to the big springtime dance. *Major* guacamole. And I need to load it up right now!" As he said this, a new jet of water sprang from yet another leak. Followed by another. And another.

What luck! "Why don't you let us handle the grow room situation while you handle your donation?"

Herb gave me a vigorous (if soggy) handshake. "I can't thank you enough. I'll be back just as soon as I take care of the guac."

"No problem!" I said brightly.

"And don't mind the pollinators," he said as an afterthought. "The bee-door is shut right now, but a few of them always manage to get left behind."

"I can't say I've ever heard of a bee-door."

"It's my own invention!"

"Huh. Learn something new every day."

"Just make sure you don't swat the little workers. You wouldn't want to send them into attack mode."

"Attack...mode?"

"Thanks again!" Herb said, and sloshed out the door.

"What the heck?" Sabina cried. "This place is full of bees!"

I looked up and saw that above all the spraying water jets, the air was abuzz with honeybees. The water sounds must have camouflaged their buzzing! They didn't seem to mind the spray. In fact, several of them had paused to sip from water droplets. While they didn't seem aggressive...there sure were a lot of them. "Hi, little bees," I crooned. "Don't worry, we're not here to swat you. Just holding down the fort till your bee-dad gets back."

"Bee-dad?" Sabina repeated.

I shrugged. "Anyway, if you guys keep your stingers away from me, I promise to keep my hands to myself. Win-win."

If Yuri was apprehensive about the grow room before, he was positively dismayed now. But we couldn't just walk away without getting to the bottom of the situation. Not with his current cheek-ish condition. He was nipping off tape strips as fast as he could manage and wrapping up leaks as quick as they could sprout, but there were just too many seams involved. At every corner and bend there was a joint with leakage potential, and it would take every last roll of duct tape in Pinyin Bay to seal it all up.

"What would rupture a hydroponic system?" I wondered. "We're not on a fault line...are we?"

Sabina slapped her hand over a particularly powerful spray. "Not that I know of. And there haven't been any new explosions lately, either. Maybe a really big truck hit a pothole nearby and shook the street."

Unlikely. The streets outside Scrivener Village were in pretty good repair.

Yuri unreeled the last strip of tape from the roll and plugged another leak, but by the time he did, his first repair had already split open. He glared at the spurting water, planted his hands on his hips, and said, “Patching holes is no use. We must turn off water at the source.”

YURI

4

We split up, and each of us went a separate direction—right, left, and dead ahead—in search of a shutoff valve. Sabina was grumbling and Dixon was chatting with the bees, but I kept quiet and focused all my effort on finding Spellcraft. While it certainly might be some other "perfectly logical thing" at fault, I knew in my gut it was *volshebstvo*. Perhaps it was counter-sabotage from the baker. Or perhaps Herb's own Crafting had backfired on him. Either way, the whole thing smacked of Spellcraft.

But how could I find it? The telltale bending of light by which I recognized a Crafting would be impossible to see among the jets of water.

I have tried to use my other senses to understand Spellcraft. Back in Russia, when I first learned of my ability, I took nothing my mentor said as fact, certain that she was manipulating me. No one helps another without the motive of somehow serving themselves. (Which was why this whole "charity" motivation of Herb's was suspect.) Never did I think Ulyana was training me from the simple desire to see me flourish. She wanted something. To believe otherwise would be foolish.

She once told me, "A Scrivener experiences the *volshebstvo* through touch, through words, through language. But a Seer will grasp Spellcraft only through the image in his mind. This is an advantage. You could bring forth your ideas without having to fully understand them yourself. All that matters is that you can envision the Seen."

Of course, I liked nothing better than to prove her wrong, and catch her in her manipulation. But Ulyana was far more cunning than I. It would be possible to paint a scene blindfolded, I decided, and spent most of an afternoon attempting to do this by way of proving her wrong. The resulting mess was a useless waste of pigment. But worst of all was her smile of satisfaction at seeing me fail.

"A Seer is nothing more than his eyes. And you are a Seer. Never forget."

Was this so different from a Scrivener?

I have never met a blind Scrivener, but Dixon's people are nothing if not resourceful. I would not be surprised to discover a Spellcrafter who was able to poke braille messages into Seens with the sharpened tip of his quill.

But the problem with being resourceful is that you often entertain far too many ideas at once, and Dixon was eager to abandon our search already. He dodged a spray of water, shook out his hair, and said, "I think this is a bust. Herb is no saboteur. He's a charitable guy."

I said, "People do what they do for reasons of their own. You cannot assume he is above sabotage just because he is free with his guacamole. The hearts of men are complicated."

Dixon gave me a knowing look. "Indeed, they are."

I shrugged off his look and did my best to penetrate the jets of water with my gaze. But just as the magic bends light, so does water. The whole grow room shimmered with reflection and refraction and made it impossible for me to make sense of things. I was tempted to give up and say it was no use...but then the thought occurred to me: while I sensed Spellcraft with my eyes, could the same be said for the bees?

The subtle signals of magic were impossible for me to see, but the pattern of the flying insects was not, once I attuned myself to their rhythms. Up towards the ceiling, they buzzed around the room in a seeming jumble...until I realized they were flying in concentric circles, one within another.

In the center of that circle was a post supporting the ceiling. And attached to the very top of the post was a tiny piece of paper. I could not see the light bending around it from where I stood... but I was certain it would be thrumming with *volshebstvo*.

"There," I called out, pointing. Dixon mouthed the word "oh!" while Sabina's eyes went wide. It took a bit of doing, but Dixon boosted Sabina onto my shoulders, I stood on tiptoe, and she gingerly plucked the Crafting from its seat.

"What's it say?" Dixon asked her eagerly.

"I'm not gonna read it with a faceful of bees! Put me down first!"

I crouched down so Sabina could dismount, though now I was certain I felt the tickle of bee's legs against my shorn scalp, and could barely restrain myself from brushing away the sensation for fear of sending them into "attack mode."

As Dixon helped Sabina off my shoulders, he said, "We'd better find a dry spot to read it."

Definitely so. Wetting down a Crafting can be a very effective way of setting the spell. We found a corner that was mostly shielded by the climbing leaves of an overgrown cucumber plant. I shielded Sabina with my body, and she drew out the Crafting and read.

"*Leaks are sprouting everywhere*. I guess we know what's up with the hydroponics."

"It's a good start." Dixon tilted his head for a better look. "Maybe we can backtrack starting with the Crafting. Do you recognize the penmanship?"

Before Sabina could decide one way or another, a new leak shot out from among the cucumbers, dousing all of us with water. She tucked the Crafting underneath her jacket and sprinted for the door.

Dixon and I were right behind her. He said, "This is a huge deal,

Yuri! Herb and Bruno are *both* the victims of sabotage! But who'd want to run both of them out of business?" Any number of people, no doubt. Never underestimate a man's potential for greed. "Once we can track down the Scrivener, I'm sure they'll spill the beans. So long as we manage to convince them we're not cutting into their territory, anyhow."

In Russia, a Scrivener would deny his own Crafting until his dying breath. But in America, where Spellcraft was legal (though not entirely ethical)? Bragging rights would certainly be claimed, at least if the Crafting were successful. And I had yet to meet an American Scrivener who could resist telling a tale...and then embellishing it for dramatic effect.

Once away from the water, we crowded around the paper and had a look.

The Seen was painted in transparent watercolors. Quick strokes, layered in an interesting way. Mostly greens. Abstract foliage. I would recognize the style, had I seen it before, but I had not. Unlike Scriveners—who were more like a large, extended family—Seers were aberrations. Wild cards who kept to themselves. And aside from Rufus Clahd, the Seer at the family Spellcraft shop, I was acquainted with no others in the city like me.

Sabina turned the paper this way and that. "Do you recognize the writing? Seems to me I've seen that letter-R before. And maybe the S. Then again, there's only so many ways to make an S."

"It's old-school penmanship," Dixon decided.

I tried to understand how he determined such a thing. Scribing was generally done longhand and it all looked traditional to me. But as I saw technique within paint strokes, he saw nuance in handwriting.

"Maybe my parents would recognize it," Dixon said.

"Or my dad," said Sabina, "with all his connections."

Fonzo was the Hand of the Penn family. Even after all this time under Fonzo's roof, I was still unclear what the Hand must actually do. Evasiveness was Fonzo's default setting, and his explanation of his duties took vagueness to an entirely new level. Perhaps the title of Hand was mostly tradition. After all, his family managed without him for a year while he floundered around trying to rid himself of a curse. Or perhaps the family had simply succeeded in covering for his neglect. Either way, Fonzo was the point person for the Penn family in the local circuit. He would be the most acquainted with Pinyin Bay's Spellcrafters. Especially the elder generations.

"Can you Uncraft it?" Sabina asked Dixon.

"It looks a little damp. I'd better not try until it's totally dry—hey, that rhymes!"

If we could not fix the Spellcraft, we would need a mundane solution. I found Herb in the loading dock hefting the last cartons of guacamole into the back of a delivery van. "Where is water valve?" I asked.

"We can't turn off the water! My poor seedlings won't stand a chance!"

"It's up to you," I said, shrugging. "But you can hardly fix the seams while water is spraying through them."

Herb's shoulders slumped in defeat. "It's just that my most stubborn crops finally took root—and they were doing so well!" He headed toward a side door and motioned for me to follow. It opened into the far end of the grow room. Water jetted in a dozen directions, like our shower head did when it was clogged with lime.

The plants did not seem bothered by the situation. They hung from their hydroponic tubes and vats, leafy and vigorous and green. Water beaded on the leaves, which created their own rivulets. The effect was like walking through a rainforest during a monsoon—if that rainforest was made up of parsley, broccoli and kale.

We pushed through the greenery as carefully as possible, until finally we reached the far side of the grow room.

"Zucchini," Herb told me, pointing to an intimidating wall of massive, vining plants. "They're the opposite of fussy. Very prolific. Fast-growing, too. In fact, you've got to be careful not to let them get away from you. Left to their own devices, they'll get as big as a baseball...bat."

He had been parting the wet greenery as he spoke, but on the last word, he froze in shock. I pushed aside a cluster of leaves and followed his gaze. On the concrete floor lay a zucchini so monstrous it looked more like a prop from a horror movie...and it had wedged itself so firmly into the space below the hydroponic tubing it might take a chainsaw to get it out.

Good thing there were two of us. It took me pushing and Herb pulling to finally free the absurd vegetable. And once we did, we saw that it had grown on top of the main water inlet, where over time, the weight of it had pushed the valve past its normal setting.

Herb turned the valve down a notch, and within moments, the jetting water spray slowed to a manageable drip. "If that don't beat all! Have you ever seen anything like it?"

I refrained from telling him about the greenhouse full of explosive tomatoes I'd encountered in Taco Town. It was bad for business to let the Handless know how common it was for Spellcraft to go berserk.

"I'll tell you what," Herb said. "Zucchini are sneaky little buggers. Who knows how long that would've gone unnoticed if you hadn't come along?" He thrust the zucchini into my arms. I staggered a bit under its weight. "You take it. It's the least I can do."

Nobody I knew would have the faintest idea how to cook such a vegetable, and the only one under our roof likely to eat it was Meringue. Even she could be surprisingly finicky. "You don't need to thank me."

"No problem at all. In fact...I *insist*."

DIXON

5

While Yuri kept Herb busy, Sabina and I headed for the restroom at the back of the store. It was a unisex affair, just a single small room with pictures of veggies on the wall. The images were vintage scientific illustrations showing the cross sections of corn, peppers and eggplant. While I've never encountered a Seen that was quite so realistic, I checked for the sparkle of Spellcraft and the presence of Scribings anyway. Luckily, the pictures were nothing more than pictures.

Too many instances of Spellcraft in close proximity can lead to unexpected results. That's why we had so many Scriveners working at Practical Penn—to keep everything separate. But once we assured ourselves we were in a Spellcraft-free zone, Sabina pulled out the soggy Crafting and gave it a blast of warm air from the hand dryer while I puzzled through the best way to Uncraft it.

Leaks are sprouting everywhere. Ample room to turn it into a couplet, plus lots of good potential rhymes. But what? I could claim the sabotage was *unfair*...but was it really? For all I knew, it was retaliation for making the brownies radioactive. It gave us a *scare*—and that was the truth—but the actual timeline of Spellcraft can be a little slippery. I didn't want to encourage things to go from startling to horrific.

Scriveners need to be really careful about any word with a double meaning. We've all been told the cautionary tale of the Scrivener who tried to Craft himself some extra luck at the craps table and keeled over dead. Now that I've had more direct Crafting experience myself, I'm pretty sure the story had been purely fabrication. Spellcraft would never mess up the word *die*...not if *craps* was also an option. Still, the story was impossible to forget.

"I wonder if I could stop the leaks by saying it was all the system could bear," I told Sabina. "But homonyms are so tricky. What if that line made all the crops stop bearing?"

Sabina gave me a look. "You're missing the obvious issue."

"What's that?"

"You don't want a grizzly bear to shamble through the door!"

She had a point. And while any bear meandering through the place should wander off once we tore up the Uncrafted spell, it wasn't wise to push our luck.

"Maybe I could add something about glare...though that's got more than one meaning, too."

"*Leaks are sprouting everywhere.*" Sabina considered the Crafting. "Why don't you just add a few letters to change the word *are* to *aren't*?"

"Not the most elegant solution," I said loftily. "But I suppose it would work." I might be crazy about my cousin...but I didn't want her to start elbowing in on my Uncrafting specialty.

I checked the paper. Totally dry. Spellcraft was always done on the best paper available, and the thick cotton rag was able to withstand a lot of abuse. In this case, though, the watercolor Seen was looking kind of spotty. There were no telltale sparkles that I could see, and it was quite possible the Spellcraft had done its work and was already long gone. If that were the case, I supposed it couldn't hurt to add those extra few letters. And as a bonus, if it failed, I could always blame Sabina.

I flipped down the plastic changing table, set my messenger

bag on top (doing my best not to think about any traces of baby poop it might come into contact with) and pulled out my pen and ink. Despite the fact that I was working on a changing table—and despite the fact that the paper in my hand might be little more now than a fancy piece of calligraphy—I did my best to center myself and focus on the work. Two letters and a stroke of punctuation. Such a small change, but one that would totally reverse the meaning.

I took a deep breath, inked my quill, and set pen to paper. There was space enough between the words to add letters. Not pretty letters, by any stretch of the imagination. But legible enough to re-route the Spellcraft, if there was any left in the Crafting to divert.

Sometimes it's hard to tell whether it's that old tingle I feel in my inking hand, or just nerves. Especially when I'm so excited! But once I changed *are* to *aren't*, I held my breath and listened. Unfortunately, judging by the distant hiss of water and the gurgle of the drains, the grow room was still functioning as an impromptu sprinkler system.

I was just about to remark that we'd given it our best shot, pack it all in, and start calling around for a plumber, when my arm gave a jolt as if I'd just whacked my funny bone. I re-read the Crafting and the follow-up line sprang into my head, fully formed and perfect. I dipped my quill again...and I Scribed.

Leaks <u>aren't</u> sprouting everywhere
In fact, things are in good repair

Sabina and I both shivered as the Spellcraft raised goosebumps on our goosebumps. The distant hiss of water went silent, and a moment later, the drain stopped its gurgling.

"Quick," I told my cousin. "Set the spell." With a decisive nod, she tore the Crafting in half. I was about to suggest flushing it to a watery grave, but Sabina tucked away the two halves of the spent spell in her jacket. "Good thinking, Sabina. We can track down the handwriting."

"I thought we might want to shove it in someone's face later when we make our big accusation. But that works too."

We packed up and emerged from the restroom just as Yuri stepped through the grow room door carrying something that looked like a cross between a pool noodle and a mutant pickle. "What do you intend to do with that?" I said.

Sabina didn't miss a beat. "Gross! I don't want to hear about your sex life."

"Sex life? I was worried he'd try to cook it up for dinner!"

My cousin has lots of opinions...and apparently, her opinionated worldview extended to this particular vegetable. "Zucchinis are good for one thing, and one thing only: leaving on other people's doorsteps."

That must not have been a popular pastime in Russia. Yuri gave her the side-eye and hauled the ginormous veggie toward the truck, where he pitched it unceremoniously into the pickup bed. The truck listed a bit to one side. "We will figure out how to get rid of it later. Right now, we need to check the bakery for Spellcraft."

I'd thought Yuri's cheeks looked painful before, but they were even redder and spottier now, and twice as swollen. Yuri's got an iron-clad constitution. One time he did come down with a case of the stomach flu—which was really weird, since we'd had dinner at my folks' house, and no one else there was affected—but other than that, nothing can lay him low.

We hurried over to the bakery, where we spread out to find the best way in. I tried the office, and found the door open—what luck! Bruno's assistant Bernadette was there, sorting through a teetering pile of orders. She spared me a quick glance and said, "If you're here for the job fair, you've come on the wrong day. We're not taking any applications until tomorrow."

Uncle Fonzo always says that anyone who takes "no" for an answer deserves exactly what they get. I wouldn't say that philosophy is entirely bulletproof, as it's earned my uncle his fair share of angry tirades. Luckily, he's charming enough that most folks don't stay mad at him for long.

I did my best to channel his charming demeanor...which may

or may not have involved me shamelessly batting my eyelashes. "Are you sure we can't just get a head start on that job application? After all, don't you want your new hire to be a real go-getter?"

She handed us a card with the job fair particulars. "We just need good bakers. That's all."

My feet were already backing away from the brownie shop in strategic retreat, because no way would I be able to pass myself off as a baker without a thorough crash-course in the subject. The last time I tried to bake anything from scratch, we ended up having to replace the toaster oven.

I bid Bernadette my best charming goodbye, then caught up with Yuri and Sabina in the truck. "If there's any chance of getting a foot in the door, we'll need to disguise that foot as a baker."

Sabina went puzzled. "Just the foot, or...?"

I rolled my eyes. "The whole body. Maybe my mother can give us a few pointers. Enough nomenclature to skate through a job interview."

"Your mother is a very busy woman," said Yuri.

Sabina shifted uneasily. "If she wasn't before, she will be now that I skipped work."

Yuri said, "We know a talented baker who never seems to be busy. And he lives not five minutes from here." He cut his eyes to the railroad tracks that separated the cut-rate shopping district from Scrivener Village, and I bit back a groan. Or I gave it my best shot, anyhow...though a sound of annoyance might have slipped out.

"Okay," Sabina declared, "I give up. Who in the heck are you two talking about?"

Someone who was strikingly good-looking and effortlessly cool.

Someone who had impeccable penmanship with gorgeous flourishes.

And someone who—darn it all—made shortbread that literally melted in your mouth.

My age-old nemesis.... "Vano Shirque."

6

"Vano Shirque?" my cousin repeated. "The time in high school when you spent every last cent of your birthday money on hair goop trying to imitate some other kid's hair, and it turned out he'd just slept on it funny...*that* Vano Shirque?"

I crossed my arms and muttered, "Why, do you know someone else by that name?"

"Don't be so sensitive, Dixon, no one blamed you for trying. His hair did look pretty cool."

Understatement of the year. Vano Shirque was the poster child for luck. Usually. Except for the time his father drowned in the Ganges and his mother was trampled by an elephant. Other than that, he's led a phenomenally charmed life.

As much as it would pain me to ask Vano for a favor, he truly was the least busy guy we knew. Plus, the fact that he was so good at everything he put his hand to would hopefully work to our advantage. Even if it did gall me.

We headed over to Scrivener Village, where half the streets were blocked off for construction and we nearly lost a tire to a missing manhole cover, but luckily, we found a parking spot around the block from Vano's apartment. It had very nearly been *my* apartment, but Vano was quicker on the draw and got to the lease before I did. And while I'd never aspired to live in a place where all the walls were created from surplus doors, maybe I would've considered it—had I realized such an apartment actually existed.

"We don't even know that Vano's home," I complained...though I made no move to text him.

We rounded the corner, and Yuri pointed to Vano's second-story window, where the silhouettes of two figures were faintly visible behind the curtain—one tall and Vano-like, and the other much shorter and vaguely stooped. Vano's great-grandmother was the head of the Pinyin Bay Spellcraft circuit, and if anyone could identify the Scrivener of the leaky Crafting, she could. So I supposed it was in my best interest to plaster an ingratiating smile on my face and ask them for help....

Though I didn't have to like it.

There seemed to be some kind of commotion going on in front of the building, though it wouldn't be Scrivener Village if a commotion wasn't going on somewhere. This particular commotion consisted of a woman having conniptions at Vano's front door.

At first I took her for your typical middle-aged businesswoman, given the fact that she was wearing a suit. But when I got a better look at her, I realized her suit was a little too clingy, her fingernails were press-on, and her designer bag screamed "knockoff." She jingled with jewelry, from the glittering stacks of bracelets on each wrist to the oversized earrings that swung like giant pendulums. And though her hair was a brassy blonde, her complexion was the same coffee-with-cream as everyone else who's had a magical quill fall from the sky.

Sabina saw her at the same time as I did and ducked behind the nearest Volkswagen. She hissed, "What on earth is Venus Monger doing here?"

I said, "Presumably she lives in the neighborhood." After all, most Pinyin Bay Scriveners did. I crouched down by Sabina, and Yuri did his best to follow suit...though we definitely should have picked a bigger car if we'd hoped to keep Yuri out of sight. "So, why are we hiding?"

Sabina said, "Because she's always got some cockamamie money-making scheme in the works. Remember when my dad bought that timeshare in Des Moines?"

"How could I forget? Dullest vacation ever."

"Well, who do you think talked him into it? One look at her plunging neckline and he was putty in her hands." That made a lot of sense. Uncle Fonzo *did* have a real weakness for the ladies. "If Venus gets a load of us, we'll be the ones to get stuck listening to whatever crazy sales pitch is on her agenda!"

My cousin takes particular umbrage to a pushy salesperson, and before I knew it, she was halfway down the nearest alley in her bid to get away. Yuri caught me by the arm and tugged me along behind her. Did I mention he has a really impressive stride? And I can't say I was too disappointed we'd need to come up with a plan B after all—one that *didn't* involve begging favors from Vano Shirque.

Sabina looped around to the rear of the building and pulled out a slender metal nail file. Everyone knows how annoying a hangnail can be, but even so, it was an odd time for a manicure. I was about to say as much when my cousin stepped up to the back door, thrust the nail file into the lock, gave it a jiggle, and popped open the door.

"Impressive," Yuri said.

Sabina shrugged modestly. "Persistence really does open all doors. But in the absence of a handy Crafting, a little lock-picking knowledge doesn't hurt, either."

As we trooped upstairs, I said, "This is a terrible idea. Vano's obviously busy visiting with his Nana—"

"His *Nana*?" Sabina chortled.

"—and no one wants to annoy the head of their circuit by being a buttinski."

Apparently, no one was moved by my totally valid argument. Yuri, I could excuse. His rash was making him do desperate things. Plus, he didn't grow up in the Craft, so he must not have understood how important it was to avoid pestering Morticia Shirque. As for my cousin, though? I'll bet she was just hoping for another opportunity to show off her B&E skills.

Sabina was in the lead. She marched up to Vano's door—the front door to his apartment, which more-or-less worked, unlike the other doors, which were repurposed as various structural elements—and brandished her impromptu lock-pick. But before she could jam it in the lock, the door swung open, and there was Vano, in all his carelessly tousled glory.

Hold on. Tousled...or frazzled?

"You're not Venus Monger," he said to Sabina.

"Well, duh!" My cousin loves nothing better than landing a well-deserved *duh*. "But you should definitely let us in, just in case Venus manages to slip into the building behind us."

With a hasty glance up and down the hallway, Vano ushered the three of us inside. Immediately, I sought out his great-grandmother, brimming with apologies, since I'm told courtesy goes a long way with Morticia. But in the front window where I'd seen her standing with Vano, instead I found a coat rack and a broom with an old afghan thrown over the top. "It's a decoy," Vano said. "While that pushy woman was yelling up at the front window, I was planning to slip out the back."

"Why are *you* hiding from her?" I asked. "Did she try to sell you a timeshare?"

"She's trying to take me out on a date."

Yikes. Venus might be bodacious, but she was old enough to be Vano's mother. And then some.

Vano ran a hand through his hair. It looked even more fetchingly disheveled. Of course. "Ever since Nana got out of the hospital, the vultures have been circling."

"That's awfully morbid," I said. "I thought your Nana made a full recovery."

"She did! They're not circling her, they're circling me. Because if Nana decides to retire after her health scare...."

Sabina looked up in surprise from a wall-door she'd been

prodding at with her nail file. "Then you'll be the Head."

But that was crazy-talk. The head of circuit is a venerable position, and Vano was my age! "How is that possible? There's no one between Nana and you? Aunts, uncles, grandparents?"

"A few cousins down by St. Louis. But even though they're older, they don't live in Pinyin Bay, so the responsibility would fall to me."

I vaguely remembered a residency requirement among all the various rules and regulations. The path of Scrivener succession is convoluted...and boring. Waaay boring. Oh, they tried to drill it all into my head in Scrivener lessons, but obviously I paid more attention to penciling flourishes onto my desk than the mechanics of position and rank within the Spellcraft community. Morticia Shirque had been the head of our circuit approximately forever—in fact, she presided over my grandparents' Quilling Ceremonies—so I'd never pictured one of my contemporaries taking her place.

Yuri edged into the room, giving the coat rack and broom a wide berth. He's not a fan of anything person-shaped that isn't actually a person. "If your grandmother is not here, then where is she?"

"She finally won her mansion back from the Loveland Corporation. The red tape was brutal and they dragged out the case for months. But in the end, it was no match for the quill."

Yuri cast a look at a patchwork of shutters that made up the lounge's wainscoting. "Then why are you here, and not back in the mansion?"

Vano shook his head sadly. "It's Nana's idea. She's under the weird impression that I need a 'bachelor pad.'"

Outside, Venus called up, "Not up for zip-lining? How about glow-in-the-dark putt putt? I hear it's very romantic!"

Vano sighed. "Unfortunately, living here means everyone in Scrivener Village can track my comings and goings." He peeked out through the window blinds and winced. "Including Venus."

"I've got an idea," I said, hoping to make it sound like I'd be doing *him* a favor, and not the other way around. "We'll make a huddle around you, smuggle you out, and help you escape to your Nana's mansion. And once we're there...you can invite us into that crazy kitchen full of wooden spoons and teach us how to make brownies. Won't that be fun?"

"I suppose I'll be harder to spot if I hide behind Yuri. Let's go."

I'll say one thing for Vano—he was a pretty good sport about riding in the bed of the truck. We threw a tarp over him (just in case any sharp-eyed, eligible Scrivener ladies were out and about) then made for the supermarket in the Handless part of town. There, we grabbed some baking supplies—and a yogurt. Because Yuri was looking beyond miserable, though I'd never be so insensitive as to mention it. Whether he believed that I was actually craving a plain, sour yogurt was anyone's guess.

As reluctant as I'd been to enlist Vano's help, he knew exactly what to buy for our baking lesson without needing to consult a recipe. It seemed awfully suspicious, though, that brownies contained no brownie mix whatsoever.

The last time we'd seen Shirque Mansion, it had been locked up tight...but not anymore. Ask me if I'm a traditional guy and I'll deny it up and down. I prefer to think of myself as a trendsetter and a go-getter. But pulling up the fancy circular drive and seeing the windows no longer boarded up and the big padlocks all gone? I'd be lying if I said I wasn't relieved the weird old mansion hadn't been lost after all.

After his sojourn in the back of the truck, Vano was, of course, no worse for wear. But he did seem unduly impressed by the zucchini. "That's a real beauty—and so early in the season. Too bad the state fair is so far off. It'll be mush by the time judging rolls around."

Yuri did not share his enthusiasm. "You want the squash? Take it."

Vano was delighted...or as delighted as he tends to get, which looks more like a fetchingly mysterious half-smile than a full-blown expression of joy.

Yuri hefted the monster zucchini and we headed for the mansion. Morticia wasn't home, but Vano had a key (much to Sabina's disappointment). The inside was a lot more open and expansive without the boards on the windows, though it was still a weird mishmash of styles. Shirque Mansion was a showcase home—in the literal sense. Morticia's father had been a builder who used his own house to demonstrate all the cutting-edge styles and finishes he offered. And while the Shirques no longer needed to live in a life-sized catalog, it would take a lot of money to re-fit Shirque Mansion as a single, cohesive house.

Money they didn't really seem to have.

Furniture was dusty, wallpaper was peeling and carpets were faded. Other than the electricity and phone lines, things hadn't been updated in nearly a century. And even the electricity looked somewhat dubious in spots. But as long as the oven worked, we'd be in business.

Vano parked the zucchini in the corner, cleared clutter from the kitchen table, and set up each of us with measuring cups, spoons, and a mixing bowl. As he demonstrated how to weigh the flour, he said, "In some ways, baking is a lot like Spellcraft. Something between an art and a science. The ingredients are like words—you need to choose the right ones and treat them with respect. But there's room for creativity too."

He pulled something off a dusty spice rack, gave it a sniff, and added a pinch of it to his bowl.

"And then there's the part where you give over to the process and take your hands off the batter. Too much beating makes the flour go tough. And you can't close the oven door without letting go of the pan."

Yuri pressed a damp kitchen towel to his cheek. "But the stakes are a lot higher with Spellcraft."

"True," Vano agreed. "Maybe Spellcraft is more like baking without a recipe—with a bunch of un-labeled ingredients, in an oven with a broken thermometer." He considered the metaphor. "Frankly, it's a real wonder Spellcraft works at all."

Vano was a patient instructor—which was no surprise, since he was as unflappable as the wings of a taxidermy seagull. (To be fair, no one at the nature center *told* me they weren't supposed to move. And once they wired them back on, you could hardly tell the difference.) I had no idea baking was so particular. It's not enough to fill the measuring cup—you need to level it off, and sometimes you "pack" it, sometimes you don't. Teaspoons and tablespoons? Apparently not synonymous. Stir, but don't overstir. And bottled vanilla tastes *nowhere* as good as it smells.

Despite learning the technique in his second language, Yuri seemed the most competent. Not a surprise. He's the only one who can make toast without setting off the smoke alarms. But I did my very best to pay attention—to mind my big T's and my little t's—and by the time I reached the end of my recipe, I was happy to find my batter looked just like everyone else's.

Everyone but Sabina, who had some kind of chunky, watery, marbled effect going on, despite the fact that Vano did everything in his power to assist, right down to helping her stir the bowl.

Once everything was mixed, we popped our pans into the oven. The range at Uncle Fonzo's house has a window in the door. It's small and grimy and nearly impossible to see through, but it's a window nonetheless. The range in Shirque Mansion was a big, fancy cast iron affair that belonged on the set of a historical movie where every character had a slightly different British accent. It was easily large enough to hold all four pans—but it had no window.

Vano noticed me hovering around the oven door. "Don't open it, you'll just let in cold air. You can tell when they're close to done by the way they smell."

Maybe. With his brownies. But he didn't account for the other three pans alongside his. I doubted his wisdom. At least I *did*, until the weird old kitchen filled with the enticing smell of chocolate. Chocolate, and...pizza?

Vano glanced at the dusty spice rack. Two of the jars had smudges of shine on them where they'd been recently handled. His—the cinnamon. And the other....

He plucked it from the rack and said, "Who added oregano?"

Sabina looked annoyed. "I thought it was mint." Yuri gave her an exasperated look, to which she said, "What? You know how much I love mint-chocolate-chip anything."

"You never know," I told her. "Maybe it'll be an awesome flavor combo!"

Before my cousin could call me out on my bald-faced lie, we were interrupted by the crunch of tires on the gravel drive as the head of our circuit pulled up to the mansion in her slightly rusted Rolls Royce.

What luck! If anyone would be able to identify the handwriting on the Crafting we found at Herb's, it was Vano's great-grandmother. And then we could really get to the bottom of things!

YURI

7

Morticia Shirque was the picture of a storybook witch. Her hair was long and steely gray, and she wore it in a single thick braid. Her frame was bony, her nose was hooked, and she even had a mole on her protruding chin that could double for a wart. But unlike a storybook witch, she couldn't just wave a wand and make spells happen. She would need a quill for that, just like any other Scrivener.

Morticia hobbled into the kitchen squinting nearsightedly. "Vano? Is that you?"

"Who else would it be, Nana?"

"Someone with very strange taste in pizza toppings. Pineapple is one thing. But chocolate is simply a bridge too far."

"It's not pizza, Nana, it's brownies. Uh...hopefully." Vano went and met her with a kiss on the cheek, which was apparently enough to confirm his identity to his squinting great-grandmother. None of the other Scriveners in Pinyin Bay would ever dream of being so familiar with the head of their circuit. Meanwhile, I glanced out the window at her car to see if any pieces of mowed-down pedestrians were clinging to the grille. How she'd managed to get home in one piece was anybody's guess.

"Excuse me, Ms. Shirque," Dixon said bravely, "but we've got a Crafting here we were hoping you could identify."

Sabina produced the torn Crafting we'd found in the hydroponics room. Morticia took it from her and squinted at it very hard. And after a long, tense moment, she handed it back and said, "It does appear to be a Crafting."

"Erm...yes," Dixon said as tactfully as possible, "we know. Any telling who it was that Scribed it?"

"Not without my glasses. Haven't seen the darn things all week."

I checked the car yet again for body parts.

"I'm great at finding glasses," Sabina declared. "Where should we look?"

Morticia shrugged. "If I had any idea, I would have found them myself!"

And so, we looked. We searched the parlor. We searched the drawing room. We searched the conservatory. Under the unseeing eyes of a half dozen misshapen plaster statues, we combed every room that was still in use. We were just about to climb the turret when Dixon said, "That's funny—funny-weird, I mean, not funny-ha-ha."

"What is?" I asked.

"Smells like barbecue."

Of course it did.

We rushed back to the kitchen only to find tendrils of smoke creeping from the oven. "Don't open that," Vano called out, but he was too late. Sabina was quick on her feet, and once she's in motion, she's impossible to stop. She heaved open the oven door and thick black smoke billowed out, filling the kitchen in a choking cloud which smelled vaguely of oregano.

As the rest of us fanned the smoke in no particular direction with any available paper—newspapers, magazines, the Crafting—Morticia shuffled in behind us. "Someone open a window before the smoke detector goes off!"

"Since when do we have smoke detectors?" Vano asked.

Morticia gave a sniff of annoyance. "The Loveland Corporation filled the place with the wretched things. I'm sure I've yet to find them all."

I glanced up at the ceiling where a tiny red light blinked amid the smoke.

Vano turned to the nearest window and tugged. "It's sticking."

I shouldered him out of the way to do it myself, but it was no use. The sash was painted shut. I felt something creak and pulled harder, though I suspected the thing that had shifted was my own sinew and bone, not the window. And when a sheen of sweat broke out on my face, it prickled like liquid flame.

Succumbing to a rash was bad enough.

Having it happen because the *volshebstvo* was working against me felt like a betrayal.

There was a ceiling fan overhead, an elaborate Victorian thing with blades of filigreed metal. Vano flipped it on. Grudgingly, it squealed and squawked into motion. Unfortunately, the smoke did not dissipate. It simply compressed toward the floor.

And then smoke detector began to bleat. It was a shrill, ugly sound that made me feel twice as disorientated as the smoke alone. You would think that with a bird who knew how to imitate the sound uncannily well, I would be accustomed to the noise. But the offer of a peanut won't shut up a real smoke alarm.

"Knock that wretched thing down!" Morticia ordered.

Sabina perked up immediately. "I'm as great at beating down pinatas as I am at finding glasses! I just need a long enough stick."

That would be a challenge. Even in the kitchen, the ceilings were high. As the alarm shrieked, we searched desperately for something that would reach—a broom, a cane, a baseball bat, anything—but there was nothing in that kitchen longer than a wooden spoon. Nothing except....

"The zucchini!" Sabina cried.

Before anyone could stop her, she grabbed the ridiculous vegetable, scampered up a chair and onto the kitchen table. "I got your back," Dixon called out as he lunged for the light switch. "Ceiling fan stopping in three...two...one!"

Sabina hoisted the zucchini—it was as tall as her and weighed nearly as much—and gave it an awkward swing...just as it became clear that Dixon had not shut the fan down, but turned up the speed instead.

A series of wet thumps joined the cacophony of squeaking and shrilling as the fan blades chewed through the zucchini. Everyone reflexively crouched and shielded their heads (everyone but Morticia, who couldn't see what was going on). Gobs of zucchini flew in all directions. It was a wonder any of us were spared, but most of us did remain unscathed. All but Sabina, who took a big chunk to the forehead, and toppled backwards off the table.

Luckily Vano was there to break her fall.

By the time they scrambled to their feet, it became clear that the fan blades had done more than just chop the zucchini. The filigreed openings, together with centrifugal force, had acted as a massive peeler. And as we all watched in bewilderment, a thick ribbon of zucchini spun from a chunk caught in the blade, wider and wider, whirling around the room like a giant weed whacker. On the ceiling. Made of zucchini.

Soon the vegetable strip reached the diameter of the room, and as it did, it began knocking things off shelves. Spice jars. Cookbooks. Wooden spoons. Dozens of small objects rained down from the shelves.

And among them, coming to rest in the center of the kitchen table atop an elaborately embroidered dish towel, were Morticia Shirque's lost glasses.

Soon the smoke settled out—it was apparently quite heavy—and Dixon managed to knock down the smoke alarm by straddling my shoulders and whacking at it with a wooden spoon.

Sabina had a red mark on her forehead that would likely bruise, and was picking streamers of zucchini from her hair.

I expected Vano to bemoan the loss of his zucchini, but he hardly seemed to notice it had been demolished.

He was too busy gazing at Sabina.

I supposed she could do worse. Though if anything came to pass between them, her cousin would be less than thrilled.

Morticia had been cleaning her glasses elaborately on the hem of her blouse while the commotion raged around her. Once she finally slid them on, she looked around her kitchen and said, "Dixon Penn? What are you doing here? And what's wrong with your grown man friend's face?"

Luckily, Dixon does not know the meaning of the word exasperation. (And given the effect his rambling had when it outlasted a stranger's patience, he truly should.) "That rash is exactly why we're here! Yuri ran afoul of a Crafting, so we're trying to track down a Scrivener and were hoping you'd recognize the writing."

Sabina handed the two halves of the Spellcraft—luckily no worse for wear—to the head of the circuit.

"It's been Recrafted," Morticia remarked.

"Oh, right!" said Dixon. "That would be me. You'll notice that not only is the rhyme quite inspired, but the meter is spot on. In fact, I'd go so far as to say the Recrafted version is much more elegant than—"

"Dixon," I murmured.

"Anyhoo. It's the author of the *original* Spell I was hoping to nail down."

Morticia gave Dixon a shrewd glance. I wondered what she saw when she looked at him? The Scrivener whose Quilling Ceremony had failed, or the Scrivener who'd redeemed himself? Either way, I had no great trust of canny old women. "This might be familiar," she said, "but I'll need something to compare it to before I give you a definitive answer. Vano, fetch me the Register of the Hands."

Gooseflesh prickled along my arms. Not due to the *volshebstvo*—I was accustomed now to its comings and goings—but the thought of witnessing a Scrivener's secrets. *Things were different here than they were in Russia.* This was a phrase that was continually proving itself to me, again and again. Russian Spellcrafters guarded their secrets with their lives. In comparison, American Spellcrafters were merely coy. And once they knew me as a Seer, they laid open their secrets to me as if I had always been one of their very own.

In Russia, I was told only as much as I needed to know to create a usable Seen. And so, in Russia, I could not say if there was a Hand in every Scrivener family. But in Pinyin Bay, this was how things were done...though Fonzo was never clear as to what being the Hand might entail.

I expected Morticia to unveil something secret—something sacred. But instead she cleared zucchini peels from the kitchen table with her forearm, then Vano dug an old notebook from a drawer and tossed it onto the clean spot. There was a coffee ring on the cover.

"The ends of the strokes have a slight hook to them that you don't see very often," the old woman said as she paged through the notebook. I was too far away to see what secrets it so casually contained, but I did notice that Dixon had gone silent and was doing his best to read over her shoulder without being too obvious...though anyone who knew him would know that the moment he falls silent is the one in which you must keep your eye on him.

Sabina, meanwhile, could care no less about the book. She was more concerned about the brownies. "Sabinochka," I chided, "you're not thinking of eating those."

"You never know. The middles might still be good."

Earlier, when we were mixing our brownies, we had each chosen a different pan (as there were no two alike) but had used the same ingredients. Even so, the things she now pulled gingerly from the oven could not have been more different.

I recognized my pan immediately. My brownies looked good—not too burnt—until I realized they had not risen. They were half the height of everyone else's. When I pried my attempt out of the pan, it came out in a shallow square which was so hard you could have used it to pave a walkway.

Sabina's brownies were burnt black around the edges, and yet they still wobbled with raw egg in the center. The oregano had risen to the top and floated on the soupy center like algae off the shoreline of Pinyin Bay.

Vano's brownies? They looked like...brownies.

And surprisingly enough, so did Dixon's.

Dancing from foot to foot, Dixon clapped his hands together. "I've never baked anything from scratch! Ever! Who'd have thought it was so easy?"

Sabina narrowed her eyes. "This makes no sense. You can't even toast a frozen waffle without smoking out the whole house."

"Then clearly the problem was the toaster," Dixon replied. He snatched up a fork and plunged it into his steaming pan of brownies. "You're just jealous because yours have a swimming pool in the middle. Whereas mine are..." he scooped out a steaming forkful and shoved it into his mouth. Immediately his eyes started to water. I believe he was attempting to say the word "delicious" through all the spluttering and retching that followed. But even his relentless optimism could not possibly make anyone believe him.

Morticia grabbed a small crumb from the pan, placed it in her mouth, and winced. "You've mixed up the sugar and the salt."

While Morticia got Dixon a glass of water, Vano lopped his own brownies into warm squares and doled them out onto mismatched china plates. Dixon wanted to refuse to try them, I could tell—but he also needed to get the taste of salt out of his mouth. He took a resentful bite, then another, and I followed suit. The texture was good, soft and chewy, but the taste was unusual. Not just chocolate, but something else, too, aside from the pinch of cinnamon. The more I ate, the more appealing it became. A hint of burnt sugar. Evidently, as Sabina's brownies burned, they had imparted a subtle, smoky flavor to Vano's—as if that had been his intention all along.

No wonder it took a valiant effort for Dixon to swallow them... though he did manage.

In the end, had we learned anything about baking under the tutelage of Vano Shirque? Only the lesson of not getting distracted while something is in the oven—a lesson that would no doubt be forgotten soon enough.

Once nothing remained of Vano's brownies but a few moist crumbs, his great-grandmother turned her attention back to the stained notebook and began flipping through in earnest. It was beginning to look like yet another dead end as she paged through to the very back of the book. But just as I resigned myself to a life of itchiness and yogurt, she let out a triumphant crow.

"Aha! I knew I recognized those hooks! The Scrivener who penned this Spell...is Ladin Silver."

DIXON

8

We left Vano and his Nana at Shirque Mansion and headed back to Scrivener Village to try to track down our man.

Ladin Silver is a regular fixture of the Pinyin Bay circuit. Not only was he the guy who wooed Sabina's mother away from Uncle Fonzo, but his photo graced the wall of every restaurant in town with an oversized gimmick entree—you know the type, eat the whole thing and it's free? Ladin was the champion of them all. He was the only person who'd managed to eat the three-pound Bamtastic Beefburger in one sitting without throwing up. Baskets of hot wings, stacks of pancakes, and entire schools of deep-fried perch, Ladin had powered through them all...and then called for the dessert menu. Rumor was he'd Crafted himself a little something to keep his competitive edge. But if you've ever taken in the full expanse of him at close range, you'd know that eating came so naturally to him that such a Crafting would be totally unnecessary.

The thing about Ladin Silver is that he tends to show up (uninvited) whenever you'd like to avoid him—but when you do need to see him, he's nowhere to be found.

Ladin lived in a three-story brick walk-up with storefronts on the ground floor and a bank of unmarked doorbells beside the entryway. The popcorn shop that was once below his place was no more, lost to a catastrophic blowout of epic proportions back when explosions were commonplace in Pinyin Bay. I did miss the shop, though only for nostalgic reasons, since the popcorn had always been pretty bad. And despite the fact that it had been many months since popcorn rained down like chewy, scorched, fake-buttery snow, seagulls still circled the building, hoping another explosion might occur.

In the old popcorn shop's place was a new, trendy-looking boutique of locally-sourced items. The shop was closed for the day, so I cupped my hands around my eyes and peered through the plate glass window while Yuri tried all the doorbells. Candles and wind chimes, coasters and paperweights. And beside the quaint, antiquey cash register was a bunch of skin care items displayed in a cardboard honeycomb display, topped with a hand-lettered sign that read, Bee Balm. Did that mean the bees were local, or just the balm-maker? Or would that be *balmist*? Most importantly, would bee balm soothe poor Yuri's inflamed cheeks? I turned to ask, and let out a startled yelp as I nearly pitched headfirst into Venus Monger.

"What the heck?" my cousin said. "Don't sneak up on a person like that!"

"You don't want to shop there," Venus told us importantly, then leaned in and whispered, "it's owned by Handless."

So were the majority of stores in Pinyin Bay. I saw no reason to feel weird about spending my money in Handless establishments. After all, they were the ones who paid me to Uncraft their wonky spells.

"Besides," Venus went on, "you wouldn't get the personalized service there that you get when you buy direct from the manufacturer."

"Uh-oh," Sabina said. "Here comes the sales pitch."

"Anything you could find here, I could recreate at half the cost."

Yuri, naturally, was skeptical. "A Scrivener should be crafting Spells, not pot-holders."

Venus was undeterred. "No need to get all flustered and flushed."

"I am not flustered."

"All good Scriveners have a healthy amount of hustle. And diversifying is the best way to protect yourself from a fluctuating market. What is it you're looking for? Pens? Note cards? Macrame?"

My initial impulse was to give her a polite brush-off, but once I thought about it, I realized it would be silly of me to pass up the opportunity to help Yuri. "I was just curious about the skin care items inside the—"

"Say no more!" Venus swung a massive handbag off her shoulder, snapped it open, and thrust her arm inside—which disappeared up to the elbow. After a hearty rummage, she came up with a small, unlabeled jar with something semi-liquid sloshing around inside. "You've heard of the health benefits touted of various natural ingredients—goji berries, coconut oil, apple cider vinegar. I've combined all these plus a proprietary herbal blend into a miracle product I call Monger's Medicament Balsam and Tonic."

Great name. And I'm not gonna lie...I've always been a sucker for anything *proprietary*. "What does it do?"

"The question you should be asking is: what *doesn't* it do?"

"Well, okay, what doesn't it—?"

"Monger's Tonic is a toxin-clearing, wellness-promoting, colon-cleansing, gluten-free, organic-adjacent alternative to any product for the home or body you can imagine. And it can be yours for a mere $99.99. Plus tax."

"That's awfully steep," Sabina said.

I nodded toward the storefront window. "The bee balm in the display is only ten dollars."

Venus narrowed her eyes. "But I can personally guarantee that Monger's Tonic is bee-*free*." That did seem like a pretty important feature. "Plus, instead of waiting till morning for the shop to open back up, you can get it right now."

"I don't have a hundred bucks." I patted down my pockets. "How about five?"

Venus didn't seem thrilled about my offer...but she did grudgingly accept my crumpled five. And, bonus, since I was now out of money, she informed us that since she was not actually a medical professional, she could make no medicinal claims on her tonic, and wasted no time in moving along to find her next mark. Er... customer.

"This was no use," Yuri said, giving a Very Stern Look to Venus's departing back. "Ladin Silver is not here. Unless we can figure out some way to track him down—"

"Guys?" my cousin said. She cocked her head at a nearby telephone pole that was plastered with so many layers of notices and flyers it ruffled in the breeze. "Check out this note."

My breath caught. "Wow—someone's selling a trampoline?"

"No, not that one." She pointed to an unobtrusive slip of paper pinned to the top of the stack. "Look at the handwriting—it's got those little hooks Morticia pointed out. It must be Ladin's."

Yuri and I joined my cousin at the telephone pole and read.

Meat is scarce
At least I know
The cabbage is
In season

"What the heck is that supposed to be?" Sabina scowled. "Some kind of haiku?"

I ran through it in my head. "Wrong number of syllables," I said. "Though if I added five more at the end...."

"It is awkward," Yuri said decisively. "Even for English."

If I didn't know better, I'd say it looked like a Crafting. But it hadn't been penned on a Seen, just a scrap of plain paper. Despite the fact that I'm always being reminded to "look before I leap," I was leery about touching the note, because something about it was clearly not right. "Maybe there's a Seen on the back." I pulled a faded business card off the telephone pole and used it to lift the edge of the paper. The flip side was blank.

I stared at the words and defocused my eyes, searching for the telltale Spellcraft sparkle, but all I got for my effort was a bunch of blurry words.

"I don't sense the *volshebstvo*," Yuri said.

"Maybe it's half a Crafting," Sabina suggested. "Just the words. Some kind of cloak-and-dagger handoff between the Scrivener and the Seer where the two of them never actually meet."

"Impossible," Yuri said. "You cannot Scribe without a Seen."

Sabina warmed to her own idea. "But you can't just stick a Seen to a telephone pole in Scrivener Village—it's too valuable. It would be gone before the paint even dried. A Scribing, though? Those things are a dime a dozen around here and no one would think twice. Especially one about cabbage."

Yuri didn't budge. In fact, I suspected he enjoyed the casual squabbles he shared with Sabina. "No one would waste their time Crafting about a cabbage. This saying is probably slang for something else—like every other word in your language. But the fact remains: you cannot Craft a blank page. The Seen always comes *first*."

They kept right on arguing, but word *first* echoed through my mind: *first-first-first*.... Hopefully that didn't mean my brainpan was as empty as my Handless teachers always said it was. And, honestly, that really wasn't fair of them. I might have the attention span of a flea, but I retained things just fine. In fact, who was it that had just demonstrated his knowledge of haikus? That would be me. Although I'd need to split up the lines a bit differently...not that they made any particular sense in their current configuration....

Not unless you looked at each line individually, and made note of the word that came *first*.

Meat is scarce
At least I know
The cabbage is
In season

Meat. At. The. In.

"Aha!" I exclaimed so loudly (and abruptly) that both Sabina and Yuri immediately stopped bickering. "I know *exactly* where to find Ladin Silver!"

9

Pinyin Inn sits at the edge of town halfway between the Bay County Prison and the wolverine fence. It was one of the many properties that Loveland Corporation had acquired in their bid to excavate the underbelly of Pinyin Bay—and like Shirque Mansion, it had fallen into foreclosure once it was realized there was nothing to find under the city but a heap of disturbing, amateurish sculpture.

Unlike Shirque Mansion, Pinyin Inn had no one interested in reclaiming it. And so it sat forlornly on the western shore of the Bay, abandoned by all....

Or so we thought—until we rounded the drive and saw several cars half-hidden in the surrounding undergrowth. There'd been some effort to make the cars look as abandoned as the hotel, but it was only a cursory attempt at best. A station wagon had a tarp thrown over the hood. A couple of stray branches had been strewn on the windshield of a dented sedan. And if I squinted just right, deep in the shadows of the utility shed, I could make out the unmistakable headlights of an old Buick....

"Sabina, isn't that your dad's car?"

She rolled her eyes. "I thought he was being awfully cagey about his plans tonight. Let's go see what these crusty old Scriveners are up to."

I've always loved a good clandestine meeting. How exciting!

At first the building looked dark, but when we got up close, I could make out the faintest slivers of light creeping out around the edges of the drawn curtains. The front door was plastered with all sorts of foreboding signs: *Private Property - Keep Out*. Which only made the whole thing that much more intriguing.

I tried the door. The doorknob didn't budge. Sabina brightened. No doubt it had been a while since so many lock-picking opportunities presented themselves to her in a single day. But as she jimmied a credit card into the crack of the doorframe, a tiny window slid open right beside her head and startled her so badly she not only jumped, but punctuated the hop with a noise like a squeak toy.

A pair of beady eyes regarded us from the other side of the door. "What's the password?" the owner of the eyes demanded gruffly.

This night just kept getting better and better! "I'm great at passwords. I'll just need a couple of hints. Is it bigger than a bread box? And do people even use bread boxes nowadays? Come to think of it, I'm not sure I've ever seen an actual bread box in the wild—"

"No hints," the doorkeeper said. "Either you know the word, or you don't."

Sabina could not let that statement go unchallenged. "Really? Maybe we're here to make sure *you* know the password. You tell us."

Unfortunately, the guy didn't fall for it. He made to slide the tiny window shut—but before he did, Yuri stuck his finger in there. He ended up getting his knuckle cracked, but he did keep us from being shut out entirely.

"Fine," I called through the gap, "I don't need a hint. I'll just make an educated guess. *Hotel*. No? How about *door*? Still no? Okay, is it *doorknob*?"

Sabina wasn't about to guess when she could argue instead. "You have to let us in. My father's in there—so, obviously, he'd vouch for us."

An exasperated sigh, slightly tinged with whiskey, wafted through the gap. "Look, kids, I don't make the rules. You need to say the password or you can't come in. So do us all a favor, take your finger, and go on home...."

Just through that door, tales were being told and secrets were being secreted, and here we were, mere moments away from a rare glimpse into the clandestine underpinnings of Pinyin Bay's Scrivener community. All that stood in our way was a single word. But with more than a million distinct words in the English language, I couldn't imagine how we'd ever—

"Spellcraft," Yuri said. "The password is Spellcraft."

"Fine," the doorman groaned. Home free! Or so I thought, until he said, "And your contribution to the potluck?"

Uh-oh.

If ever there was a perfect time to whip out a giant zucchini! Unfortunately, the incorrigible courgette was now nothing but a bunch of zucchini streamers festooning the kitchen of Shirque Mansion. In theory, I kept a granola bar in my messenger bag to ward off any potential low blood sugar moments, but in practice, whenever I reached for it, I came up with nothing but a wrapper and a vague memory of a pronounced craving for a granola bar. I delved into my bag anyhow to buy myself a moment to think... and, lo and behold, came up with a carton of warm yogurt which, technically, *was* food.

What luck! I brandished the yogurt triumphantly and said, "Here's our contribution!"

The eyes squinted. "Yogurt? That's it?"

"Of course not." I dove back in my bag and came up with the snake oil Venus sold me...which hopefully did not contain any actual snake. "Once you mix in this proprietary herbal blend, it's an unparalleled dressing and dip. Now let us in."

With much rolling of eyes and another whiskey-tinged sigh, the old Scrivener opened the door.

The Pinyin Inn harkened back to times when a hamburger cost a nickel and people rented rooms by the week. The original decor must have been interesting once, but now it bore little resemblance to its original glory. The place had been revamped several decades ago—think country cottage chic, with whitewashed wood, stenciled borders, and lots and lots of gingham—and no one had given it so much as a coat of paint ever since. The whitewash was so yellowed and the gingham so faded, their origin looked more 1880's than 1980's, and the fact that the place was now lit solely by candlelight only deepened that impression. But we Scriveners learn to make do with what we have. Given the laughter coming from the old dining room, everyone was having a grand old time despite the lack of electricity and the cringeworthy decor.

I could hardly wait to see what top-secret undertakings were transpiring. A long-lost rite? An obscure ritual? I rounded the corner eagerly, and found a half-dozen Scriveners seated around a table. Candles flickered. Cigars smoldered. And in the center of it all?

A pile of plastic chips, which rattled as Ladin Silver threw in a handful, declaring, "I'll see your bet and raise you ten."

At my side, Yuri made a sound of annoyance. "All this secrecy... for a card game?"

The poker players all looked up, Uncle Fonzo among them—and he seemed particularly glad to see us. "Well, would you look who's here! You all remember my daughter, and my nephew, and his grown man friend—"

"No stalling, Fonzo," Ladin told him. "Either see the bet, or fold."

With a groan of resignation, Uncle Fonzo laid down his cards. "Fine, fine. It would be unsportsmanlike to clean you all out before we've even gotten started."

The other poker players all chuckled. I knew each of them to some degree. They were ubiquitous fixtures at any Pinyin Bay Quilling Ceremony, the type of paunchy, middle-aged guys who'd hand you a thin envelope with a couple of bucks inside, tell a few questionable jokes, and then try to be surreptitious about spiking the punch bowl.

It was like any other poker game you might imagine, save for one thing. Each player had a piece of Spellcraft stuck to his person. Oh, and the one guy now sniffing curiously at Venus's goji berry concoction. But mostly it was the visible Spellcraft.

The sentiments were all pretty much what you'd expect. *This hand is a winner.* Or, *The cards are with me.* Or, *Luck is my lady tonight.* Crafting for luck is big business, so it wasn't the presence of the Spellcraft that surprised me, just the fact that everyone had his lucky poker spell on full display...though I wouldn't be surprised if they also had a few backup spells tucked away for safe keeping.

As the Scrivener who'd answered the door raked in a hefty pile of plastic chips, Uncle Fonzo shook off the loss of the hand with cheerful brusqueness. He parked his stogie in an ash tray, stood and brushed cracker crumbs from his lap, and said, "Whatever it was that led you to track me down must've been pretty important, so I suppose I can tear myself away from the game."

With zero attempt at tact, Sabina blurted out, "We weren't looking for you, Dad. We have a question for Ladin Silver!"

Now everyone was curious—but accusing another Scrivener of sabotage was serious business—and I'd like to think I was more tactful than my cousin. "Maybe we should ask Ladin in private," I suggested.

"Nonsense," he declared, larger than life as always. "We're all among friends here. I've known this group for ages and I'd trust them with anything."

"Really," I said, "this is a delicate matter."

That insistence only made Ladin more determined to make me air his dirty laundry in front of the whole group. He dug in his heels and said, "I'm not shady like your uncle, all secretive and sly."

"I'm nothing of the sort!" Uncle Fonzo protested.

Ladin went on. "Anything you need to say, you can say in front of my pals."

I would have tried once more to lure Ladin away from the table, but Yuri'd had just about enough of our American attempts at politeness. He shoved the leaky Spellcraft under Ladin's nose and said, "We know this is your Crafting—and don't try to deny it.

Your writing was verified by the head of your circuit!"

A forceful Yuri is truly a sight to behold. Ladin backed up as far as his chair would allow—but only to get the Crafting into the sweet spot of his bifocals. "Sure! I remember that one. The veggie man was what you'd call a skeptic, but I guess I showed him. How's he doing?"

"How would you expect?" Yuri said dangerously.

For some reason, Ladin wasn't the least bit intimidated. "Hopefully a lot better, now that I fixed his leaks."

Sabina read the Crafting aloud with great indignation. "*Leaks are sprouting everywhere.* You call that a fix?"

"Absolutely." Ladin gestured to the potluck spread on the sideboard. "I needed some potatoes for my famous spuds au gratin, my credit card was declined, and Herb was complaining that his leaks wouldn't sprout—so I struck a bargain and paid with a Crafting. If that's not a win-win, I don't know what is."

A groan worked its way from the back of Yuri's throat. "It is a misspelling."

I read through the Crafting again. "Everything looks kosher to me."

Yuri shook his head. "The very first word: *leaks*. It should have been L-E-E-K-S. Like the vegetable."

"Are you sure, Yuri? I've most certainly never eaten anything called a *leek*." Then again, vegetables weren't exactly my greatest area of expertise.

The Scrivener who'd answered the door said, "I've eaten leeks before. My lady-friend puts them in her potato soup."

"Your lady-friend knows how to cook?" Ladin Silver asked with a predatory gleam in his eye.

"Forget I said anything!" The doorman went back to his cards.

Fine, so an obscure vegetable known as a leek might actually exist, and some hearty soul might be so brave as to eat it—on purpose, even. But a Scrivener misspelling a Crafting? Unheard of! Growing up, we had spelling drilled into our impressionable Scrivener heads just as forcefully as vocabulary and cursive. Handless kids at public school got away with the occasional quiz, but once they dispersed to piano lessons or soccer practice, budding Scriveners were shuttled off to another hour of Spellcraft training—not to mention the weekend workshops and summer camps. Homonyms and homophones were topics of many a lesson. I should know—Cuthbert Rath called me a *homonym* for most of seventh grade.

Not that he was wrong.

There was even a handy rhyme we were taught as a cautionary tale against using homonyms: *When two words are spelled the same, it's time to use a different name.* By *name*, obviously, they meant *word*. Though that didn't rhyme. Although, if the first line were reworked to end with *absurd*.... At any rate, it was ludicrous to think any Scrivener would be careless enough to actually misspell something as critical as a—

Sabina elbowed me and pointed to the Crafting protruding from Ladin's breast pocket.

Grate luck is at my fingertips!

Eesh. Maybe the whole *leek* theory did hold water after all.

Yuri was not entirely convinced. "How did the farmer fail to see your mistake?"

"Mistake is an awfully strong word," Ladin said. "Do you think Spellcraft knows the difference between an A and an E?" Actually, Spellcraft was infamous for exploiting mistakes like that. Everyone knew the *volshi-boogaloo* loved nothing more than a loophole. But Ladin wasn't looking for an actual answer to his question. "The intent is what really matters. And as for the farmer—he was such a skeptic, he made a big point of not even looking at the Crafting. I guess I showed him!"

Boy, I'll say.

I would have loved to stick around and absorb the private conversation among the Scriveners—though I suspected most of it revolved around old-man topics like cigars and liniments, and maybe off-track betting—but it was time to head home and do our best to prepare for tomorrow's job fair. Yuri's cheeks were looking really painful. And as for Venus's miracle tonic, judging by the guy scraping the last dregs from the bottom of the jar with a stale tortilla chip, the concoction must've made a pretty good salsa.

"Say, Uncle Fonzo, before we go, would you mind calling Dr. Slaughter and asking if there's any other home remedy we can try?"

His stack of poker chips was pretty diminished, and I think he was grateful for the opportunity to sit out a hand. "I'd been meaning to check in with her anyway. Things have really been heating up for us in the romance department, if you know what I mean."

"Dad!" Sabina cried. "Ew!"

Ignoring her, Uncle Fonzo pulled out his phone. He set it to speaker—presumably to prove that he was *not* shady—and dialed.

She picked up in a single ring. "Fonzo...I thought you were at poker night."

"I am! Say hi to the boys, Glenda!"

"Um...hi. Listen, Fonzo, take me off speaker for a second, would you? I need to tell you something."

"I've known these guys since the dark ages. Anything you need to say, you can say in front of them."

"But, Fonzo—"

"I have no secrets from my friends."

"I'd really rather not."

"No, I insist!"

"Well...if that's how you want it." After an especially awkward pause, Dr. Slaughter cleared her throat and announced, "I'm late."

Late for what? If she knew Uncle Fonzo was on a boys' night out, it wasn't as if she'd expect to meet up with him. I was about to ask when Sabina sucked in a huge gasp—seriously, a major whoop, like she'd just given up on a breath-holding contest—and she'd gone white as a sheet.

I said, "I get the sneaking suspicion I'm missing something."

My cousin snagged me by the elbow and hauled me toward the door. "I'll tell you later. Let's get out of here."

YURI 10

Back at our flat, Sabina informed us what women mean by the word "late" when spoken in a particular tone of voice—and the *period* involved had nothing at all to do with the end of a sentence. She declared she had no desire to be stuck with babysitting duty, then stomped downstairs in her combat boots to slam her bedroom door, play her music far too loud, and probably scream into a pillow.

Dixon shook his head. "I'm having a doozy of a time wrapping my head around this, Yuri. Uncle Fonzo is *way* too old to be a new dad."

"Apparently not."

Once Fonzo absorbed what was going on, I had no doubt he would be thrilled. American Spellcrafters adore their children—and while they were loath to use the word "blessing," if ever I heard a Scrivener utter such a loaded word, it would be in regard to the promise of new life.

The thought of a wailing newborn just beneath my floorboards should have left me apprehensive. I had no patience for babies. They were helpless and demanding. They gave off all sorts of objectionable noises and smells. And they turned every adult in their vicinity into a babbling, cooing simpleton.

And so...why was it *eagerness* which I felt stirring in my belly?

I had no desire to be a father myself. I was reared with no good example of how to parent—my mother was cold, and my father lashed out with both words and fists. But there was no doubt in my mind that when I opened my heart to Dixon, I gained not only a *vozljublennyj*, but a family. This family had so much love, there was easily enough to spare for another child. In fact, no doubt the baby's arrival would only cause that love to multiply.

I paused beside Dixon as he rummaged through our refrigerator (which was actually two mini refrigerators stacked on top of each other) and said, "Will it make any difference that the mother is Handless?"

"Not in the least." Dixon pulled out a container, sniffed it, and put it back. "As far as the circuit is concerned, the more, the merrier. Any child of a Scrivener is considered a full-fledged Spellcrafter—and their partner, too."

"Scriveners are so clannish. I am surprised they would not prefer to limit themselves to other Scriveners."

"Maybe it's something to do with making sure there's fresh DNA in the bloodline. You wouldn't want to start getting inbred, and a kid with one formerly-Handless parent is no more likely to fail a Quilling Ceremony than a full-blooded Scrivener." Dixon's expression clouded. His own failed Quilling Ceremony was still a painful memory. But then he glanced up at Meringue, dozing in the rafters with her head tucked under her snow white wing, and he immediately brightened. Because if his official Quilling Ceremony had succeeded, he would not have ended up at Precious Greetings that fateful day—and the two of us might never have met.

"Just picture it, Yuri. Can you imagine how much fun a baby will be? Those chubby little legs? Those itty-bitty toes? Those inky-dinky little toenails??"

"What if its mother does not wish to move in and raise the child with Fonzo?"

"Of course she will! You know how charming Uncle Fonzo can be! Plus, she's got her medical career to think of, so she'll want all the extra help she can get. We Scriveners work much more flexible hours." As evidenced by the fact that Sabina wandered away from the office whenever the impulse took her.

Dixon hugged himself in anticipation. "A new baby! I can't wait to teach him how to talk. Him...or her. Or, ooh, I know—what if Dr. Slaughter has one of each? Maybe she learned a special way to make that happen in medical school."

"While she was learning about birth control?"

"And when do I get to start calling her Auntie Slaughter? Maybe the baby can have her surname as its first name. Slaughter Penn—how about that? Hip, trendy, unisex—and, bonus, if the baby ever decides to be a pro wrestler...."

Dixon turned on an overhead light to get my reaction to his name suggestion. At the sight of me, the wistful joy in his expression turned to concern as he pressed the backs of his cool fingers to my face. "Maybe I shouldn't have surrendered that yogurt to the pot luck after all. Your rash is getting worse."

I stepped into our bathroom and carefully unbuttoned my shirt, dreading what I would see in the mirror. My cheeks were as red as the crimson paint pan in my small metal paintbox, but that was hardly a surprise. The skin felt hot and angry, as though I was enduring an unending moment of humiliation. And it was no longer just my cheeks looking red, and blotchy, and swollen—but my neck, too.

As I scrutinized my reflection, Dixon slipped into the bathroom behind me...holding a bowl.

"That had better not be the concoction from that Monger woman," I said.

"Come on, Yuri, I'm an incurable optimist, but I wasn't born yesterday. Plus, those Scriveners at the poker game finished every last drop."

"We have no yogurt. If you have found anything in our refrigerator that seems like yogurt, it can only be some milk we have forgotten about."

Dixon bathed my reflection in a tolerant smile. "Don't worry, I know how you felt about putting yogurt on your face. So I did a little web search, and found that oatmeal might be soothing."

"How is oatmeal any better than yogurt?"

"Well, for one thing, we already had some in the fridge. Good thing you made that triple-batch this morning."

"If this is a magical affliction, it's a waste of time to pursue a mundane cure."

Dixon fluttered his dark eyelashes—a move which never fails to melt my resolve, though I do my best not to show it. He pitched his voice low, just the slightest bit sultry, and said, "If I'm going to waste a little time with someone...there's no one I'd rather do it with than you."

He eased my shirt down to my elbows and lay a stroke of chilled oatmeal across my bare shoulder...then warmed it quickly with his tongue. A shiver coursed through me that had nothing to do with the *volshebstvo*.

Dixon is creative to the point of being fanciful...which, I have found, is one of the very reasons I adore him.

Half an hour later, after nearly braining ourselves in the shower—oatmeal is surprisingly slippery—we dried off and settled into our bed. I rolled to face the door, not because I did not want Dixon to see me, but because he loves to spoon against my back. The gentle rasp of his stubble buffed my shoulder blade and his contented sigh played down my spine. And there, in the dark, in the safety of our room, on the very cusp of sleep, I found a bit of wayward courage. I could have let it pass, but I chose, instead, to speak.

"It is clear that neither of us has any chance of being hired as a baker based on our skills, but I know you, and I know you do not take *no* for an answer. I also know you are not only persistent, but charming."

Into my back, Dixon murmured, "You're just saying that because I do naked things to you." He sounded like he was smiling.

I squeezed his hand to my chest. "I'm saying that because it is true. Even if I did not love you—" Against my back, Dixon tensed. Only briefly. More of a quiver. But thankfully, he did not make a big deal of what I'd inadvertently admitted. "—even then, I would be amazed at your ability to win people over and get what you want."

With another happy sigh, Dixon mashed himself into my back more firmly and settled into the deep breaths of sleep.

Love is a complicated thing. I have always thought love made a man weak, or at the very least, uncomfortably vulnerable. But maybe, I now suspected, that uneasiness was a fair price to pay.

DIXON

11

You really don't appreciate how early bakers get up until you have to pry yourself out of bed well before sunup. It was the next morning, technically—though it felt more like the middle of the night—and even Meringue couldn't be bothered to stir and mimic the alarm clock. It was tempting to duck under the sheets and pretend I'd hit the snooze button (and not the off-switch)... until I found Yuri's face in the dark, and pressed my fingers to his disturbingly hot cheek.

Apparently the oatmeal hadn't been much help.

There was some debate about whether we should include Sabina. Of the three of us, she was by far the worst baker. I thought she might make us look better by comparison, while Yuri was concerned that her badness would paint us all in a negative light. But since she proved impossible to pry out of bed, we ended up heading over to Bruno's without her.

There's a mirror beside my uncle's front door—a promotional thing from the seventies bearing the logo of a long-gone shoelace factory—but its placement is perfect for double-checking your hair on the way out.

Unfortunately, it gave Yuri second thoughts about leaving the house at all.

The red spots on his cheeks were livid. They were so raised now, they actually looked shiny. They looked pretty painful, too, poor guy....

"This plan will never work," Yuri said. "No one will hire me to touch food looking like this."

I gave his biceps a squeeze—but gently, in case the rash had spread. "It has to work. There's no telling how bad your condition will get, let alone how long it will take to get better." If ever. Because magical afflictions didn't exactly follow the usual laws of nature. "Too bad I lost that prosthetic beard yesterday to the duct tape. I don't think the costume shop opens again until ten. Darn it, I knew I should've sprung for the three-pack.... Wait, I know." I snatched a scarf from beside the door, a slinky, silky boho thing that belonged to Sabina, and wrapped it around his head.

"Dixon—"

"Don't worry, you can totally pull it off. Just pretend you're European. Er, wait, you are European."

"I am Russian."

"There you go—perfect!"

We headed over to Bruno's Brownerie, where the owner's assistant, Bernadette, met us at the staff door looking pint-sized and adorable. "Cute scarf!" she told Yuri. "But with health regulations being what they are, anyone with facial hair longer than a quarter inch is required to wear a beard guard."

Normally, I wouldn't have been caught dead in something called a beard guard—but we'd left the house in such a hurry, I hadn't had a chance to shave. And Sabina's comment yesterday about the proliferation of my one-day beard was no exaggeration.

While I might have felt reticent, Yuri couldn't get that thing on fast enough. It was a gauzy, meshy fabric, fine enough to see through, but it did obscure his condition. If you didn't know to look for it, you'd never realize his cheeks were covered in angry spots. Once our beards were girded, we filled out our name tags, stuck them on and headed in.

At the next branch in the hallway, Bruno was watching applicants file in with a look of gentle bewilderment on his broad, friendly face, directing the stream of hopefuls into a workroom large enough to hold us all. As I passed him, I couldn't help but notice a door behind him labeled in extremely stern lettering: Staff Only.

"What's in there?" I asked. "I'll bet it's super interesting!"

His tiny, bright button-like eyes lit up. "It sure is. No other brownerie has anything like it—"

"Never you mind," Bernadette said briskly, herding us along. "We don't let just anyone in on our trade secrets. Land one of the job vacancies and *then* you'll get the grand tour."

The workroom she hustled us into held three rows of long stainless steel tables manned (or womaned) with about a dozen job applicants. I'd been hoping we wouldn't have so much competition, and that the appalling hour would weed out some hopeful bakers. Unfortunately, the other potential candidates were early birds. Not only had they arrived well before us, but they looked disturbingly awake.

The best way to scope out our rivals, I reasoned, was to be friendly. Actually, that's my go-to approach for pretty much everything. But in this case, it really did seem like the best course of action. Ingratiating myself to the top dog should make me seem like a good team player—never mind that I know nothing about teams, since Spellcraft is more of a relay race than a football game. The current group of hopefuls had turned to check us out as we walked in, but they fell back into the dynamic they'd established just as soon as they looked us over.

A woman named Joan was the first to resume speaking. She was maybe my mom's age—but unlike my mom, she'd let her hair go natural salt-and-pepper, wrapped in a tight bun at the top of her head. She wore a folksy, embroidered smock that screamed artsy-fartsy (or perhaps artisan-fartisan, if you want to be technical, since baking is more artisanal than artistic). And while I had no preconceptions of what a baker might look like, she did strike me as the sort of person who'd have a sourdough starter bubbling away in a dark corner of her kitchen.

"I would never use hard winter wheat in a croissant," Joan was saying loftily. "In fact, in the Basque region, soft winter wheat is the norm. Of course, in Slovakia, they prefer red wheat to white...."

My only experience with flour was that while "whole" wheat flour might sound impressive, it was *not* welcome in my mother's home—I found that out the hard way. Though on the bright side, it did get me out of grocery shopping duty. Anyhow, this woman was dauntingly knowledgeable, and I clearly had no hope of out-baking her. But I could absolutely schmooze her.

Maybe we could forge a connection by talking about Europe, I figured—since Yuri was European-ish and I was very well-traveled. I sidled up to Joan's table and said, "Wow, Joan, you really know your European wheat. Have you been to Slovakia?"

"Several times." She proceeded to tell me a bunch of dull facts about Slovakia which I immediately forgot.

Yuri, meanwhile, scoped out the adjacent table, which just happened to be vacant, and leaned into it with his arms planted wide so as to discourage anyone from cozying up to him. Not that his ridiculously butch stance would work on me. In fact, it might just have the opposite effect—if it weren't for the silly beard guard. Then again, I'd been forced to wear one too, so I couldn't exactly throw stones. Maybe later I could get Yuri to strike that same pose without the guard....

I was contemplating whether or not the card table in our kitchenette would bear the full weight of Yuri's assertive leaning when one final hopeful joined us in the baking room—and that person was none other than Venus Monger.

Yuri's forbidding territorial stance was all for naught. Venus strode up to his work table, jingling with bangles and baubles, and plunked her massive purse down right beside him with the force of a knockoff wrecking ball. Yuri moved, grudgingly, and conveyed his annoyance at being displaced with a short but expressive sigh—so expressive that it made Venus finally look at the person she'd been elbowing in on. "Oh, aren't you the Seer—er...?" Only once the question was out of her mouth did she notice she was in the company of a bunch of Handless—all of whom were now way more curious about Yuri than they'd been a mere five seconds before. "Sea urchin, uh, trainer. Yes. That's right. That's what you do, isn't it? Whip those spiny little critters into shape?"

Yuri answered with an even more eloquent sigh. But before he could come up with any sort of plausible response—either to play along or totally deny the urchin-wrangler thing—Bernadette brandished a tiny air horn, pushed the button...and nearly sent the entire room into cardiac arrest.

Once our ears were done ringing, she said, "Okay, gang, now that I've got your attention, let's talk brownies. Bruno's Brownerie has done incredibly well in a very short time, and the reason for that is quality, consistency, and attention to detail...."

Somehow, I'd ended up front and center of the crowd, so I politely nodded along with Bernadette as she went on about what she was looking for in a job candidate. But it was early. Really early. And she was, frankly, pretty boring. Not only that, but I was way more interested in figuring out why Venus Monger might be there. Venus was the poster child for entrepreneurial endeavors. So why would she even dream of putting in an application to work for someone else?

I pondered that for a good few moments before I realized Bernadette was still talking. "...so if you do your best to align yourself with Bruno's standards, you stand the best chance of donning the apron. Now, for the first part of the job fair, we're going to see how well you listen." Fantastic! I'm a great listener. "I'll take you through the supplies and tell you where everything is, then give you a simple recipe to convert. Step right this way and we'll get started."

Logically (and logistically) I should have been the first person to follow Bernadette out the door. But before I knew it, I was being shoved aside as Venus Monger hustled and bustled her way to the front of the line. "Don't worry," Joan told me. "All the rushing in the world won't make her any better of a baker. Knowledge and precision are the keystone habits of a competent baker."

Precision was no problem—I was able to cant my writing at any given angle so accurately you'd swear I kept a protractor up my sleeve. But knowledge? Hopefully I'd get away with faking it.

Our group of a dozen hopefuls crowded into a big pantry full of very industrial-looking bins of ingredients. Bernadette pointed out where everything was, assuring us that it was all fresh, organic, and local. Except for the fair-trade cocoa, which apparently didn't grow in Pinyin Bay. Maybe that problem could be solved with Spellcraft...but before I got too lost in my fantasies of starting my own magical chocolate plantation, Yuri elbowed some bakers out of the way and eased up beside me. This was probably for the best, as I had no idea where to go about recruiting Oompa Loompas to help me run the operation. Yuri cocked his head toward Venus, then whispered through the beard net, "That woman is up to no good."

That was really assuming the worst...but at the very least, she must have an ulterior motive.

"Venus would do anything for right price," he said decisively. "She must be the one behind the sabotage, and she is here to cover her tracks."

The Scriveners in the Pinyin Bay circuit were basically a large, often estranged, and somewhat dysfunctional family. While I hate to think ill of any one of them...I did have to admit that Yuri's notion made an awful lot of sense. If someone hired Venus to make Bruno's Brownies look bad at the big expo, it was in her best interest to clean up the evidence. And like my mom always says, the only one interested in your own best interest is you...and, naturally, your mother. But since I'd never met Venus's parents, I could only presume she was acting on her own behalf.

"I hope you've all been paying close attention," Bernadette announced—and I realized I'd missed pretty much everything she'd said up to that point. "Because I only have three positions available."

And given Joan's extensive knowledge of baking, she was sure to land one of them! Which meant it was imperative we knock Venus out of the competition to make sure both Yuri and I were hired.

Bernadette herded us back into the workroom and said, "Before I have you all start baking, first I'll need to make sure you can convert a recipe." She handed out recipe cards, papers and pencils. "Let's say you're making a double batch of this basic butterscotch blondie. Jot down exactly how you'd go about it."

The original recipe was hand-written—clearly penned by someone who hadn't been subject to daily calligraphy drills, at that. Obviously, I'd improve on the penmanship. But the numbers were a bit concerning, once I realized that some of the measurements were in fractions, like the 1/2 cup of butter (and, wow, that's a lot of butter) or the .5 tablespoons of salt. How was it that both of those figures doubled to become the number 1? As I pondered how decimals and fractions could both exist in the same universe, Yuri cleared his throat and asked, "Beside the baking powder—is this teaspoons or tablespoons?"

Oh no, he'd exposed himself for the rank amateur he was—even after getting a lesson from Vano. But instead of showing him the door, Bernadette smiled broadly and said, "Very good! If something is ambiguous or confusing, always ask for clarification. That's a teaspoon."

Now that she mentioned it, the letter I'd taken for a sloppily inked capital-T next to the baking powder was a lowercase with a particularly short stem.

Bernadette kept her eye on Yuri, and when he finished his conversion, she took a look at his paper and said, "Very good. You've made it to the next round."

12

Yuri was in—which meant we were halfway there! Or a quarter of the way, given that there was apparently more to come. Though maybe it would be best expressed as a decimal....

Bernadette collected the rest of the converted recipes and paged through them, giving each one only a cursory glance. "You'd be surprised how easy it is to mess up a simple conversion. For instance, the double of .5 is not .10. Whoever this belongs to? You'd better brush up on your math if you ever hope to work for Bruno's." She held up the sheet in question and a shame-faced hopeful sheepishly left the room.

"Here's one that took the conversion one step further, and doubled two tablespoons to a quarter cup. Joan? Great work."

Joan accepted her victory with a curt nod, as if she hadn't expected anything less.

After a few more flips, Bernadette paused, then lingered. "Now this is some beautiful writing." Ooh! Handless notice that about me all the time! All. The. Time. I could hardly wait to be ushered through to the next phase. I was schooling my features into what I hoped would be enthused (but gracious) acceptance when Bernadette said, "Venus? Congratulations."

Good thing for the beard guard, otherwise my jaw might've hit the floor. As I scrambled to hide my dismay, Bernadette paged through the remaining conversions. "We've got one more semi-final spot." Just one?? "And so the last candidate will be...Dixon." She gave the paper another long look—no doubt to reassure me that my cursive was on par with Venus Monger's—then said, "But you definitely need to tone down the loop-de-loops. Legibility always takes precedence over flair."

My writing was *supremely* legible, thank you very much. But while the criticism stung, at least I was in.

Once all the other potential candidates filed out the door, I asked Bernadette, "So, when do we start?"

"Not so fast! There's four of you, and only three positions open—and I'll need to see your baking skills in action."

Uh-oh. Unless those skills involved the creation of brownies that could double as salt-licks, I was in big trouble.

With only four of us left in the room, Bernadette was able to spread us apart so we each had our own table—which really put a crimp in my plan to copy off Joan. Passing out recipe cards, Bernadette told us, "This is our most requested brownie, the Nut'n Honey, made with heirloom black walnuts grown in the nearby township of Success, and honey harvested right here. If you haven't worked with raw honey, just warm it gently in a hot water bath if you need to dissolve any crystals."

What luck! There'd be no chance of me mixing up my salt with my sugar if we were baking with honey instead.

I headed for the pantry to gather my ingredients. Venus (being obnoxiously pushy) didn't care who she had to plow down to get in and out of that pantry as soon as possible. Joan was clearly in the zone, scooping out her dry ingredients so fast I swore she'd sprouted extra arms. I followed behind, realizing I had no idea what the labeling on any of the bins actually meant, since I'd been thinking about Oompa Loompas at the time...but I did my best to just grab from the same bins Joan had been rooting around in, figuring I'd sort it all out back at my workstation.

My handwriting might have been too fancy for Bernadette's liking, but I'd just have to show her that I knew how to measure. Unfortunately, by the time I got back to the table, I realized I had no clue what all the various white powders might be. I'd just have to use the process of elimination. Cocoa was brown. Butter was buttery. Honey was liquid. Eggs were round. Salt was granular. Baking soda, baking powder and flour, though? They all looked the same. Even if I was able to copy Joan move for move, I had no idea which scoop of dusty white powder was which.

I was still puzzling over my ingredients by the time the other three bakers were stirring up their batter, so clearly a decision would need to be made. If I didn't know which was which, I'd just have to put in equal amounts of everything. That way, at least one of them would be right.

And then there was the raw honey, which was actually pretty intimidating. It was chunky and cloudy, with bits of wax inside. If anything like that ever turned up in my mother's pantry, she'd heave it into the trash for sure—and that's really saying something, as she considers expiration dates to be nothing more than suggestions. But, surprisingly enough, I was familiar with the concept of the warm water bath. When I was a kid, I used the technique to melt down my crayon stubs into multicolored mega-crayons to play Scrivener with my cousin. The color-changing line was a pretty creative representation of Spellcraft, if I do say so myself.

But despite what Vano had claimed during our baking lesson at Shirque Mansion, I was beginning to wonder if there really was a place for creativity in baking. With all the math and chemistry involved, the process felt much more like a science than an art.

So, I dutifully bathed my honey, creamed my butter, chopped my nuts, cracked my eggs, measured my dry ingredients, and stirred. And lo and behold, when I sifted in the cocoa powder, (*sifted*, mind you) my brownie batter actually smelled like brownies!

I was feeling pretty optimistic—but when I snuck a little taste for myself, I was in for a surprise. A big, nasty surprise. Because while my batter may have smelled like brownies, it tasted more like aluminum foil. Pretty sure that *wasn't* the flavor profile I was supposed to be going for.

Baking was definitely not an art. With art, you could pass anything off as a success if you knew how to justify your process. But even without running it through the oven, I could tell that no amount of fancy verbal footwork would ever convince someone that this batch of brownies was edible.

While I'm not averse to bending the rules, I've never been a fan of cheating. But even through the beard net, I could see that Yuri's cheeks were livid with swollen, hot splotches of Spellcraft-induced rashiness. I may not like it, but for Yuri, I'd do what I had to do to get in that bakery and put an end to his misery. And no way would I manage that with my current brownie batter, though lucky for me, Venus's batter was directly behind me—right within arm's reach.

Though I could hardly grab it right out from under her nose. Not without a good distraction.

I checked my ingredients, pinpointed the white mystery powder that was closest to the edge of my table, feigned a massive yawn, and elbowed it over the side. The container hit the floor with a plasticky clatter, spraying white powder that was possibly flour, or baking soda, or talcum. Everyone turned to look...and then turned back before I'd even had a chance to grab my brownie pan.

Dang it!

"Butterfingers!" I said, hoping to make a bigger spectacle out of the spill. "Don't you just hate it when that happens? Especially on shag carpeting. Not that I have shag carpeting in my kitchen. Or anywhere in my apartment, for that matter. But my dad has a few shag carpet squares in the basement. Those are the ones you always trip over...."

Talking was proving to be an inadequate distraction, since the only one paying me any heed was Yuri. And he was giving me his patented *I-know-you're-up-to-something* squint. If he was the only one looking at me, I realized, I could give him a message.

Unfortunately, I couldn't just come out and say it. I've found out the hard way that even when someone looks completely tuned out, they'll snap back to attention the moment you slip and reveal something you'd meant to keep secret. Maybe I could signal Yuri in Russian. Too bad the only Russian words I knew were naughty, and not appropriate to the situation at all.

Stumped, I glanced down at the spilled powdery stuff on the floor...and realized I wouldn't need to *speak* my secret message after all. I waved at Yuri, crouched low, and scribbled DISTRACT THEM with my fingertip in the powder. His brow furrowed—but I recognized the look as a thinking-furrow rather than a confusion-furrow—and I quickly dashed away the message with the side of my hand before anyone else could see.

I waggled my eyebrows at Yuri expectantly.

He scowled harder.

I added a particularly pleading puppy-dog look.

He gave a subtle head shake (with a silent sigh), then pointed at a window on the far wall and called out, "Erm..look. Pinyin Bay Perch."

This time, everyone did look—and when they didn't immediately see a guy in a fish costume, they kept right on looking! Heck, they even went over to the window! I made the switch with time to spare. Did I feel bad for swapping my tinfoil brownies for Venus's undoubtedly better (or at the very least normal) brownies? Only somewhat. Yes, it would mean I'd finagled my way into a job that should technically go to her. But it wasn't as if I was planning on keeping my bakery job once we got Yuri's rash under control. Besides, Venus had a dozen other streams of income to fall back on in the meantime.

"No mascots that I can see," Venus called back, "but it looks like someone's having a major meltdown on the street. And I think it's Dixon's cousin!"

13

Yuri and I flocked to the window, and sure enough, the old Buick was parked just down the street, and Sabina and Uncle Fonzo were squaring off in the middle of the road beside it. I couldn't tell what they were squabbling about with each of them yelling over the other, but since they were both pretty opinionated, it wouldn't be the first time they butted heads.

"I'm sure it'll work itself out," I told Joan, who looked particularly concerned. "After all, they haven't killed each other yet!"

It would have been so much easier if Venus hadn't called attention to our family ties and I could just pretend I didn't know the people shouting on the street. Luckily, Bernadette swept back into the room before I had to fabricate any excuses for my family members. "All right, everyone, the proof is in the pudding—or, in this case, the brownies." She put a little colored wooden pick in each pan to mark whose was whose. At least the sludge in Venus's pan didn't dissolve the toothpick! "Let's pop our batter into the ovens and see what we get."

"Hold on," Joan said as Bernadette tried to collect her pan. "My batter seems to be bubbling and I'm a little concerned—"

Bernadette would have none of it. She snatched the pan from

Joan with a firm yank. "I gave you all more than enough time to mix up a simple batter. If you had time to look out the window, you had time to double check your measurements."

Yowsa. For someone who looked like a little kid playing dress-up, Bernadette could be quite the drill sergeant. I never realized brownie baking was such serious business.

She tucked the brownies into the oven and set a timer. Within moments, the bake room filled with the enticing aroma of chocolate. And aluminum. But mostly chocolate. Bernadette said, "Let's take a break while we're waiting for this batch to bake." Great rhyme! Though my enthusiasm for it dimmed somewhat when she glanced at the spillage on the floor. "But first, I'll show you where we keep the brooms."

I've always been good at sweeping, aside from that weird line of dust you get at the end that you keep chasing around with the dustpan—the one that doesn't get any smaller no matter how hard you sweep. I can usually get away with scattering whatever refuses to be swept up, but I'd never seen a floor so clean. All around the edges, where a normal floor would have at least a few crumbs or cobwebs, was nothing but gleaming linoleum.

No baking ingredient was gonna get the better of me!

As I skootched around on the floor chasing the stubborn line, I took the opportunity to search for errant Spellcraft, but came up empty-handed. And I also kept one eye on the oven in case smoke started pouring out the door. But by the time I was so bored with sweeping I could barely manage even one more stroke, we were still smoke-free.

"Dixon!" Yuri called from the doorway. "Come outside and talk some sense into your family before they ruin our chances of getting hired."

"I'm sure they'll listen to you, seeing as how decisive and commanding you are. Actually, scratch that—" It was the perfect excuse to stop sweeping. "I'll come out and help you smooth things over." But just as I edged the final bit of flour under a nearby worktable, something glinted in the dust. Interesting. I blew gently on the dust, and something shimmered iridescent in the light. Not Spellcraft—but a single translucent insect wing.

How strange. A few deceased houseflies or ladybugs can usually be found on the windowsills of my mom's kitchen. I was surprised, though, to find bug parts in Bruno's scrupulously clean workroom.

Before I could puzzle too hard over the insect wing, Yuri hauled me outside, where Sabina and Uncle Fonzo were still going at it. Sabina was particularly riled up, and her angry voice really carried. "I'm just saying, you'd be fine at Glenda's. All of you. In fact, I'll bet it would be a lot easier to baby-proof than our place."

"Nonsense!" my uncle said. "I raised you in that house, I'll remind you—and look how you turned out!"

"I've got a big scar on my knee from the time I fell through a rotten step in the basement!"

"And you learned a valuable lesson about snooping around in your old man's toolbox, didn't you?"

"I didn't give a baboon's butt about your toolbox—I was looking for my Frisbee!"

I leaned into Yuri and said, "Why did they come here to have this argument?"

He shook his head. "They both claimed we would take their side, so when we didn't answer our phones, they brought the argument to us."

Meanwhile, my uncle said, "Glenda's got one of those sterile condos that looks like a model home. How would a kid pick up any life lessons in an environment like that?"

Since time was running out on our break, I took it upon myself to try and bump their discussion into a more productive direction. "Where would Dr. Slaughter want to raise a baby?"

With great enthusiasm, my uncle said, "Glenda is an agreeable lady—she'll love that old house just as much as I do."

Sabina snapped, "You just want the tax write-off!"

"Everyone loves a tax write-off," Uncle Fonzo allowed.

Sabina was not appeased. "And you want to use me as an indentured babysitter!"

Ah...now we were getting to the heart of the matter.

My cousin has never been too keen on babies. When Aunt Rose gave her a baby doll for her fifth birthday, the next day it turned up in the oven, melted to a misshapen lump. Aunt Rose claimed Sabina was just looking for a quiet place for her dolly to sleep. But my cousin later told me that she didn't like the way it was looking at her.

Which was probably one of the many reasons she and Yuri got along so well.

"I'll move out," Sabina said. "That's what I'll do."

My cousin lives paycheck to paycheck—and that's without spending any money on meals. Or clothes. Or anything, really, but the occasional zucchini to leave on an enemy's doorstep. Pinyin Bay real estate didn't come cheap...which meant she'd be angling to move back into the attic by the time the baby was due.

I loved my cousin. But I shared the attic with Yuri now. Just him. (Okay, and technically Meringue. But she fell asleep the minute you threw a sheet over her cage.) That space was our alone-time haven—and that's how I wanted it to stay.

I eased myself between my cousin and Uncle Fonzo and said, "Look, there's still plenty of time before the baby gets here. Weeks? Months? A year? Can't say I paid too much attention to the pregnancy section in Health class. Anyway, point being, no one needs to make any rash decisions right this second."

Sabina boffed me in the arm—ow. "Whose side are you on?"

"There are no sides, and there's absolutely no reason we can't all come out ahead. I adore babies—and I'm confident I would make a fabulous babysitter. Plus, I work from home, so you know I'm always available—"

"As Dixon said," Yuri interrupted. "No decisions must be made right now."

I knew that tone—one of his many leery tones, this one intended to stop me from biting off more than I can chew—but before I could tease him about being spooked by a harmless little baby, I saw his hot, painful-looking rash had spread well beyond the beard guard, and was now creeping up his temples!

"You're absolutely right," I told Yuri. "We'll have plenty of time to plan for the baby. Right now, let's get back inside and find that Spellcraft."

Poor Yuri. He was putting up a brave front—but that was his go-to reaction to pretty much everything. Behind the gruff, tough exterior, my big, brawny bruiser of a man was hurting. Not only that, he was scared.

No more messing around. Yuri was my number one priority. And I might not be known for my focus, but darn it all, I would not stand idly by and watch my grown man friend suffer. So help me, I would ferret out whatever Spellcraft was responsible for Yuri's condition if it was the last thing I did. Which was a weird expression, come to think of it, since of course I'd want to Uncraft the spell once I ferreted the thing out. And also, I've never been a fan of ferrets—they're just a little too sinuous for my taste. Maybe I'd be better at ottering....

"Well?" Bernadette called from the doorway, "Are you coming inside, or what?"

"Oh. Right. Absolutely."

I sent my family on their way, then marched back into the brownerie with a full head of steam, intending to search that place up and down, leaving no crumb unturned, just as soon as I was hired.

Bernadette gathered us all in the workroom. The first thing to hit me was the heavenly smell of the Nut'n Honey brownie, which I remembered from the job fair. Unfortunately, it was followed by a whiff of something weird and metallic—kind of like an aftertaste, but in my nose instead of my mouth.

And it smelled an awful lot like my batter had tasted. But wa-a-ay stronger.

Especially when Bernadette swung open the oven door, and a blast of metal-brownie-scented air hit the room.

All of the pans had gone into the oven looking like brownie batter—and three of those pans still looked like brownies. But one particular pan had morphed into a science experiment gone berserk. It was like one of those baking soda volcanoes collided with the expanding aerosol foam my dad used for sealing gaps around the basement windows. Whereas all the other brownies were flatish rectangles, the brownies I'd mixed up were exuberantly 3-D. They'd puffed up so high, they engulfed the shelf above them, and when Bernadette tried to liberate the pan from the oven, the entire top rack pulled out right along with it.

With a yank, Bernadette freed the crazy brownie-mountain from the hot metal. The top skin of the brownie stayed behind. But losing that top layer released a blast of steam—which smelled like a hot metal skillet roasting a bunch of ball bearings—as the monstrous brownie deflated like a yoga ball on a thumbtack.

It was bad enough I'd cut off one of Venus Monger's potential streams of income. But I'd also made her look completely inept—and for that, I felt truly guilty. Spellcrafters might play fast and loose with things like income taxes and local ordinances...but we did have our pride. I'd have to make it up to her somehow. Not with something as extravagant as buying a timeshare in Des Moines, obviously, but I could acquire some of her outrageously priced snake oil without too much haggling.

I felt so terrible about what I'd done that I actually winced when Bernadette pulled out the identifying toothpick, gave it a look, and said, "Anyone can have a bad day, but it's pretty clear this person has a lot of work to do before they should set foot again in a professional kitchen. Better luck next time, Joan."

Joan?

At that moment, I realized I hadn't been the only one playing brownie batter switcheroo. If Joan's toothpick ended up in my science experiment, Venus must've swapped the pans when the rest of us were watching my family argue out the window!

That really didn't seem fair. If the Penns were going to provide a useful distraction, it should have been for *my* benefit.

Poor Joan was horrified. "I don't understand," she stammered out. "There's been some mistake."

Bernadette dropped the flaccid brownie skin into the sink with a metallic hiss. "That's a major understatement."

"If the bins were mislabeled—"

Bernadette wasn't having it. "If that were the case, explain the fact that no one else had an issue. Mistakes happen. But you need to take ownership for them, not try to explain them away. Thank you for your time, Joan, but unfortunately, your services will not be required."

In Scribing, vocabulary is everything. It's usually a great feeling to come up with the perfect word. But at the sight of Joan's face as she left the room, the term *crestfallen* sprang to mind...and pinpointing that specific word felt decidedly un-great. Once Yuri was cured, I'd have to make it up to her.

Presuming that curing this magical affliction was even possible....

Bernadette startled me out of my doldrums with a brisk clap of her hands. "Well, that settles it. Welcome to Bruno's Brownerie, everybody!"

"Aren't you even going to taste my brownies?" Venus asked.

"No need," Bernadette waved at the thing smoldering in the sink, "since one of them was clearly inedible. There's just enough time for the grand tour, gang, so step lively and follow me."

YURI

14

I was unsure how Dixon managed to switch pans with Joan during the few seconds in which I distracted the room, though there was no doubt in my mind it was precisely what he had done. Dixon is a man of many talents...but cookery is not one of them.

In his shoes, I would have played it safe and tried to knock Venus out of the competition. Not only had she been standing closer to him than Joan, but the results would be more believable, since Joan was clearly the superior baker.

But Dixon does nothing by half-measures. This unabashed confidence never fails to amaze me. Sabina is much the same, always sure of herself and her opinions. Both raised by a loving family with encouragement and praise, not threats and indifference. This new child of Fonzo's would be nurtured just as the two cousins had been. Perhaps to an even greater degree, with Dixon's unflagging support. Sabinochka might grumble, but I suspected she, too, would ferociously champion her new sibling just as she did everyone she loved.

I had never thought myself fond of children. These stirrings of anticipation I now felt were most definitely unexpected.

Also unexpected was the level of secrecy with which these bakers guarded their secrets. Bernadette handed out some contracts and said, "I'll just need the three of you to sign our standard non-disclosure agreement, and we'll be on our way."

Dixon, naturally, was eager for a chance to show off his signature. He was not the only one eager to sign. Venus dashed off her name boldly, then held out the pen to me. I thought she was being helpful, until she said, "If you're in the market for a quality writing implement, look no farther."

I do not normally carry a pen, but the child's marker given to me by Fonzo's lady friend was still in my pocket. Though when I attempted to use it, the ink proved to be transparent, more like that of a highlighter pen. Water-soluble, too, like paint. Where the contract had picked up a bit of moisture from the work table, the ink immediately spread out into a yellowish cloud. And the green apple scent cut right through the smell of metallic brownies which permeated the room.

Dixon came to my rescue by pressing one of his many mundane pens into my hand. "Yuri lives with a Scri—uh, scriptwriting pen enthusiast." Bernadette did not seem to notice the near slip. "He'd hardly want for something to write with!"

Dixon was, indeed, a pen enthusiast. The pen he handed me overwrote the spreading green blob with ease.

Once we all signed, Bernadette collected the contracts, then happily ushered us all into the hallway, headed for the staff-only door which had previously been blocked by Bruno. She led us into a room that was stacked floor to ceiling with large cloth sacks, which she presented with a sweep of her hand. "Our first crucial ingredient is our flour. This is a proprietary blend milled especially for Bruno's, to ensure both quality and consistency."

"Question," Dixon said. "Do the wheat plants have flowers on them? And if so, is it not confusing that a plant would produce both *flowers* and *flour*?"

"The flowers are very tiny. I've never heard of anyone confusing them with flour."

I should have known something was amiss when Dixon did not immediately launch into a running commentary about the quirkiness of language. By the time I saw him scrutinizing one of the giant cloth sacks, it was too late. Bernadette noticed him just as I did. "Wait! You don't wanna pull that—"

A white cloud enveloped us.

"...string."

I slapped my hand over the corner of the sack that was now gaping open, and within a few minutes, the dust began to settle. It was only because of the beard guard acting as a filter that I did not choke on the airborne flour. Bernadette waved away the cloud, coughing. "That's how you open the bags!"

"Sorry," Dixon said meekly as she found a clamp to re-close the sack. "It was like having a hangnail. But made of thread. On a flour sack."

"I can see we'll need some ground rules," Bernadette said. "Rule number one—don't touch anything unless I say so!"

"Got it." Dixon said. "No touchee." But when Bernadette turned toward the next door, he gestured to his eyes with the vee of his fingers and then pointed at the room, reminding me to watch for Spellcraft. I swept the room with a glance, but the only atmospheric shifting I could see was the settling clouds of flour.

Though as I walked through to the next room, that flour seemed to drift into a shape like an arrow, guiding me forward. At least, I thought it did...until the motion of my passing made it disperse.

Bernadette led us onward. "Be especially sure to keep your hands to yourself now. We're passing through the egg room."

If ever there was an accident waiting to happen....

Hundreds of eggs—white, brown and pale sea-glass blue—were stacked two meters high in narrow wooden pallets. Bernadette was much more confident than I that we would make it through the egg room unscathed. She turned to the group and said, "At Bruno's, we contract with three local poultry farms, and we visit them all regularly to make sure our hens are being treated right. Happy chickens lay happy eggs."

Dixon was, unsurprisingly, impressed. "Hey! That egg is the very same color as my favorite shirt!"

Despite "rule number one," he impulsively reached out to grab the egg. With visions of an entire wall of eggs crashing down on our heads, I was quick to grab him. So quick that the green marker launched itself out of my pocket...and rolled directly under Venus's feet. She stepped down on the bright plastic barrel and rolled forward an inch, flinging her arms out to catch her balance. Bangles rang together. Bracelets jingled. I shielded Dixon with my body and steeled myself to be covered in yolk. But mere inches from the egg wall, Venus righted herself with a final jangling swoop of her arms.

The only casualty was a single round bracelet, which flew from her wrist, rolled toward the next door, circled a few times, then settled to a halt at Bernadette's feet. She picked it up and handed it to Venus. "Rule number two: no dangling jewelry. It's a safety risk."

"I never knew baking was so serious," Venus said with a sigh, while I retrieved my marker. It gave me an opportunity to scan the room's lower half for Spellcraft, but in that respect, I came up empty-handed.

Bernadette gave us all a hard look. "Absolutely no fooling around in this next room. With all the heavy equipment, things could turn dangerous."

I glanced at Dixon—he looked far too eager—and surreptitiously took hold of the back of his shirt, just in case I needed to restrain him.

When the next door opened, the smell of chocolate enveloped us. Not sweet like candy, but dark and rich, bitter and complex, like coffee or wine or freshly turned soil. The room was dominated by a large metal machine with a conveyor belt on one end and a hopper on the other. Bernadette turned on a power switch and the conveyor belt chugged to life. "While we can't grow the cocoa here in Pinyin Bay—totally wrong climate—we can grind and roast our own nibs. This gives us the freshest possible ingredient, which we can even tailor to our various recipes. These dials control how quickly the nibs make their way through the roaster. A fan cools them to the optimal grinding temperature, and then they're precision ground to our exact specifications."

Bernadette was clearly very proud of this machine, and she grew more and more emphatic as the explanation went on. "Bruno invented this system himself. It's really a marvel of modern culinary engineering! I'll let you see it in action—but the settings are very precisely calibrated. It's absolutely crucial you don't touch anything."

I tightened my grip on Dixon's shirt.

Tendrils of heat were now rising from the body of the roasting machine. Bernadette took a large scoop of "nibs" from a nearby vat and spread them on the conveyor belt. Immediately, Dixon strained toward the machine, but I held him firm.

"Hey! What're you doing, Yuri?"

"It is for your own good."

"But the machine—"

The ponderous chug of the roaster changed in pitch as, suddenly, the internal gears sped up. The mouth of the machine glowed red, and the smell of roasting chocolate filled the room.

And then a thin wisp of smoke rose from the machine.

"Is it supposed to do that?" Venus asked.

Bernadette scrambled over to the controls. "Something's wrong!"

Over the sound of the motor, Dixon called, "It's the middle dial! You hit it with your pinkie while you were enthusing about your machine."

For once, Dixon's interference would have averted a crisis instead of creating it. And my preventing him from meddling had only made matters worse. It was such a convoluted turn of events, I knew in my gut it could not be coincidence. And so it was no surprise that when smoldering cocoa nibs blasted out of the machine, they all shimmered with the telltale distortion of the *volshebstvo*.

Two inventors, both specializing in food, set up shop directly next door to one another? No doubt there was a rivalry. Where there was rivalry, there was sabotage. And in Pinyin Bay, where there was sabotage, there was Spellcraft.

Perhaps we should not have been so fast to clear the hydroponic farmer of wrongdoing.

Nibs shot in every direction. They were small—but they were hot, pinging off our exposed skin like tiny coals. Good thing I had a beard guard—I could focus on shielding my shaved head from the assault without worrying about my face.

Bernadette lunged for the controls and shut the roaster off—but not before she endured a spray of hot nibs. "Eep! My eye!"

"I've got you," Dixon called out as he yanked a bottled water from his messenger bag. In one quick motion, he cracked the top, and sent a stream of water arcing toward Bernadette.

She took it square in the face.

Beside her, the slowing roaster began to hiss.

The whole debacle smelled disturbingly good.

Dixon put an arm around a soggy Bernadette and said, "Let's get you to an eye-wash station." Then he caught my eye over the top of her head and mouthed the words, *Find the Spellcraft!*

15

Bernadette might be occupied...but I could hardly search the place with Venus Monger watching me. "You should go help them," I said firmly. Americans tend to listen to me when I use this tone.

But Venus was the most persistent Spellcrafter I had ever met—and that's saying a lot, considering I live with a man for whom pestering is practically an art form. "Oh no, Seer. You're not getting rid of me that easily. You guys are obviously running some kind of racket. And whatever it is, I want in."

"There is no *racket*."

"The heck there isn't! If you're an avid baker, then I'm the Mayor of Pinyin Bay. A single Seen is more lucrative than a whole day slaving over a hot oven—and you don't need to get up at the crack of dawn to do it. I wasn't born yesterday—something's definitely up!"

I did not know how long Dixon and Bernadette would be gone. While I had no good reason to trust Venus, she was a Scrivener, and it would be valuable to have a Scrivener's help. Also, I realized, I did not need to trust her. I just needed to strike the correct bargain. "I am looking for a Crafting. If you help me find it, I will pay you."

"Ten thousand dollars," she said, without missing a beat.

While I knew she was just starting her bargaining from a high position, I did not have time—nor the patience—to talk her down to the five dollars in my pocket. "I would not pay you with money."

She gave me a long, skeptical look, then shrugged. "I don't generally prefer my men quite so lunky, but I suppose you'll do. Though you'd have to lose the beard guard."

"That's not what I meant! I am offering you a Seen."

Her avaricious eyes lit up. "Ah! Now you're talking! I'm definitely in. Where do we start?"

"Search the room," I said, and began slinging around hundred-pound sacks of cocoa nibs to ensure there was nothing lurking between them.

Venus did nothing to earn her Seen. Or so I thought. While she appeared to be simply staring at the floor, it turned out she was scoping out the situation. "Before you wear yourself out throwing chocolate around, come take a look at this."

The floor was set with square tiles on the diagonal. The hot cocoa nibs had settled into the cracks between the squares, but only a few of them. Enough to form the distinct impression of an arrow—one which did not drift away as easily as the flour. An arrow pointing at a door on the far wall. A door marked *Apiary.*

"What does apiary mean?" I asked.

Venus shook her head. "It always comes down to the monkeys...."

It made no sense to house monkeys at a bakery. I plugged the word into my phone's dictionary. "That cannot be the definition—"

Venus paid no attention to me. She was already opening the door...from which we heard the gentle hum of a distant, droning buzz.

I took a step back and said, "An apiary is not for apes...but for *bees.*"

Movement.

The far wall was made entirely of glass, behind which thousands of insects undulated in a brownish ripple of motion. When Bernadette had said the honey was harvested "right here," I presumed she meant Pinyin Bay. Not the brownerie itself.

I am not afraid of a bee. While I do not wish to be stung, I could certainly handle the pain. It was the sight of so many, moving together with a single intelligence, dipping in and out of sticky, moist cells in the honeycomb...depositing their larvae....

"It is no use," I said. "We will never find the Crafting in here—"

"There it is!" Venus pointed triumphantly to a small, framed bit of calligraphy tacked to the glass.

I certainly would have noticed it without her help...once I had a moment to get my bearings.

I swallowed down my insect-induced nausea and forced myself to approach the undulating wall of bugs. The Crafting was on the bee-side of the pane.

Of course it was.

And a dozen bees had wriggled their way between the Crafting and the glass, thwarting my attempt to read it. "Can you hazard a guess as to what these words say?" I asked.

"I don't have to guess!" Venus declared. "I wrote them."

I had never met a woman with such gall. "Why would you do such a thing?"

"Bernadette commissioned me, of course. It's bad business to give away your Spellcraft for free."

"So she is sabotaging Bruno?"

"I have no idea what you're talking about. She's crazy about Bruno, but the man has zero business acumen, so she had to take matters into her own hands. There's no sabotage, just a standard business-enhancement Crafting. That's all."

At the top of the hive was a clear plastic pipe, almost like a chimney—the same piping used in the hydroponic warehouse. It exited through the wall facing the other business. It must lead to the bee-door Herb had told us about in his grow room.

As I tracked the path of the bees, I realized Herb and Bruno were not in competition with one another at all. They were in a collaborative relationship—the ultimate win-win—with one of them utilizing the bees and the other reaping the honey.

But if this was not sabotage.... "Why would anyone hide a harmless piece of Spellcraft within a living wall of bees?"

"*The hives are flourishing*," Venus read—or recalled. "Where else would it go?"

I would not put it past this woman to stretch the truth, so I forced myself closer to the glass to try to read what I could for myself. But when I neared the glass, the rash on my face flared to life, hot and angry as the sting of a thousand bees. I grunted in pain and tore off my beard guard.

Venus saw my cheeks and let out a startled gasp. "Yikes—what are you so allergic to? I've never seen such a terrible case of...hives."

Our eyes went to the Crafting.

Behind the shimmy and shake of the industrious bees, the Crafting itself glimmered with magic. The words were just as Venus had claimed—*The hives are flourishing*. And the Seen? A cluster of reddish blobs—which could have been painted by none other than Practical Penn's inscrutable Seer, Rufus Clahd.

Indignantly, Venus said, "I thought it was a bunch of bee hives. Obviously, that's what I asked him to paint. Not an allergic reaction."

"Tell that to the *volshebstvo*!"

"I can't have people saying my work needs Uncrafting. It would be terrible for business!"

"I care nothing for your business." My cheeks were blowing up like a pair of fleshy balloons. "We must fix this thing *now*!"

"Fine," she said petulantly. "I'm willing to add the word *bee*. But you'd have to be an idiot to stick your hand in there."

Where was a giant zucchini when you needed one?

That thought reminded me of the hydroponic grow house next door—and Herb's admonition not to swat his bees...the ones who had lingered behind after he shut the bee-door.

My cheeks had swelled to such ridiculous proportion I could hardly see to pull up Herb's business on my phone and call him. After three rings which seemed like an eternity, he answered. "Herb's Herbs and Veggies, where freshness is always in season!"

"It is Yuri," I said bluntly.

"Yuri! How's that zucchini treating you?"

The words that followed were nearly painful to grit out. Because until I met Dixon, I would consider them the words of a fool. "I need...a favor."

"Of course. Can't rave enough about how you and your grown man friend saved my skin by finding the problem with my irrigation system. Anything I can do."

"Open the bee-door."

"The bee-door?"

"It is urgent." Must I say it? "Please."

"It's a little early yet for bees—but if it means that much to you—"

Herb rambled about the bees' schedule, but I had crammed the phone back in my pocket to press the palms of both hands against my blazing cheeks as if I could squash them back into place. It was not just painful. It was pain and pressure and itching and heat—all of it underscored with the growing tingle of *volshebstvo*.

My eyes were squeezed shut tight when Venus said, "Would you look at that? All the bees are high-tailing it out through that clear plastic tube."

Not all. Some, I saw, were still tending to their *larvae*. But the majority of them seemed eager to go visit the flowering plants next door...enough of them that I could yank open the glass panel—the earthen floral smell of honey was dizzying—and steal the Crafting from the hive.

I thrust the sticky thing at Venus. "Quickly. Add the word."

"Obviously, I can't do it here. I don't have my quill on me."

"You carry a handbag big enough to kidnap someone and you do not have your quill?" Without waiting for her to answer, I snatched back the Crafting, hoping I could summon Dixon before I was utterly incapacitated by the hives. I thrust my hand, sticky with honey, into my pocket to retrieve my phone, though I worried how many precious minutes it would take Dixon to retrace his steps through the brownerie to reach me. When I pulled out my phone, something else was also stuck to my honeyed hand....

The green marker.

Obviously, it was possible to Uncraft a Scrivening. But never had I realized it was possible to re-envision a Seen. Normally, I would take time to consider what I was about to do, and probably talk myself out of it. I am naturally averse to things that have never been tried, especially when the stakes are so high. I would rather allow someone else to experience the inevitable failure. But at that moment, the *volshebstvo* was thrumming through my left arm in an impulse too fierce to deny.

The green marker was not dark enough to obliterate Rufus Clahd's work, but it was stuck fast to my hand—and these things happen for a reason. I smacked the small picture frame against my knee to expose the Crafting and the thin glass shattered. As I shook away the fragments, I tore off the marker cap with my teeth. The scent of green apple welled up, cutting through the cloying scent of honey—mixing and mingling into a tempting aroma much better than either one alone.

As the scents combined, I understood. I did not need the ink to cover the original Seen. I only needed to enhance it.

I would like to say I directed my own hand, but this would be a lie. Seens do not come *from* me. They come *through* me. As I brought marker to paper, ink flowed through the barrel just as surely as my paints would flow through a brush. The ink was not only transparent, but water-based, and the friction of the felt with the wetness of the ink began pulling at the pigments laid by the brush of Rufus Clahd.

The intent of the Scrivener was already there—bee hives—and the *volshebstvo* on the page was eager to resolve the friction between Scrivening and Seen. Marker and paint mingled, green over red, its opposite on the color wheel. And together, the two made brown—many shades, from the color of the wooden frame to the deep golden hue of honey.

Though I was doing little more than scribbling over the Crafting with a marker, it was hard work to control the Spellcraft. Sweat sprang to my brow, and a meandering bee paused on my temple to sip at my perspiration. But it did not sting.

Unlike most men, the wild creatures of the earth respect the *volshebstvo*.

I dug boldly into the Crafting. Magic drained from my arm as the colors shifted, and the Spellcraft reimagined itself. It was much different from creating a Seen from scratch, where the control rested solely with me. More like coming upon a strange pan of unbaked brownies, trying to determine what might be missing, and mixing in that ingredient before the pan went in the oven.

Or perhaps it was more like pulling the pan out just before the brownies have set and remixing the molten batter.

At any rate, the relief, when it came, was immediate and profound. I might have dropped the Crafting, but it was stuck with honey to my right hand.

The pain and itching subsided in moments as the Spellcraft settled into its intended purpose, and my face cooled to the temperature of the skin around it.

The bee drank his fill and buzzed away.

I always suspected I was especially sensitive to the energy of the *volshebstvo*. How else had it called to me from across the ocean? No wonder it had no problem nagging at me to come and set it right from the other side of the city.

By the time Dixon returned with Bernadette, we had the glass swept up and the Crafting back in place. Venus might not have a quill in her handbag, but she did carry an assortment of small picture frames. (I did not ask why.)

Bernadette was disheveled and her hair was damp. Her cheeks were pink, but this was from the eye wash station, not the *volshebstvo*, judging by the twin tracks of mascara trailing down her face. "I see you found our honey room," she said with a weak smile. "Though I'm not sure why the bees are gone so early. I hope they haven't escaped!"

I reassured her that they went through the proper tube, and she sagged with relief. "It seems like everything that could've gone wrong today, did. Spectacularly. And it might sound hokey, but I think everything that happens, happens for a reason. I'm sorry to say I've changed my mind about expanding Bruno's Brownerie, so I won't be taking on any new staff. But as a reward for coming out so bright and early, I've got a 10%-off coupon for each of you."

You would have to buy a lot of brownies for that ten percent to be worth your while...but they *were* very good brownies, and surely we should not leave empty-handed. Though from this moment forward I did plan to avoid the signature Nut'n Honey brownie. Just to be safe.

Dixon asked, "Can we at least take home the brownies we made?"

"Sure," Bernadette said wearily. "They're all yours."

"What a relief. I'm starving!" Venus grabbed her pan and was already halfway out the door. Time is money, and she was not the sort to waste valuable earning potential exchanging pleasantries if there was nothing for her to sell.

We collected our warm brownies and headed toward the door, with Dixon calling out a promise to return the pans just as soon as we were done with them. Making our way through the brownerie, as soon as Bernadette was out of earshot, he lowered his voice and said, "Your rash is, like, a thousand times better. Whatever you did—it must've worked!"

What I had done—Reseeing a Seen—was completely out of my realm of experience. I was not sure whether I felt excited, or terrified. I would need to mull it over before we talked it through, so for now, I changed the subject by saying, "I would be surprised if my brownies are even edible...and I'm guessing yours were the ones that blew up bigger than my cheeks."

Dixon winced. "Unfortunately. But I didn't mean to knock Joan out of the running. I was aiming for Venus—darn it, I should've known she'd be cutthroat enough to swap with Joan." This said with absolutely no acknowledgement that he'd used the same tactic himself. "Maybe it's a moot point, since it turned out there was no job to be had anyway."

I nodded toward the pan in his grasp. "So who made those?"

Dixon pulled out the colored toothpick and waved it at me. "While Bernadette was in the eye-wash, I swapped toothpicks with Venus, so these must be Joan's. Unless Venus switched them first, and this is a quadruple-switcheroo. In which case, I suppose she really has outsmarted us all." Dixon popped the toothpick in his mouth and sucked off the crumbs...and his eyes nearly rolled back in his head with delight. "Nope, these are definitely Joan's. D'you suppose I should track her down and give back her brownies? Not that I know where she lives." He hugged the warm tray possessively to his chest. "And when you think about it, she's totally skilled enough to whip up a batch of perfect, glorious, gooey, sweet, chocolatey, oven-fresh brownies anytime the mood strikes her...."

We stepped outside and I squinted against the early-morning sun. Once my eyes adjusted, I noticed two people chatting under the awning at Herb's Herbs—Herb, and Joan. Herb's thin chest was puffed out proudly against his tie-dyed shirt as he expounded about something, probably dull things about vegetables. Joan tittered at whatever he said and tucked a lock of graying hair behind her ear. I said, "It appears Joan's morning was not entirely wasted."

Dixon peeked out from behind me, shielding his brownies with my body. "Wow. Those two foodies go together like chocolate and, uh...pretty much anything. I can't even imagine how factual their discussions will be."

Satisfied that Joan would not wish to be interrupted over a job which did not exist and pan of brownies she could easily recreate, we climbed into the truck. The smell of fresh brownies filled the cab, though if I tried, I could still detect the lingering scent of green apples.

Dixon pressed the backs of his fingers to my cheek and said, "So I guess everything's back to normal." I expected him to then tuck into the brownies, but instead he set them on the dash with a wistful sigh. "But just think, Yuri. Nine-ish months from now, you'll no longer be the most recent member of the Penn family!"

We were on the brink of some interesting times...and I found I was not entirely dreading them. I captured his hand and pressed a kiss to his fingers, and his wistful smile turned slightly naughty as he clambered across the bench to take my face in both hands and kiss my mouth, slow and deep.

When we ran out of air, he gave my face an extra squeeze and said, "I hadn't realized how much I missed being able to smush your adorable cheeks!"

I caught his hands in mine and cleared my throat uneasily. "Tell me something, Dixon." Certain things would be difficult for me to hear, but if anyone could soften the blow.... "Am I...lunky?"

"Not at all, Yuri." Dixon's smile turned naughtier still, hinting all the many ways in which he would like to grab hold of my not-so-thin places. "In fact, I'd say the more accurate word is *hunky*."

The English language is a confusing thing. Words sounded the same but were written differently. Or they were spelled the same, but had different meanings entirely. The alteration of a single letter changed everything. Even the very same word might mean the opposite, depending on how it is spoken. And in the hands of a Scrivener, words were literally magic.

I may not know what this *hunky* specifically meant without double-checking the definition. But seeing the smile sparkling in Dixon's dark eyes...I most definitely understood in every way that mattered.

FORGING AHEAD

DIXON

What is talent? Is it something you're born with, a skill that just comes naturally? Or is it the result of hours of practice—of focus and interest and keen self-discipline?

Maybe it's a bit of each.

I was born a Spellcrafter, though that birthright was followed by years of training. I'm not sure if it was nature or nurture that made my failed quilling ceremony sting so badly. I suspect that despite the lack of a quill, some part of me knew that not only was I indeed a legitimate Spellcrafter—but a talented one.

Though I don't suppose animals have so much ego and backstory wrapped up in their success.

I'd spotted the ad for Creature Feature Talent Show in the Pinyin Bay Journal as I was perusing the latest juicy exposé. You wouldn't think a city the size of Pinyin Bay had quite so many secrets and scandals. But now that my friend Charlotte (of the tinfoil hat fame) was their top investigative reporter, all sorts of shocking secrets were being uncovered.

And some of them were even true.

It was tempting to read more about the famous painting

someone had uncovered in the back of their garage...but like so many of Charlotte's articles, it was light on speculation and heavy on dry facts, so my eyes kept drifting to the little ad instead.

Does your four-legged friend perform tricks? Can they carry a tune—or even speak a word?

The presumption that all pets had four legs was awfully mammalist. Meringue could do all those things and more. She knew several words, in fact. Insulting words...but words nonetheless. Her singing was melodic, her dancing was hypnotic, and her tornado siren imitation never failed to send us scurrying down to the basement.

Show me a dog who could do all that—*and* pluck a magical quill from its own pinfeathers.

I didn't think so.

Yuri is just as appreciative of Meringue's talents as I am. He may claim he feeds her just to give her something to do with her beak other than squawking...but given that he'll dispense a peanut every time Meringue calls out, "Nom nom!" I'd say she had him wrapped around her little finger...er, wing. So, Yuri would undoubtedly believe in Meringue, however, he's still an artist. And as such, he can be particularly sensitive to the criticism of others, especially when they hold themselves up as arbiters of taste.

Judgers gonna judge, I always say...but since Yuri would only look at me funny and question the grammar, I'd decided it was best to spare him the anxiety of entering Meringue in a talent show. Not by not-doing it, of course—but by sneaking out the door with the bird in my messenger bag while Yuri was in the shower. There was a thousand-dollar prize on the line, and with Uncle Fonzo's lady-friend in the "family way," we'd need that money.

Auditions for the Creature Feature Talent Show were being held in a big tent outside the scratch 'n dent grocery outlet where they sold expiring perishables, discontinued flavors, and unlabeled cans. It's in an oddball part of town, pretty far off the beaten track. Since my mom is one of their top customers, and since I'm a loyal son who was often roped into helping with the shopping, I found my way there, no problem. Despite the relative obscurity of the locale, though, it seemed like half of Pinyin Bay had turned out in hopes that their family pet might break into show business.

The parking lot was overflowing. There were dogs. There were cats. There was even a miniature pony. But I was the only one with a bird, so I had high hopes that Meringue would make a big impression.

Until I ran into Rufus Clahd, anyhow.

Rufus has a really weird afro. Sometimes you can gaze into it and see the shapes of other things, like you'd do staring at clouds—but with hair. He was also the Seer who'd worked at my family's shop ever since I could remember...if by "worked" you mean "napped on the Murphy bed in his office." But since Yuri has confirmed that painting Seens is actually pretty tiring, I supposed I should cut our official Seer some slack.

As long as you didn't mess with his stuff, he was a pretty chill guy. If there was a weird angle to come at a given situation, Rufus always managed to find it. So he hadn't brought a dog or a cat or even a miniature pony...but something in a very small covered cage. The thing about Rufus is that you can never quite tell what he'll do next—and whether it'll be genius or nonsense. While I knew darned well I should just ignore him and get on with winning the show...of course I had to see what was in that cage.

"Hey, Rufus," I said casually. "Whatcha got there?"

"A breakfast sandwich from the gas station on the corner. I do believe they use a different sausage than the food truck by the shop."

"Er...the other hand."

"Ah, yes!" he said cheerfully, blowing out a few soggy biscuit crumbs. "Why, this delightful creature is truly one of nature's miracles. Behold!" He shoved the sandwich in his mouth, plucked off the cover, and swooped the small plastic box right under my nose. "The chameleon."

The lizard was clinging to a small plastic branch. Despite the fact that Rufus was swinging it all around, it managed to stay so still it looked as fake as the decorations...except the way its nearest eye was swiveling all around.

Had I encountered this particular chameleon before, I wondered? My parents' Spellcraft shop was full of random exotic pets we'd inherited from Precious Greetings. "Did that critter come from Practical Penn?"

"I presume it came from an egg."

"And you're sure it's a chameleon? None of the creatures at Practical Penn camouflage themselves."

"It's a common fallacy that chameleons try to mimic their environments, but when excited, they do indeed change color. I can't imagine a more inspiring companion for an artist."

"Absolutely," I said, hoping I sounded sincere. Referring to the Seens he painted as *art* was a stretch. But since their main purpose was to power a Crafting, they didn't need to look like much. Which was good. Because they didn't much resemble anything at all.

As Rufus meandered off, trailing crumbs, a woman's voice called out, "Dixon? Is that you?"

I peered into the crowd and found not one more familiar face, but two. And they were one another's spitting image.

Pansy and Violet Strange are identical twins who are no longer completely identical, thanks to a misfired bit of Spellcraft that left one of Violet's eyes an unnatural shade of purple. While I couldn't see their irises from across the parking lot, I did note that the sisters weren't dressed the same. Violet was pursuing a career as a fetish model, and Pansy had aspirations of being a professional baton-twirler. So, I figured Violet was in jeans and a T-shirt while Pansy was the one in the majorette getup...unless it was Violet in costume, catering to a highly specific kink.

Thankfully not. Once I was in range, I saw the twin covered in gold braid had two brown eyes.

"Hey, Dixon—where's your grown man friend?" Violet called over as she tried to wrangle something large and furry out of her tiny hatchback.

"Back at the apartment...doing something, ah...Russian—say, is that a large dog or a small bear?"

The creature in question flopped out of the back seat in a flurry of slobber. Its tail whomped back and forth hard enough to bruise, and it peed ecstatically the moment its feet hit the ground.

Violet and Pansy both gave an identical wince. "That's Cosmos," Pansy said.

With a sigh, Violet added, "He's kind of excitable."

Pansy pulled a slobbery baton out of the car. "But I'm sure he'll calm down by the time we get in front of the judges. We've been practicing our act all week."

Uh oh. It had never occurred to me to practice any sort of routine. Hopefully Meringue could win over the judges by just being her charming self.

The dog was on one of those spring-loaded leashes that reels out from a plastic holder. As Violet attempted to unwind the leash from her left foot, Pansy shook the spit off her baton and said, "Cosmos, speak!"

The dog flopped onto its side, grinning maniacally, and thrashed Violet's foot with his tail.

"I'm sure he'll do great!" I said with lots and lots of enthusiasm, and went to take my place in line.

I've never been much good at waiting, but luckily there were all sorts of interesting people to talk to. Unfortunately, upon learning that I was a Spellcrafter, several of them demanded I Craft something on the spot to ensure they passed the audition. By the time the long line crept forward enough to get us through the door, there were only a few available spots in the show, but at least a dozen requests for Craftings.

Maybe I should've shown up with a bunch of Seens in my bag instead of a big sassy cockatoo. There'd be way better odds of making a profit. But if I had, the judges would be deprived of Meringue's dulcet voice!

As if she could sense me thinking about her, Meringue began to stir. What's the expression—are your ears burning? Birds didn't have ears. Just ear-holes. Though Meringue sure made good use of hers when she heard Yuri muttering to himself in Russian.

This was a family-friendly event, so hopefully none of the judges were Russian expats. I was craning my neck to see if any of them looked particularly Slavic when my view was blocked by a broad expanse of polyester shirt tucked into Sansabelt slacks, and the whole ensemble topped with a fur-collared vest. "Ladin Silver?" I said. "What are you doing here?"

"With a thousand smackeroos at stake? Auditioning for the talent show, of course!"

Darn. I was hoping he'd finagled his way into a stint as a judge, since we Spellcrafters always look out for our own. Unless we're competing for the same prize—in which case, may the craftiest man win. But Ladin didn't have a pet with him. Hopefully his tendency to bend the rules would knock him out of the competition and leave me one step closer to the big payout.

The line had inched forward so we were now inside the tent, nearing the judges' table. Unlike reality show judges, this particular trio didn't laugh or roll their eyes or stand up and insult people. They just scribbled on their clipboards, and called out, "Thank you, next!" approximately thirty seconds into every act, as a bunch of disappointed hopefuls shuffled out the door.

Somewhere behind me, I heard Violet and/or Pansy saying, "Cosmos—sit. Cosmos? Cosmos! Sit!"

Ahead of me—having cut the line, though I couldn't exactly prove it—Ladin rocked expectantly on the balls of his feet. And then his gaze shifted slyly back to me. "You did know this was an animal act," he said, "didn't you?"

"I could say the same to you." I'd been playing coy, keeping an ace up my sleeve—or a bird in my bag—hoping to outmaneuver a guy who, for his size, was surprisingly maneuverable. But before I got too smug, my bag took it upon itself to make an announcement.

"Nom nom!"

I patted down my pockets in search of a peanut and came up with nothing but a lip balm and half an eraser. "Not right now," I whispered into the bag.

"Nom nom!"

"Just as soon as we're done here, we'll swing by the store and—"

"Nom nom!"

For an animal with a brain the size of a Raisinette, Meringue is pretty darned smart. Unfortunately, she'd never quite grasped the concept of delayed gratification. (Then again, neither had my cousin. But Sabina could be distracted with compliments about her hair, whereas Meringue simply took such observations as her due.)

I lifted the flap of my bag and found a beady little bird-eye giving me a reproachful look. How that cockatoo manages such a wide range of expressions without being able to smile or frown or waggle a pair of eyebrows, I'll never know. But since it was clear I'd never appease her without coughing up a peanut, I decided to try and distract her instead by whispering, "Night-night."

This is what I told her at the end of a long day as I covered her cage with a sheet so she could settle in for the evening. Hopefully the darkness of my messenger bag would be enough to convince her to keep quiet until it was our turn in front of the judges...though there may have been some grumbling in Russian as I closed the bag again.

Before I knew it, Ladin Silver was mounting the stage, which creaked alarmingly under his ponderous weight. Like so many Spellcrafters who use the gift of gab to secure their clientele, Ladin is a natural showman. And when he addressed the judges, he laid that salesmanship on really thick. "Ladies and gentlemen, you've seen many a furry friend today—cats, dogs, and even an intrepid goat."

Actually, I was pretty sure that had been a Dalmatian in a goat costume. But a rustling sound in my bag sidetracked me before I could comment on it. It was a papery sort of rustle. A *fine* papery sort of rustle. The kind of rustle you'd hear when you clean out the paper shredder. That didn't make any sense, though. I wasn't carrying any shredded paper in my bag.

Though I was carrying around a piece of...*uh oh.*

I make a big impression.

The Crafting was meant for the painfully shy salesman who'd

helped us get a great deal on a slightly used writing desk. But I had the sinking feeling that I'd need to go back to the drawing board before I swung by the furniture store. Unless the papery thing Meringue had gotten hold of was my shopping list instead....

Onstage, Ladin produced a miniature piano—where on earth had he been hiding that?—and declared, "Anyone can traipse into a pet shop and buy an animal. But it takes a special kind of brilliance to tame a creature from the wild."

As I lifted the flap of my bag to see exactly how shredded the contents might be, Ladin's fur collar sprang to squirrelly life as he chose that exact moment to brandish a peanut....

And my bag exploded in a cloud of Spellcraft shreds and feathers.

"Nom nom!" Meringue cried triumphantly as she dive-bombed the stage. How a cockatoo can smell a peanut at thirty yards without a nose I'll never know. Bits of set Spellcraft rained down on my head, ensuring that *I* was the one who'd make the "big impression." Meanwhile, Ladin Silver was surprisingly calm about the burst of exclaiming white feathers hurtling toward him...however, his fur collar most definitely was not. The semi-tamed squirrel bolted right down his leg, across the stage, and into the crowd.

"Cosmos, stay!" one of the twins cried.

Ladin might be calm—Cosmos, though, was anything but. The dog gave a bellow and was off like a shot. And while Violet had the wherewithal to hold on tight, there was a heck of a lot of leash wound up in that holder. It spooled out like fishing line, whipping back and forth through the crowd in the dog's wake.

If only Ladin thought to let go of the peanut. Spellcrafters are notoriously...frugal. Instead of relinquishing the treat, Ladin spun in a circle, protecting it with his massive body. Meringue was coming at him from every which direction, though, and Ladin hardly stood a chance.

But the squirrel? Apparently semi-tame rodents have pretty good survival instincts. The squirrel quickly determined that while Meringue was only after the peanut, Cosmos was another story. It knew enough to put both distance and roadblocks between him and the perceived threat...which meant weaving in and out of the legs of the crowd: contestants, animals, and judges. And Cosmos was hot on its furry little heels.

The leash lashed back and forth, smacking into the lizard cage in Rufus Clahd's hands. The top popped off, spinning high into the air, while the chameleon, startled, scrambled up Rufus's arm and across his shoulders, changing colors all the while. By the time he scooted down Rufus's pant leg, the swivel-eyed lizard had gone from a boring, solid green, to a scintillating stripey pattern of blacks, yellows and reds. And while it might be scientifically accurate that he wasn't deliberately camouflaging himself by trying to mimic his surroundings, the floor of the tent was a surprisingly good match.

Rufus dropped to the ground so fast I thought he'd fainted, at least until he started commando-crawling through the squealing crowd in pursuit of his chameleon. Meanwhile, the squirrel was desperate for some camouflage of its own, and it must've mistaken the Seer's afro for a small, mobile tree—or maybe a convenient crawling bush. It flung itself at the hair, but Rufus is pretty hard to shock. He took it all in stride, crawling after his lizard with the squirrel clinging to him like an avant-garde hat.

Up on the stage, Meringue was bound and determined to get her claws on that peanut. As tiny, off-kilter piano notes chimed under the onslaught of her impressive black beak, the holder Violet was gripping ran out of leash, and the line snapped taut. Violet's heels were dug in hard, and Cosmos had some incredible momentum, but something had to give. That "something" was everything in between them. Things went flying every which way. People, animals, tables and chairs.

And judges.

As the fur, feathers and Spellcraft shreds settled, a stunned silence fell over the tent as everyone tried to figure out how they'd ended up on the floor. (Except Rufus, who'd sprung back up with a squirrel on his head and a chameleon in his arms.)

The silence was broken by the repetitive plink of a single piano key.

Time for damage control. I hopped up onto the stage and said, "Jingle Bells! You all heard it—the first seven notes, anyhow. Let's all give a big round of applause to Meringue, the Caroling Cockatoo!"

Those judges who'd seemed so bored a moment ago were suddenly a lot more engaged. Unfortunately, they were also pretty angry. Not a single person clapped, either—unless the hearty smack of Cosmos's tail against the floor counted as applause.

When a stray peck landed on Ladin's thumb, he juggled to keep hold of his tiny piano—and peanuts scattered everywhere. Meringue happily launched off in pursuit of her nom-noms as a couple of determined-looking folks in security windbreakers strode my way.

A single peanut rolled toward me, coming to rest against my shoe. I scooped it up, grabbed my bird...and shot the security guards my most conciliatory smile while I beat a hasty retreat.

YURI

2

As accustomed as I might be to chatter (both avian and human), when I woke to find Dixon out making a delivery and Meringue's cage still covered, it was a peaceful morning in our attic flat. Until I heard Sabina clomping up the stairs, anyhow.

"Wait until you hear my idea," she announced in the doorway.

I took a slow sip of my tea.

Without any prompting on my part, she went on. "Everyone is buzzing about painting these days, but paint is expensive. And canvas is downright ridiculous. I thought of a way of using stuff we already have and turning it around to make some money."

"Why is everyone buzzing about painting?"

Sabina's shoulders sagged. "You're missing the point, Yuri. I had an idea. Me. And it's all mine—not just something my cousin managed to get me all worked up about."

True, Sabina was more likely to bring up the rear than to take the lead. "Fine. I am curious about this idea."

She swung a dusty canvas bag onto the folding card table, where it came down with a resounding thud. Crumbs jumped on the vinyl surface, and a small cloud of dust puffed out. "Rocks," she announced proudly.

I peered into the bag's opening and, yes, it was full of rocks. And some dirt. But mostly rocks. "So you...throw them at the painting? Or maybe the artist."

"Well, no...though that sounds like *way* more fun than what I was thinking. Dang it."

I patted the chair beside me. "Come, Sabinochka. Tell me."

One of our folding chairs is loose-jointed, with stripped screws and a bent leg, and even Meringue cannot light on it without the whole thing collapsing. But Sabina and this chair were old acquaintances—I suspect they even grew up together—and when she lowered herself onto the seat, the chair moved with her as though it was an extension of her body. She sat down, tipped up on the back legs, rested her combat boots on my lap, and said, "Now that my dad's knocked up his lady-friend, there's gonna be expenses. The Handless have baby showers, and gift registries, and gender reveal thingamajigs. But you know how Scriveners are so big on the importance of words and meaning. Our main to-do is the Naming Party. Back in the dark ages, this happened after the baby was born. But nowadays they throw the party just as soon as the sonogram can tell you what's between the kid's legs."

The more she explained, the less I understood. "And so...the rocks?"

"To sell, of course. Everyone but the parents are expected to splurge big-time on the Naming Party. But not with Spellcraft income—that would be bad luck."

Spellcrafters explained away many things with "luck." I suspected the real reason the tradition came about was that if all the Scriveners in a given circuit were in need of cash at the same time, it could easily lead to a price war which would devalue the work of everyone.

Sabina said, "The luckiest money comes from getting something for nothing. With just a bag of rocks and a can of leftover house paint, there's zero overhead."

Maybe not. But I was dubious about the part where anyone would actually pay for painted garden gravel. Then again, Americans had so many useless possessions, they were always on the lookout for something they did not already own.

As I dug some old paint out of the crawlspace, I was thankful that Meringue had chosen that day to sleep in. The bird has an uncanny knack for getting into anything that will make a mess. For that matter, the same could be said for Dixon. Hopefully our painting would be done before he got home.

We spread yesterday's Pinyin Bay Journal over the table and dumped out the bag of rocks. While I sorted through the pile looking for something smooth and graceful, Sabina grabbed the first stone she saw and began to paint. Or, at least, she tried. Instead of the paint sticking to the rocks, the dust and dirt on their surface was clinging to the paint and gumming up the brush. "This is nowhere near as easy as they made it look on the internet," Sabina said.

"We must clean rocks, then let them dry. Otherwise, paint will not stick. And perhaps a coat of gesso—"

"That sounds expensive," Sabina groaned. "And we've got better things to do than wash rocks all day, and then sit around and watch them dry! Maybe there's someone on Friendlike with a bunch of clean rocks to get rid of."

Abandoning her half-painted stone, she pulled out her phone and typed a request on her Friendlike page. I continued my search for some useable rocks. "Don't get your hopes up," I told her. "You can't rely on social media. It might be hours before anyone sees this posting. And even when they do, people do not simply have bags of clean rocks just lying around—"

Sabina's phone gave off a ding. She called up her Friendlike messages and said, "Awesome! The rocks are on their way."

"How is that possible?"

Sabina tucked away her phone and tossed her sticky rock into the trash. "I dunno. Some Irish guy says he's bringing them over."

"Who is this *Irish guy*? And how does he know where you live?"

In Sabina's eyes, the particulars were of no concern and the matter was already settled. "Don't be so paranoid, Yuri. It's

Friendlike. Which means, he's like a friend. Whoever he is."

"And he is coming to case the house so he can rob it later."

"Good—maybe he'll take the davenport and we can get a new couch."

"Does this 'guy' have a name?"

"It's Van."

"And what kind of name is *Van*?"

Sabina sighed dramatically. "I know you're only looking out for me, Yuri—but this isn't Russia, it's Pinyin Bay. People around here get a kick out of helping each other. It makes them feel important. Besides, even if he is scoping out the house, once he gets a load of you, no way would he risk robbing the place. So when you think about it, I'm doing us all a big favor."

Her logic was just as convoluted as her cousin's. Sabina was too trusting. Too young. And I would not stand by and watch while her naiveté was shattered by some suspicious Irishman.

We were still arguing about the general trustworthiness of humanity when the doorbell rang. Sabina swerved around me and thundered down the stairs, eager to demonstrate that I was being too cautious and that her Friendlike "friend" had only the best of intentions. At the foot of the stairs, she yanked open the door dramatically...and said, "Vano Shirque? What the heck are you doing here?"

Vano stood, framed in the doorway, with the morning sun shining through his tousled hair, bringing out russet highlights in the Spellcrafter-black locks. I was accustomed to him looking effortlessly striking—with Dixon complaining about it all the time, I cannot help but notice. This morning, however, there was something else about him, too.

Something...uncertain.

"What do you want?" Sabina asked, with less tact than even I would have used.

Vano shuffled his feet, scratched the back of his neck, and said, "Hey...Sabina. I, uh...."

"Well? Spit it out. I haven't got all day. I'm waiting for this guy

Van to drop off my—" she fell abruptly silent, looked him up and down, then said, "Hold on. *You're* Van O'Shirque?"

"Sorry," Vano said. "You've lost me."

"It's all right here on my phone!" She pulled up the app to accuse him of catfishing her, tapped his profile...then scowled and said, "Your username really needs an underscore. And why is your profile pic a four-leaf clover?"

Baffled, Vano said, "For luck. Why else? We've been talking on Friendlike for a week now and you didn't realize—?"

"Never mind," Sabina grumbled, then shifted her attention to the bag in his hand. "Are those the rocks I asked for?"

"I found them under the downspout, nice and clean, just like you wanted."

Sabina was only slightly less annoyed. "Okay, then." She took the bag from his unresisting grasp. "Thanks."

As she reached for the door to shut it, I saw Vano's face fall...and, so help me, I took pity on him and said, "Three pairs of hands can do more work than two."

"Okay, whatever," Sabina said with a shrug, and headed back upstairs without a backward glance.

Three pairs of hands were indeed better than two—especially once Sabina's attention wandered. She can be incredibly persistent when she wants to be. However, this was not usually the case when manual labor was involved.

The stones Vano brought were much nicer than the ones Sabina had pried from a neighbor's garden. They were river stones worn smooth by water and time, just the right size to fit comfortably in the palm of a hand. If a gullible Handless shopper were to pay actual money for something as silly as a rock, this was the perfect rock to sell them.

Vano did not question why we were painting rocks—he simply set to work. He was efficient, too, dipping one half into the paint as if he was frosting a cupcake, allowing it to dry, then dipping the bottom half. And when it came time to add decoration, he improvised a graceful flourish, different every time, unique to the particular shape and character of each stone.

I fell into a rhythm with my painting. My own style is more representational, and I am unaccustomed to working on a rounded surface. But I chose the stylized motif of a sun and simply repeated it from rock to rock, losing myself in a trance of color and paint....

Or perhaps I was succumbing to fumes.

The room spun a bit as I crossed the floor to open the louvered window, and I stood there for a moment drinking in the fresh air, hoping I had not starved too many brain cells in the pursuit of a money-making scheme that could never hope to succeed—all because Sabina was so much kinder to me than any of my real siblings, and it was impossible to deny her anything.

As the fresh air pulled us all from our fume-induced trances, Sabina said, "It's awfully quiet around here without Dixon. Where did you say he was?"

"Delivering a Crafting." I checked my watch. He had been gone for quite a while—but this was probably for the best. If he witnessed the effortless way Vano flourished the rocks, he'd carry on about it for the rest of the day.

I fetched some newspaper from the recycling and shifted some rocks to the coffee table to dry. As I snapped open the arts section (which was little more than a half page above the used car ads) a prominent photo caught my eye.

"I know this man," I said.

Sabina looked up from her half-painted rock. "Drew Draws—he's the guy who found a goldmine in his own garage."

In the photograph, Drew clutched a small canvas to his chest, looking slightly stunned.

I scanned the headline: *Rare Painting Discovered by Local Artis*t

Artist? Only if your definition of art was loitering around the boardwalk and drawing the same figure over and over. I had spent an excruciating afternoon at his side sketching a busload of tourists who only seemed to care that you drew them with plenty of hair.

Sabina joined me, and Vano joined her...and together, the three of us read.

Pinyin Bay is famous for many things, from the colorful streets of Scrivener Village to the bright yellow Ferris wheel on Pinyin Beach. But a piece of Pinyin Bay history that had fallen through the cracks has been all but forgotten, until now.

Nearly three decades ago, internationally acclaimed painter Shul Cadfur made Pinyin Bay his home.

"Shul Cadfur?" Sabina scoffed. "What in the heck kind of name is that?" Clearly, she was still annoyed with herself for misreading Vano's username as Van O'Shirque.

Cadfur has always been reclusive. Even at the height of his popularity, he stayed out of the public eye, claiming that his art should speak for itself. His generous contributions to Pinyin Bay were responsible for many beautification projects and improvements. After donating the funds to place the Wishing Bell on display outside the Historical Society, Cadfur quietly retired from the art world and has not been seen or heard from since.

The last Cadfur painting was a hyperrealist rendition of Pinyin Bay's abandoned landfill at sunset, said to be a commentary on the human condition. The canvas fetched six figures at auction. Despite the painting's success, no more work was forthcoming. The young artist was quoted as stating he wanted to retire on a high note. Up until now, the only clue that the elusive artist is still among us is the continued funding of the Entropy Organization, his charitable foundation working to cure chronic misalphabetization.

Should modern authentication practices prove the new Cadfur painting to be the genuine article, its lucky owner may be Pinyin Bay's newest millionaire.

I cut my eyes to Sabina. "This is what inspired you to make us paint all these rocks?"

"Okay, I'll admit, I was throwing rocks at the Mayor's billboard when I overheard someone gushing about a painting and I didn't really pay much attention to the details."

"But it's a great idea," Vano said. "People are always eager to buy a handcrafted item."

Some of our rocks might pass for a paperweight—mainly the ones Vano had flourished. But spreading house paint was nothing like painting Seens, and my rocks were forgettable, at best. And Sabina's looked like something made by a distracted monkey.

Vano was obviously trying to appease her. And she didn't particularly notice. "Why don't I ever find million-dollar paintings under piles of random junk?" she demanded. "It's not for lack of trying. I'm always poking around where I don't belong."

Before Vano could come up with more dubious words of encouragement, our doorbell rang for the second time that morning. Sabina stopped complaining about her lack of rare paintings and said, "Why hasn't your bird mimicked the doorbell yet? She's usually twice as loud as the real thing."

As the doorbell rang again, all eyes went to the sheet-covered cage.

Vano was closest, and he whisked off the sheet with the flair of a magician. Except when he revealed the cage beneath was empty, it was not because he had caused her to disappear...but because the cage door was open...and so was the nearby window.

As my heart sank down to the soles of my feet and I wondered how I could possibly explain to Dixon that his beloved pet had flown away, the doorbell rang yet again.

Briskly, Sabina said, "Now, before you panic, keep in mind how attached Meringue is to both of you. She knows how good she's got it here. I'm sure she hasn't gone far. I'll just drop a post on my Friendlike page to see if anyone's noticed a wayward cockatoo—"

"Wait," I told her. "If you post that, Dixon will see."

"I can put it on my profile," Vano said. "For some reason, Dixon never got around to adding me."

Now was not the time to tell him that Dixon had been ranting and raving about the request ever since it had appeared, wondering what ulterior motive Vano might have for making contact.

The doorbell rang yet again. What if a helpful neighbor had

spotted Meringue? Even better, what if they already had the bird and were returning her to her rightful owner?

I hurried down and opened the door...but there was no bird. Instead, I found a figure in disguise. Oversized sunglasses, trench coat, and fedora. But even had I not just read his name in the newspaper mere moments before, I would have recognized him by his obscenely short shorts...and the fact that his fedora was covered in sequins. "Who could this possibly be?" I said dryly.

Oblivious to my sarcasm, the man on my front step pulled down the sunglasses and whispered loudly, "Why, it's me, silly! Your dear mentor, Drew Draws."

3

"You are hardly my mentor—" I began.

"No time for pleasantries, my strapping young apprentice!" Drew prodded me in the chest with a briefcase he'd been holding. "Let me in before some crazed gallery owners eat me alive!"

If he was worried about being eaten, perhaps he should consider wearing some pants. But I knew how the man operated. He was annoyingly persistent, and it was easier to invite him inside than convince him to go away.

Upstairs, Sabina and Vano were checking in the cupboards and under the furniture to see if Meringue was simply hiding, though I knew in my heart she must be gone, since she had more difficulty holding her tongue than Dixon. Sabina looked up from the stack of dorm refrigerators and said, "Hey, that's the guy from the article!"

"I see my fame precedes me! Or should that be infamy?" Drew fanned himself with his fedora and plunked down at the table. Luckily not in Sabina's chair. "What's with the rocks?"

"They're for sale," Sabina said. "Want one? We'll cut you a great deal."

"I can't possibly think about shopping at a time like this. My phone has blown up with interview requests and art scouts are banging down my front door."

"Why is that a problem?" Vano asked him.

"Are any of them even remotely interested in *me* as an artist? Not one single bit. All they care about is Shul Cadfur. I've been upstaged by a man who hasn't touched a brush in nearly thirty years."

Sabina, naturally, had an opinion. "Whoop de do! Who cares if this Cadfur guy is the flavor of the day? Sell off his painting and you can laugh all the way to the bank."

"If only it were that easy," Drew said with a dramatic sigh. "I've seen what they're saying in all the news outlets—that I won't see a cent unless the painting is authenticated. I don't know what to do. The authenticator will be here in just a few days."

He brushed a few painted rocks aside, set his briefcase on the table, and snapped it open. It contained only one thing: a canvas. And the painting on it was so painstakingly realistic it looked more like a photograph—albeit one that was a bit too bright, a bit too precise, detailed to the point of unnatural clarity.

The subject was a very *nineties* young man, from his soul patch to his head-to-toe faded denim. The fabric was so finely rendered you could practically count the frayed threads. His baseball cap was backwards, and his mirrored sunglasses reflected the phantom image of whoever was viewing him—presumably the artist himself. The man in the painting stood, arms crossed, in front of a graffiti-covered brick wall with a cocky smirk on his face and a can of spray paint in his grasp.

"I suppose you can't blame critics for making sure a talented artist like me hasn't attempted a forgery," Drew said. I bit back a snort. The only "art" Drew produced were sketches of tourists with big scribbles of hair. "After all, what creative hasn't dabbled in the art of self-portraiture?"

Sabina did a double-take. "Hold on—that's *you*?"

Drew blinked, startled. "Well, who else would it be?" I supposed the word DRAWZ tagged on the wall behind him in stylized graffiti made more sense now. Drew struck the pose of the confident young man in the painting...but only succeeded in making himself look like a ludicrous middle-aged crackpot in short-shorts. When he saw we were all looking at him dubiously, he added, "And how on earth would I know it was a genuine Shul Cadfur if I hadn't seen him paint it myself?"

Most certainly, there was a story there. But before we could grill him on the details, the door downstairs banged open, and Dixon's tread sounded on the stairwell. I would know it anywhere. It always paused slightly before the squeaky step, as if wondering which stair was the loud one, then came down on it hard just the same.

"No one say anything about the bird," I said.

"What bird?" Drew wondered.

Moving quickly, I tossed the sheet over the cage. It settled just as the upstairs door opened.

All of us turned to Dixon, who offered us a nervous smile. "Wow. I didn't realize the apartment would be quite so...populated."

"Rock painting party," I said.

"Okay, then." Dixon sidled toward the bedroom, protectively clutching his messenger bag to his side. "I won't keep you."

There was an awkward pause, cut off by the ding of an incoming Friendlike message on Vano's phone...echoed by a muffled, slightly off-key *ding* in Dixon's bag. As Vano checked his messages, another ding sounded, and another. Meringue sightings? Hopefully. Vano edged toward the door and said, "Anyway, uh...turns out there's something I need to, erm...do."

"I'll help," Sabina said quickly. Not from any desire to be helpful, but because she didn't want to be around when Dixon figured out Meringue was gone. The two of them hurried out the door.

Hopefully all those Friendlike alerts were from people who'd spotted Meringue. She was loud, curious, and impossible to overlook. But she also had a tendency to fly up into the rafters and taunt us when we tried to get her to do anything she did not wish to do.

At the table, Drew remarked, "I get the feeling I showed up right in the middle of something."

I lowered my voice and said, "Whatever you do, don't mention the—"

"What on earth?" From the bedroom, Dixon's comically loud exclamation interrupted my admonition. "Meringue! What do you think you're doing in here? You know this is Daddy and Papochka's private space!"

"Don't mention the what?" Drew asked, bewildered, but I was already halfway to the bedroom with my heart hammering against my ribcage.

I burst into the room and found Meringue standing there in the center of the bed with Dixon scolding her with a wag of his finger. When the bird saw me, she spread her wings wide in a stance Dixon calls the "bird hug" as she waddled towards me. "Nom nom!"

I found a stray peanut in my pocket and handed it over. These days, I buy them with the shells already removed. Meringue took the nut delicately with her beak, then grasped it with one foot and proceeded to peel off the skin with her agile tongue. I expected Dixon to remark on the fact that there was no food allowed in the bed—a rule we put in place after the unfortunate whipped cream incident that left our sheets reeking of rotten milk, even after we'd washed them. But instead he offered me a forced smile and said, "Meringue must have let herself out of her cage this morning. Because you didn't. And I certainly didn't. So it's clearly the only logical explanation."

"Yes," I quickly agreed. "Clearly."

"Okay, then." Dixon clapped his hands together briskly. Meringue, busy crumbling her peanut, hardly noticed. "Now, why is Drew Draws in our kitchen?"

As I told Dixon about the million-dollar painting, his eyes went wide. Not only at the thought of the money, but the promise of intrigue. "We totally have to help Drew get that painting authenticated. You can't just leave your good friend high and dry."

"He is *not* my good friend—"

"And then we can invite him to the baby's Naming Party...and suggest we all go in on our gift together." With that, Dixon scooped Meringue up off the bed, trailing peanut crumbs, and strode out into the flat.

Left to his own devices, Drew had taken it upon himself to rearrange all of our painted stones from best to worst. He said, "This rock operation is in serious need of some quality control. Tourists are always eager to throw away their money, but they expect some kind of presentable souvenir in return. These should fetch you a buck or two." He gestured at the rocks Vano had painted. "But these?" he pointed at mine. "You'd need a convincing narrative to pawn these off on anyone. Claim they were done by a child prodigy and you might get a few sympathy sales. As for the rest of them...." We all looked at Sabina's rocks. To say they were clumsy would be generous. "No good. Unless you claim they were painted by an elephant, in which case, you might get a few novelty sales."

Since an elephant had been responsible for the unfortunate end of Vano's mother, I doubted that story would work so long as he was on our team.

"The rocks are adorable," Dixon said. "Well, most of them. But what we should really be focusing on is that painting. Everyone's buzzing about it now, so you need to strike while the iron is hot and do whatever it takes to establish its provenance."

Drew seemed startled by Dixon's enthusiasm. "Well," he said to me. "Maybe your young man friend isn't so airheaded after all."

Dixon blinked. "Hey—"

"Unfortunately, there's a problem. Shul made a point of not putting his name on this painting. I remember the conversation like it happened just yesterday. I jokingly asked him to sign it in case he became a 'big time artist' someday—and he laughed and said he couldn't imagine anything as pretentious as signing a gift for a friend."

Dixon said, "But you saw him paint it. That's gotta count for something."

"You'd think so, but no. There's nothing to prove Shul and I were cohorts but my word. I've been searching high and low for old photos, letters, anything. But I've come up empty-handed. All I have of our time together are my memories." Drew shook his head sadly. "Memories that only I seem to give two figs about."

I said, "There must be other ways to authenticate a painting."

"Nothing they could do in Pinyin Bay," Drew said. "Without a signature, this thing isn't worth a cent more than the canvas it's painted on."

"What about sentimental value?" Dixon asked cautiously.

"Surely I'm not so maudlin as to pine over an old friend who dropped off the face of the earth without so much as a quick goodbye. If this painting were signed, I'd have it at the auction house before you could say, *Hasta la vista!* In fact, if you've got a paintbrush handy, I'll go ahead and sign it myself—"

"Hold on," Dixon said. "That can't possibly work. Any specialist worth his salt will be able to tell it was signed with a different paint."

Drew nodded toward the crusty cans of paint we'd been using for the rocks. "Not at all. Back in the early days, when we were young, starving artists, we'd use whatever paint we could get our hands on. Including house paint."

I picked up a can and looked for a date. "But surely this is not thirty years old...wait, never mind." Dixon's family truly never threw anything away.

Still, Dixon was not convinced. "Experts will be scrutinizing that signature long and hard. You can't just dash off any old John Hancock and expect it to pass muster. If it's not perfect, you'll ruin any chance of ever being able to sell that painting. Even worse, you'll ruin your reputation too, and from here on out, everyone will think you're a fraud."

"Then it's no use," Drew said. "And I'm stuck with this painting that's nothing more than a reminder of my disappointment."

Dixon simply cannot pass up the chance of showing off his handwriting prowess. "Hold on. I'm something of a handwriting expert," he said with his best attempt at humility. "I'd be willing to help you out—but first, I'd need to see some examples of Shul's real signature."

Drew said, "Well, the most famous Cadfur is the Mayor's official portrait. It's been hanging in his office since parachute pants were in style."

Yuri pulled up Pinyin Bay's municipal website on his phone and called up the portrait. "This picture is cropped so I can't see the signature. We will have to go look in person."

Drew shook his head. "Everyone knows it's impossible to get an appointment with Mayor Dunce."

"Maybe so." Dixon rubbed his palms together in anticipation. "But I'll bet his gatekeepers are no match for my advanced-level pestering. Let's go!"

Once Dixon followed Drew out the door, I made sure the window was shut tight, then dug up a treat to lure Meringue into her cage. But the peanut was unnecessary. I found her already there, fastidiously arranging a bed of shredded papers. "That had better not be the electric bill again," I told her.

"Nom nom."

I pushed a peanut through the bars and she hurried over to take it from me, which gave me a better look at the pile of shreds. Whether it was an important piece of mail, I could not say. I was too distracted by the fact that it was not merely a mound of shred, but a nest....

A nest which contained a single, tiny egg.

DIXON

4

Lucky for me there'd been so much going on at the apartment when Meringue and I got back from the talent show—and thankfully, no one had questioned how Meringue had ended up in the bedroom. Yuri would take it pretty hard if he knew Meringue had been banned from competing in any future talent shows. She'd been pretty unaffected by the whole thing, though—which meant she was much less of a diva than I'd always presumed.

Pinyin Bay is hardly a sprawling metropolis, and the trip to City Hall was shorter than my mother's temper when a customer bounces a check. Spellcrafters are generally none too fond of municipal government, as we'd rather abide by our own traditions, not Handless rules and regulations. We preferred a handshake to a contract, and cohabitation to marriage. And I've never once known a Spellcrafter to pull a permit to remodel their own home... case in point, my current apartment, which no doubt violated any number of codes.

Unfortunately, some Handless rigmarole you simply couldn't avoid. I hadn't been at City Hall since I'd renewed the business license of Practical Penn half a dozen years ago, but the lobby was exactly like I remembered...and I mean *exactly*. From the buzzing fluorescent light overhead to the city's dusty motto on the pediment: To Bay, Or Not to Bay.

And off behind the clerk, framed by an open doorway, hung the very painting we'd come to reconnoiter: the official mayoral portrait.

Mayor Dunce had been in charge of Pinyin Bay ever since I could remember. In fact, I might have even voted for him once. I distinctly remember this because my mother was none too pleased when she found out I'd registered to vote when a couple of intrepid political types set up shop outside the frozen yogurt bar. "Just because someone tells you to sign something doesn't mean you should," she'd told me. "What's next, you're gonna join the Navy when you show off your signature to a cute guy who turns out to be a recruiter?"

Still, I was a restless eighteen-year-old, experiencing growing pains in more than just my shins. At the time, Pinyin Bay seemed positively podunk, and I was balking not only at my small-town roots, but all the unwritten rules of being a Spellcrafter. I couldn't wait to march up to that ballot box and choose a candidate.

Which one—Dunce, or his opponent? Can't say I remember. Just that I felt really grown-up while I did it.

I do recall that Mayor Dunce took that election...but only because he'd won not only that race, but several before it, and every one since. The photo hanging in City Hall was from those early days, with slicked-back hair, big shoulder pads, and a dazzling smile of teeth so white and square they looked more like piano keys. (The big white keys, I mean, not the shrimpy little black ones in-between.)

Drew Draws—who'd naturally have an opinion about a portrait, being a portraiture artist—regarded the picture with his hands on his hips. "That's as old as the painting I just found in my shed. You'd think Dunce would spring for an update."

"True," I said. "That painting's been in use since I was in diapers. But it could just be he likes how it looks. After all, my mom refuses to renew her driver's license ever since she gained a few pounds."

Though maybe that was also because she took umbrage to the thought of the governmental bureaucracy dictating her ability to drive.

A handful of people had business there before us, paying property tax, licensing their dogs, complaining about their utility bills. We inched our way forward, until finally we got to the window... and found a wizened little man at the counter poking at an ancient keyboard. Up until now, Morticia Shirque was the oldest human I'd personally met, but this guy was giving her a run for her money. He peered at us through filmy bifocals and wheezed, "Can I help you?"

I squared my shoulders and said, "We need to see Mayor Dunce at once!" Wow, that rhymed! But I stopped myself from saying so, as people don't take me seriously when I helpfully point that out. "We're here on very important business."

The clerk squinted. "And what business would that be?"

And...I had nothing. So I turned to Drew and said, "Well? Tell the man!"

Drew rolled his eyes elaborately. He elbowed me aside, put on a Very Important Voice, and announced, "I need a festival permit."

The clerk said, "You'll have to come back in a few months. We only take permit applications from October to December."

"Don't I know it? You people have shut down every great idea I've ever proposed, from the Big Bay Splash Fest to the Rainbow Bay Pride Parade. The Boardwalk used to be a real feather in Pinyin Bay's cap, and now look at it! Blasted half to smithereens by the Loveland Corporation, with all the performers and artisans crammed onto what's left of it, just a few battered planks, struggling to make an honest living. We need an infusion of cash—we need to rebuild—and the best way to do that is with a Bring Back the Boardwalk Festival!"

Wow, I hadn't realized Drew could be so persuasive. I was ready to empty my wallet on the spot...not that my twenty bucks would fund more than a plank or two. The Boardwalk was one of those Pinyin Bay institutions I always thought I'd outgrown (especially during my European Wanderlust phase). But having rediscovered that funny old stretch of beach, I now realized how special it was.

And how sad that it was still in disrepair.

But as I turned to Yuri to remark that we really should do something about the boardwalk, I noticed that he hadn't been listening to Drew's impassioned speech at all. Instead, he was staring hard at something tacked to a nearby acoustic divider.

While Drew continued to argue with the old man behind the counter, Yuri drew me aside and said, "Look at that calendar."

The calendar in question was your standard promotional giveaway, the type to flood your mail slot every December. A real win-win, when you think about it. The business gets to put its logo where a customer will see it several times a day, and the customer gets a free calendar. "You might not have promo calendars in Russia—"

"Of course we do."

"—but they're pretty commonplace around here."

Yuri closed his eyes and silently counted to ten. Probably in Russian. "Look at the month. It has not been changed since January."

A few years ago, I may or may not have owned a fireman calendar that stayed on Mister February for the rest of the year. Who needs to know what day it is when you could be gazing at those bulging biceps instead? But the image on this particular calendar was nowhere near as enticing, just a boring old picture of the Recent Center shopping mall at the edge of town—a place that hadn't seen much traffic since feathered hair was in vogue. And the slogan was just as dull as the picture:

We like things
just the way they are.

As I puzzled over the world's most uninspiring calendar, Yuri said, "That is not January of this year. It's January 1996."

I let out a small gasp of surprise as the tingle of Spellcraft whispered across my awareness, distant, but unmistakable. Pinyin Bay was infamous for having more red tape than a stationery outlet, and everyone complained about having to drive all the way to Strangeberg to shop at the big box stores. The only businesses who did muddle their way through the bureaucracy (like the Loveland Corporation) must've managed only because they had Spellcraft of their own, since Spellcraft will find loopholes within loopholes to try and keep itself straight.

Whoever owned the Recent Center back in the day was probably long gone, but their legacy remained in Pinyin Bay's every outmoded ordinance and denied permit. How clever—I mean, underhanded—to make a gift of the Spellcraft and get the "lucky" recipients to hang it up themselves.

There's not really much rhyme or reason as to how far the effects of a single Crafting might reach. Some spells are as ephemeral as twilight, while others stick around like the dog days of summer… times a thousand.

And apparently this one was phenomenally sticky.

Not only did this decades-old Crafting keep new businesses from setting up shop in Pinyin Bay, but it caused City Hall itself to grind to a standstill. The clerk should've retired twenty years ago. Mayor Dunce had been re-elected multiple terms running. And speaking of which, it was a wonder the computers were still running at all.

Would it be harder to Uncraft such an old spell, like prying a stubborn rock out of the ground? Or had the Voobaloobadoo worn thin all those loopholes in reality, and once I rejiggered the words, change would push out like a toe through a worn sock?

My brain wanted to change "We like things just the way they are" to "We like to adjust the way things are," but unfortunately, this was Spellcraft, not an anagram. (And, actually, my idea wasn't even a proper anagram, like "eleven plus two" shuffled to read "twelve plus one.") I couldn't rearrange the calendar. Only add.

Simple declarations seem susceptible to simple negations, as in "We don't like things just the way they are." But would the addition of the negator actually work? Or would it make City Hall truculent and disgruntled, and leave Pinyin Bay open to outsiders who only wanted to make a quick buck?

Maybe such entrenched magic could be eased out of its rut with a simple qualifier. *We like things just the way they are...sometimes.*

"I know what you're thinking," Yuri said.

"That my Recrafting would sound even better if it rhymed?"

"There is no way you can get behind his desk and alter that Spellcraft without half the city seeing you."

True. The longer Drew filibustered with the clerk, the longer the line behind us got—and the more impatient everyone in it was looking. While I was itching to write something about new ideas "going far," I could hardly do it in full view of all those Handless.

Where was a fire alarm when you needed one?

Nowhere, apparently, thanks to safety codes several decades out of date.

I was about to announce I heard a distant tornado siren when Yuri blurted out to the clerk, "Of course the mayor is not interested in this festival."

Drew and the clerk stopped arguing and turned to him, baffled.

Yuri steeled his resolve and went on. "Who would wish to promote something so uninspired as a festival on the boardwalk? Just because it is a time honored tradition, there's no reason to do it again. No one is interested in the same booths, the same performers, the same popcorn and cotton candy—"

The clerk had punched a few numbers into his ancient phone system and was already murmuring into his handset. Brilliant! Yuri had convinced him by acting like the festival was business as usual. And by the time he ran out of weird things to say, the old man gave us a nod and said, "Mayor Dunce will hear your proposal."

He buzzed us in and directed us toward the painting.

"I just about had a heart attack back there!" Drew loud-whispered as soon as we were out of earshot. "Warn a guy when you're about to use reverse psychology."

Gotta leave it to the Handless. They could be incredibly good at making excuses for Spellcraft.

Mayor Dunce's office was just as drab and dated as the rest of City

Hall. The acoustic ceiling was yellowed, the curtains were faded, and the wall-to-wall carpeting had a threadbare strip running down the center from the tread of several decades' worth of shoes. It was all frankly pretty overwhelming...so much so that when the figure at the desk moved, I nearly had a heart attack myself.

The Cadfur painting dominated the room, larger than life. A *lot* larger. But the man behind the desk was a withered, shrunken version of the man in the portrait, as if someone had created a Mayor Dunce scarecrow to put out on their porch for Halloween. The hair was the same bottle black. The glasses were the chunky tortoiseshell frames that had gone in and out of style at least three times. And the suit was the same expanse of blue polyester and shoulder pads. But Mayor Dunce was rattling around inside that suit like the last peanut at the bottom of the can.

"Gentlemen," he said smoothly, baring his piano key teeth, which looked even larger now that the rest of him had shrunk with age. "What's this I hear about a boardwalk festival?"

Drew Draws was nothing if not a quick study. He took the line of reasoning Yuri had used with the clerk and totally ran with it. "Hardly worth your time, Mayor, I'm sure—progressive thinker such as yourself. But I'd be remiss if I didn't petition for the time-honored, traditional Boardwalk Festival—a stodgy affair, really, something that would only appeal to the folks who've lived here all their lives. No doubt you'd rather attract the Millennials to Pinyin Bay with a handcrafted artisanal water-cocktail bar instead."

"Millennials? *Water* cocktails?? No, no, that just won't fly—Pinyin Bay already has a bad reputation for watering down its drinks. We can't compound the problem with water cocktails." From a stack on his desk, the mayor grabbed a brittle, yellowed carbon-copy form and said, "Schedule your festival for the same weekend you always do and it's a done deal. Just make sure you have a good, old-fashioned beer tent. No water cocktails."

Mayor Dunce dashed off his (rather forgettable) signature, which was pretty disappointing—but he made up for it big time when he pulled out a mayoral seal and embossed the Pinyin Bay city crest over the top of it. I'm a real sucker for anything stationery-related, and to see such a unique tool in action was riveting. Drew Draws would get his festival after all, and we'd saved the day without even needing to Uncraft any—

Yuri kicked my foot and startled me out of my self-congratulatory reverie. He jerked his head toward the Cadfur painting.

Oh. Right. I was so invested in our decoy festival that I'd forgotten all about the signature. I edged closer to the portrait. Not only was the painting itself huge and cumbersome, but the frame contained enough lumber to build a raft and sail to Strangeberg. Very stately. Unfortunately, it was also so big that it obscured all but the very tippy-top of Shul Cadfur's signature.

I elbowed Yuri and gestured toward the hidden signature with my eyes. He gave a squint of annoyance, then cleared his throat and said, "I have heard it was traditional to celebrate the signing of a permit with a tour of City Hall."

"Absolutely," I agreed. "That's how it's always done." Hopefully, it wouldn't occur to Mayor Dunce that this was patently untrue... either because he'd signed so few permits in his umpteen terms in office, or because he was so tangled up in the web of Spellcraft that it was easiest not to struggle against it.

Up until that point, Drew Draws had been a perfect accomplice, playing along with whatever schemes we came up with despite his disadvantage of being in the dark about the Spellcraft—but now he thought we were still using reverse psychology. "Who'd want to tour this dump? Not me. I've got places to go and people to see."

Mayor Dunce looked affronted. "I'll have you know, City Hall is Pinyin Bay's most symmetrical building. Someone who can't appreciate that might not be the sort of person I'd trust to chair a festival—"

Before things spun way out of hand, I blurted out, "Drew was just telling me on our way over how much he appreciates symmetry, weren't you, Drew?"

"I was?"

"And you were really eager to see a good example of it in person."

"I...was. Yes. That's right. Because these things are very important to me. As an artist. And a symmetrical human being."

Gotta hand it to Drew. He was really good at rolling with the punches.

In fact, he worked himself up so effectively about the whole symmetry deal, when he whisked the mayor away for his tour, we could hear him enthusing all the way down the hall—which was fantastic for gauging just how much time we had to monkey around with the Cadfur painting!

I casually toed the door shut so the people in line couldn't see what we were doing, and Yuri eased the heavy painting off the wall. It left a dark square behind—kind of like those really organized pegboard tool walls with an outline drawn around each tool. My mom always thought those things looked too much like a crime scene...which made my father twice as eager to install one in the basement. We know full well he did it just to get mom's goat, as he hasn't touched a single one of those tools in years. His sense of humor can take some getting used to. Anyhow, this particular square was left by the passage of time, with the paneling around it sun-faded half a shade lighter than the surrounding faux wood.

Yuri flipped the painting around and scowled at the back of the portrait.

"What is it?" I asked.

"Something is wrong. For such a large canvas, it is flimsy and cheap." He picked at the edge. "And the material is strange. Like plastic." He turned the painting right side up and ran his fingers down the front. Spellcraft Seens are made with paints that soak into the paper and leave a smooth, flat, uninterrupted surface for the Scrivener to write on. Oil paintings, on the other hand, tend to have hills and valleys in the texture of the brush strokes. But the Cadfur on the mayor's wall had a surface smooth enough for Scribing. "This is not a real painting. It's a print made from a photograph."

"That's weird," I said, "but we can wonder about it later. All we care about now is the signature!" With Drew Draws still enthusing in the distance, I pulled out my pen knife and bent back some of the metal tabs holding the fake painting in place. As Yuri pushed the canvas from the frame, I readied my phone to take a snapshot of the signature....

Only to discover that beneath the wooden frame, instead of a signature, there was yet another frame...and this one was a photo, so there'd be no prying it off. Whoever had reproduced this painting had shot the framed original, and only another fraction of an inch of the artist's signature was visible. I snapped a picture anyway, though I didn't see how it would do us any good.

"Coming here was useless," Yuri grumbled, and shoved the canvas back into the frame. Drew's voice was getting closer now, and we had barely enough time to slap the fake painting back on the wall and position ourselves to stand there looking totally innocent.

"Well?" Drew demanded, once we were safe in the truck. "Don't keep me in suspense. Did you get it?"

Yuri and I exchanged a look. "We ran into a little snag," I said, and pulled up the photo I'd taken to let Drew see for himself.

"Spread me with jam and call me a tart!" Drew grabbed the phone from my hand and zoomed in on what little we could see of the signature. It was mostly frame. "I endured a tour of City Hall for this?"

"Afraid so."

Drew slumped back against the seat and fanned himself with his sparkly fedora. "Now what?"

"Now nothing," Yuri said. "The Dunce painting was our only hope."

If only I could see just a li-i-ttle bit more of those letterforms, I might be able to extrapolate the rest of the signature. After all, if we were having such a hard time finding a clear example of Shul Cadfur's handwriting, maybe the authenticator was, too. I took back my phone from Drew's unresisting grasp and zoomed out to get a better sense of the artist's hand. Unfortunately, with just the very tops of the letters showing, the only thing I could say for sure was that the spacing between the letters looked neat and precise.

Drew was scrutinizing the photo over my shoulder. "No wonder the frame in Dunce's office was so wide. It had to be to cover the edges of the painting. You can even see a bit of the surrounding wall here. And that wallpaper—talk about tacky!"

How odd. This photo did indeed contain about half an inch of wall. The wallpaper behind was either modern shabby chic or truly old, with a faded pastoral pattern in navy on beige. Old-fashioned? Yes. But tacky? "As wallpaper goes, I've seen a lot worse."

"Individually, I suppose they're fine. But come on, people, pick a lane!"

When I zoomed out some more, I saw there was a totally different old-timey wallpaper behind the left half of the photo, this one a mauve silk moire. Two wallpapers, one wall. I knew immediately where the painting had been photographed. I quelled a groan and said, "Yuri? We'll need to head over to Shirque Mansion."

YURI

5

Though the Shirques had always been decent enough to me, I had no great love of their ancestral home. To demonstrate various building techniques and finishes, Shirque Mansion was made in a sprawling patchwork of clashing styles. And though Morticia Shirque had been doing her best to offload the disturbing sculptures which were a legacy from her father, every now and then you'd turn a corner and find a pair of blank plaster eyes staring you in the face.

I was familiar with Shirque Mansion, and I still found it strange—but Drew was encountering it for the very first time. He took it in with a glance and said, "I've heard of eclectic, but this is ridiculous. It's like a half-dozen different architects put this place together. Blindfolded."

I pulled up the curved driveway and did a slow circuit around the house, and saw Morticia Shirque's rusted Rolls Royce was not in its customary spot beneath the carport.

"I guess we'll just have to try all the doors," Dixon said. "And then the windows."

I gave him a sharp look. "We are not breaking into the head of the...ah...gardening club's home."

Drew did not seem to notice my near-slip. "If this is how their master gardener keeps her flowerbeds, no wonder the hostas around the boardwalk are half dead."

I usually had no problem keeping Spellcraft secrets from the Handless. Perhaps boardwalk folk were so much like Scriveners that I nearly mistook the cartoonist for one of us. Both groups were leery of outsiders. Both knew how to think on their feet. And both were looked down upon by society at large...until something was needed, and then they were treated as a sort of guilty pleasure. Scriveners and boardwalk folk were close cousins...speaking of which, I wondered where Sabina had ended up. I pulled out my phone and said, "I will ask Vano to let us in."

It took Vano several rings to pick up, and when he did, it was amidst some kind of commotion. "Yuri? Hello? Yuri, can you—?"

He sounded...flustered. Which, for him, was unusual. "Vano?"

A flapping, squawking cacophony obliterated his reply. Then a shuffle as Sabina grabbed the phone away and announced, "I know you love that dumb bird of yours, Yuri, but I don't think I can handle looking for her much longer!"

...and with that, I realized I'd neglected to tell them Meringue was home safe and sound, and had been for hours. I could hardly say it now in front of Dixon, either. Though if I made it look like Vano was ordering a Seen, he'd think I was just trying to keep secrets from Drew. "That is correct," I said. "I am available to paint...houses."

"What?" Sabina called over the cries of birds. "Fainting mouses? I can't understand you!"

I covered the phone with my hand and announced to the passengers, "I will take this outside."

"That's great," Dixon said quickly, cranking up the radio. "My favorite song is on."

Drew was bewildered. "The jingle from the car wash?"

"Totally! Let's sing along! *When your car is shmutzy and your hose is broke—*"

I climbed out of the truck and left Dixon to distract our

companion feeling both grateful...and guilty. Yes, I was somewhat annoyed with myself for not calling Sabina and Vano sooner. But mainly I felt bad about lying to Dixon. White lies are something I had no use for in Russia. But failing to mention that Meringue had gone missing felt like something much more serious than complimenting Florica's cooking to spare Dixon's feelings.

But my *vozljublennyj* did love that "dumb bird" of his...more than words could express. And since Meringue was home safe now, it made no sense to upset him.

A series of squawks and trills sounded over the phone, only somewhat camouflaging Sabina's cursing. "Sabina," I said, "where are you?"

Over the commotion, she yelled, "Once Vano posted on Friendlike, his inbox went nuts! It's ridiculous! People are bringing us birds from all over Pinyin Bay just for an excuse to make goo-goo eyes at him—and not just the Spellcrafters trying to hook up with him for his family name, either. Plenty of Handless are smitten with him too. And most of the birds are just random pigeons and seagulls—hey, watch it, pal. That's *my* trail mix!" A brief scuffle ensued. When Sabina came back, she sounded even more frazzled. "Good thing we had them meet us at the car wash parking lot. Otherwise we'd be drowning in feathers."

And good thing Sabina had already completed her quilling ceremony. Birds are known to have a long memory.

I said, "You can stop looking for the bird—she found her own way home."

"That's a relief—I was worried you just wanted to talk me into telling Dixon his bird flew the coop!"

Perhaps it was for the best I did not mention that Meringue had been home safe for quite a while. "Right now, we need you to get us into Shirque Mansion."

"All you have to do is take a credit card and jimmy it down the doorframe—"

"Legitimately."

Sabina groaned. "Now you tell me. As soon as you said the

cockatoo was okay, I figured I could ditch Vano in his sea of admirers and make a run for it. The last thing I wanna do is go back and pull him out!"

"A million dollars depends on it."

"Fine," she grumbled. "We can sure use the cash, and it's not like I've had any luck unloading those dumb painted rocks. Good thing I've been keeping my elbows limber in case Pinyin Bay ever started up a roller derby."

A few minutes later, the old Buick rounded the drive with Sabina at the wheel. She climbed out and slammed the door. Hard. Vano followed sheepishly and let us into the mansion.

"We need to find a portrait of Mayor Dunce," Dixon said.

"No problem." Vano motioned for us to follow him up the grand staircase, shedding a few downy feathers from his T-shirt and hair. "Back when I was little, my grandfather heard that manor houses in England set a special room aside in case the queen stops by, and insisted we do the same. Thus, the Mayor's Room came to be. Though I don't remember Dunce ever actually staying in it. In fact, I probably spent more time in that room than anyone else."

"Pretending to be Mayor?" Drew asked—clearly a Handless question, as most Spellcrafters would rather pluck out their nose hairs one by one than hold office.

Vano shook his head. "It was just a good place to hide to get out of doing any chores."

He led us all the way up to the fourth floor, where the various stretches of wallpaper looked surprisingly subdued...until I realized I only thought so because I was viewing the patterns through a thick coat of dust.

The door to the Mayor's Room was twice as grandiose as any of the others, with elaborate paneling and thick, hand-carved molding. The wood was inlaid with patterns of mahogany and rosewood, and the doorknob was faceted crystal. I reminded myself not to get too wrapped up in admiring the workmanship, because in Shirque Mansion, anything pleasing would change to some other style or color soon enough. Besides, it was wise to keep one eye out for lurking statuary.

Initially, the door would not budge. But before Sabina could offer her opinion about how best to navigate the lock, Vano put his hip into it, and the door opened with a startling pop and a cloud of dust.

Once we were all done coughing, we took in the stately room. The four-poster bed was just as I imagined it, ponderous and heavy, carved with winding vines. But the bed linens were clearly two sets stitched together up the middle, dark and masculine on one side, soft and feminine on the other.

"Grandpa was a pretty progressive thinker for someone who insisted on a Mayor's Room," Vano said. "He wanted to cover all his bases in case a female mayor ever took office."

Indeed, the whole room was split down the middle, half dark blues and greens, half pale florals. And at the foot of the massive bed, at the juncture where the wallpapers met....

Was nothing at all.

We all looked up. The ceiling above was damaged. A rusty stain of damp spread across it like a map of an undiscovered continent, and crumbling plaster hung down in great chunks.

"Nana must have moved it when the rain came in," Vano said.

Hopefully the old woman remembered what she'd done with it. "Well," I suggested, "ask her where it is."

"But not through Friendlike," Sabina grumbled.

Vano tried calling...and in the distance, a phone rang. "Uh oh, Nana left her phone in the charger again. No telling where she might be. But feel free to look through the mansion. In fact..." he eased toward Sabina. "We'll cover more ground if we split up."

"Good idea!" she said—and snagged her startled cousin by the elbow, much to the alarm of both him and Vano. "Come on, let's go!"

The three Scriveners ventured off in search of the painting, leaving me with Drew. I expected some waspish remark from him, but instead found him staring at the spot on the wall where the painting no longer hung with a curious look on his face.

"It's awfully good of your friends to drop what they're doing to help me find the painting," he said. He had no idea how eager Dixon and Sabina were to avoid doing any actual work. "All this fracas reminds me of what it was like, back in the day, to have my own partner in crime. Shul tried to apologize to me after he called me a sellout, but I was so full of righteous indignation, I refused to listen." Drew sighed. "I didn't realize friendship was such a precious commodity."

I am the last person anyone should come to for sympathy. "Everyone has regrets. But sometimes there is no way to repair the past, and the only thing left to do is move forward."

Moving forward was also the only way we could hope to find this painting. Shirque Mansion was a sprawling collection of rooms and hallways, stairways and chambers. Door by door, we worked our way through the third story, through the travesty of architecture and decoration. And every time I thought I was inured to the process, I stumbled across another distorted plaster statue. But eventually we covered the entire floor, with no mayoral portrait to show for it.

Hopefully, Dixon was having better luck.

DIXON

6

Divide and conquer—usually a pretty good plan. After all, that's how Spellcraft worked, with each person doing their own respective part. Seers painting. Scriveners writing. And Handless compensating us for our specialized skills. But in this particular instance, I really wished the group had stuck together. Because I had no desire to spend the afternoon with Vano Shirque...but I was also anxious about being alone with Yuri after fibbing to him about the talent show.

Don't get me wrong. While it might seem like I voice every fleeting thought that goes through my head—in this case a car wash jingle I'd no doubt be singing in my sleep—I can be pretty tactful when the situation calls for it. Like when Sabina's Spellcrafting fails to employ a stunningly obvious rhyme. Or my dad drags home something from a neighbor's trash that clearly should have stayed on the curb.

Or I realize that Yuri wasn't just being a stick in the mud...he was actually looking out for me. And rightly so.

Clearly, I'd need to come clean, sooner rather than later. I just needed some time to figure out how to frame it in the best possible light.

And speaking of frames...there's more paintings in Shirque Mansion than all the art galleries in Pinyin Bay put together. Not that there are all that many galleries, and one of them specializes in soap carvings. But still.

"None of the paintings are worth much," Vano told us. "Nana's father picked up most of them on the cheap from students and unknowns. He was more interested in showing off the different frame treatments than the art itself. Kind of like those generic families you find in picture frames at the drug store."

Sabina said, "One of those fake families hung in our house for ages, a bunch of dippy-looking Handless and a matching golden retriever. We all figured they were some of my mom's relatives. Turned out she just thought the dog was cute."

We trooped through a series of sitting rooms, each done in a different style of tacky, and I noticed Vano noticing Sabina. When we sent up the SOS to Vano to let us into the mansion, the last person I expected to find him with was my cousin. Okay, technically, the last person would probably be Elon Musk. Or maybe the pope. But Sabina was definitely top-ten.

We saw painting after painting, but none that featured the mayor. Once we were back where we started, Vano tore his eyes off my cousin long enough to say, "Well, that's about it for this wing. I guess we could check out the turret in case there was something I missed."

Vano's old bedroom was in the turret. And if he was canoodling with Sabina, I drew the line at touring the place where his prior conquests took place. Besides, there was a slender door off to one side of the ballroom I was fairly sure we hadn't checked. I quickly pointed it out. "We haven't looked in there."

Vano said, "Nana dropped the key to that door down the toilet a couple of years ago. No one's been in there since."

Sabina's attention had been flagging, but at the mention of pickable lock, her second wind came roaring in with a vengeance. "Wow, I hardly ever get to try my hand at a skeleton key lock." She reached down her shirt and whipped a lockpick out of her bra—Vano had the good grace to blush—and then she thrust the tool inside and started feeling around. "Compared to modern locks, the mechanisms are easy. Except when they're stuck, or broken or...." She paused. Focused. And gave the pick a hard turn.

With a profoundly satisfying click...we were in.

The room was octagonal, with low velvet cushions all around. The silk wallpaper was printed with stylized flowers and cranes, and each wall held a slightly clumsy painting of a Victorian "Oriental" scene—camels, bazaars, Turkish baths with half-naked ladies lounging around. Vano pointed to a platform in the middle. "There used to be a hookah there. But when I was a teenager, Nana sold it off—partly for the money, partly to make sure I didn't get any ideas about using it."

Spellcrafters might consider Handless ordinances and laws to be mere suggestions, but one thing we did share with our non-magical neighbors was the desire to keep our kids on the straight and narrow—even though our concept of that path might allow for a few extra twists and turns.

Of all the paintings, only one of them was a portrait: a guy in a turban with a peculiar half-smile on his face, and eyes that seemed to follow me as I crossed the room.

I hopped one way, then the other, and then I realized they didn't just *seem* to follow me. "Don't look now," I whispered, shielding my mouth from the painting, "but we're not alone."

"Don't worry," Vano said. "It's a kinegram."

"Kine-what?" Sabina asked.

"The painting's eyes are covered with a special lens that changes what you see. No matter which part of the room you're in, the gaze follows you."

No doubt the moving eyes were twice as alarming under the effects of a hookah. I would've asked how much he wanted for it, but I suspected Yuri would never go for it, optical illusion or not. But we couldn't just let it pass without a thorough inspection. My cousin and I positioned ourselves in front of the portrait, then took a step to either side, and another, and another.

"Still looking at me," I said.

"Me too." She kicked a cushion out of her way to put more distance between us, and a slip of colorful painted paper fluttered out. When it settled, it was stuck vertically between two floorboards. Sabina pulled it out with a yank and read:

For the son of my son's daughter, grant these things three:
A passel of luck
A life of ease
And a beautiful Scrivener girl to share it

Vano shifted awkwardly. "Um, sorry. Nana's been a little overprotective since my parents died."

Sabina shoved the Spellcraft at him like it was a hot potato. "Yeah, well, fat lot of good it'll do you hidden in a locked room. Anyway, no Dunce portrait. Let's move on." She jostled her way out of the room—wow, her elbows were really sharp—but as she did, I couldn't help but notice that the tippy top corner of the Spellcraft she'd crammed into Vano's hand was now torn.

Vano noticed, too. He said, "It must've been sitting around for years. I'm sure the magic's long gone." I wasn't so sure. You don't get to be the head of the circuit for nothing. "Besides...Sabina has a will of her own. An old piece of Crafting won't change that."

Aaand...he had to go and come right out with it. Sheesh! "Say, would you look at the time? That Dunce painting's not gonna find itself—"

"You probably know her better than anyone. What would I need to do to make her notice me?"

As apprehensive as I was about finding that Crafting, now I wondered if it was actually a stroke of good luck—for me, I mean, not Vano. "If you cook her a special meal, make sure it's especially healthy. And vegan. In fact, the more bean sprouts you can cram in, the better."

"I never would've guessed. She told me her favorite meal was a quarter-pound cheeseburger with extra cheese...and a side of cheese."

"And it's hard to go wrong with presents. Sabina goes nuts for anything cute and cuddly."

"Really? She doesn't strike me that way at all. I figured she'd have more of a punk aesthetic."

"Bonus points if it's pink."

Vano was perplexed. "I spent half the day with your cousin and somehow it's like I don't know her at all. My instincts about Sabina were way off—I nearly blew my chance with her. Good thing I asked."

He was buying it: hook, line and sinker. I couldn't think of a more masterful stroke of misdirection. I should have been incredibly proud of my quick thinking.

But since when did pride feel so bad?

Darn it, I just didn't have it in me to screw up his chances with my cousin. While it was a real shame to pass up on the opportunity to ensure there was less Vano Shirque in my life, it sounded like he really had gotten to know Sabina pretty well in a short amount of time. Was my cousin the "beautiful Scrivener girl" the Crafting had been waiting for? Beauty is pretty subjective, but I'd always thought Sabina was a real cutie—and she was obviously a Scrivener, too. She could do worse than to end up with someone who saw her for who she really was.

"Vano, forget about teddy bears and health food. Just listen to Sabina. Appreciate her. Maybe give her the occasional stubborn door to open. But most of all, be yourself."

It was a surprisingly tender moment...interrupted by a painting of a belly dancer announcing in Sabina's voice, "Be yourself? Who else would you be?"

The painting's eyes were definitely not kine-whatevers, given that they blinked. Plus, I'd recognize my cousin's eyeliner anywhere. "How'd you get in the wall?" I asked her.

"Elbowed a loose piece of paneling out of the way and here I am."

"Did you find the portrait?"

"Nope." She paused to sneeze against the back of the painting. "Just a bunch of dust bunnies and a few wooden spoons."

She sneezed a few more times, nearly camouflaging the sound of a creaky old car coming up the driveway...and then bonking something large and metallic that sounded suspiciously like my uncle's old Buick. That vehicle was an absolute tank. I should know—I'd taken out many a mailbox during my stint as a WheelMeal delivery driver. And if those people really cared about their mailboxes, they wouldn't plant them so close to the curb.

Vano and I went to the window, and sure enough, Morticia Shirque's Rolls Royce was kissing the fender of my uncle's Buick—ugh, now there was a mental image I really needed to scrub from my mind. The Rolls sat there for a while as if Morticia was trying to figure out exactly how the Buick got there. Then gravel crunched as she threw it into reverse.

When Morticia's rear bumper connected with Yuri's truck, she hit a spot of concentrated duct tape that gave off a soft plastic thud. A few flakes of rust rained down from her undercarriage, and the truck emerged from the encounter only slightly misshapen.

Another pause...then she lurched forward and bumped the Buick again.

Vano said, "I'd better go stop her before she turns her car into an accordion," then hurried out of the room.

In Sabina's voice, the belly dancer painting said, "Getting to paw through all the junk in Shirque Mansion was fun and all, but I'm good and ready to grab that Dunce portrait and get out of here."

Because she'd blundered into the conversation I'd just been having about her with Vano and was feeling vulnerable? Unlikely—Sabina didn't do vulnerable. If she'd overheard much of anything, she'd be sure to rub someone's nose in it.

We headed downstairs. Yuri and Drew caught up with us, and we all trooped into the kitchen to talk to Morticia and finally get our hands on that painting. "Well, if it isn't the Penn boy," she called out in greeting. I'm always somewhat surprised when Morticia recognizes me—possibly because she's nearly a hundred. But while her driving skills leave something to be desired, her mind is still as sharp as a rusted undercarriage. "How nice of you to visit my Vano."

"That's right," I said. "That's exactly what I'm doing here." It just so happened that the only time I "visited" Vano was when I needed something from him. "Say, listen, we were hoping to get a look at the portrait from the Mayor's Room, but it's not there."

"That's the problem with having such a complicated roofline. Too many opportunities to spring leaks. It's tempting to just lock up the top floor and throw away the key."

Why'd she have to go and say that? Now my cousin would hardly be able to resist coming back for an actual visit.

"Where is painting?" Yuri asked, dropping his article.

"Well, let's see." Morticia settled herself at the table, closed her eyes and thought back. "The shingles came down about five years ago during that terrible windstorm—"

"I remember that storm," Sabina said. "Our old patio set blew away, but we found a new one scattered around the yard."

Morticia said, "The rains came a few weeks later. But it was another couple of months before I noticed the leaking." She thought some more, then shook her head. "I'm sorry, at least half a dozen rooms were affected, and I was so annoyed with the roof for leaking, I can't recall what I did with that painting."

Vano had slipped into the kitchen while she was talking. "Nana, did you have dinner? Maybe once you eat, you'll remember."

I sure knew who *didn't* have dinner—all of the rest of us. Yuri's stomach made that abundantly clear by growling. Loudly. In English. "Think," he demanded. "We *need* painting." His accent was thick—it does that when he's hangry—which gave us the perfect opportunity to skedaddle. Yuri could always swing by to pick up the mayor's portrait later. Without my cousin in tow.

But before I managed to herd us all out the door, Vano checked the fridge and announced, "I can whip up a quick frittata...unless anyone's got a problem with eggs."

"I could eat," my cousin said, and plunked down at the table.

Drew piped in, "Me too." Boardwalk folk never turn down a free meal. Then again, the same can be said for Spellcrafters.

And that's how I got stuck spending the whole entire evening at Shirque Mansion.

The frittata was delicious—of course it was—but unfortunately, it didn't help Morticia remember what she'd done with the portrait. "Let me see...where would I have put Dunce for safekeeping? The east side of the ballroom is usually pretty dry, though there was that incident with the termites back in '53...."

"Maybe you should sleep on it," I suggested.

Morticia shrugged. "I can't imagine it would be very comfortable. I'm positive that portrait is here somewhere, and I won't rest until it's found. Vano, be a good boy and fetch us some coffee. And your almond biscotti."

Well, I supposed it would be rude to leave without dessert.

As Vano saw to the coffee looking annoyingly handsome, his great-grandmother did her best to recall where she'd stashed the painting. "At one point I kept it in the linen closet, but it fell on my head every time I pulled out a fresh afghan. And it hung in my bathroom for a while—but who wants that man ogling them in the tub?" She shuddered. "Him and all those big, square teeth."

Try as she might, Morticia just couldn't recall the last thing she'd done with the mayor's portrait. There were simply too many nooks and crannies in Shirque Mansion where a painting could disappear. By the time the coffee was ready, I despaired of ever finding that darn portrait and was prepared to drown my sorrows in delicious coffee and homemade cookies. But as Vano approached the table, Drew cocked his head and said, "My dear boy, you call that a tray?"

Everyone's eyes went to the shallow, boxy thing that could barely hold a stack of coffee cups and a really tempting plate of chocolate-dipped biscotti.

Vano said, "All the trays and platters are stuck behind a cupboard door with a broken latch."

"Why didn't you say something?" Sabina demanded. "I'm great at prying open broken latches."

The makeshift tray looked more like half a puzzle box. Or an in/out office basket. Or maybe...a stretched canvas.

I craned my neck to look at the underside and found the toothy image of Mayor Dunce looking back at me. But that couldn't possibly be right. The official Dunce portrait was easily three or four times the size of the thing in Vano's hands. Everyone scrambled to empty the "tray"—or maybe to get first dibs on the cookies—and Vano flipped it over.

"Now I remember," Morticia said. "I left it in the pantry after I pulled off the frame and sold it. The gilt fetched a pretty good price."

The Shirque portrait was not only disappointingly shrimpy—but like the portrait hanging at City Hall, it too was only a printed photo of the real Cadfur painting.

Drew said, "At least this is one generation closer to the original."

"Maybe so," I said. "But the signature is so tiny I can hardly see it." Not only that, but it was still half-covered by yet another frame.

"And would you look at those hideous walls," Drew said. "I'd need therapy if I spent my day surrounded that sickly shade of institutional green."

Puzzle pieces began sliding into place before I even know what they meant. Institutional. Therapy. And some truly ugly walls. I met Yuri's eyes, hoping maybe I was wrong...but saw he'd come to the same conclusion.

He winced and said, "Original painting is hanging in Strange Manor."

YURI

7

I re-secured my bumper with a few strips of duct tape and headed home. Drew rode with Sabina in her father's Buick. It should have been a relief to be rid of Drew's grandiose chatter, but being alone with Dixon for the first time today was surprisingly awkward.

I longed to unburden myself and tell him about Meringue's escape, but what good would that really do? Americans claim that honesty is the best policy—but only because they like to parrot phrases that rhyme, with no intention of actually following their own advice. Was I anxious to admit what happened because Dixon needed to know, or simply to soothe my own conscience?

And since when did I care about my *conscience*?

Only once we pulled up to the flat and Dixon finally spoke did I realize he'd been uncharacteristically silent. "Would you look at that? Talk about dusty!" He patted his lap and a tiny cloud rose from his trousers. "I'd better grab a shower before I get Shirque Mansion particles all over the attic." And with that, he sprinted upstairs.

I followed, relieved for the chance to check on Meringue without Dixon noticing. I found the bird roosting on the uppermost perch of her cage with her egg unattended in its pile of fluff. While I grew up in the city and knew little about hatching eggs, this behavior did not seem to bode well.

Dixon might only be giving himself a quick rinse, so I had to do something, and do it fast. If Meringue had access to a male bird, the egg could be fertile. And since I had no idea where she'd flown off to, I should operate under the possibility we had a fertile egg on our hands.

I did a quick search to find out what I should do. Most pet bird sites recommended removing the egg and replacing it with something inert. They were concerned with the bird obsessing over a non-viable egg that went rotten. Meanwhile, Meringue was doing the complete opposite and ignoring her own egg.

In the bathroom, the shower cut out and the blow drier powered on. I needed to make a decision...and I found I could not bring myself to pluck out the egg, toss it out the window and be done with it. Evidently, my heart was set on keeping it. I knew Dixon—and I knew how hard he would take it if the egg did not hatch. It was best not to get his hopes up.

Incubating the egg myself would be challenging enough. Doing so without Dixon noticing would be impossible.

His cousin, however, could very well get away with it.

Before Dixon could finish drying his hair, I'd scooped the egg into an old cigar box—fluff and all—and headed downstairs to pass this problem to Sabina. I found her in the kitchen, shielding a half-eaten biscotti from me with her body while trying to act natural. The Penn family shared many things...but a truly good homemade dessert was pushing it. And I could use her guilt to my advantage and get her to take care of the egg.

"Meringue now has an egg to show for her adventures, but she is lacking in motherhood skills. I cannot care for this egg myself. Not only will Dixon start asking questions...but I am weak with hunger."

Sabina rolled her eyes. "I suppose I can stick the egg under my desk lamp. But once we've got a mini-marshmallow on our hands, won't you just have more explaining to do?"

"Dixon will be too excited about the chick to care."

"True." Sabina took the cigar box. "But when the bird-baby hatches, I draw the line at spitting worms into its mouth."

Thankful that Sabina had taken the egg without much of an argument, I tried to head back to the flat...only to find my path blocked by Fonzo, who was attempting to wrangle something up from the cellar. Without much success.

"Yuri!" he said gleefully. "Come give an expectant father a hand. This darned crib weighs a lot more than I remember. It must've been absorbing moisture in the basement over the years."

If Fonzo had not told me the item he was dragging upstairs was a crib, I would have taken it for an old crate of some sort. Or maybe a pile of scrap lumber.

"Watch out for splinters," he warned me.

A protruding nailhead dug into my palm. "Where will you put this thing?"

"I was just clearing out some space in the downstairs office."

The "downstairs office" was actually a coat closet where they stored old computer parts they were too cheap to recycle. And by "clearing out," Fonzo meant "shoving things to one side."

"Are you sure the nursery will fit?" I asked doubtfully.

"Where there's a will, there's a way."

Perhaps, but even the most willful person was still subject to the laws of physics. "You will need to get rid of this pile of monitors."

"Nonsense. Babies learn through osmosis. What better way to ensure the little tyke grows into a tech-savvy adult than to start exposing them early? Kids these days need skills, Yuri. They need enrichment. They need tutors and braces and ponies." Fonzo paused and mopped his brow on his sleeve. "Phew...I think I need to go sit down."

I climbed over the "crib," leaving it wedged halfway into the coat closet, and followed Fonzo out onto the front porch. It was a narrow thing, barely a stoop, but the lawn furniture there—the pieces deposited by the windstorm—were surprisingly sturdy. It made a comfortable enough place to sit and think about life. Or, in Fonzo's case, to contemplate the cigar he'd been working on for the past several weeks.

"I'm excited for the baby," he declared. "Who wouldn't be? Sabina was an accident—and look how great she turned out! Not many guys my age get a second chance at fatherhood, y'know. Especially with a lady as classy as Glenda. I'm lucky, Yuri. That's what I am." He clutched my knee desperately and repeated, "So...incredibly...lucky."

Fonzo was trying to convince himself, not me. That is probably the main reason I took pity on him. "Did Sabina require tutors and braces and ponies?"

"Not once I told her she'd be stuck cleaning up all the horse poop. Maybe I should've considered the tutor, though. The Handless school almost made her repeat algebra, but then I showed her the best place to hide a cheat-sheet—right between the cheek and gums, just like a pinch of chewing tobacco—"

"Your daughter is a fine young woman. Not because you spent money on her," which, undoubtedly, he did not. "But because you gave her your time and attention. You don't need all these expensive things. You have family. *Good* family."

Fonzo toyed with his unlit cigar. "But times change, Yuri. Back when Sabina was a baby, I could just toss her in the back of the Buick and take her along to the dog track. But nowadays everyone expects parents to volunteer in the classroom and show up at soccer games. We're supposed to figure out the *new math*." He ran a hand through his hair. A few strands caught between his fingers and pulled free. He shook them out with a sigh. "Hard to believe, Yuri...but I don't have quite as much get-up-and-go as I used to. I don't know if I'm up for raising another kid."

"But you have help now. You have Dixon and me. And...Sabina."

Fonzo sighed heavily, and I wondered if he was thinking the same thing I was: Sabina was not the sort to fawn over a baby and he could expect little help from her. So it surprised me when he followed up the sigh with, "Sabina has always been my little girl. Just Sabina. I don't know if I want that to change."

"I know your family," I said firmly. "There is always room for one more."

DIXON

8

The next morning, we fortified ourselves with a breakfast of eggs and toast to prepare for our portrait-hunting venture, though Yuri was looking uncharacteristically queasy as he pierced his yolk and the bright yellow gooeyness ran out.

Probably just nerves. To say our last visit to Strange Manor was harrowing would be putting it mildly. Yuri had flayed the skin off his hands rowing across the bay in a frenzy. I'd nearly drowned in a pit full of bones. And then there was the dead body. Hawthorn Strange had been scary enough when he was still alive. The mental image of the corpse's bony hand, poised to clutch the cursed quill, still made me clench in all the worst places.

Frankly, I'd never expected to darken the Strange doorstep again. We couldn't even claim to be visiting Violet and Pansy, since the sisters had moved out right after the whole curse debacle. But we did have one ally at Strange Manor, a sunny optimist named Molly we'd met at the Hunting Party.

Hopefully rooming at that cringeworthy ex-mental asylum with our ex-tenant Mr. Greaves hadn't soured her disposition.

Drew Draws showed up at our doorstep bright and early in

skimpy cutoffs, an oversized PBU sweatshirt, and a bedazzled baseball cap.

"Don't you have portraits to draw?" I asked.

Drew sighed dramatically. "How can I possibly focus on my work now? Something funny's going on with Shul's paintings and I won't rest until we get to the bottom of it."

As a Spellcrafter, I was used to things turning up in improbable places for the vaguest of reasons. But Handless have a much stricter notion of cause and effect. It was getting more and more challenging to make excuses as to why the painting's provenance was so convoluted. But since a loud, sparkly diversion might come in handy at Strange Manor, we figured we might as well let Drew come along.

As towns went, Strangeberg was perfectly forgettable—save for the ragged coastline of the bay with the foreboding Strange Manor at the top of the highest bluff. It was as if a giant child had gotten their two playsets mixed together—one Fischer Price, and one Edgar Allen Poe.

"On clear days," Drew said, "You can see the silhouette of this old place from my tent on the boardwalk. I always thought it was abandoned!"

"We should be so lucky," Yuri said.

I hoisted the tray of coffees we'd grabbed on the way. "Molly should be making a coffee run any minute now."

"How do you know?" Drew wondered.

"Friendlike! Every day she posts a picture of her latte. And once we've saved her the trouble, she'll be thrilled to let us come in and snoop...er, tour her new apartment inside Strange Manor. There's her bike right there—the cute little red number with the daisies on the basket. Any minute now...."

We were all so focused on the bike that when someone knocked on Yuri's window, we nearly ended up wearing the lattes.

You'd think that outside the awful manor, in the cheerful sunlight, Dahlia Strange wouldn't be anywhere near as intimidating.

And you'd be wronger than a wig on a bowling ball.

Dahlia Strange was tall and cadaverous, with deep-set eyes always flashing in righteous indignation. She was also the Head of the Strangeberg circuit, which meant she was definitely not one to be trifled with. Which is a strange expression, when you think about it. Because I had a trifle once in a little cafe outside Brussels and it was actually pretty delightful.

While I was thinking about whipped cream—which is much better on a trifle than in bed—Yuri reached for the ignition in hopes of making a fast retreat. I nudged his hand away. "Your elbows are sharper than your cousin's," he muttered.

"We can't just drive away now. Dahlia's already seen us." And, in fact, she was making the universal hand-signal for *roll down your window*. When Yuri didn't comply, I reached across and gave the window a few cranks—enough to talk, but not enough for her to reach in. I may be overly eager to please authority figures. But I'm not stupid.

"Did my daughters send you?" she demanded through the window-crack. "Because they told me they weren't picking up Cosmos until ten. That's seventeen and a half minutes from now. Seventeen and a *half*."

Unless you were telling time by the grandfather clock in the dining room, in which case, all bets were off. But although it was tempting to point out how she'd used that clock to renege on her deal with my uncle, I couldn't help but be curious why she was acting so defensive. "I've met Cosmos—super friendly, not very slobbery at all—but he hardly seemed like a stickler for punctuality."

"Then you're not expecting me to produce a dog?"

"No," I said carefully, since what I'd hoped to turn up was a painting. "But I'll go out on a limb and hazard a guess that if I *were* expecting a dog, I'd be out of luck."

"Completely," Dahlia snapped. "In fact, I have no idea where he's run off to."

Drew leaned across me, throwing sparkles across the dash with his sequined baseball cap. "You can hardly be expected to keep track of a dog in a huge place like this all by yourself. And with only sixteen minutes, fifty seconds to find it, well...no one could blame you if the poor creature simply doesn't turn up."

When Drew's sympathetic words sank in, Dahlia went from combative to compliant in the wink of an eye. "I can't do this to my daughters. They've always been so critical of my attempts to provide them with a proper, stable home. And if I lose their dog, they'll never speak to me again."

"Children," Drew commiserated. "If they only understood half of what we sacrificed to grow them into reasonably well-adjusted adults."

Dahlia was caught so off-guard by this unexpected show of solidarity, she actually teared up.

And once Drew saw he had her, he said, "You check the grounds. We'll make sure he's not hiding somewhere in the house."

Which was how we ended up with full and unchaperoned access to Strange Manor.

"Wow," I told Drew. "That was incredible, how you won Dahlia over to our side. I didn't realize you had kids."

"Of course I don't. Bad enough trying to provide for myself on an artist's income, let alone a child—what with their piano lessons and tattoo removals and orthopedic shoes. If the boardwalk has taught me anything, it's that you need to make an effort to read people. To give them what they want."

As we ventured into the erstwhile mental asylum now known as Strange Manor, the temperature dropped with each step we took, until I felt sorry for Drew in his barely-there cutoffs. But years of being buffeted by the wind off the bay had made him pretty sturdy, and though his goosebumps had goosebumps, he didn't complain.

While Shirque Mansion unspooled like a ball of yarn rolling down a spiral staircase, Strange Manor was just the opposite. Blocky. Square. And chillingly institutional. Every last inch of it painted the same nauseating green.

I said, "Maybe the twins can tell us where to start looking."

But Yuri stopped me as I pulled out my phone. "We cannot get them involved. If they realize dog is not here, they may drop what they're doing and hurry over, cutting into what little time we have."

The other obvious choice would be to Craft something to point us in the right direction. But we could hardly do it right in front of Drew and expose our trade secrets to a Handless. As I considered how best to distract him so Yuri and I could get down to business, Drew pointed to the floor and said, "Look at all that fur."

Springtime is notorious for shedding—at least, that's what Uncle Fonzo had been saying lately every time he brushed his hair. And Cosmos had a lot more follicles than my uncle. His brownish-grayish-whitish fur had formed mini-tumbleweeds that drifted along the baseboards.

"Remember," Yuri said. "We look for painting. Not dog."

Drew was already following the fur. "Who says we can't do both? Besides, if we're the first ones to get our hands on the dog, that means no one else can find it and put an end to our snooping."

We tracked the fur down a long, desolate hallway. There were no portraits on the walls, though there had been a sad attempt to make the place look "inviting" by hanging countrified wooden planks with words stenciled on them like *welcome* and *gather* and *home*. But just slapping a word on the wall doesn't make it true. Not unless it's penned with a magical quill over the painting of a gifted Seer. And even then, the results aren't exactly reliable.

At the end of the hallway was a stout door. Good thing it wasn't locked, otherwise my cousin would never forgive us for not bringing her along. The door opened onto a dimly lit landing, all concrete cinderblock, painted the same sickly green as the rest of the place. The whole manor was chilly, but this stairwell was positively dank, leading down, down, down.

Yuri ran a hand over his scalp and said, "We have no reason to think dog was ever here."

Drew pointed to the foot of the stairs. "Except that big rubber bone."

Well...he had us there.

With every step down, the temperature crept lower, the light grew darker, and my anxiety crept higher. And when I'm nervous...I talk. "I'm sure there's absolutely nothing creepy in the cellar of an old mental asylum. Like padded cells, or straitjackets, or ping-pong tables. In fact, we'll probably just run across the arts and crafts room. Crayons and construction paper and...I wonder if the paste is still good? Not that I've ever eaten paste. Okay, maybe I did touch it to my tongue that one time, but Cuthbert Rath ate such a big wad he was constipated for a week. And you really can't blame a guy for being curious when it smells kind of like toothpaste—"

Undaunted, Drew pushed past me, grabbed the dog toy, and shoved through the door at the foot of the stairs. "Here, doggie doggie!"

The room beyond was pitch black. And, frankly, if Cosmos had been hiding in there, we would've heard the clumsy skittering of dog toenails on concrete by now. But as Yuri had so eloquently put it, we looked for painting. Not dog. And it was quite possible the walls down here were still that same shade of sickly institutional green....

Overhead lights flickered to life. Turned out it wasn't an arts and crafts room we'd stumbled into after all.

It was a morgue.

Not an old morgue that was being used for storing garden equipment, either.

A morgue that was still in use.

A stainless steel worktable in the middle of the room held a sheet-covered thing that couldn't possibly be anything other than a body. Yuri said something Russian and made a hand-gesture like a headbanger at a heavy metal concert. I backpedaled, knocking into a rolling cart of metal instruments that let out a ridiculously overloud clatter. And Drew crossed himself vigorously as he sidled away. As he did, the fabric draped over the body somehow caught on his foot. All at once, the sheet fell away....

And on the table was the gnarled corpse of Hawthorn Strange.

"Quick," I said, "put it back the way you found it! You do *not* want to mess with that particular dead body...and, er, don't ask me how I know."

Dahlia Strange had a mean streak a mile wide—coupled with a pronounced dislike of the Penn family. If she found us messing around with her dead father's body, we'd be goners ourselves! I whirled around, eager to make tracks, and nearly collided head-first with—

Molly.

A perky blond Handless and not a scary Spellcrafter! I was dumbfounded with relief, sinking to my knees even as Cosmos pranced into the room, nails clicking, and gave my face a thorough tongue-bath. If I wasn't so stunned, I would've taken back that thing I said before about him not being slobbery. But mainly I was beside myself with gratitude that Dahlia hadn't caught us sticking our noses where they didn't belong. (Not that a nose *ever* belongs inside a corpse—but where curses are concerned, corpses are particularly un-noseworthy.)

Molly did a double-take. "Dixon? Yuri? Guy from the boardwalk? What are you doing here? Did my Smush-Bear invite you over?"

For reasons I'd never been able to comprehend, the ever-optimistic Molly was entirely smitten with Mr. Greaves. How two people with such radically different personalities ever managed to get along was entirely beyond me.

If this was the work of Mr. Greaves—and if Molly saw him for the twisted soul he truly was—could she survive the shock of what her Smush-Bear had been getting up to?

I spread myself out to shield Molly the best I could from the sight of the withered corpse and said, "Step away, Molly."

"What for?"

"You really don't wanna—"

"Hold on." Molly had been holding two coffee cups—good thing I'd stopped short of plowing directly into her—and she knelt to place one on the floor. Cosmos bounded over and thrust his snout inside.

"Your dog has a caffeine habit?" Drew said doubtfully.

"Not my dog," Molly said, stroking the critter's ruff. "He's borrowed. And it's not coffee, just a squirt of whipped cream from the sweethearts at the cafe drive-through. Cosmos loves to feel included."

The dog in question was currently making a bunch of moist gulping sounds. He came up seconds later with a snootful of foam and an expression that clearly said, *Is that all you got?*

Molly straightened back up, and Yuri took her firmly by the shoulders and marched her away from the desiccated body in the middle of the room. At least, he tried. But Molly misinterpreted the gesture as a friendly hug. Yuri's not much of a hugger—even with me, he'll just kind of squash me into the nearest flat surface. But Molly didn't know that. Naturally, she reciprocated, which made Yuri go stiffer than what was left of old Hawthorn.

But Molly was huggy enough for both of them. "Great to see you again too, Yuri!" She gave him an extra-long squeeze and a chipper pat on the back. "It's been a while—we should definitely get together more often."

If Yuri had been willing to hug her back, it's possible he could have steered her toward the door. He was entirely out of his element, though, rendered helpless by a simple hug. But while Yuri was frozen, Drew was quick on his feet. He pitched something toward the door and cried, "Fetch, doggie! Fetch!"

For one horrific moment, I thought he'd snatched a handy femur off Hawthorn Strange...and if the quill had such a nasty curse on it, I couldn't imagine what protections Dahlia had placed on her father's body. But then the object bounced, and I saw it was just the purple rubber bone. Though why Drew had been holding onto it in the first place was anyone's guess.

If Drew had been hoping to provide a distraction, he'd done it, all right. Cosmos went berserk, exploding into a flurry of clackety dog toenails and a spray of whipped cream slobber. The diversion would have worked...if only the edge of Hawthorn's shroud wasn't now wrapped around the dog's tail. And with the strength of a windshield wiper on a turbocharged Humvee, the tail whipped back and forth, whisking the thin cotton sheet from the body and waving it around the room like a flag of surrender.

I danced away from the rippling fabric, both to avoid the death cooties and to shore up Yuri, who was looking more than a little green around the gills. The sheet continued to sweep across the room. And when it caught on the rolling cart holding what was left of Hawthorn Strange, it had gained so much momentum, it catapulted the old man's body into motion. The cart skidded to a stop. The body wobbled stiffly, then settled with a dusty rustle, dead center in the circle of all our horrified gazes.

All but one...who looked upon the disturbing remains with a beatific smile.

Molly.

9

Optimism is one thing—but Molly's cheerfulness bordered on delusion. Drew was baffled, Yuri was on the verge of passing out, and I was so flummoxed I actually found myself tongue-tied. But Molly gestured grandly toward the body and turned her sunny smile on us. "Doesn't my Teddy do the most wonderful work?"

I stammered ineffectively, wondering why on earth his "work" entailed grave-robbing. Mercifully, Yuri filled in the blanks. "Ed Greaves is mortician."

"Well *that's* a relief," Drew muttered. "Sometimes my imagination is a little too fertile for its own good."

His and mine both.

"Teddy isn't just a mortician," Molly gushed. "He's a post-life aesthetician." She stepped to the head of the rolling cart and leaned in, planting a hand on either side of Hawthorn Strange's wizened head. "When the Loveland Corporation tore down Final Slumber, we thought Teddy would need to change careers. It's not like you can embalm people in your living room...not within city limits, anyhow. But Dahlia Strange is the most understanding landlady, and she was absolutely delighted to help Teddy set up shop here in the sanatorium's old morgue. He can't *technically* embalm anyone. But there's no law against freshening up a mortician's previous work."

"Lemme get this straight," Drew said. "You expect people to pay your guy to dig up their dead relatives and give them a makeover?"

"Exactly! Just look what magic he can work!"

Members of the Strange family tend to get gaunt and stringy with age, so their late patriarch didn't look much different than he had while he was still complaining about the weather and slurping soup at Pinyin Vittles. Except for his nose, which had shrunk down to the cartilage. But I hardly noticed that at all now, what with the garish spot of rouge on each cheek vying for my attention, and the ludicrous toupee.

Maybe Mr. Greaves was still perfecting his technique—and I couldn't imagine there were many test subjects available for him to work on. Not many folks would be as eager as Dahlia Strange to exhume their family members just for the sake of giving them a little touch-up. At least, I hoped not.

Molly, naturally, saw no problems—only opportunities. "No one else in Strangeberg is offering such a unique service—we've really cornered the market."

"I'll bet," I said weakly.

"And I was able to set Teddy up with a really spiffy website. Customers can order their dear departed loved ones' makeovers from a dropdown menu and pay for it electronically. E-graves—sounds really high tech, don't you think? And the best part is, I figured out what to call it by rearranging the letters of Teddy's last name."

Molly sighed happily as she basked in the glory of Hawthorn Strange's painted remains. As she did, Drew nudged my foot to get my attention, sketched a frame around himself, and mouthed the word *Dunce*.

Oh. Uh...right. With all the weird discoveries we'd just made, I'd very nearly forgotten why we'd ventured into Strange Manor in the first place. "Say, Molly, you really seem to have hit it off with Dahlia and her family."

"Such a warm, welcoming bunch of people. I just knew Teddy could be friends with Spellcrafters if he gave them half a chance... and lived somewhere with thicker walls."

"Be that as it may," I said diplomatically, "although you and Mr. Greaves get along with Dahlia like corpses and toupees, I'm sure you've noticed a few, shall we say, *idiosyncrasies* when it comes to her taste in portraiture."

Molly picked up the shroud and shook it out like she was making a bed. "How do you mean?"

"The big, forbidding, gothic portraits in the dining hall are totally understandable. They're family. But then there are the random ones that probably have a really convoluted backstory—"

"Oh! Like that one of dogs playing poker in the padded room upstairs. Except with pigs. Because dogs would be totally normal."

"Right, just like that. Except with people. By themselves. Not playing poker."

Molly thought very hard. "No, nothing like that. Except that one time I did get a glimpse.... No, I'm sure it was nothing."

I said, "You never know if something's nothing until you describe it. In great detail. To all your friends."

"Well," she said, "when you put it that way. Once I was passing by Dahlia's bedroom and her door was just a li-i-t-tle bit open. I would never dream of peeping into someone else's bedroom. Not unless I was at a party and they told me to go toss my coat on the bed. And even then, I'd shield my eyes so I didn't accidentally see anything too private." I personally couldn't fathom how anyone could resist a little snoop, especially when presented with such a great opportunity, but I figured I should keep that opinion to myself. "I was right outside her door and I happened to sneeze, which jerked my head around. And before I could look away, I caught a glimpse of a portrait inside."

"A portrait of whom?" Yuri demanded.

"I don't know. It was just a glimpse."

And it would look awfully suspicious if we tried to pry the location of Dahlia's room from her just after she'd admitted to seeing a portrait there. But Dahlia wouldn't be tromping around outside forever looking for Cosmos, and we had to get in while the getting was good.

I supposed I'd have to resort to good, old-fashioned groveling.

But before I could plead my case, Drew plucked a papery liner from a tray of gruesome-looking instruments, whipped a marker out of his pocket, dashed off a sketch and shoved it into Molly's hands. "Here you go, sweetie. Your cute little button nose was so inspiring I simply couldn't help myself."

Confused, Molly looked from the paper to Drew and back again. "Oh. Wow. That's me?"

Back when Yuri went undercover as a Boardwalk artist, Drew's tacky portraiture had been the subject of many a Russian-punctuated rant. According to Yuri, *all his people look the same*. And, *Americans actually pay money for this?* And, *no one has that much hair*.

From my point of view, the drawing in Molly's hands was nothing but a loose scribble—and so there was no wonder she seemed confused. But then the bewilderment morphed into a shy smile that deepened into a broad, infectious grin. "This is absolutely stunning, Drew! I can't wait to show Teddy."

There's positive...and then there's positively delusional. But as I craned my neck, I realized I'd just been seeing the drawing from an odd angle. When viewed the right way around, what had looked at first glance like a scribble was actually a loose and gestural portrait. One that captured Molly's sunny disposition perfectly.

"You should totally hang that up," I said in all sincerity.

"My thought exactly," Drew agreed. "But first we'll need to see how all the other portraits are hung."

Molly said, "There are no other portraits in our room."

"Doesn't matter where they are," Drew said with great authority. "Even in an entirely different part of the house. If you place this one too high or too low in relation to the rest, it'll throw off the whole feng shui."

Molly gave him an impulsive hug. His sequined baseball cap threw sparkles on her rosy cheeks. "I'm so lucky to have you looking out for me. I would have just put it up wherever it looked nice and ruined everything!"

Drew sure was good at getting people to do what he wanted. Maybe he would've made a successful politician—if only that weird calendar hadn't kept Mayor Dunce in office longer than a Scrivener baseball game. (Since we're not generally very sporty, it can take a few extra innings to break the 0-0 tie.) "Drew," I said, "why don't you and Molly go check out the portraits in the dining room while Yuri and I check out that other portrait—and, don't worry, Molly. I'll keep my eyes averted the entire time. And Yuri will only look in Russian."

Molly wasn't entirely sold, I could tell. Not until Drew said, "Yuri is an artist too, you know—I can't say I taught him everything he knows, but I did manage to give him a few valuable pointers. So he's uniquely qualified to assess that painting."

"It's just like doctor-patient privilege," I said brightly. "But between paintings and artists."

"I'm not familiar with that," Molly said—darn it, we were losing her—but then her attention wandered to the distant sound of Dahlia calling for Cosmos. "Um, did you guys hear something?"

"I'm sure it's nothing," Drew said smoothly. "Dogs have a phenomenal sense of hearing, and your borrowed dog isn't reacting to it at all." In all likelihood, that was because Cosmos had never picked up on his own name. Either that or he figured it was actually *Cosmos, no!* and didn't take kindly to it being shortened. But before Molly could second-guess him, Drew swept her off toward the dining hall, leaving Yuri and me to find the mayor's elusive portrait.

Over the years, attempts had been made to get Strange Manor to look more manorly, but renovations petered out by the time you reach the second story. In my opinion, Dahlia would've gotten a lot more bang for her buck by repainting the walls instead of booby-trapping her mausoleum. The majority of the floor was creepily unlived-in, just a bunch of cells with bare walls, a single cot, and a very sturdy door. It only took us a few tries to find Dahlia's bedroom. And a few seconds to realize we'd finally hit paydirt.

Dahlia Strange's room was crammed with furniture that clearly aspired to be anywhere other than a defunct mental asylum. It was heavy and imposing, bulky enough that I wondered how it had managed to fit through the narrow cell door. But despite all the self-important furnishings, the walls were still that same, sickly institutional green as the rest of the place.

And hanging on the far wall, gazing at us across the expanse of Dahlia's red satin bedspread, was the square-toothed image of Mayor Dunce. My first thought was that Dahlia Strange must be somehow using it to curse the mayor from afar. Not only was she the head of the Strangeberg Spellcraft circuit, she was the village president. So, obviously, she and Mayor Dunce would be bigger rivals than the quarterbacks of opposing football teams. And she was clearly not above flinging curses when the mood took her.

I was sure the portrait was just there so Dahlia could plot against her enemy...but Yuri had a totally different take on it. "When you look at the mayor just so, his forehead is shaped an awful lot like Pansy and Violet's."

"What're you saying, Yuri? That Mayor Dunce is Pansy and Violet's—?"

"Looking for something, gentlemen?" At the sound of Dahlia's voice, I nearly jumped out of my own skin.

"Oh!" I said innocently. "Hello! We, uh, heard a noise and, ah...."

"Dog," Yuri supplied.

"That's right! Dog! What sort of dog wouldn't want to hide in such a handsomely appointed room?"

"If you're going to claim you were looking for Cosmos, don't waste your breath. I recognize snooping when I see it." Dahlia Strange strode into the room, imperious and brittle, then crossed her bony arms and gave Yuri a withering look. "Seers are notorious for spotting those ridiculous little details everyone else chalks up to mere coincidence, so I'm hardly surprised to find you digging the skeletons out of my closet."

If ever the time was ripe for a remark about what Mr. Greaves was doing in her basement....

"I'm not ashamed to admit it," Dahlia went on. "I was young. Ambitious. And Chauncey Dunce was a dashing politician who swept me off my feet. But when I told him we had a baby on the way, he wouldn't hear it. Threw a big fit and refused to see me anymore. I know Handless don't value their families like we do, but I was still distraught that Chauncey would be that way about his own flesh and blood."

Yuri said, "Can you remember if he gave you any kind of reason?"

"How could I forget? He claimed he wanted everything to stay exactly the same between us, and a baby would change everything."

Because he liked things *just the way they were*.

Yeesh.

Dahlia sighed. Her crossed arms looked less like a stance of aggression and more like an attempt to give herself the hugs that she'd been denied all these years. After everything she'd put my family through, nearly costing my uncle his hand, I wouldn't have thought I had it in me to feel sorry for Dahlia Strange...but oddly enough, I did.

"Dahlia," I said gently, "he'll always be Violet and Pansy's father. But that doesn't mean you need to carry a torch for him forever. Maybe it's time to move on."

"I'm sure you're right," Dahlia said. "Having Chauncey staring at me from that wall day in, day out—it can't be healthy. For some time now, I've been thinking about giving it to one of my daughters. But then I can't decide who: Violet or Pansy."

Funny how we can all be blind to an obvious solution until someone else points it out. I said, "The twins share an apartment. You don't need to choose. Give it to both of them...and get on with your life!"

Yuri quickly agreed. "That would be the smartest thing to do. But they would never accept it in such a terrible frame."

Good thinking! Unfortunately, at the first sign of difficulty, Dahlia always defaulted to the nuclear option. She crossed the room, heading right for the portrait. "If the girls won't take that awful thing, then I'll just have to burn it!"

"Not so fast!" I said. "I'm sure it'll be fine with no frame at all. In fact, the plain canvas on the wall would look modern and chic. The twins will be eager to take it off your hands." Dahlia seemed doubtful, since her heart was now set on torching the thing. "Show her, Yuri."

Yuri eased himself around Dahlia, careful not to brush up against her, and grabbed hold of the painting. The massive frame was pretty stodgy and it looked like it weighed a ton, but Yuri plucked it off the wall like it was nothing. I figured it was just all those push-ups he does. But then his brow furrowed as if he'd expected it to be heavier, too. When he spun it around, instead of the wooden struts and framework you'd expect to find on a stretched canvas, there was nothing but a sheet of poster board held on by a few staples.

Yet another print! Yuri met my eyes grimly.

"A poster," I said with forced brightness. "That's even cooler."

"It is?" Dahlia said doubtfully.

"Absolutely," I said. "I'm sure the twins will be ecstatic." Before Dahlia could second-guess herself, Yuri gave the poster a tug, popping off the staples, rolled it up and stuck it under his arm. I gestured toward the door. "Now let's find Cosmos before Pansy and Violet get back."

Dahlia headed off to look for Cosmos, leaving Yuri and me alone. My enthusiasm at finding the Dunce portrait had drained away upon learning it *still* wasn't the real painting. "All this trouble for yet another copy? What if there is no original, and the copies go on to infinity?"

Yuri pressed the backs of his fingers to my cheek. "Remember. We do not need original. Only to see the signature." He unrolled the edge of the poster. Unlike all the other versions we'd seen, there was no photographed frame hiding the borders of the canvas. We could see all the way to the edge, and even a smidge beyond, and my frustration turned to excitement as Yuri carefully unrolled the brittle paper. I pulled out my phone to snap a picture of Shul Cadfur's signature.

I had the screen trained on the very spot I would find it when the poster was completely unrolled. The anticipation was so thick I could barely hold the phone still. In fact, I figured it was my own shaky hand that was causing the signature to blur...until Yuri uttered something in Russian that he always scolded Meringue for repeating.

I lowered the phone and looked with only my eyes. The signature was there, all right.

But the lower half was hidden by a blurry green streak.

YURI

2

So. A plant of some kind had been in the foreground when the original painting was photographed to create the poster. Of course it had.

Dixon considered the edges. "No frame, with only the tiniest sliver of wall showing. And it's brown. I'd wager there's hardly any place in Pinyin Bay *hasn't* had brown wood paneling on at least one wall over the life of the home. So unless you wanna start knocking on doors at one end of the city and search house by house—and I'm guessing someone will take umbrage over our interruption of their dinner—it looks like your buddy Drew is out of luck."

Dixon is the epitome of persistence. If he was ready to give up, we must truly be out of options. I was about to roll the poster back up and call off the search when I noticed something on the very edge of the print. A small, curved shape. A circle, just the edge. No, not a circle, a hole.

I pointed it out to Dixon, expecting a barrage of ludicrous suggestions as to what this hole might be (up to and including something to do with wolverines), but he recognized what it was immediately. "Oh, it's not paneling after all, it's pegboard. Just like in my father's...basement?"

And so, once we reunited Dahlia with her daughters' dog, we collected Drew and set off to visit Dixon's parents.

Breathless, Dixon barged into their home, calling out, "You guys will never believe what's downstairs!"

Florica and Johnny Penn were in the middle of a pre-dinner game of Scrabble—and Dixon's mother does not allow herself to be rushed. "Hold your horses, Dixon. I'm right in the middle of my turn."

I gather that players usually keep their letters to themselves, so as not to play anything their opponent might then use. But the Penns made no secret of checking out each other's tiles. In fact, they reveled in it.

Johnny peered at Florica's hand and said, "Hah, you got the Q! If you don't play it now, I'm blocking that U for sure."

Florica narrowed her eyes and said, "Don't rush me. I'm thinking."

While his mother thought, Dixon introduced Drew and then made the rounds, cramming himself behind the table to kiss the top of his father's head and give his mother's shoulders a squeeze. He paused behind her and said, "I love a good Q-word! What'll you play?"

"Aside from the Q, I've also got these two pesky Bs to get rid of."

"Bulb? Slab? Ooh, I know—blab!"

Drew was eager to find the mayor's portrait and get it over with, but he could not help but be curious. He leaned in and said, "You can do better than that. Sable? Squab?"

Though Florica was technically his opponent, Johnny chimed in, too. "I know—useable!"

"Stop distracting me with all your piddly little words," Florica snapped, and the room went silent. Her shrewd eyes flicked from the board to her tiles as she arranged and rearranged her letters, while Johnny looked pleased with his seven-letter suggestion. But his face quickly fell when she slapped all her tiles down on the board, triumphantly declaring, "Squabble! I'm out—I win. And *that's* how you do it!"

"Hooray!" Dixon said. "Congratulations, Mom! But now we all need to see something in the basement."

I did not relish the thought of going downstairs. The Penn's basement was daunting, filled with a great dune of things: broken metallic geese and souvenir ashtrays embossed with the image of the Pinyin Bay Ferris wheel, rusted mops and trivets and compasses and tiny musical instruments; there were fortune-telling charms and bottlecap towers and painted clothespins rising from a seabed of cast-off junk. And while the pegboard should be easy enough to find, there was no guarantee that the painting was still here...though I suspected the blurred grayish greenery in the foreground belonged to the crumbling wreath that threatened to put my eye out every time I went in the basement.

I had resigned myself to spending the rest of the evening shifting teetering piles of boxes back and forth when Sabina called. "First of all," she said when I picked up, "you need to look at the bright side. If one bird makes an obnoxious amount of noise, two will be even louder. And peanuts don't grow on trees. Er... they don't, do they?"

I withdrew to a quiet corner of the living room between two mismatched recliners, lowered my voice and said, "What happened?"

"It's this dilapidated fuse box. My dad must've used the waffle iron this morning—that thing always burns one side of the waffle and leaves the other side raw—and my desk lamp conked out. I didn't realize until I got home."

"Maybe we can salvage the egg. See if it is still warm."

"Ew! I'm not touching it. It's covered in bird germs!"

It was a challenge to keep my voice down as I said, "You are willing to eat food that expired last year but you will not touch an egg?"

"Everyone knows syrup doesn't go bad. But fine, if it'll make you happy...." Shredded paper rustled, and then Sabina sighed into the phone. "I'm sorry, Yuri. It's stone cold."

"It might still be good," I said, though this was looking doubtful now, at best. "Turn the lamp back on and I will deal with it when I get home."

I hung up, wondering why I cared so much about this egg. We would certainly have enough to deal with when Fonzo's new baby came along. But more importantly, Dixon was not aware of the egg, so it wasn't as though he would feel let down when it didn't hatch. There was nothing I could do about it now, so I put it out of my mind.

At least, I tried to.

"What on earth is this supposed to be?" Dixon's mother said as she bustled into the room, squinting at her phone. "Morticia Shirque posted a picture of a 'frittata' on Friendlike and now all the Spellcrafters in the circuit won't shut up about it. Apparently everyone's got a favorite recipe, too. I can't just sit there and say nothing—everyone will be expecting me to chime in. I'll be a laughingstock if I admit I've never even heard of the darned thing."

"Find a picture online, post it, and say it was delicious."

"That'll never work, Yuri—they all know exactly what my countertops look like, right down to the scratches where Dixon climbed up the cupboards in baseball cleats when he was seven years old pretending he was a sherpa. No, I'll just need to whip something up. Good thing you're here. It never hurts to have another pair of hands to help pick out the shells."

The kitchen was not as cluttered as the rest of the house, though it was just as dim and dated. I could have told Florica there would be less shell in her eggs if she didn't smash them against the edge of the bowl with such force—but this was her domain, not mine, and out of respect, I held my tongue.

An egg splashed down into the bowl with a wet plop. All my efforts to keep myself from thinking about Meringue's egg were for naught. "Tell me," I said. "When Dixon was growing up, if you knew something would upset him, would you spare him the truth?"

"Sometimes. But I'm his mother—it's my job to protect him

from the big, bad world. You're his partner, though. You're equal. And that means you take turns being the strong one. Only you can decide what's right."

Florica Penn was a wise woman.

"So," she said briskly. "Your emotional dilemma is all squared away. Now what sort of meat should we use—bologna, cocktail weenies or Spam?"

DIXON

11

"Let me get this straight," my father said, once Drew and I filled him in about the Dunce portrait. "You think that old painting in the basement is the real deal—and that it's actually worth something? I hate to break it to you, Dixon, but I found that thing in the trash behind the store back when you were still in diapers. In fact, I was ditching one of those very diapers when I saw it sticking out of the dumpster!"

Dad might not be entirely convinced that the mayor's portrait was an original Shul Cadfur, but he was tickled to lead Drew and me downstairs. He's always happy for an excuse to show off his basement stash, and I was impressed to see how much it had grown since the last time I'd been in its majestic presence.

"Wow, Dad. Just...wow."

"Fair warning, kiddo: it's been a few years since I've seen your painting, so it's buried deep. Respect the stash and she'll see to it your patience is rewarded. Just pay attention to what you're doing and don't make any sudden moves."

The piles and stacks reached up into the ceiling joists, covered in cobwebs, bursting with all the various objects my father painstakingly and methodically scavenged. Was that a spool of kite string I spied? You can never have too much string. Ooh, and there were salad tongs, hardly used at all! And did my eyes deceive me, or was that a cookie jar lid at the very top of the pile?

Unfortunately, Drew did not share in my excitement. "No one told me we'd have to go through a landfill to get to the painting! I think I need to sit down."

"You can't give up now," I declared. "The painting is close—the real painting, and not some weird facsimile. This is where you dig in your heels and gear yourself up for one final, big push."

Drew muttered, "How Yuri can manage in the face of such unvarnished optimism, I'll never know." With a sigh, he began to pick through the nearest pile.

While I've never been good at stacking houses of cards—I tend to get excited and accidentally blow them down—my Scrivener training ingrained in me a certain respect for balance. Enough to see that when Dad piled up his stuff, he took a lot of creative liberties. It was slow going, shifting the stacks, but once we began to glimpse hints of pegboard peeking through all the stuff, we found our second wind.

Or, at least, I did.

Now that our prize was in sight, Drew was suddenly too curious about the gewgaws and doodads all around him to help us unearth it. "Heavens to Betsy, is that a weathervane? I've never seen one up close—and why anyone would care which way the wind is blowing, I have no idea. Though I suppose it would be helpful if you were starting fires. Or flying kites. Or flying flaming kites, in which case, the string you found earlier would be a great help, and what a spectacle it will be—"

"Drew?" I said. "The authenticator will be here first thing in the morning. If the paint's not dry on the signature, then instead of being known as the guy who found a million-dollar painting in his shed, you'll be the guy who tried to fake a Shul Cadfur."

Just as I said that, my father found one of those magical strata within the pile—a sideways ladder that would shift a whole bunch of stuff at once. "Grab that rung," he called out, and with the finish line close enough to taste, Drew rallied and helped us heave off the entire top of the stack and relocate it to a different (just as precarious) pile.

And then...there it was, in all its mayoral glory. Not another copy, but the original Shul Cadfur painting. Its colors were richer, its texture more pleasing, and the details so crisp and clear it was as if you could fall into the scene and shake hands with the mayor of my childhood while he grinned at you with those big, square, piano-key teeth. We'd tracked that darn portrait from one end of Pinyin Bay to the other and back again—and it had managed to elude us for so long, I half-expected it to give us the slip. But there, just along the lower edge, I spotted Shul Cadfur's signature. Intact...and perfect.

"Well, I'll be," my father said. "You were right."

I drew closer, chafing a prickle from my forearms I mistook for anticipation—until I got close enough and realized that underneath the signature, more letters were half-hidden in the tiny, precise brushstrokes. "Dad, look." I pointed.

Carefully, my father and I lifted the canvas off the pegboard. The original portrait was big, at least three feet tall. It was way heavier than any of the copies, even unframed. Now that we knew there was an active Crafting peeking through the brushstrokes, we had to be extra careful not to set it until we knew what was what.

All the facsimiles had looked enough like oil paintings to fool everyone, even us...at least until we were close enough to see the brushstrokes were photographic. But now that I was in the presence of the original, I could see the copies could never hope to do it justice. Like the painting of young Drew leaning against the graffiti-tagged wall, the portrait of Mayor Dunce vibrated with tension. The light seemed to come from nowhere and everywhere at once, and the edges were so crisp, my eyes blurred themselves in search of relief.

My father liberated an old desk lamp from one of the piles, plugged it in, and shone the light directly on the signature. Or, more accurately, the Crafting beneath it. The brushstrokes were tiny, making up the herringbone texture of the wool on the mayor's suit. And tucked in between were fine, faint letters that read:

Seen for a fake

It wasn't a curse, not exactly. Not only were curses written in multiple hands by multiple Scriveners instead of a single cohesive calligraphy, but they're way more blatantly...well...cursed. Obviously, though, this particular Crafting was definitely not one you'd want gracing *your* portrait. And clearly, the Scrivener had known he or she was treading on thin ice. Since it didn't name names, it was within the letter of the law (Crafting by name can get you in big trouble, which was why this particular wordage was so vague) but an unsympathetic judge might not see it that way.

It shouldn't come to that, since the Crafting had apparently been affecting the portrait instead of the man—to the point where it spun out a bunch of copies to throw the scent off the original. But some judges are so anti-Scrivener, you never know.

As I wondered how I'd ever get my father to part with it, Drew murmured, "Now it all makes sense."

I said, "It...does?"

Drew sighed heavily. "Now I understand what drove us apart." He wasn't looking at the Crafting, I realized, but the painting as a whole. "The rift between Shul and me wasn't only the result of artistic differences. There was a woman involved. I was jealous, I'll admit. Not because I was carrying on with my friend—Shul and I didn't have *that* sort of relationship—but because this crush of his distracted him so from all the things that really mattered. And the fact that the woman was torn between him and some other man only made Shul obsess about her more. *That other guy is a phony,* he said. *A fraud. A sell-out.* That's why I reacted so badly when he called *me* a sell-out too." Drew narrowed his eyes at the painting. "Shul didn't mention his rival was also the newly-elected mayor."

Which would make Dahlia Strange the third side of the love triangle. Or was that the hypotenuse? I'd never been much good at Handless trigonometry.

More importantly, was Shul Cadfur a Scrivener himself? If so, someone in the circuit must know him. Or was he a clever Handless who'd collaborated with Spellcrafters to underlay his painting with a Seen and ink the words between his brushstrokes? It would be difficult to establish who'd done the Scribing, since no one's usual calligraphy was that tiny.

But maybe the origin of the Crafting didn't really matter. The question was whether we should set the spell, Uncraft it, or simply let nature—and Spellcraft—take its course.

Although...maybe that course put the portrait in this particular time and place for a reason. And the one who was supposed to do something about it was *me*. Unfortunately, I couldn't Uncraft something in front of a Handless, and getting rid of Drew would be a major challenge. He was utterly riveted by the painting, staring like he was waiting for it to speak to him and tell him the meaning of life.

Before I could think up a good fib to get him out of our hair, Drew took off his sequined baseball cap and looked at the portrait even harder. "Why's it all sparkly? Is that glitter paint?"

Huh—talk about a plot twist I hadn't seen coming. No wonder he and Yuri struck up such a quick friendship. Yuri must've seen the Seer in Drew without even knowing that's what he saw. If the local circuit knew Drew sold sketches on the Boardwalk for twenty bucks a pop, he'd be overrun by Scriveners in no time. Yuri could explain things when I Uncrafted the mayor's portrait later. Right now, we had an authenticator to fool. Er...convince.

Once we were fortified with a spectacular hot dog frittata—Vano could really take a lesson or two from my mother—we cleared the dining room table, unearthed some old paint from Dad's workbench, and settled in with paint and brush to render Drew's canvas more authentic.

Some might call our plan forgery, but was it really? The work really was in Shul's hand, after all. We were just going to augment it with a few quick strokes of paint at the bottom. Naturally, both of my parents wanted in on the action and offered to help with the signing. Dad was enamored with Drew's painting just as soon as he'd heard it was found under a tarp at the back of a shed. And for a small fee, Mom occasionally "assisted" customers with signatures on wills and divorce papers, citing that Handless legalities were needlessly convoluted.

With major bragging rights at stake, the three of us each endeavored to prove our rendition of Shul's signature was the most authentic. Dad's facsimile signature started strong, but devolved into his own handwriting by the end. He's not exactly known for his follow-though. Mom's attempt was good. Maybe too good, as most folks' signatures vary from instance to instance, while her Shul Cadfur was unflinchingly faithful to the example.

As for me, I took in the characteristics of the signature itself: the curl of the capital S, the long ascender on the lowercase d, the overall height and spacing and proportion. But then I thought past all of those technicalities to what I knew of the artist. Someone who was methodical and controlled, yet considered himself a rebel. Someone pitted against a political figure for the affections of a young Scrivener. Someone who was sorely missed by the friend he'd grown apart from.

If my mind were a camera, it would've just zoomed out—way out—from an unflattering close-up to a wide shot of the entire neighborhood. Maybe even the whole continent.

Maybe this is why my Uncraftings always work. I see all the little details—but I can take in the big picture, too.

Yuri recused himself from judging our Shul-signatures, but it was Drew's painting at stake—his million dollars—and he was plenty judgmental all on his own.

"Honestly, I thought Dixon had the attention span of a goldfish—the cracker, not the marine creature—and this task was far too challenging for the likes of him." Hey! "But I can't deny that his signature is uncannily good."

And so it was settled. I would be the one to sign the painting of young Drew.

All my life, I'd been trained to write. Even without Spellcraft, this act of forming letters and words, of creating something from nothing, was the most primordial form of magic. As I put paint to brush, then brush to canvas, I opened my awareness even wider, zooming from the neighborhood view to the planetary view. Maybe even the solar system. I might not be Shul Cadfur, but the same impulse of creation sang through both of us, so in that sense, whatever I daubed on that canvas was authentic in every way that—

"What on God's green earth are you doing?" Drew cried.

I came back to myself with a start, realizing I wasn't holding a paintbrush, but my precious quill—dripping with old housepaint! And instead of Shul's signature, the letters I'd scratched onto the canvas read:

Art and artist are one

While Mom threw a conniption fit over what I'd done—and Dad scrambled to lay his hands on some paint thinner that wasn't entirely evaporated—I whispered to Yuri, "Why didn't you stop me?"

"I thought this was your plan."

"Hardly! When I touched the painting, I was overcome by some sort of daydream-trance."

Yuri nodded. "And the *volshebstvo* took over. But what does it mean?"

When Drew piped up, I realized he was the only one among us who wasn't freaking out. "I know exactly what it means." He reached toward the Crafting but stopped just short of touching it. "There's no possible way I can part with this portrait, not even for a million dollars. Shul was the best friend I've ever had. Bad enough we went our own separate ways. Art and artist are one—don't you see? Selling this off would be like losing him all over again."

I was about to suggest that a million dollars would bring plenty of new friends crawling out of the woodwork when there was a knock on the front door. A strange and syncopated sound, knocked by someone who clearly marched to the beat of their own off-kilter drummer.

Everyone stopped exclaiming at each other and fell silent.

The knock sounded again.

"For heaven's sake," Drew said. "Someone get the door!"

Certain that I was on the cusp of a momentous revelation, I hurried over to the door, fully expecting Shul Cadfur in the flesh to be gracing my parents' front doorstep, and whisked open the front door....

Only to find Rufus Clahd standing there looking fuzzy-haired and vaguely befuddled with a chameleon cage in his hands. "Hello there, Dixon! Good to see you made it back from the talent show in one piece. I can't say the same for the judges. One of them lost a contact lens and another is missing an upper denture."

From the other room came, "What talent show?" in Yuri's voice.

"At any rate," Rufus went on, "I've come to return this small fellow to your parents—though I shall sorely miss both his colorful antics and his ebullient personality."

On his plastic branch, the chameleon shifted his weight. One of his eyes swiveled.

Rufus handed me the cage with a sigh. "Having him around has made me realize just how solitary my life has become—"

As he spoke, a few tiny lights danced across his cheek, like a miniature galaxy fleeting past. I took it for Spellcraft—after all, a Seer could very well activate his own face with a wayward swipe of paint—but I quickly realized it was only the sparkle reflecting off Drew's glittery sequined baseball cap as he came up behind me.

In a tone that was unusually serious, Drew said, "Maybe it's a sign you shouldn't be spending so much time alone."

Across the threshold of my parent's front door, the two middle-aged men took each another in—Drew in his short shorts and sequins, Rufus in his rumpled linen suit and cloud-shaped hair... Rufus Clahd, the letters of whose name rearranged themselves in my mind like Scrabble tiles to form the perfect anagram, *Shul Cadfur*.

Rufus (after all these years, I could hardly think of him as *Shul*) took in the sparkly spectacle of Drew Draws and said, "I read about you in the PBJ. After we argued, I thought you would have used that painting I made you for target practice."

"Most certainly not," Drew said, primping his sequined hat. "Consider the subject." But his bravado was short-lived, and he dropped the breezy attitude with a sigh. "Besides...you were right. I am a sell-out. I can't tell you the last time I connected with my artistic nature and drew something from the heart."

"Molly's portrait," I blurted out, then realized I was butting into a delicate conversation. "It really was impressive," I added. "Uh... carry on."

Rufus smiled sadly. "Over the years, I've regretted those harsh words between us more than you can imagine. I've followed the trajectory of your career, and come to see that you bring joy to your patrons. Could there even be a more noble calling than that?"

"Oh, please." Drew rolled his eyes. "I don't fund some impressive charity. I draw caricatures on the Boardwalk."

Maybe so. For now. But if Drew was looking for a change, there was a whole new vocation awaiting him—one that would make the Scriveners of Pinyin Bay very, very happy, indeed.

12

There was only one print shop in Pinyin Bay with a machine big enough to spit out all those portrait copies, and luckily, it was still in business. With the owner's help, over the next couple of weeks we were able to trace the route Mayor Dunce's painting took on its way to the dumpster behind my family's store.

Back around the time my parents opened the doors of Practical Penn, Shul Cadfur discovered his true vocation was Spellcraft, not portraiture, and reinvented himself as Rufus Clahd. He'd just completed one last commission: the portrait of the newly elected mayor. When he found out Mayor Dunce was the one standing between him and Dahlia Strange, he cancelled the commission, talked Uncle Fonzo into Scribing on the painting, and pitched the whole thing into the dumpster behind the shop, which was where my dad found it.

Spellcrafters are always calling on one another during Quilling season, and it must've been during one of these visits that Hawthorn Strange snapped a photo of the portrait and gifted it to Dahlia for Pansy and Violet's Naming Party. Dahlia hung it in her room with the hope that the twins' father would eventually come to his senses.

Soon thereafter, Vano's grandfather, Silas Shirque, was

decorating his mayoral room in Shirque Mansion. He spotted the portrait at Strange Manor while he was playing poker with Hawthorn Strange and got lost on the way to the bathroom. He tried to buy it—and when Dahlia refused, he came up with the same strategy as Hawthorn and made the second reproduction, which he hung proudly in his mayoral bedroom.

As the Hand of his family, Ladin Silver had occasional business with the Shirques. He'd also been waiting for months to have his petition heard to throw out a hefty stack of jaywalking fines. In hopes of greasing the wheels at City Hall, he reproduced the second reproduction and gifted the newly printed canvas to Mayor Dunce himself.

Whether or not that helped with the fines, the printer really couldn't say.

And so, both my father and Drew were each now the owner of an original Shul Cadfur painting.

It turned out Drew had no need for an authenticator at all—not with *Shul* himself to vouch for the painting. And though it meant coming out of retirement, Rufus Clahd was eager to start mending fences with Drew, so he sacrificed his anonymity to stand up for his old friend.

The plan seemed pretty solid. What we didn't count on was the effect of Shul's return. With the mystery surrounding the artist gone, the value of Drew's portrait dropped precipitously. Which was all for the best, since he no longer entertained any ideas about selling.

My father, however, was thrilled over the prospect of something from the basement stash finally earning its keep. Unfortunately, the Dunce portrait wasn't quite the goldmine we'd hoped it would be. The mayor's office informed my father that the reproduction that had graced its walls for so many years was perfectly fine, and they had no need to replace it with the original.

Essentially...they liked things *just the way they were*. Which was how, a few weeks after this whole portrait business began, Yuri and I ended up at City Hall in disguise.

Practical Penn had more promotional calendars than walls to put them on, including a toilet calendar from a plumber who'd once fixed a leaking spigot—and not very effectively at that, which was why Mom refused to hang it up, though Dad couldn't bear to throw it away. For our plan, it was perfect!

There was some healthy debate about who'd get to wear the coveralls, but eventually Yuri prevailed, and I had to settle for some mirrored sunglasses. We showed up just before closing. Yuri planted himself at the back of the line like he was waiting to pull a permit, while I headed directly to the little boys' room. I checked under all the stalls for telltale feet, found none, and then slipped a screwdriver out of my inner pocket and got to work on one of the taps. Once I liberated the handle from the faucet, water sprayed out like a decorative fountain—success!

I hurried back out to the lobby just in time. Yuri was almost at the head of the line, looking pretty nervous, as he doesn't actually know the first thing about pulling a permit. "Bathroom emergency!" I declared...though when I saw the looks of disgust on everyone's faces, I hastened to add, "Not in my pants—in the men's room. There's water everywhere! Is there a plumber in the house?"

"I am plumber," Yuri declared stiltedly.

"Then you'd better go handle the situation. I'll just wait over here by the counter to, ah, keep everyone company while you work." I leaned against the clerk's desk as the last couple of customers renewed a dog license and paid a parking ticket. And when I realized the doddering old clerk wasn't just clearing phlegm from his throat but trying to get me to leave so he could lock up, I said, "I'm just sticking around to make sure your bathroom situation turns out okay."

"Oh?" he asked suspiciously. "And why is that?"

"Because I'm so civic minded! Er, say, while we're waiting, I was hoping you could clarify whether today is the third or the fourth. Because I'm always getting those two dates mixed up."

"You...are?"

"Absolutely. Because the numbers three and four—while they

may not look or sound alike—are more similar than you might think. They're both numbers. They both come after two and before five. *Third* has five letters and begins with a 'th' while *fourth* has six letters and ends with the very same sound, so you can imagine my confusion." When I saw my explanation had caused him to start glazing over, I went in for the kill. "Maybe if you just brought that calendar over here, I could sort this whole thing out once and for all."

Dazed, the old clerk plucked the calendar off the wall in hopes of shutting me up. With a yoink, I pulled it from his arthritic fingers and sprinted toward the exit. As I passed the men's room, Yuri emerged, wet and scowling. "Maybe this fine plumber has a calendar you can use," I called over my shoulder as I hurried out the door.

Once he set the clerk up with the toilet calendar, Yuri joined me in the truck, still making that face. "You could have just left the faucet running—there was no reason to take it apart."

"And that's just one example of how thoroughly I commit to my roles! So, did our guy take the bait?"

"Did we leave him any choice?"

I sighed happily and patted his damp knee. "You're so right, Yuri—we *do* make a fantastic team."

That Crafting had been entrenched at City Hall for decades. Removing it from the premises was a step in the right direction, but lucky for the folks who worked there, Yuri and I had the wherewithal to Uncraft the spell once and for all.

I'd been mulling over my options ever since I'd first seen the Crafting. Because *We like things just the way they are* was written on two separate lines, and more importantly, because I didn't need to make it look like part of the slogan, I had ample space to change the Scrivening without causing any weird loopholes.

With the calendar spread out on the dash, I inked my cockatoo quill (the housepaint had peeled off without a fuss) then quieted my mind and tuned in to the sensation of Spellcraft playing along my nerve endings. Once all the pieces slid into place, I added some text of my own.

We like things to run smoothly.

When necessary, we adjust the way they are.

Yuri and I both exhaled. It felt like all of City Hall had finally been able to let out a breath as well. I passed the calendar to Yuri, and with great satisfaction, he tore the whole thing in two.

Talk about sexy! I made a mental note of the way his forearm muscles flexed for future reference. "Well, Yuri, all's well that ends well."

I was wondering if they ever said that in Russia—probably not, given their love of depressing literature—when Yuri said, "We are still no closer to finding a gift for the new baby's Naming Party."

"I've got an idea. Maybe instead of buying the baby a gift, we can help them set up the nursery. Since we're so handy and all."

Yuri raised an eyebrow at that suggestion. But he didn't disagree.

Back home, we found my uncle ensconced at the dining room table with Drew Draws. Bits of paper surrounded them, some blank, some painted, and some full-fledged Spellcraft. Drew had been "discovered" by me, and as the Hand of the Penn family, it fell to Uncle Fonzo to show him the ropes.

It may have been the first actual Hand duty I'd ever seen him perform.

There's a short hall off the parlor that leads to Sabina's room, a coat closet filled with useful electronics, and a bathroom with a busted lock on the door. Everyone knew that if you were making any bathroom noises you didn't want the rest of the household to be aware of, you'd run the water. Not that it really covered up any of the unfortunate sounds—but it was the thought that counted. Currently, the bathroom door was shut. Since there was no water running, my cousin could be heard muttering to herself on the other side.

"About this Naming Party," Yuri began—I just love the forceful way he cuts right to the chase.

"Can't say it's been at the forefront of my mind," Uncle Fonzo said. "What with all the other excitement going on lately—"

Drew's discovery had been pretty thrilling, but his actual training was as dull as watching paint dry. Things had frankly been pretty ho-hum ever since the paintings got sorted out, so this sounded suspiciously like an excuse. Come to think of it, Dr. Slaughter had been pretty scarce lately, too. I was about to try and dig deeper by clarifying exactly which excitement my uncle might be referring to when I paused to sniff the air. "Uncle Fonzo, did you try to make waffles again? Something is smelling just a little too toasty."

"Look!" Yuri pointed toward Sabina's bedroom door, where wisps of smoke were curling out from around the edges. My mother's always said that my curiosity is so insatiable, if a tidal wave ever rose out of Pinyin Bay, I'd be the one running *toward* it to try and get a better look.

She's not wrong.

I dodged around Yuri's index finger, dashed down the hall, and yanked open the bedroom door. Luckily there wasn't a full-fledged fire behind it, though the room was pretty darned smoky.

The culprit was a box of shredded paper sitting way too close to a desk lamp. I grabbed the box and darted out of the room, thinking I'd fling the smoldering paper out onto the lawn before it did any real damage. Unfortunately, when I yanked open the front door, Vano Shirque was standing there with his fist poised to knock—and I took that knock smack to the middle of my forehead.

I flailed for balance as I tipped backward, scattering charred paper, and went down hard. Yuri leaped toward me to try and break my fall like an action hero, but he came up short. At least, I'd presumed he was aiming for me...at least until I saw I hadn't been his target after all.

He'd landed belly-down on the worn carpet with his arms outstretched and a small something caught in his hands. Whatever it was, it must've been buried under those burning shreds—and it must've been pretty hot. With a Russian exclamation, Yuri rolled to his knees and began tossing it back and forth, blowing hastily on his palms.

It was at that moment that Dr. Slaughter showed up. What luck! If ever you're going to fall down backward or burn your own palms, it's better to do it in front of someone with medical training, even if that someone has been known to prescribe *yogurt*.

"Is it always this crazy around here?" Drew asked my uncle...who had apparently lost something behind the davenport and didn't answer.

Dr. Slaughter slipped past Vano, stepped over me, veered around Yuri, and planted herself at the foot of the davenport with her hands on her hips. "Fonzo? You can't avoid me forever. We need to talk."

"Glenda!" my uncle said with forced cheer as he popped out of hiding. "What a pleasant surprise. I've been meaning to call—"

Dr. Slaughter wasn't buying it. "Save your excuses. They'll only make you look worse. And besides...they're not necessary. It turns out I'm not pregnant after all."

A stunned silence settled on the room. Surely she hadn't just said what I thought she'd said. There was a baby—there had to be. We were all so eager to meet the little tyke!

My uncle was the first to recover. "How could you make that kind of mistake? You're supposed to be a doctor!"

"My first test was a false positive. And my cycle is irregular thanks to perimenopause."

I doubted anyone in the room was familiar with the term, and as far as anyone knew, she'd just made it up—but it did sound awfully medical.

"Listen, Fonzo," Glenda said, gently touching his arm. "It was pretty obvious you didn't want the responsibility of being a father again. And while you're incredibly charming...I'm not sure I was ready to make our relationship quite so...permanent."

Uncle Fonzo looked chagrined—and even a little bit relieved. As for me, though, I struggled to wrap my head around the fact that this baby I'd been so excited to meet didn't actually exist. And poor Yuri took it even harder than me, kneeling there on the floor over a small white pebble with tears in his eyes.

Vano knelt beside Yuri, put a hand on his shoulder, and said, "It's okay." He prodded the pebble and flipped it over. The underside was painted with the word *Love* in flawless calligraphy with a stunning flourish. "No harm done."

Yuri did a double-take. "What?" He grabbed the painted

stone—presumably it had cooled down—and clenched it hard enough to turn it into a diamond. "How did *rock* end up in Meringue's nest?"

Drew said, "I put it there ages ago, back when all of you were scurrying around looking for your bird. That empty cage was so depressing I thought I'd snazz it up a little."

Evidently my talent show excursion with Meringue hadn't gone entirely unnoticed. Whoops. I'd tell Yuri all about it later, once he had a chance to cool down. Given the way he was currently clutching that stone, if I were Drew, I would've ducked behind the davenport with Uncle Fonzo.

Before there was a true emergency for Dr. Slaughter to attend to, Sabina came stomping out of the bathroom, right into the fray of things. She planted herself in the middle of the group in her ripped jeans, hole-riddled T-shirt and scuffed combat boots, looked around the room defiantly, and said, "Anyway. I'm late."

Late for what? I wondered...until the meaning sank in. And then excitement that was so freshly quashed began to bubble up again over the thought of those itty-bitty tiny fingers and inky-dinky little toes. Uncle Fonzo might not be ready for another round of fatherhood, but Sabina would be an excellent mother, fierce and loyal and always up for throwing acorns at the neighbor's garage. And Yuri and I would be even more excellent uncles!

I couldn't possibly imagine settling for everything staying just the way it was like the poor folks at City Hall. Not when change held so many bright and shiny possibilities, and our circle of friends and family was always expanding.

I was beside myself with joy, though I could tell I should save my congratulations for a future time, one in which my cousin didn't look quite so stabby. And inquiries about the baby's paternity would need to wait, too. Fortunately, Sabina is notoriously bad at keeping secrets. When it was clear no one else had anything to say—nothing that they dared to speak aloud, at any rate—she gave a disgruntled huff, then boffed Vano Shirque squarely in the shoulder and added, "Thanks a lot, *Vano*."

MAYOR MAY NOT

DIXON

1

Who can resist a piping hot churro straight from the deep fryer? Or a golden brown, deep-fried funnel cake? Or a melty, chocolatey fried Snickers bar? Or a thick, chewy slab of fried dough covered in frosting and cinnamon and colorful candy sprinkles? Not me.

And judging by the fact that he was currently covered in powdered sugar, not Yuri.

A-dorable.

"Say, Yuri," I ventured, as the mineral-seaweed scent of the water cut through the olfactory wall of fried food. "Isn't it funny that of the million and one places each of us could be, we both ended up in Pinyin Bay?"

He scowled as if to say, *Hardly funny when I was lured here against my will and bound by Spellcraft to serve a Handless tyrant*...but he didn't go so far as to actually speak the words. Because while that might've been technically true, no one would argue that things had totally turned out for the best.

It was the perfect day for a fundraiser. The Pinyin Bay boardwalk creaked beneath our feet. Though it was still patchy in some places and completely blown up in others, with any luck, repairs could begin soon. And in the meantime, no one complained about our festivities spilling out into the asphalt lot of the municipal salt pile. I worked my hand into the crook of Yuri's elbow, enjoying the bulge of his biceps in a way that never got old, then gave his arm a squeeze and said, "Even the boardwalk will be back to normal before you know it."

Yuri eyed the crowd. "I am not so sure. Turnout is not as good as we had hoped."

"Really?" I took a better look around. "Come to think of it, there was an awful lot of elbow room at the urinal—"

"We live ten minutes away, could you not have waited?"

"Anyhoo, Drew's going to be phenomenally upset if we don't make our numbers."

Drew Draws was the driving force behind the Rebuild the Boardwalk Extravaganza...if by driving, you meant blustering around with lots of big hand gestures in a glittery visor and lamenting that a creative's work is never done. Drew had been selling tourist caricatures from a stall on the boardwalk for more than twenty years, though late last summer we discovered there was more to his talent than just making his subjects' hair look big.

Of course, Yuri and I helped wherever we could. Yuri with Seer advice, and me insisting on adding the word *Extravaganza* to his fundraiser's title—because who doesn't love an extravaganza?

Through nippy fall days and long winter nights, Drew had split his time between learning the Seer craft and making the extravaganza a reality. He'd been planning to use the big event to announce his "retirement" from caricature and become a full-fledged Seer. It was perfect timing. He could make the announcement when he turned over a big novelty check to the contractors who'd won the bid to restore the boardwalk to its former glory...or at least its former garish kitschiness. That check couldn't be paltry, though, not when the numbers would be big enough for everyone to see—even in the blurry, weirdly-framed shots they published in the Pinyin Bay Journal.

The fundraiser had been months in the making. If it flopped, we'd never hear the end of it. Not because we were personally responsible, but because the new Seer spent so much time with my uncle, and the attic floor isn't very well insulated. And Drew can be pretty darned loud when he gets excited.

"Word of mouth is what we need," I decided.

"Where else would words come from?" Yuri wondered. "Or do I really want to know?"

"Just another charming expression in English. It means we need to get these people hyped up so they let all their friends know how much fun they're having." I grabbed the nearest stranger, a sunburned guy wearing socks with sandals, and asked, "Isn't this the coolest extravaganza you've ever attended?"

The great thing about questions is that they're not just for finding answers. In this case, I was hoping to help this guy realize exactly how much fun he was having. I knew for a fact there hadn't been an "extravaganza" in Pinyin Bay's recorded history (I'd even looked it up!). So, even if he was just having an okay time—by sheer default, Rebuild the Boardwalk would still be the coolest.

Strangers usually agree with me—especially when I startle them—but instead of just saying whatever it might take to disengage, the pink-nosed guy took in all the festivities and said, "The games are rigged, the food is cold, and the only ride is the Ferris wheel. And I could ride that anytime."

"There's a bouncy castle right over there."

"With a weight limit of a hundred pounds. I'd hardly call this an extravaganza. A fair, maybe. Or even a festivity. But *extravaganza* is really pushing it."

Far be it from me to get involved in a discussion about vocabulary with someone so pedantic. I knew full well how important it was to be accurate with my word choices. How could I not, with all the vocabulary Spellcraft tutors had drilled into my young, impressionable brain?

Turning away, I scoped out a woman in big sunglasses and bright pink lip gloss. She probably had a whole bunch of friends on Friendlike! Plus, she was tiny enough that she could hop around in the bouncy castle if the mood took her. I plastered on a big, non-threatening smile, trotted up to her, and said, "Could there possibly be a more perfect day for an extravaganza?"

Hooking a finger over the arm of her sunglasses, the woman slid them down her nose, scanned the bay, and said with a shrug, "I guess it's fine."

There's just no pleasing some people! But there were dozens of folks milling listlessly around...or maybe they were just relaxed. Surely there'd be a potential influencer somewhere in the crowd. It was just a matter of finding someone suitably enthused to take my message to the people—

"Dixon Penn!" boomed a familiar voice, startling me so badly I nearly ended up wearing Yuri's funnel cake. Ladin Silver peeled out from behind a concession stand belly-first, brandishing a Technicolor snow cone in each hand. I was hardly surprised to see him there, as Ladin had a particular knack for games of chance. Rumor has it his old trailer was raided for suspicion of illegal gambling—stoat racing, to be exact—but he's never confirmed or denied that allegation.

"Just the person I wanted to see!" Ladin boomed at me.

"Wow. Uh...really?"

"Hasn't Drew Draws been spending all his free time over at your uncle's place?"

It was no secret among the circuit that Uncle Fonzo was training a new Seer. In fact, it was pretty big news within our Spellcraft circuit. "That's right."

"Good. Then you're sure to run into him at some point. Hold this." He shoved a snow cone at me, and reflexively, my hand came up to grab the paper holder. The ball of ice on top was a bright green so electric it couldn't possibly be found in nature, and it smelled like a confusing melange of coconut and oregano. Once Ladin had a free hand, he dug an envelope out from his Sansabelt slacks and thrust it toward me. I grabbed it as reflexively as I'd grabbed the snow cone. "See that Drew gets this." He patted me on the head with a sticky palm. "There's a good boy."

I gave back the green snow cone and he ambled off, pausing every few steps to lick one, then the other, until eventually he meandered behind the listlessly capering Pinyin Bay Perch, and I lost sight of him.

Yuri scowled down at the envelope in my hands. "What is it?"

"Maybe it's a bribe. Local businesses donated all kinds of interesting stuff for the big raffle—and you know how easy it is to rig those things." I held the envelope up to the light, but unfortunately the paper was too thick for me to see though. "What do you suppose the going rate might be to fix a local raffle? There were some really cute curtain rods in one of the gift baskets—"

"We only have one window," Yuri reminded me. "And it has shutters."

I tucked the envelope into my messenger bag. "True. But things are always better when they're free."

"But it is not free if a bribe is involved."

I was about to say we'd have to agree to disagree when we came upon the bandstand. Normally, this was where Pinyin Bay Elementary held their graduation ceremony and the civic orchestra played rousing marches on the Fourth of July. The crowd was thicker here, and everyone was abuzz.

I craned my neck to see what they were all so excited about, but the guy in front of me was particularly tall.

But not taller than my grown man friend.

"Hot dog eating contest?" Yuri said incredulously.

"Only in America!" I declared. While that probably wasn't the case...I was sure he'd been thinking it. And I never like to disagree with him for long.

"Excuse me...pardon me," I said as I squeezed my way to the front of the crowd, while Yuri strode in behind me with significantly more force and fewer apologies. I'd never seen a real, live competitive eating event, and I had so many questions. Were the hot dogs boiled or grilled? How much mustard was involved? And could anyone actually say the word *wiener* without tittering?

I was nearly to the edge of the bandstand when someone snapped, "Watch it, buddy, I'm standing here," and I found myself elbow to elbow with my cousin.

"Sabina!" I said enthusiastically. And, "Vano..." less so. He'd been stuck to my cousin like glue ever since he put her in the family way. While I was used to having him around nowadays, he still managed to outdo me at every turn. Granted, I'd really upped my flourishing game lately in the face of such stiff competition. What stuck in my craw was the fact that Vano was anything but competitive. Currently, he was fanning Sabina with a map from the tourism kiosk, and he was going at it so earnestly that he'd worked up a sweat...which made his hair fall into an effortlessly attractive tousle.

Of course it did.

Self-consciously, I smoothed the sides of my hair and checked for any wayward strays. I supposed that the important thing was that Vano was willing to take the brunt of my cousin's mood swings. I've heard that some women get a certain glow about them when they're pregnant. Sabina's glow was more of a glower.

"Where've you guys been?" my cousin said. "This sun is brutal. I need Yuri to cast a shadow."

Without missing a beat, Yuri glanced up at the sky and positioned himself to block the sun from landing directly on her.

I said, "It seems like you've been pregnant forever. How much longer until the baby is due?"

Sabina shrugged. "Hard to say. Depends on whether I got knocked up on the davenport, or under the boardwalk, or in the back of the Buick."

Vano smiled to himself. "I still say it was on the circular staircase in the solarium at Nana's house."

"Forget I asked," I said weakly.

"Can the doctors not give you a due date?" Yuri wondered.

"Doctor!" Sabina scoffed. "Who has time for all the ridiculous hoops a doctor would make me jump through? Tests and sonograms and prenatal vitamins and whatnot. It's all just a racket to pad their bills."

Beneath the burgeoning sunburn on his nose, Yuri went pale. "I thought Americans had programs for things like this. What about insurance?"

"Insurance is a sucker's bet," Sabina said dismissively.

I patted Yuri on the arm. "It's fine. There's a midwife in our circuit who handles these sorts of things."

Yuri narrowed his eyes at my cousin. "And when was the last time you saw this midwife?"

"I've been meaning to get around to it. But things have been so busy, what with the new Seer and the festival...."

"Extravaganza," I reminded her.

Ignoring me, Sabina grabbed the brochure out of Vano's hands and began fanning herself harder. "I've had all I can take of this weather. If they don't start the contest soon, I'll need to forfeit."

"Hold on," I said. "You entered?"

"Drew needed more bodies to make it look good, so he waived my entry fee. I figured, free hot dogs, why not?"

Who *doesn't* love a good hot dog? Other than a vegetarian. And probably a pig...although they do say pigs are notoriously omnivorous. At any rate, even though hot dogs were as American as apple pie and sky-high health insurance, Yuri—who can be surprisingly picky—was happy to demolish half a pack at a sitting.

Sabina fanned herself harder as some helpers wheeled a groaning covered cart onto the bandstand to some hoots and cheers from the swelling crowd. Through the ancient, crackly PA system, Drew's voice announced: "Folks, our big event will start in five minutes. Now it's time for the contestants to gather backstage."

I expected my cousin to waddle toward the starting gate at full speed, but surprisingly enough, she turned on her heel and started pushing through the crowd in the opposite direction. "Sabina!" I called out. "Where ya going?"

"Can't you smell that?" she demanded. I smelled nothing but the ambient marine funk of the bay. "Hot dog water! Gross! It's enough to make me hurl!"

The crowd in front of her thinned out in a real hurry.

"But wait," I said, "what about your spot in the eating contest?"

"One of you will have to fill it. I'm outta here."

2

Vano put a protective arm around my cousin, and together, the two of them fled the scene. "Well, Yuri," I turned to him and said, "I guess it's up to you." I then saw he was eyeing the hot dog cart up on the stage with the same look he'd give a misshapen statue holding a bucket of squirming earthworms. Given that there was a smudge of chocolate at the corner of his mouth and he'd already let his belt out two notches, I could see he wasn't quite up for the task. I patted his shoulder and said, "By which I mean, up to me."

Following the sound of Drew's voice calling out directions, I hurried over to the bandstand, stepped around a very official looking stanchion (that *never* gets old) and joined a group of hopefuls waiting to compete.

I've never been competitive by nature, especially among Handless. I just wasn't particularly great at running or jumping or anything that involved a ball flying toward my vulnerable head. I might've done well at spelling, but Pinyin Bay struck spelling bees from the school district's extracurricular activities before I was old enough to compete. Budget cuts, they said. But my mother maintains the Spellcrafter kids, with all their after-school lessons, were making the Handless feel inadequate.

Behind the stage, a loose knot of hot dog hopefuls waited for their fifteen minutes of fame. Pinyin Bay is hardly a sprawling metropolis, and I recognized most of the people there. The chubby guy from the gas station on the corner of fourth street where I bought my gum. A server from a nearby pancake house. The old guy from the hardware store who was always sharing way too many personal details about his grandchildren.

And Biff, one of Sabina's (many) ex boyfriends. Back when she'd broken up with Biff, citing "gnarly manfoot" as a bridge too far, I'd actually been a bit disappointed. Biff might not be all too swift, but he was cheerful and good-looking and surprisingly well-to-do. Luckily, they'd parted on amicable terms, and when he saw me, he broke into a big smile and waved me over.

"Dixon! I was wondering if any Spellcrafters would enter the contest."

Come to think about it, everyone else gearing up for the big event was Handless, and the only reason Sabina had agreed to participate was because her entry fee had been waived.

Biff dragged me over to one of the few people I didn't quite recognize. He said, "This is Sherman Bolter—we went to high school together, and now he's a world-famous competitive eater."

"Any friend of Biff's is a friend of mine," Sherman said. He looked like he'd prepped for the contest by starving himself for the past month and a half. He was about my age, and thin to the point of gauntness, with sharp cheekbones and sunken eyes. But his face was absolutely dominated by a big, bushy beard.

As we shook hands, I said, "I had no idea it was possible to make a living by eating."

"It's not for everybody, that's for sure. But I've got an advantage."

"Your beard?" I guessed. I could just picture it funneling food toward his mouth like a third appendage.

"The beard does offer some protection from splashback," he admitted. "But I was referring to the fact that I have no taste buds."

No wonder he was so thin. "That's terrible," I said. "Is it a hereditary condition?"

"Not at all. Years ago I had a freak Pop-Rocks accident, and woke up in the hospital three days later with a tongue smoother than a baby's bottom. What I lose in traction, though, I gain in tolerance. My nausea factor is practically nil."

Unlike my cousin's. I was beginning to see what a wise decision it had been for her to pass the baton to me.

Biff looked concerned. "There's really nothing doctors can do for you?"

"Nothing short of a tongue transplant. And given the possibility of ending up inheriting someone else's speech impediment, it's not worth the risk. Not to mention the thought of having someone else's tongue in your mouth."

Good thing Yuri wasn't within earshot. He'd have nightmares for weeks over the mere thought.

Sherman went on, "I don't usually bother participating in any eating contests without a substantial cash prize, but I've made my quota for the year, so I'm available to do some competitions just for fun."

It was a far cry from showing up for the free hot dogs.

He took in the loosely milling crowd with a sweep of his hand. "In my career I've traveled far and wide and scarfed down a great number of things, from oysters in Bangor to blubber in Anchorage. But I'm beyond thrilled to ply my trade in my hometown of Pinyin Bay. As cities go, it's no Topeka, but when I watch the sun set over the bay from my kitchen, framed by the canopy of the myrtle trees in Pinyin Park, I feel that I'm well and truly at home."

Then we had something in common, since I'd done my share of rambling around and come to the very same conclusion. "My entry was kind of last-minute," I said, "so I haven't had time to prepare. Any advice for a newbie?"

"The secret is to eat the hot dogs and buns separately," he told me. "And dip the buns in water."

"Why would you give me your trade secrets?" I wondered.

He flashed a grin. "Even when I pace myself...I still eat circles around my competition."

Maybe so. But there were prize baskets at stake here, too, and even the runner up would have a pretty spiffy haul. The first-place basket was obviously the most desirable, with over five hundred dollars' worth of gift cards and other sundry items. The second-place basket wasn't bad either, brimming with gift-sized jellies and jams. The third-place basket also had a pretty good curtain rod...which I was now coveting just on principle.

Numbers were distributed, and as we pinned them to the fronts of our shirts, a thin recorded fanfare played over the PA system. Footfalls sounded on the floorboards of the bandstand, and I craned my neck to get a look at what was going on. From where I stood, though, all I could see were feet. There was a squeal of feedback...and then a voice boomed through the microphone.

"Citizens of Pinyin Bay...." A very familiar voice! I'd been expecting Drew to announce the competition, but those dulcet tones could be none other than Mayor Dunce himself! The mayor of a town this size might hardly qualify as a VIP, but Chauncey Dunce had been so set in his ways all these years—so completely inaccessible—that spying him up on that stage would be like getting a glimpse of the Loch Ness Monster.

"Thanks for turning out for our fair city's Rebuild the Boardwalk Extravaganza. You're in for quite a treat, as you're about to witness one of Pinyin Bay's treasures in action: competitive eater, Sherman Bolter."

The mayor then launched into a speech about the historical significance of the boardwalk, but frankly, it was difficult to pay attention to anything but the shoes. Some policemen were standing by, and their shoes were easy to spot: plain black oxfords with nonskid soles. And Pearl from the historical society was there too in sensible low-heeled navy pumps, slightly worn. And then there were the bright green foam clogs, an atrocity even at home, worn in full view of the whole city. I'd figured they were on Drew's feet, given that he has an interesting sense of style (to say the least). But then I heard him say, "Okay, people, put on your game faces, 'cause it's showtime!" And I realized he was behind me.

Then who on earth was wearing those cringeworthy clogs?

"Come on, come on, look alive," Drew said, shoving the contestants toward the steps. "The skywriter is just about ready to make its big entrance, and I don't want to blow it. Those things don't come cheap." He paused when he got to me and said, "Dixon? What are you doing here? And where's your cousin?"

"I'm taking Sabina's place," I said cautiously, wondering now if this had actually been a good idea.

Drew threw up his hands in frustration. "That's ridiculous. Fonzo's been taking bets on how long it'll take her to barf, and I've got a pretty penny riding on her keeping those wieners down." No titter. But judging by the short-shorts, it was pretty plain Drew was really hard to embarrass. "Not to mention the fact that having a pregnant woman in an eating competition would really make it memorable. Who cares about watching a bunch of forgettable people wolfing down food for ten minutes? Heck, most folks can see that at Sunday dinner. I was counting on that bet! I'm not meeting any of my projections, and without that win, I'll be even farther behind."

"Maybe I can help. Did you need her to barf or *not* barf?"

"It doesn't matter. The bets were on Sabina. And as entertaining as it might be to watch a dapper young man toss his cookies, it's just not the same."

He thought I was dapper! About time someone finally acknowledged this out loud. Now if only I could get someone who *wasn't* wearing a glittery visor to agree....

Plans of being noticed for my snappy dressing were all but forgotten when I mounted the bandstand and realized that the person in the crazy foam clogs was none other than Mayor Dunce.

Thanks to a persistent bit of Spellcraft, the mayor had worn the same few shoulder-padded power suits for the past three decades. But now that I'd Uncrafted the spell, evidently he was free to explore his, er...*casual* side.

While the mayor might have looked like an extra out of The Godfather in his boxy pinstripe suits, over the years, his limited wardrobe had saved him from many unfortunate fads.

Now, that protection was no longer in force.

Mayor Dunce had turned out for the event in a Pinyin Bay Baseball cap and T-shirt with the city slogan *To Bay or Not to Bay*, and acid washed jeans ironed to a sharp crease. Frankly, the only thing I recognized on him (other than his voice) was the set of big, square choppers he was flashing in a grin that was surprisingly charismatic...if you were into weird little trolls in foam clogs, that is.

We contestants took our places behind a long table covered in a red and white checkered plastic tablecloth. There were several huge cups of water at each spot—and we each had a trash can at our side, just in case things *didn't* go south. I ended up between Biff and Sherman, but there was an empty slot on Sherman's other side.

"Why don't you move over there?" I suggested in a whisper. Because while I knew I had no chance of actually winning, standing next to a world-class competitive eater would make me look twice as bad.

"Tip number three," he said. "Follow all the rules so you don't get yourself disqualified. Drew put me here—and here is where I'll stay."

Huh. Maybe if I could trick Sherman into shifting over one spot, I'd have a better chance of scoring a prize basket. Drew considered himself a free-thinker, though. He was unlikely to disqualify anyone for not following directions. Plus, Sherman was likely to be a crowd favorite, and Drew was all about pleasing his public. Still, thanks to the no-show, I had a fifty-fifty chance of winning *some* sort of prize—and those seemed like pretty good odds to me.

As I sized up the gift baskets one more time and Mayor Dunce began wrapping up his intro, the bandstand trembled. We all turned to see a massive form lumbering up the stairs...none other than Ladin Silver, who situated himself in the empty spot and deposited what was left of his two snow cones in his trash can.

I had a feeling my odds of winning a gift basket just took a nose-dive.

"The boardwalk is an integral part of Pinyin Bay history," the mayor said grandly. "And so, without further ado...."

His paused dramatically. The pause stretched as his expression went puzzled. Drew began mouthing something from the sidelines with lots of eager gesticulations, which the mayor ignored. And then he pulled a little cue card from his unfortunate jeans, brightened, and said, "On your marks!" just as a small propellor aircraft roared past overhead. Smoke spewed from the back—a startling amount of smoke—but as the plane made a loop-de-loop, I realized it was deliberate. Evidently, skywriters were one of those things I'd only seen in cartoons. Encountering one in real life was quite a sight!

"Get set...."

As the triple-loop became a cursive capital-E, a heaping tray of hot dogs was placed in front of us.

"Eat!"

The declaration was echoed by an *eat*-shaped trail of smoke in the sky.

"C'mon, Dixon," Biff said cheerfully. "Time to chow down!"

Which was precisely what Sherman Bolter was already doing... and fast! He went at his hot dogs two handed, dumping them out of their buns and cramming them into his mouth. I'm not sure he even chewed. I just knew they were going down fast. Biff, meanwhile, had pulled out his f'knife. While you might think a novelty implement would just slow him down, he'd had a lot of practice with that thing. He whittled down his hot dogs into bite-sized pieces in no time flat.

I'd better get eating if I hoped to win a prize.

Since I'd given most of my food tickets to Yuri, I was still hungry, and the first hot dog went down pretty good. Unfortunately, in that amount of time, Biff had eaten two. And Sherman? "That makes twelve for the Bolter!" the mayor cried over the PA. Stiff competition, but I had no f'knife, and the thought of dunking my buns was really unappealing. Still, maybe I had a chance at the smallest prize.... "And fourteen for Ladin Silver!"

Whaa?

I leaned forward to glance around Sherman and try and see what method Ladin was using to get a leg up. But while Sherman was frantically cramming and gobbling and dunking, Ladin was chomping down big, happy, gusto-laden bites—and making all sorts of satisfied "Mm!" "Ahh!" "Yum!" noises while he was doing it!

There was a fourth-place runner's up basket I could potentially score. Granted, it consisted mostly of mothballs donated by a specialty closet shop. But since Yuri had a thing for wool socks, if I won, at least they wouldn't go to waste.

As I pounded another hot dog—third? fourth? I'd lost count—the gal from the pancake house started hopping up and down, making room for more, as Mayor Dunce announced she was at ten!

I already felt full. Even if everyone else put down their wieners (heh) I had no chance whatsoever of winning anything at all...so I figured that if I had to lose, I'd just need to make sure I looked good while I was doing it.

I picked out Yuri in the audience, looking slightly fretful that he might witness a barfing, and managed to catch his eye. Batting my eyelashes, I nailed him with my most seductive look. Once I was good and sure I had his attention, I waggled my eyebrows and slowly raised the hot dog to my mouth....

Only to be upstaged by a loud boom in the sky above us.

The skywriter had just finished the words *Eat Up* and had spiraled into a cattywampus pattern that scrawled out the phrase into something more like *Eat Upoovommmm*.... The plane leveled out—what a relief!—but then the smoke cut off abruptly as something tumbled from the craft.

A true professional, Sherman kept right on eating. So did Ladin Silver—mainly because he couldn't be bothered by something so trivial as the sky falling while he was getting his wiener on. (Hee hee).

The thing from the plane didn't seem too scary, until it gained velocity and I saw how big it really was: a hefty 5-gallon drum. Fortunately, it wasn't heading for the thick of the crowd, but rather off to one side where people were already scampering out of its way as it hurtled to earth. It looked like it was going to come down right in the middle of a volleyball sand pit—perfect spot. But then a last-minute gust of wind off the bay changed its trajectory and sent it spinning off toward the bouncy castle.

Reflexively, I crouched down behind my mound of uneaten hot-dogs and plugged my ears with my fingers, expecting the mother of all pops. But pop never came. Instead, the 5-gallon drum bounced!

A bounce which sent it straight at the bandstand.

I backpedaled faster than you could say, "Upoovommmm." In fact, all the contestants scattered—everyone but Sherman, who wasn't going to allow something as trivial as a plummeting metal object slow him down...and Ladin Silver, who had no intention of letting anything get between him and a free meal.

Of all people, Biff was the first one to grasp the situation and see the massive metal drum was heading right for Mayor Dunce. Without hesitation, he dropped his f'knife and vaulted over the table to bodily tackle the mayor, whose baseball cap stayed aloft on the errant breeze for just a moment, then settled center stage.

Which was exactly where the metal drum came down, smashing a huge hole in the stage floor and sending splinters flying.

"I could have been killed!" the Mayor said, followed by a very effusive string of curse words.

And just his luck, somehow his mic was still on...managing to pick up every last syllable.

YURI

3

When that five-gallon tank bounced toward the stage, I panicked, shoving people left and right in a bid to leap in front of Dixon and take the brunt of the impact myself. There was no way I could possibly make it in time, but the urge to keep him from harm was a reflex I could not control. The heavy drum did not angle toward Dixon, though—it went directly at the mayor. And Dunce only survived due to some quick thinking by Biff...of all people.

The splinters settled. With a hot dog in each hand, Ladin Silver strode up to the fallen tank, which was now half-buried in the stage, and read: "Smoke oil. Danger: contents under pressure." He stuffed a hot dog in his mouth and patted the tank heartily. "Good thing it didn't—"

With a pop like a firecracker in a trash can, the metal canister ruptured, spewing its liquid contents from one end of the stage to the other in a shower of glistening grease. Mayor Dunce went down like a sack of ham. Biff tried to help him up, but slipped and fell on top of him instead.

Biff was a sizable man and the mayor was well past his prime.

They both flailed helplessly until I slid my way over and plucked Biff off the top of the heap. Good thing I'd had plenty of ice skating practice during my frigid winters in St. Petersburg. The stage was like an ice rink. A very splintered ice rink...covered in hot dogs.

I maneuvered my way over to Dixon, who'd crouched behind a pile of buns and escaped the worst of the blowup. We grabbed onto one another for balance, and he pointed up at the aeroplane, which had leveled out and was heading for the field behind the salt piles. He said, "I sure hope the pilot's okay! I wonder what happened?"

As though it could be anything but the *volshebstvo*. I locked gazes with Dixon. He lowered his voice and said, "Not-speaking of which... do you feel a tingle?"

Our eyes went to the messenger bag at his feet. As casually as we could manage (given the fact that oiled people were flailing and shouting all around us) we crouched down behind the table and checked the bag. Now that I focused, I saw the light bending strangely around the envelope from Ladin Silver. "That is no bribe," I said.

Dixon peeked over the top of the table. "Agreed. All the prize baskets took the brunt of the oil. They're ruined, but Ladin doesn't seem to mind. In fact...he's still eating."

Above the hubbub, Drew's voice cut through all the other sounds. "Heavens to Betsy—could this day get any worse?" He skidded and slid toward Dunce in an effort to help the mayor onto less slippery ground.

"Sabotage?" I suggested to Dixon, though with Ladin's track record, it was more likely a misfire than a deliberate attempt to undermine the "extravaganza."

Dixon slipped a thumb under the seal of the envelope. "Let's take a look for ourselves."

The paper was heavy cotton rag, hot-pressed, smooth, designed to take ink with a minimum of bleeding and splatter. It was the paper of choice among the Spellcraft community—the paper on which Fonzo had been training Drew.

The sketch of the bandstand in the Seen was gestural and loose in Drew's signature marker-style, with a vibrancy and energy that seemed to vibrate off the page. A burst surrounded the stage that was meant to be confetti...but looked suspiciously like the spray of oil which had followed the canister's eruption.

In Ladin Silver's hand, the wording read:

Rebuild the Boardwalk is a big hit!

"At least it is spelled right," I muttered.

Dixon winced. "This is a totally innocent Crafting. It's almost like the Spellcraft deliberately misunderstood their intent. Do you think it's Drew's inexperience or Ladin's sloppiness at fault?"

I shrugged. "We will never know."

"One thing's for sure, Drew won't be happy about tanking his own fundraiser. At least there's plenty of room for me to add another line and Uncraft it. Something very specific about earning lots of money and making everyone happy." He rummaged around for his quill, but as he fished it from the bag, a single drop of oil slid to the end of a strand of hair hanging down on his forehead. The droplet wobbled there for a moment...then fell onto the Crafting.

It landed directly on a spot where Seen and Scrivening touched. The oil spread ridiculously fast, and it acted as a solvent. Both inks—marker and quill pen—reacted immediately. The colors bloomed like a cloud of bright smoke pouring from the back of a stunt plane, while the letters warped until they were unrecognizable in any language. The inks combined into an oil slick of rainbow colors that danced upon the page, but just for a moment. Once the oil soaked in, it left the paper limp and translucent, and the Seen muddy and smeared.

We felt the magic leave in a rush as the spell set itself. The *volshebstvo* had fled—yet the oil remained. People flailed, trying to stay upright...many of them failing. And though the magic was gone, its aftermath would most certainly linger.

***

Drew was not pleased with how the "extravaganza" turned out, to say the least. *Rebuild the Boardwalk* was his legacy to the town, his official exit from the public eye as a caricature artist. It was meant to be a triumph, but thanks to the skywriting accident, it was instead a disgrace.

"And to add insult to injury," he complained, "Dunce won't even get back to me with the final figures for the big novelty check." He pulled a sequined fez from his head and attempted to fan himself with it...though the shape of a fez was not particularly conducive to fanning.

"Maybe he's busy," Dixon suggested. "That oil must've been pretty tough to clean up."

"It's not as if he's mopping it up himself!" Drew huffed. "Emails are going nowhere and he won't pick up the phone. I'll need to march down to City Hall and get some answers in person."

He was seated at Fonzo's dining room table with an array of freshly drawn Seens drying in front of him. Dixon's uncle had been working him hard—and likely selling off his "training" Seens for a tidy profit—and Drew was in no condition to march anywhere. If he did not lie down soon, he would fall over.

"I will go," I said. "I am good at getting answers out of people."

Dixon's eyes lit up in the way they do when he thinks I am speaking like I'm in an action film. I managed not to sigh.

When we pulled up to City Hall, a cluster of people were standing outside, gathered in front of the doorway at the top of the marble stairs. I would have taken it for a protest, had they been holding any signs. But they were simply milling around and complaining.

"I've tried three times this week and it's been locked up every time!"

"What if it's a new holiday? How can anyone keep track?"

"It's no holiday. Dunce is gone, I tell you. The Easy-Meal boxes are really piling up on his front porch."

"No kidding—and they're getting a little ripe, too. The pesto linguine wasn't bad, but the artichoke risotto was already starting to turn."

I stepped into the crowd, cupped my hands around my eyes and peered through the glass. The lobby of City Hall was dark and still. If the mayor had succumbed to a heart attack, he could very well be lying on his office floor, sprawled out beneath the reproduction of his portrait. Though why no one would have found him by now was beyond me. Never mind the implausibility of City Hall shutting down entirely just because the mayor did not show up. This was Pinyin Bay, after all, where Spellcraft prevailed more often than logic.

"Should I call Sabina?" Dixon whispered. "She'd never forgive me if she missed a chance to break into the mayor's office."

A new arrival paused at the foot of the stairs and called up to all of us, "Looking for Dunce? Don't bother—my wife works at the Quick Mart over by the interstate. She says the mayor stopped there with a bunch of luggage strapped to the roof of his car. He bought three extra-large coffees and hit the on-ramp doing at least eighty. And no one's seen the guy since."

"When was this?" I asked.

"Right after the big oil spill."

I glanced again into the darkened interior of City Hall. If Mayor Dunce did not want to be found, I saw no point in trying to find him. He had certainly served the city longer than anyone could reasonably expect. And now...it appeared that Drew Draws was not the only one whose legacy to Pinyin Bay would be an oil-soaked fiasco of an extravaganza.

4

I would hate to be the one to tell Drew his big check would need to wait. He was too sparkly. And melodramatic. And loud. And so it was with great relief I received a call from Sabina saying, "I need you to lift something heavy before Vano pulls a groin muscle," and Dixon and I headed over to Shirque Mansion.

Back when first I'd seen the mansion, it was a boarded-up, piecemeal husk of a building owned by a corporation only interested in excavating beneath it. Nowadays, returned to its rightful owners, it was still a tossup of clashing styles. But at least it looked lived-in.

Much of that was due to Sabina. Without her, Vano drifted through the cavernous place leaving few traces of himself behind—other than the homemade meals which graced the half-Victorian, half-Colonial kitchen table. As for Morticia, she kept busy minding the affairs of Pinyin Bay's Spellcraft circuit, and was seldom home. But while Sabina had been content enough in her closet-sized bedroom at Fonzo's house, she was young and full of life—and opinions—and the mansion did not feel as empty with her in it.

I had thought I would miss Dixon's cousin if she no longer lived two floors below us. It was not that she had moved out from under her father's roof, though, but rather flowed seamlessly now from one place to the other as the mood took her. And today she was in a mansion sort of mood.

She greeted us at the front door looking flushed and slightly sweaty. Shirque Mansion contained a great many things. Air conditioning was not one of them. "What a relief you got here as quick as you did," she said. "We were poking around some out-of-the-way rooms to see who could find the ugliest doily when we ran across a crazy, mixed-up nursery that hadn't been used in ages. The furniture was all intact, so Vano got the bright idea that we could refinish it good as new by the time the baby came."

The thought of a bunch of Frankensteined stuffed animals staring at me from the shelves with mismatched eyes made me shudder. "Are there...dolls?"

"There were," Sabina said. "But we shoved them all under the bed in one of the other rooms."

Hopefully not one in which Dixon and I would eventually sleep.

"Never mind the dolls," Dixon said sternly. "Are you sure you're supposed to be breathing in all those paint fumes in your condition?"

Sabina wrinkled her nose. "Heck, no. The mere thought of it is enough to make me upchuck. That's why we're doing it in the backyard, where I can supervise from the porch. In the shade. With a plate of cookies and a big glass of peppermint iced tea."

While the cookies were tempting, I was more concerned about this so-called furniture.

I joined Vano in the sample nursery, which was nightmarish enough even without dozens of dolls' button-eyes staring through me. The walls were covered in murals from turn-of-the century picture books, all populated by chubby, pink-cheeked ragamuffins baring creepy little milk teeth in maniacal grins. And the crib, dresser and rocking chair were a jumble of clashing colors and styles.

Vano shrugged and said, "If you squint, it's not so bad."

"I will buy you the furniture," I said. I might not have the cash on hand, but a determined Seer can always make money living among so many Scriveners.

"These things haven't seen any use since my parents were young." Vano ran a hand along the playpen rail. "Breathing new life into them would make Nana really happy."

I quelled a sigh.

The furniture was far heavier than it looked, not to mention covered in cobwebs. We struggled up and down a narrow staircase, because even though there were two lifts in the mansion, neither of us was gullible enough to trust them. Once everything was in a pile at the foot of the stairs, we hauled it toward the side yard, where Dixon and Sabina were chatting on the porch. "Dixon," Vano called through the rickety screen door. "A little help?"

"Never mind," I added quickly, then lowered my voice so only Vano would hear. "If he gets involved, it will take twice as long."

"He could at least hold the door."

"Even that would only slow us down." I opened the heavy toy chest we'd laboriously dragged downstairs and pulled out an old wooden tennis racket. "Prop the door open with this. It will not distract us with fanciful advice."

Piece by heavy piece, we hauled the furniture out onto the lawn under the watchful gazes of Dixon and Sabina. The paint was blistered and peeling and the pieces were covered in dust, but they were solid—nothing like the cheap ready-made furniture you could buy at a "big box" store. And a coat of fresh paint would go a long way toward making it look new again.

"How exciting," Dixon declared happily as I set down my side of the crib with a grunt. "Just think, pretty soon we'll be laying down a little bundle of joy in that crib and singing it to sleep."

"Hopefully not all that soon," Sabina said. "I still haven't thought of any good names."

While the cousins chatted, Vano and I dragged the final dresser alongside the rest of the furniture. "You see?" I said to Vano. "We handled this ourselves, no problem—"

BANG!

We all jumped as if a five-gallon tin of oil had just dropped from the sky. But it wasn't a random falling object at fault—it was the brittle old tennis racket, snapped in two, letting the screen door slam shut.

"Everything is fine," I said testily as I plucked out the broken racket and pitched it over my shoulder.

"No it's not," Sabina said. Since she will often disagree with me just for form's sake, I presumed she was gearing up for one of our usual cheerful arguments. But when I saw the look on her face—and the puddle at her feet—I realized she wasn't just being fractious. "My water just broke."

Dixon scrambled to his feet. "Tear up some sheets! Boil a pot of water! And make sure all the windows are closed!"

"Why the windows?" Sabina asked her cousin.

"So your luck can't fly away."

Vano looked puzzled for a moment, but he quickly shook off his confusion and said, "I'll call the midwife."

As Dixon and Sabina discussed the pros and cons of Lamaze breathing—apparently Sabina had not yet made time to attend any birthing classes—Vano, with phone to ear, began to pace. A stranger might think he was just shifting his weight. But I knew him well enough to see he was worried.

"What is it?" I asked quietly.

"She's not answering." He cut his eyes to Sabina and Dixon. "I'll just shoot her a text and...uh...."

As soon as the message left his fingers, an auto-response popped up in return.

Due to an unfortunate misunderstanding about a missing prescription pad, I am indisposed until the Handless judge sets my bail. If this is an emergency, please contact my part-time assistant at the following number.

"*Part-time* assistant?" I read aloud.

Vano tapped the phone number. "I'm sure it will all work out."

I bent my head to listen in on the call, not quite sharing his optimism.

Someone picked up in two rings—at least that was a relief. But then...she spoke. "Venus Monger's hypnotherapy and real estate service. Sell your home...or just think you did!"

Vano said, "I think I have the wrong number."

"Vano Shirque?" said Venus, delighted, "is that you?" Venus had "a thing" for Vano. Or, more accurately, for the prospect of insinuating herself into the first family of Pinyin Bay's Spellcraft circuit by any means necessary.

"I was looking for the midwife's assistant," he said.

"And you've found her! I'd be happy to avail you of my services, just as soon as this multilevel marketing seminar wraps up."

"But Sabina's in labor. Can't you just ditch?"

"Not when I'm the one teaching it! And frankly, the students are starting to look a little antsy...."

"Never mind," I snapped.

"Have it your way," Venus said. She had a good sense for when a sale would be too much trouble to close. "And keep in mind that my notary public services are buy one, get one half-off till the end of July."

Vano hung up, dazed. "Now what?"

"Now," I said, "we go to hospital."

There was plenty of room in the old Buick for all of us, and with Vano at the wheel, every streetlight turned green just as we approached it. We reached the hospital in minutes, and as Sabina huffed and puffed, breathing theatrically against the pain, an orderly rushed out with a wheelchair to take her inside.

Though only as far as the admissions desk.

"Don't worry," the nurse said confidently. "We've got plenty of time for paperwork. Labor lasts for hours with your first baby." Sabina paused in her huffing and puffing to stare at her in panic. The nurse added, "Sometimes days."

Sabina turned to us and snapped, "Somebody do something!"

"I know," Dixon said—and I steeled myself for a useless suggestion. "We should see if Dr. Slaughter's on duty."

Oh. Good idea.

As far as we knew, Glenda was no longer *examining* Fonzo during her off-hours...but she was someone we were all acquainted with, and that counted for something. While Dixon chatted his way past the nurse and headed off to find the doctor, I let Fonzo know what was going on. By the time Dixon returned with Glenda in tow, a Monte Carlo on balding tires had screeched up to the door.

It not only contained the rest of the Penn family—Fonzo, Florica and Johnny—but Vano's great-grandmother as well.

This child of Vano and Sabina would be the first to herald a new generation in either family. And to a Scrivener, family is everything. At a different time in my life, I might have been vaguely envious of this. Even disdainful. But I was now included in this family (though Scriveners are notoriously cagey around outsiders) and I was just as excited about the new arrival as any of them.

Glenda, however, had never been "one of us." She is also not what you'd call an intimidating person. She keeps her pockets full of cheap little toys to give away, and addresses everyone as if they're a harmless, fuzzy animal. She put a stethoscope to Sabina's belly, checked her pulse, and in a surprisingly adult tone of voice, said, "Calm down and breathe normally, you'll make yourself hyperventilate."

Sabina stopped huffing and puffing.

"Good job." Glenda patted her on the head. "Now, when is your estimated due date?"

"I've never been much good with dates," Sabina said.

"Me neither," Vano agreed quickly.

Glenda narrowed her eyes. "Okay...I'll check with someone who does know. Who's your obstetrician?"

Sabina snapped her fingers like she was trying to remember. "Name's right on the tip of my tongue. Y'know. That one baby doctor person."

Unfortunately for Sabina, Glenda did not suggest any particular "baby doctor person" for her to claim to have been seeing. Meanwhile, the nurse was busy clicking around on the computer. "I can't seem to find Miss Penn's records."

Every Scrivener in the room tried, and failed, to look casual. Johnny even managed to whistle guiltily.

While Glenda was no Scrivener, she'd been around them enough during her time with Fonzo to have some idea what was going on. She leaned in and whispered, "Have you seen any doctor during your pregnancy? Any doctor at all?"

"Define *seen*," Sabina said.

Glenda grabbed the wheelchair's handles and declared, "What this patient needs is fresh air." Considering that she had also prescribed yogurt, I was very leery of this announcement. At least until I realized she was just wheeling Sabina out of earshot from the Handless nurse. "Listen, Sabina. You need to start taking care of yourself. There are programs you can sign up for, if this is about the money—"

It wasn't...not exactly. It was about being a Scrivener, and all the notions and traditions that entailed. Fortunately, while Sabina reacted to a barrage of whispered admonitions like a pregnant deer in headlights, Morticia Shirque was not about to let the mother of her great-great grandchild be bossed around. "We have a midwife all lined up," she said imperiously. "One with plenty of experience—in fact, she even delivered Vano, and he turned out just fine."

"I'm all for having a midwife, if that's what the mother wants," Glenda said. "But where is your midwife now?"

Every Scrivener suddenly became very interested in the sky. Or the brick wall. Or a spot of old gum on the pavement. And then Johnny's tuneless anything-but-innocent whistle started up again.

As the elder family members drifted away to avoid any potentially incriminating questions, I saw I would need to take a stance on their behalf. "Midwife is indisposed," I said firmly. Americans tend not to question me when I take a certain tone of voice.

Glenda nodded. "You may not need her just this minute anyhow. How far apart have your contractions been?" she asked Sabina.

"No idea."

Vano, however, had been paying attention. "From three to fifteen minutes apart."

"I see," Glenda said. "And where, exactly, have you been feeling them?"

Sabina was excited to finally be able to answer a question without making up some elaborate excuse. "Right around the baby bump!"

"Just what I thought," Glenda said. "These aren't labor pains—they're Braxton Hicks contractions. It looks like you won't be meeting your new baby just yet."

"But my water broke!"

Glenda glanced down at Sabina's soggy sweatpants. "Actually, it hasn't. Amniotic fluid doesn't usually smell like peppermint."

Dixon's cousin is never gracious about being told she's wrong, so in case we needed more free medical advice from Glenda in the future, I hauled Sabina up from the wheelchair and hastened to get her out of there before she burned any bridges. "Make sure you stay hydrated," Glenda called after us as she wheeled the chair back inside.

Once she was out of earshot, I said, "First yogurt...now water."

Dixon stroked his chin-stubble thoughtfully. "What actual proof do we have that she's a doctor and not just a woman in scrubs hanging around the ER?"

Sabina waddled away from the hospital as fast as her swollen feet would take her. "At least no one managed to get my credit card number. And I haven't had a whatchamahoozy since we got here, so it's possible Glenda's onto something." By the time we got to the parking lot, she was flushed and sweaty. "I don't know about you guys...but all this running around has really worked up my appetite. Let's go get some pancakes."

DIXON

5

Happy Jack's (home of Pinyin Bay's hottest griddle) is the city's most notorious pancake house...not because the food is anything special, but because shady men from out of town are continually mistaking it for a "massage parlor." The purple velvet curtains and the skimpy waitress uniforms probably didn't help. According to the servers, though, lots of cleavage meant big tips, so they didn't complain much about wearing them.

The server currently taking our order had a butterfly tattoo on her bosom that flexed its wings every time she breathed. I'm not generally mesmerized by cleavage, but the butterfly was awfully distracting.

"Say," she blurted out in the middle of her special-of-the-day pitch. "Weren't you in the hot dog eating contest?"

My eyes snapped up to her face and I realized we'd met at the extravaganza. "Oh! I didn't recognize you—" *with so few clothes on?* "—in that uniform! Especially with your hair up."

Good save.

"Talk about a fiasco," she said. "Every last prize was ruined. I was all set to nab third place, too—and it's so hard to find nice curtain rods nowadays."

Sabina snapped her menu in hungry annoyance so it was standing up rigidly between her hands and said, "Should I get the blueberry or the buttermilk?"

"Get both, you're eating for two," the server said automatically, seeming much more interested in gossiping about the failed fundraiser than in getting us fed. She turned back to me and asked, "Have you heard about the pilot?"

"Not a thing. Is he all right?"

"A few bumps and bruises—and they're saying he passed the sobriety test, too. It took a while to figure out exactly what went wrong, but eventually the truth came out."

I swallowed hard, wondering if anyone knew that truth had been riding around in my bag.

The server leaned closer, butterfly wings heaving, and said, "Apparently...there was a spider."

Relief flooded me. Not for the spider, who'd likely been squashed by flailing pilot hands. But for the fact that Spellcraft hadn't been exposed—a piece that I'd been carting around, no less—while the head of the circuit watched my reaction with her shrewd little nearsighted eyes.

"Well," Morticia said, once the server was gone. "I suppose now is as good a time as any to get down to business."

Yuri cut his eyes to me, but I could only shrug in return. As far as I knew, we were only there for the business of filling our bellies with pancakes and mediocre coffee. I did my best not to squirm, hoping beyond hope that I wouldn't end up getting blamed somehow for Ladin Silver's failed Crafting. But instead of dressing me down, Morticia took a fortifying slurp of her decaf and turned to my uncle instead.

"The baby will be here anytime now," she said. "And when it does, our families become one." Marriage was more a Handless institution—my parents being a notable exception—but for Spellcrafters, it was *children* that sealed the deal. "When this happens, I plan to retire."

You'd think that we would all be prepared for this announcement, given that Morticia was the oldest Spellcrafter in the circuit. And yet, the whole table shifted uncomfortably as we all took in the news.

Vano was the first to speak. "But Nana, the circuit needs you."

"Pah! I've served it long enough—and I've still got a bucket list longer than my arm. The only reason I've held out this long was that I knew you weren't ready to take over."

Vano swayed a little in his seat and went the color of the non-dairy creamer on the table setting. "And now I am?"

"Let's just think this through, Morticia," my uncle said. As the Hand of the Penn family, he was the only one familiar enough to call her by name. "The baby's not here just yet. We've got plenty of time to plan," he said smoothly.

A little too smoothly.

Why was he going into damage-control mode?

He said, "We all know there's more to running a circuit than just showing up and looking handsome. Why, you've got to keep all the local Spellcrafters from stepping on each other's toes, and the Hands of the families are going to walk all over your great-grandson, good-looking or not."

Morticia's actual duties were never quite clear to me, and I'd always assumed she was more of a figurehead. Then again, Uncle Fonzo never really went into what happened while he was doing Hand business, either...other than playing lots of poker.

"Your concern is touching," Morticia told him. "But let's not sugar-coat what's really going on. You're worried that once Vano steps up, he'll not only be head of the circuit—but Hand of the family."

As my uncle made the face he makes when we catch him drinking straight from the orange juice carton, the ramifications sank in. It was really none of our concern who the Hand of the Shirque family might be.

But if our families merged, then their Hand was our Hand. Which meant Uncle Fonzo...my parents...*me*—we'd all have to answer to Vano.

A stunned silence fell over the table, broken only by the bright chatter of the server as she hauled over a groaning tray of food and began dealing out the pancake orders, butterfly wings flapping. Sabina was the only one who seemed unfazed—either that or she was just especially hungry—and she dug in before her plate fully hit the table. But the rest of us just sat there in shock as Morticia fixed us each in turn with a steely squint that challenged us to defy her authority. Either that or she couldn't quite tell who was who, and was just hedging her bets.

Once the waitress was gone, Morticia settled at last on my uncle and gave her head a rueful shake. "I understand your concerns, Fonzo—and frankly, I agree. Vano is a good boy, but he's still young, and there's a lot of new responsibility coming his way already. What he really needs to be right now is not the Head, and not the Hand, but a father. Which is why I have decided to split the Hand."

I'm guessing she wasn't talking blackjack. Mom, Dad and Uncle Fonzo each sucked in a breath. The rest of us, however, were in the dark.

"What split, exactly, did you have in mind?" my uncle said carefully.

"Someone to lead the circuit, and someone to speak for the family. And neither of those should be Vano. For the Head, we need someone with experience. The Hands of the families can be tricky—something you know quite well—and the Head will need to think one step ahead of them. For that reason, the person I choose to succeed me, Fonzo...is you."

My uncle (who'd been totally gearing up for an argument) lit up like a dubiously wired electrical socket. "It's gratifying to hear that the esteemed head of my circuit thinks I'm worthy of such an honor," he said grandly.

My father was just as excited. "And I've been ready to take on the Hand duties for the Penn family ever since my brother's extended... er...vacation."

All's well that ends well—but it's not over until the fat lady sings. *Really* unfortunate Handless expression. Though if the shoe fits....

"Now hold on right there," my mother snapped. "What makes you think *you're* the one for the job? I have just as much of a right to the position. Not only am I a member of the Penn family just the same as you are, but I was the one who did all of Fonzo's *Hand-jobs* while he was gone."

Now was probably not the best time to correct Mom on the terminology. Not while she was this full of beans.

As both of my parents dug in their heels in preparation for a heated (and very public) debate, Morticia raised a wrinkled hand for silence and said, "Each of you holds a legitimate claim to the position. Normally, I would let you all battle it out amongst yourselves. But matters like these tend to cause wounds within families that can take generations to heal. And since your family will soon be my family, I will not stand by and allow that to happen. There's a Spellcraft tradition as old as the Quilling Ceremony, but much less common. When the household can't agree on the succession of the Hand, it's left for the kee-poo to decide."

"The...kee-poo?" Dad repeated, while Mom narrowed her eyes as if she thought she was being punked.

"I hope there's no actual poo involved," Sabina said between mouthfuls of pancake.

Since my cousin was on the cusp of producing a great-great-grandchild, Morticia was willing to ignore the attitude. "Whoever finds the kee-poo will be the one to lead the family."

"That sounds...fair," Dad said, though he seemed awfully perplexed.

"Fine." Mom cracked her knuckles, eager to get down to business. "What exactly is this kee-poo thing and how to we go about finding it?"

"You will know it when you see it," Morticia said. "Now, go. The kee-poo is waiting."

My parents stared at her for another few beats, just in case she had further instructions to divulge. But when none were forthcoming, they both shot to their feet and scrambled to the door. Dad was the quicker one...but Mom was closer to the exit. And she was totally willing to block the entire doorway to keep him from gaining an edge. Luckily, she crammed herself into the passenger seat of the Monte Carlo before Dad could take off without her—but just barely. She was still struggling to settle the seatbelt over her bosoms without strangling herself as Dad peeled away from the curb.

"Glad I didn't need to referee that particular match," Uncle Fonzo said. "But now we've only got one car, and it'll be a tight squeeze."

"That's okay," I said quickly. Normally, you could fit a small army in the Buick—but Sabina was awfully big these days, plus I doubted Morticia wanted anyone sitting on her lap. "Yuri and I can walk."

The check arrived, and Morticia waved it toward Uncle Fonzo with an imperious gesture. In my family, we preferred to go Dutch so there was no argument about who paid last time. But the addition of Morticia made this official Spellcraft business, and for the time being, my uncle was still the Hand, which made him responsible for the bill. Uncle Fonzo glanced at the total and winced. "Are you sure there's no expectant mother discount?" he asked half-jokingly...but no dice.

He handed the waitress several twenties. While we waited for his change, Morticia said, "All right. That's settled. Now, your first job as Head is to find a good candidate for Pinyin Bay's next mayor."

Evidently, once the city council decided Mayor Dunce was unlikely to come back, they scheduled an emergency election for next week. Just goes to show how fast City Hall can move if they're not under the sway of a restrictive bit of Spellcraft!

As Vano helped both Sabina and his Nana to the car, Uncle Fonzo smiled and nodded at them benignly—and the second their backs were turned, he swung around to Yuri and me, whispering fiercely, "Okay, kids, this election assignment is a really big deal. We need someone pliant. Someone sympathetic to our people. And most of all, someone capable of winning. If I pick the wrong horse in this race, Morticia will change her mind about me for sure."

"That's a big responsibility," I said.

"Huge! To make matters worse, all my acquaintances are

Spellcrafters, all but the losers—er, hopefuls—who shop at Practical Penn. And no self-respecting Spellcrafter would let himself get roped into Handless politics. But you're from a different generation, a more inclusive generation. And you know plenty of suckers—ah, fine upstanding citizens—who'd be willing to serve as mayor of Pinyin Bay. You've gotta help out your poor Uncle Fonzo. Do some reconnaissance and find a candidate for our circuit to back."

From the car, Sabina called, "Come on, Dad, Dixon and Yuri don't need such lengthy goodbyes. They live right upstairs, for crying out loud!"

Uncle Fonzo clapped us each on the shoulder and whispered, "I'm counting on you." Then he plastered on a big, carefree smile, turned around and strode toward the Buick.

6

Once the bunch of them drove way, Yuri ran a hand over his shorn scalp and said, "Now what?"

"We'll just need to make a list of the Handless we know who would consider the mayoral job an upgrade. There's my friend Charlotte at the Pinyin Bay Journal...who could very well be spotted in a tin foil hat, so I suppose she's not the best choice. And there's Brad the Cad, who's been out of a job ever since his Hunting Party real estate gimmick went bust—though he'd obviously double-cross us the minute he got a chance. Ooh, I know, our waitress seemed nice. Maybe she'd want the job."

Yuri frowned—more of a frowny-frown than a thinking-frown. "Tattoos. Cleavage. Happy Jack's. She'd scare away all the conservatives. Spellcrafters might sympathize with her as a candidate—but Spellcrafters hardly ever vote."

True. Otherwise there'd be no need for kee-poos.

Yuri said, "You enjoy meeting people. There must be someone you know who would make an electable candidate."

If the server wasn't mayoral material, maybe someone else from the hot dog eating contest... "What about Sherman Bolter? Mayor Dunce called him a Pinyin Bay treasure—so he's got the support of the current administration behind him already."

Yuri frowned again. In thought, this time. "He does have an impressive beard."

"He does! Plus, he's just crazy about Pinyin Bay."

Yuri did a quick search on his phone. "His number is not listed. How do we find him?"

We could have just asked Drew what it said on his entry form... but that's no fun! I recalled how Sherman waxed eloquent about the view of Pinyin Park from his kitchen, and declared, "I know exactly how to triangulate his location!"

Pinyin Park is located in a Handless part of town on a tiny block of land where a petting zoo once stood. As parks go, it's nothing to write home about. A set of monkey bars, some picnic tables covered in graffiti and a few rusted charcoal grills. But though the greedy petting zoo goats were long gone, the grass grew lush and green from all the fertilization they'd once provided.

"Those must be the myrtle trees he was talking about," I said, pointing. "Now we just need to figure out where the sun sets!"

Yuri grabbed a stick and thrust it into the ground so we could see which way the shadow fell. (And he claims he's not a real-life action hero!) That narrowed things right down. And even better, there was only one actual house that fit the bill, nestled between a sweet little fruit stall on one side and a dog boutique on the other.

Pleased with myself for finding Sherman with only those few clues to go by, I marched up on the tidy little porch, abuzz with anticipation, and pressed the doorbell. Even the bell was cute, and as the jaunty little uplifting tune played, I congratulated myself on coming up with the perfect candidate. Someone who not only took pride in Pinyin Bay, but who Pinyin Bay could take pride in too.

There was a rustle of the quaint gingham curtain, and the door was opened by a woman. A middle-aged woman, not quite old enough to be Sherman's mother. Maybe they were dating. Who was I to judge, so long as they were happy?

"I don't need any encyclopedias," she said curtly, and tried to close the door. But I was pumped up with self-congratulation, so

I was quick to slide a foot between door and doorjamb.

"We're not selling encyclopedias."

"Plungers either." Traveling plunger salesmen were a thing? They never seemed to come around when I needed one.

"We're not salesmen," I said.

She crossed her arms and looked us up and down. "Then why are you wearing suits? You're not gonna try to sell me on your church, I hope."

Perish the thought! "We're just looking for Sherman."

"Who?"

That sense of self-congratulatory elation was draining away faster than a sink within reach of a good plunger. "Sherman Bolter." Her brow furrowed, and I added, "The world-class competitive eater."

Realization dawned. "Oh! The guy with the beard!"

"That's right. We thought he lived here, but apparently our stick was wrong—erm, never mind, long story. Do you know where we can find him?"

She gestured toward the fruit stand. "He's always poking around behind Berry Good just after closing, so he should be here any minute. Now if you don't mind, I need to go soak my feet!"

Never let it be said I stood between someone and her foot bath.

Yuri and I bought ourselves a little bag of plums, then parked ourselves on the bench across from the fruit seller to wait for closing time. I held up a plum and said, "Some folks might say plums are a crapshoot, but I like to think of them as more of a surprise. You never know if you're in for sweet or sour until you take the plunge and bite in."

"The same can be said of many things." Yuri swallowed the bite he'd taken of his plum—likely sweet, given that he wasn't making a sour-face—then turned and locked gazes with me.

The lowering sun picked out golden flecks in his hazel eyes. It highlighted the sheen of plum juice on his lower lip, too, which was curved into a subtle smile. I should probably check and make sure that plum of his really was as sweet as it looked. But as I leaned in to capture a taste from his lips, I was startled by a loud bang across the street.

Yuri's mesmerizing hazel eyes snapped to the fruit stand. "That came from behind the store. Let's go."

I made a mental note to revisit those plums later.

Alleyways are fascinating places, since they're the side of a business the owners don't expect you to see. The alley behind Berry Good didn't disappoint—while it was nothing special to look at, it smelled like fruit punch. And though there was an undertone of fermentation, it was faint enough to ignore.

Unfortunately, the swarming clouds of fruit flies were not quite as easy to overlook.

And there, amongst the cloud, was a figure tipped into a dumpster with his head buried deep and his butt in the air. When he righted himself within the swarm of flies, clutching a crushed orange in one hand and a burst pomegranate in the other, he revealed himself to be none other than Sherman Bolter.

"The guy from the extravaganza," he enthused at me. "Dixon, isn't it?"

I nodded weakly. "And this is my grown-man friend, Yuri."

Yuri took a step back so as not to encourage any sticky introductory handshaking.

Sherman didn't seem to mind. "What a pleasant surprise! This alley doesn't get a lot of random foot traffic, so I assume you've been looking for me."

"That's very perceptive!" I said.

"And I know exactly why you're here."

"You do?"

"Of course! You want to make an appearance on my Blig-Blog channel: Pinyin Freegan!"

The more he spoke, the less sense he made. "Actually...I, um...."

He shoved the pomegranate into my hands and pulled out a phone. I'd never seen such a mucky screen. "Don't be shy—I don't mind. Everyone wants their fifteen minutes of fame. My viewers love it when I have guests on, and I'm always happy to do anything

I can do to educate people about freeganism."

"Oh. Well...okay."

Sherman thumbed on his camera aimed it at himself, and said, "Greetings, Pinyin Bay Freeganeers! Dixon and Yuri are joining me tonight to watch me eat this perfectly good orange that someone was willing to simply throw away." He shoved his phone at Yuri, noting, "It's so helpful to have an extra set of hands."

Yuri took the sticky phone, but only because he'd been stunned into compliance...though he did look a bit green.

Sherman tore into that squashed orange, happily spraying juice and fruit flies. Yuri and I both took another step back from the splash zone. As huge bites of pulpy orange disappeared into the funnel of Sherman's huge beard, he said, "I'm sure you both have some idea how much edible food is thrown out each and every day. Rather than let our precious resources go to waste, I've dedicated myself to eating only food that is destined for the landfill." He fished a bruised apple from the dumpster and thrust it into my free hand. "Even if there's a blemish or two, that doesn't mean you need to throw the whole thing away. Try it!"

"No, that's okay," I said hastily, as it was a bit softer than I generally like my apples. "I'm full of plums."

"Suit yourself." Sherman snatched the apple away from me. "But the more different fruits you consume, the better. Freeganism promotes variety—you never know *what* you'll find—and a varied diet is a healthy diet."

As Sherman waxed eloquent about the virtues of a trash-picked menu, Yuri leaned in and whispered, "There is no way the city will elect a man who scrounges for his food like an animal."

"Not necessarily," I said. After all, my father has been known to slow the car when he spots an enticing find on the curb. "No one likes paying taxes. We could play up the fact that Sherman is frugal. I'm sure plenty of cheap folks would like that."

Yuri wasn't convinced. "But he is eating from the trash so as not to waste food, and yet he is entering these eating competitions which are extravagantly wasteful—and doing both of these things in a very public way. No one likes a man who talks from both sides of his mouth."

Yuri had a point. A very sticky point. I slipped the pomegranate back into the dumpster just as Sherman took his phone from Yuri, swung his video back to me and said, "Are you sure I can't interest you in a little apricot chaser?"

Eating fruit out of a dumpster was bad enough...fruit that was fuzzy to begin with seemed twice as unappealing. "Really, I'm fine. In fact, I've exceeded my fruit quota for the day—and you know what they say: fruity is as fruity does." Okay, I'm pretty sure no one ever said that. Cameras make me so darned nervous!

Unfortunately, Sherman didn't take the hint. "If you're full up on fruit, then maybe what you need is protein." He looped an arm through mine so I could see where he was aiming his camera. The alleyway swung wildly for a moment, past the foot soak lady's garage, and then landed on another dumpster two doors down. "Luckily for us, there's a wealth of protein right at our fingertips."

I struggled to recall what the other little shop might have been, but Yuri must've been one step ahead of me, because he gave a strangled little groan. "He is eating dogs!"

"Your foreign friend has a crazy sense of humor," Sherman said.

"Oh, you know Russians..." I said vaguely, straining to disengage.

But lifting all those dumpster lids had given Sherman's wiry arm incredible strength. "Freegans are known to utilize roadkill—especially when it's fresh—but most of them draw the line at dogs." Most? "Besides, there are no dogs here. Only dog biscuits!"

You know your day is circling the drain when the suggestion to chow down on dog treats comes as a relief—to me, anyhow. Not Yuri. He may be heroic in the face of certain doom...but he's phenomenally easy to squick.

To Sherman, I said, "I'll stick with people-food, thanks."

"Nonsense! The biscuits here are a gourmet product, made only with top-quality bone meal and the highest grade of suet!" Sherman let go of my arm to flip up the dumpster lid—and when he did, Yuri grabbed the back of my jacket so hard he lifted me off my feet. For a big guy, Yuri can move awfully fast. We were out of that alley in three seconds flat.

Too bad that was nowhere near enough time to escape the crunchy chewing sounds that followed in our wake.

YURI

7

Although I was sorely in need of fresh air, Dixon and I soon realized we had ended up farther from home than either of us cared to walk. Me, because I did not wish to wear through my shoes, and Dixon, because even after what we'd just witnessed, he somehow found himself hungry. Luckily, we were not far from his parents' house...and even Florica's cooking would look like a feast compared to the things we'd seen Sherman stuff down his throat.

Once we were sure the competitive eater was not pursuing us, Dixon pulled some wet wipes from his messenger bag and handed one to me. I barely resisted the urge to strip down and swab off my whole body, but managed to stop at the wrists. When I first came to America, I thought wet wipes were ridiculous. But this was not the first time I found myself silently thanking whoever had been responsible for this invention.

Dixon tossed his used wipe into a nearby trash can with a sigh. "I really thought Sherman would be the ideal candidate given that he was already on the radar in Pinyin Bay. But there's famous...and then there's infamous!"

I shuddered. "How could he actually swallow such things?"

"He has no taste buds." What? "Anyway, lucky for us we found out about his Blig-Blog channel before it was too late. If we picked him as a candidate, Uncle Fonzo never would've lived it down."

Perhaps Fonzo should find his own candidate. Then again, I trusted someone I'd chosen myself over whoever he might come up with, so having this job foisted on us may have been for the best.

As we turned down his parents' street, Dixon cocked his head and said, "I don't hear any hollering. I'll admit, I was concerned when I saw how quickly Mom and Dad skedaddled from the pancake house. D'you suppose that means this whole kee-poo business is settled?"

"Hard to say. Whatever we do, we must be careful not to pick sides. Your family might be close, but Morticia was right. Fighting over the next Hand may still do serious damage."

"At the very least, it'll hurt someone's feelings."

Indeed. "Best to leave the choosing to the *volshebstvo*."

His parents' house did look promisingly sedate as we stepped up to the front porch. True, there was a half-broken lawn chair held up by a cinderblock, and the hanging flower baskets held nothing but dry brown stalks, but this was typical for the Penns' home.

"I sure hope they've worked it all out," Dixon said nervously as I brushed a stray pomegranate seed from the fold of my lapel. It pinged off the welcome mat. "My parents can each be pretty darned persuasive in their own way."

I plucked a stubborn strand of who-knows what from the back of his sleeve, then thought better of it when it disintegrated in my fingers, leaving behind a tacky residue which was surely crawling with microbes and spores.

The door was unlocked and we let ourselves in. I had been prepared for raised voices: taunting, bickering—all of it friendly enough, though still heartfelt. What we heard instead was a sound like the kitchen being ransacked.

We found Florica Penn standing on a chair which creaked under her weight as she struggled to knock a stockpot off a high shelf with a rolling pin.

"Mom! What're you doing?" Dixon rushed in to steady the chair. I rushed after him to prevent him from being flattened if she toppled over.

"What do you think I'm doing?" Florica swatted at the pot and the chair gave off an ominous groan. Ducking the rolling pin, I tipped the pot off the side of the shelf and caught it in my opposite hand. Once Florica was safely on the floor—leaving me to wonder how successful I might be in hiding all the chairs so she didn't try such a thing again—she pulled off the lid and flipped the pot over. A bunch of leathery wishbones, an old balsa wood airplane and a stack of canceled checks fell out. She stared at the pile for a long moment, then swept it all in again and handed the stockpot to me to put right back where I'd found it.

"No kee-poo?" Dixon said.

Florica sighed. "Obviously not. Otherwise I'd be rubbing your father's nose in it right now instead of excavating this darned kitchen!"

Even a fool could see we had blundered right into the situation we'd both agreed to avoid. I wanted nothing to do with this kee-poo. Not until the matter of the Hand's ascension was settled and done. I wanted Dixon there even less. He is deeply attached to each of his parents. To help one would leave him in a mad scramble to keep from showing favoritism. There was no way to please both of them, so it was best to help neither.

Florica said, "Your father is convinced the kee-poo will fall from the sky—like the feather in a Quilling Ceremony." She tapped her temple shrewdly. "But I've figured out that the kee-poo is one of those things that's been right under your nose all along, but you only realize it's there when the time is right."

I told Dixon, "If Johnny is not here, we should call Sabina to pick us up—"

"Hold on a sec." Dixon cocked his head and asked his mother, "You're saying you think it's already in the house? How big are we talking—the size of a pea? A grape? A watermelon?"

"None of those things," she said. "It's not a tumor. You can't use fruit as your point of comparison."

Dixon shrugged. "It's been a fruity kind of afternoon."

And not in a good way.

"I wonder why people do that?" Dixon said. "With the fruit, I mean. Would it be any more comforting to hear your growth is the size of a baseball?"

"Dixon," I said. "Stop distracting your mother. She has things to do."

Casually, Florica drifted between Dixon and the dining room door. And there was no getting around that woman unless she conceded to let you pass. "You know...this search would go a lot faster with three pairs of hands."

If it were anyone other than family, I would glare at her in stony silence until she stood aside, and then remove myself from the situation. But I cared what Dixon's mother thought of me, which meant I had to be...nice. Or at least civil. "We all know how the *volshebstvo* operates," I told her. "If you are destined to find the kee-poo, it will happen. Whether I help you turn over all the saucepans or not."

"Maybe," Florica said. "Or maybe the whole point of the ritual is that the person who can drum up the most family support is the one who really deserves to be Hand."

Dixon was thumbing through a gelatin cookbook with a fruit bowl on the cover. "So is it closer to a grapefruit or a lime? A baseball, I mean. Or are we talking more like a small, underripe melon? Wouldn't it be funny if a baseball was more like a banana? That would really spice up the game...and help an enterprising player slide into the thingy where the umpire stands."

"Don't blame him," Florica muttered. "I discouraged him from playing any sports that could potentially screw up his writing hand."

Dixon said, "Have you considered the possibility that the kee-poo is a banana?"

"Now I have," his mother said. "And the answer is no."

"Are you sure? Because when you think about it, most fruits are roundish, but not bananas. And they're really the only fruit you can hold up to your ear and pretend you're talking on a telephone—just think how silly you'd look trying something like that with a cantaloupe. So if you're searching for something unique—"

"Dixon," she said testily, "it's not a banana."

With great effort, Dixon clamped his lips shut to stem his argument. Though I could see in his eyes that he was not entirely convinced.

"Listen," Florica said. "I know you don't want to play favorites, but hear me out. Your father is incredibly set in his ways. Every morning, he eats the same boiled egg and rye toast for breakfast. He's been cycling through the same three neckties for so long they've come back in style again. And every time he opens a bottle of booze, he tells the same awful joke."

Dixon smiled softly. "Liquor? I hardly know 'er."

"That's the one." Florica sighed. "Don't get me wrong, your father is steady and reliable. He's a good man. But being a Hand is about way more than just showing up on time. You need to be clever and resilient. You need to be creative. Think about all the innovations we've made to the shop. The magazines in the lobby. The tip jar. The arrangement to get all the leftover pizza from the place next door. Whose ideas were they? Mine—all mine. And I accomplished those things in spite of Johnny."

"Those are hardly major decisions," I said.

"No? Just think—how many of last week's meals were pizza?" Florica did have a point. Take-and-bake pizza was a mainstay of our diet. And while it had grown tedious to consume so much mediocre pizza...even Sherman would have approved of the price. "Face it, you two—if it weren't for me, the whole family would starve!"

Or at least need to pay for all our food.

Dixon was wavering—I could tell—but I knew that if he caved in to Florica's demands, he would only end up feeling guilty around his father. "We will help neither you nor Johnny," I said firmly. "What if someone had rigged Dixon's Quilling Ceremony? It would not have worked, and the quill would be nothing more than a feather. But even more importantly, if he'd bonded with a different quill already, the *volshebstvo* would not have been able to quill him in his time of greatest need."

Dixon chimed in, "Besides, Mom, don't you always say the best way to help someone is to let them handle things themselves?"

Only to discourage them from asking her help to begin with. But Florica Penn had been tripped up by one of her own sayings, so we were able to call for a ride and extricate ourselves before she dredged up any more reasons we should side with her.

8

The Buick pulled up with Vano at the wheel and Sabina beside him, fanning herself furiously with a piece of junk mail, looking very sweaty, disgruntled and pregnant. "Boy, what a relief that you guys called and gave us an excuse to leave," she told us. "My dad's been driving me nuts ever since the whole false alarm business."

"Your father cares about you," I said.

"Well, sure—but that's not it. Ever since Glenda figured out I'm not seeing some dumb Handless doctor, she's been blowing up his phone with advice."

"Isn't that a good thing?" Dixon asked. "Medical advice doesn't come cheap—er, so I've heard."

"Maybe not," Vano said. "But Fonzo's worried that once he and Glenda start talking, the two of them might pick up again where they left off."

"I like Glenda," Dixon said.

Sabina rolled her eyes. "Only because she gives you erasers shaped like little cars."

"Just that one time. And it was a tiny roller skate. Not a car."

Sabina ignored this. "She's not like the floozies Dad normally dates, so he finds her intimidating."

I wondered what this said about Sabina's mother...and decided it was better not to comment.

Sabina went on. "Learn to time my contractions, she says. Stay hydrated, she says. Get up and walk around, she says."

If there were any doubt Glenda had sent those messages, the fact that she recommended things like walking, looking at a watch, and drinking water would have convinced me she was the source.

Vano said, "But Glenda's not the only one we've heard from. Nana pulled some strings—a *lot* of strings—and the midwife will have her bail set in the morning."

Sabina fanned harder. "And lemme tell you—what a relief *that* is. A Handless hospital might be fine for sprained elbows and freak skywriting accidents, but I don't plan on going anywhere near it when I pop out this baby."

Sabina might think she was being rebellious...but was she? Or was this just an example of the way traditions become ingrained?

I would need to trust that Sabina's care would fall into the hands of the best person for the job...though I've never been much good at trusting.

Vano took us to Shirque Mansion, where he and Sabina would be spending the night hiding from Glenda's helpful advice, then handed off the Buick to us. The family has gotten more than its fair share of use from that car, but apparently, it is indestructible. The only part of the car which has totally given up the ghost is the driver side seat—and since the Buick is considered "classic," the cost of repairing it would be enough to buy an entire used car, so the family makes do.

The springs in the seat had become unbearable, but removing them left the driver falling through to the floor. Tennis balls had been jammed over the sharp ends to prevent anyone from being impaled, with duct tape holding the balls in place. A nylon seat from a lawn chair was lashed over the top with plastic zip ties. The tennis balls could be felt, even through the chair seat, but even the thinnest cushion raised the driver too high.

No one knows where the afghan came from that now topped off the whole ensemble. Either that, or no one would admit to making the thing. It was simply that ugly. Scraps of cheap yarn, bits of string, and random lengths of twine had been crocheted into a haphazard assemblage of distorted squares, each with a lopsided flower in the center.

Russians divide the spectrum of color differently than our English-speaking counterparts. Yet there were some colors in this afghan which did not seem to exist in either language. This was the case in the stray bit of yarn sticking to Dixon as he emerged from the car.

I plucked it off his rump and let a passing breeze carry it away.

Naturally, Dixon could not let such a gesture go without remarking on it. He planted his palms on the hood of the car, arched his back, and canted his posterior in my direction. "Are you sure there's nothing else you need to grab?"

Back at Precious Greetings—back when Dixon was nothing more than a naive young man Emery Flint was hoping to entrap—had anyone asked if his attitude would grate on my nerves, I would not have even deigned to answer. *Of course* I could never tolerate such silly, unbridled flirtatiousness. And yet, somehow his playful resolve wore me down. In fact, it has come to pass that I do not merely tolerate Dixon's lighthearted affection.

I live for it.

I fit myself over his body, just loosely enough for him to turn in my arms and drape his wrists over my shoulders. Although my eyes had closed, I could tell that when our lips met...he was smiling.

We hastened upstairs. Pausing only to refill Meringue's dish (just in case her carrying on proved to be particularly distracting) we headed straight for the bedroom.

Dixon often has many ideas for "spicing up" our love life. I have learned not to dismiss them out of hand, no matter how outrageous. While many of his crazy schemes are as ridiculous as they sound, some of them prove to be well worth the effort.

Tonight, though, we dispensed with the role-play and repurposed household items, and made love with our fingers laced together and our eyes open.

Afterwards, we lay with one another, Dixon trailing a fingertip along the tattoos on my chest. He would be the first to speak. He always was. But tonight, he took an unusually long time to gather his thoughts. When finally he did, he said, "I can tell you're not too keen on the whole midwife thing. And I just wanted to say...thanks for letting my cousin be the one to make that call."

Dixon may come off as an airhead, but every now and then he reminds me that he truly is paying attention. I caught his hand and gave it a squeeze. "I am not in the habit of forcing my help where it is not welcome. What is more difficult is withholding help from your mother. She has been good to me." Better than my own.

"Some people underestimate my mom. But when she's got her mind set on something, look out!"

"The apple does not fall far from the tree."

Dixon absently traced an invisible flourish around my ink. "It wouldn't be fair to cave in to either of my parents, not to mention the fact that if we did, we'd be going against the wishes of the head of the circuit."

I kissed his knuckles. "Then turn your thoughts away from it and don't let it trouble you. Focus instead on what we can do—namely, finding a mayor."

"A mayor who doesn't get his jollies rooting around in the trash! What we need is someone respectable."

Given the circles in which we ran...finding anyone even remotely "respectable," at least by Handless standards, would be quite a challenge. My customers were fellow Spellcrafters, so they would never stand a chance, even if they did agree to run. And Dixon's were even worse: the desperate Handless who'd commission a cut-rate Crafting so shoddy it would need to be unmade.

I was marveling over the fact that between the two of us, we could not come up with even one upstanding person when I reached for a glass of water on the nightstand, knocking off a tiny object which bounced just once, then settled.

When I peered over the side of the bed, I spied it there on the floor: an eraser shaped like a roller skate. Dixon poked his head up over my shoulder and caught his breath. "Yuri...are you thinking what I'm thinking?"

He loves asking me this. And I suppose I like being asked, since he only does so when we are of one mind. I nodded. "Who would possibly be more respectable than a doctor?"

Bright and early the next morning—closer to noon, actually, since we were distracted by a new dance Meringue had invented—we headed back to the hospital to speak to Glenda.

"Now, let's get our cover story straight," Dixon said as we pulled into the lot. "You're an heir to the Russian throne in exile, and I'm your bodyguard...and while we can't be certain, it's possible assassins dusted your light fixtures with a drug that can be absorbed through your fingerprints."

"Dixon...."

"Not a lethal drug, mind you—we don't want them to airlift you to St. Louis before we get to talk to Dr. Slaughter—but something with the potential to cause wicked hallucinations."

"Dixon...."

"And when I give the signal, you can start acting like you see animals popping up in the lobby. What kind of animals do they have in Russia? Ooh, I know, Siberian tigers!"

"Dixon!" I snapped—and he paused, eyes alight with visions of tigers traipsing through the lobby of his mind. "First of all, there has not been a Russian monarch since the Romanov dynasty. Second, they can plainly see our truck from the front desk, and no Russian prince would even deign to spit on such a vehicle. And third...we were just here yesterday. They are bound to recognize us."

Dixon considered all of this, then said, "So what you're saying is, they'd totally buy me as your bodyguard."

"Come," I said. "We will go in through the front door—as

ourselves—and ask to see Glenda." Dixon gazed wistfully at a small plastic spring he'd been planning to tuck behind his ear as his "bodyguard" disguise—I think it was once part of a keychain—but thankfully, I'd convinced him to leave it in the glove box.

Fortunately, I myself had never needed to make use of Pinyin Bay's hospital. While it was well-equipped by Russian standards, more like a private hospital than a state institution, I was leery of all the red tape involved in seeking treatment.

We approached the admissions desk under the watchful eye of the nurse we'd spoken to yesterday. What a relief I had not acquiesced to the bodyguard scheme. All we had to do was walk up to the desk, as *ourselves*, and—

I glanced sideways at Dixon. "Are you limping?"

"I'm not limping! You're limping."

"You're both limping," the nurse said. She picked up her phone. "I'll call for some wheelchairs."

"No, no, that's okay," Dixon said quickly. "We're fine. We were just hoping to talk to Dr. Slaughter...in a personal capacity. Not professional. So there's no need for you to scan my insurance card—which I guarantee is perfectly legitimate."

The nurse shrugged and checked her computer. "You're in luck. Dr. Slaughter is on her lunch break, so you can find her in the hospital cafeteria."

"I was not limping," I grumbled as we headed for the elevator.

Dixon did not seem to notice. He lived for reconnaissance missions such as these. "The more I think about Dr. Slaughter, the more excited I find myself."

"Do not get your hopes up." It was never any use to say this to Dixon, but I did anyhow. "Why should she give up her medical career to serve as mayor?"

"She doesn't have to give it up entirely, just take a little hiatus. Plus, I'll bet if you put together all the mayoring Mayor Dunce did during his back-to-back terms, it would hardly fill a year. Uncle Fonzo always said Glenda was a smart lady."

"I believe the phrase was, *Too smart for her own good.*"

"She might very well be able to figure out how to keep her job at the hospital, plus do all the mayor business in her spare time. Not only is she a well-respected member of Handless society, but she appeals to so many different demographics. Kids. Moms. And middle-aged men with naughty doctor fantasies."

True. But more importantly, she'd shown herself to be friendly to the Spellcraft community. Handless tend to either love Spellcraft or hate it. Many are downright fearful. And while I had never known Glenda to commission any Craftings for herself, not once did I hear her make a snide remark about our profession. Despite the fact that she was far too good for Fonzo Penn, she'd always treated him—indeed, the whole family—with nothing but respect.

I did not wish to get my hopes up, either. And yet, if we were able to convince her she could serve more of her community as a politician than as a doctor, she did seem like a very good choice.

And the Penn family could be quite persuasive.

The hospital cafeteria was not too crowded, and I found myself eager to have a meal other than take-and-bake pizza. We spotted Glenda at the salad bar and rushed over to grab our plastic trays and join her before she got away.

It turned out there was no need to hurry—by the time we reached her, she had not moved whatsoever. As we slapped down a tray on either side of hers, she blinked as if coming out of a trance. "Oh! Hi, guys. How's Sabina doing?"

"She's fine," Dixon said reassuringly. "Absolutely great."

"Good—I'm glad to hear it. First pregnancies can be a real challenge for the new mommy. And with Fonzo's phone acting up again, I wasn't sure he could relay my messages."

"Actually," Dixon said, "We're not here about my cousin. What we were hoping to ask you was...ah...."

As he spoke, his attention drifted to the salad bar. I followed his gaze. The refrigerated case was filled with all the things I've come to expect at a low-budget American cafeteria. A few bins of lettuce, some underripe tomatoes, imitation bacon bits and squeeze bottles of ranch dressing. But unlike most American salad bars, the items in this case had been meticulously arranged. Each ingredient was color coordinated from left to right, with the brightest greens on the left, blueberries and red cabbage next, then moving through the rainbow for reds, pinks, orange and yellows, and finally ending on the right with a miniature rainbow of artificial candies. I wondered who on earth would take the time to arrange things so fastidiously, then saw that Glenda had placed an identical array of produce on her plate—and was situating the final green peas a single pea at a time.

She handled her tongs with great precision.

An orderly leaned in and whispered to me, "Just work around her. If you wait for her to get out of your way, your lunch break will be over before you even get to the cash register. Ask me how I know."

Glenda scowled at the salad bar and swapped the bowl of peas with the bin of sliced cucumber.

I scooped up some hard-boiled eggs while Dixon tonged a wedge of iceberg lettuce onto his plate, then drenched it with salad dressing and bacon bits. Once he did, we paid and adjourned to a nearby table to wait for Glenda to stop messing about.

The orderly was right. She fussed at the salad bar so long, Dixon and I were done eating by the time she finally joined us.

Dixon eyed Glenda's plate. The salad ingredients were arranged like a clock, one wedge per color, with each division so straight it could have been made with a ruler. "Gee," he said. "That's some salad."

Glenda paused with her fork partway to her mouth and scowled. "Too much kale? I can't tell you how often I misjudge how much kale I'll need. It always fluffs up and shifts around on the walk to the table. Except when it deflates."

"I'm sure you have just the right amount of kale!" exclaimed Dixon...who, in all the time I'd known him, had never allowed kale to pass his lips.

"I'm not so sure," Glenda said, eyeing the salad bar like she was considering a return trip. "It looks a little on the small side."

My patience was running thin. "Just eat a bit of the others to make them even."

Glenda looked again at her plate, baffled. "That does seem like it would work. And it would be so much easier than trying to pay for a single leaf of kale. But when I eat, invariably the food moves around, and so it's even harder to tell when the segments are uneven. Although if I put everything on its own plate...no, no, that won't fly. The cafeteria manager gets so testy when you take more than one or two extra plates. Maybe I should have gone with the soup...."

"I'm sure the salad will be great," Dixon said. "Especially if you actually eat it."

Glenda smiled softly. "You sound so much like your uncle—always happy to put a positive spin on the situation and help me to stop overthinking everything. Not very realistic, in my opinion. But still...the world needs people who see the glass as half-full."

Unlike Glenda, who undoubtedly lost sleep pondering how to ensure whether the fill level was at exactly the halfway point.

She ate a radish slice and a few bean sprouts, then said, "Now, what was it you wanted to ask me about?"

Dixon met my eyes and I gave my head a subtle shake. If Glenda was this indecisive about her salad, how could she ever hope to handle all the responsibilities of running a city? "You know what?" he said brightly, "Never mind. There was a little project I was going to pitch to you, but I can see you've got a lot on your plate."

Alarmed, Glenda looked down at her salad.

Dixon hopped up and nudged me in the shoulder. "We'll let you get back to your lunch," he told her.

Glenda gave us a distracted wave. "Make sure Sabina comes in for her prenatal checkup...and say hi to your uncle for me."

Once Dixon and I were safely back in the truck, we both let out a long, uneasy breath. He said, "Guess that goes to show you don't really know someone until you watch them eat a salad."

"Is that one of your mother's sayings?"

"If it's not, it should be. I could see how attention to detail would be important for a doctor. But could you imagine Dr. Slaughter trying to run the city? She'd be out on the lawn with a yardstick and a pair of cuticle scissors instead of...whatever it is that mayors are supposed to do."

I nodded. "And even if she could be convinced to focus only on her own duties, she would surely overthink everything. At least you could say one thing for Dunce: the man knew how to make a decision. Even if that decision was always *no*."

DIXON

9

"What a shame," I said wistfully. "Dr. Slaughter would've gotten a real kick out of riding around on a parade float and tossing treats into the crowd. So long as they were sugar-free and presented zero choking hazard."

"It is all for the best," Yuri decided. "No one likes to show up at a parade and end up with a pencil in the eye."

We were debating where to go for second lunch (since salad hardly counted at all) when an urgent text from my cousin came in. *You won't believe what these deadbeats brought over.*

Which deadbeats? Where? Why? Inquiring minds needed to know. And in the course of learning these critical facts, if we were lucky, maybe we'd score some leftover pastry.

A few minutes later, we pulled up the crunchy gravel drive at Shirque Mansion. It was warm and the sun was high, so Sabina and Vano were ensconced on the shady porch with a tall, sweaty pitcher of iced tea and—yes!—a big plate of muffins. Not just any old muffins, either. There were pale yellow muffins bursting with fresh blueberries. Cornmeal muffins with a crust of crunchy sugar baked into the top. Chocolate muffins bursting with chocolate chips still warm enough to be gooey. It was a cornucopia of baked delight, so good I wished I had three hands to fully appreciate the—

"Dixon!" Sabina snapped. "Stop stuffing your face for half a second and get a load of these presents."

"What presents?" I said...blowing out a few crumbs.

"Kinning presents." My cousin rolled her eyes. "What else?"

"What is this Kinning?" Yuri asked...also through a mouthful of muffin.

Vano explained. "Traditionally, when a couple is expecting, the circuit provides them with three gifts: food, clothing and shelter."

"That sounds useful," Yuri said.

Sabina snorted. "Oh yeah?" She plucked an adorable yellow onesie out of a flowered gift bag in a fanfare of crumpled tissue paper. "Then how do you account for *this* monstrosity from Venus Monger?"

Um...was that a trick question? "Looks fine to me."

"Other side," Vano murmured.

"Oh, right." Sabina turned it around. The front of the cute little outfit was emblazoned with *Try Monger's Tonic!* in humongous block lettering.

"Good thing babies can't read," Yuri said.

Sabina tossed it down in disgust. "And if that's not bad enough, take a look at what apparently passes for food around here." She pulled out a crumpled bag from Bam Burger from under the table and waved it in disgust. "This is what Ladin Silver dropped off. Not only was it from the five-dollar value menu...but half the fries were eaten!"

Unfortunately, I can't say I was particularly surprised. Spellcrafters are known for their ingenuity, not their generosity.

Sabina said, "Picking out the givers is a Hand-job—" people really needed to stop calling it that... "so it was up to my dad to figure out who'd cough up the best loot. You think he would've put a little more thought into it. What the heck! I hate to think what the next bozo will try to pass off as a gift."

As she finished complaining, a distinctive sound reached our ears: the sound of a squeaky wheel. And it was getting louder—a metal on metal squalling that sounded like nails on a chalkboard... if that chalkboard happened to have a truly persistent itch.

The squeaking reached a painful peak, and as it did, a baby buggy rounded the corner—with Drew Draws at the helm. The new Seer paused at the edge of the lawn, snatched a glittery purple cowboy hat from his head, and fanned himself vigorously. "Well, would you look at the bunch of you," he called over, "with nothing better to do than lounge around on your wicker furniture and soak up the shade while the rest of us are hard at work."

The "rest of us" meaning him, I guess—if you considered wheeling around a squeaky buggy to be work. With a big, annoyed shove, he plowed the buggy across the lawn, accompanied by the dissonant chatter of the wonky wheel. That thing was so loud, it was like he had his own soundtrack. Though what sort of movie it might appear in, I couldn't decide. Maybe some sort of experimental art house film. In which case, the sequined hat and short shorts suddenly made a lot more sense.

Halfway to the porch, the baby carriage gave an especially loud squeak, then hunkered down stubbornly in place. With a snippy sigh, Drew strutted around the buggy. We all found somewhere else to look when he bent over to peer underneath. But when it finally felt safe to open my eyes, I discovered he'd whipped out a familiar little jar. "Ran into an interesting lady over by the T-shirt kiosk in the mall while I was shopping," he explained. Before I could break it to him that Monger's Tonic was even less useful than snake oil, he'd dipped in a forefinger to slather some on the offending wheel.

He gave the buggy a push...and somehow, against all odds, the squeaking had vanished.

Once that was settled, he turned to survey the yard. "And what's with the half-painted furniture strewn all over the place? What're you lazybones waiting for—Christmas?" I was tempted to interject that we didn't celebrate Christmas...but he was on a roll. "Sabina's as big as a house. She'll pop any day now. You don't want to be running around with a wet paintbrush when the stork shows up!"

Without waiting for any of us to agree, he proceeded to crack open a paint can and start stirring.

I hadn't really given much thought to finishing the furniture right that very moment, since it's a real challenge to eat and paint at the same time. But because I'd feel guilty about lounging around while Drew did all the work, I finished my muffin, and then my other muffin—and then headed over to pick up a paint brush and assist. Vano joined us, and after he polished off the last muffin, so did Yuri, leaving my cousin to supervise from the porch.

As we painted, Drew asked, "So, have you settled on a name for your baby yet?"

Sabina (who never much cared for getting "the third degree") said, "That's for me to know and you to find out."

Vano explained to Drew, "A lot of Spellcrafters use the father's surname as the first kid's first name. But I wouldn't saddle anyone with the name Shirque Penn."

"That's a relief," I said. "Especially with literally every other name in the world to choose from. Just keep in mind, words have power—and the name of a Scrivener carries a lot of weight. It's got to be powerful, memorable and as deep as the ocean. A name with gravitas. A name for the ages."

"Dixon," Sabina said, exasperated, "we've been through this a million times. The baby is not going to be named after you."

Well, you can't blame a guy for trying.

Back when Yuri and Vano first dragged all that baby stuff outside, it had looked more like a bunch of spare parts you'd unearth in my father's basement than a pile of furniture. I'll admit, my hopes hadn't run very high. But now, with four of us industriously scrubbing away the grunge and applying a fresh coat of paint, something surprisingly good was beginning to take shape. Without all the dust and cobwebs, without all the garishly clashing finishes, the old furniture looked new again, with elegant lines and good bones.

"It's amazing what a coat of white paint will do," I said proudly.

Drew rolled his eyes. "You don't know the half of it. Furniture isn't the only thing getting whitewashed around here. Everyone's buzzing about the upcoming election. Apparently Pinyin Bay polls are showing most voters leaning toward a convicted felon."

Sabina waved his concern away. "You know how arbitrary Handless laws can be. Swing a bat and hit a baseball, and you're a big ol' hero. But aim it at a few ugly mailboxes instead...."

Lucky for my cousin, she'd been a minor when the whole mailbox fiasco took place.

Drew said, "Normally, I wouldn't look askance at a man with a record. Most of the boardwalk folk I know have spent some time in the hoosegow. But those were for crimes of passion...or intoxication. Having a white-collar criminal represent my fair city, though, is beyond the pale."

Gooseflesh raised on my forearms as Yuri asked, low and dangerous, "Who exactly is this felon?"

Drew shrugged dismissively. "Some ne'er-do-well by the name of Emery Flint."

Everyone went silent—everyone but Drew. My cousin must've told Vano about what happened to her dad, because even easygoing Vano looked spooked. As Drew rambled on about why anyone dumb enough to get caught filing a fake tax return was obviously not mayoral material, I kept my eye on Yuri.

Back when Emery Flint bamboozled away my uncle's quill, our whole family had suffered at the loss of our Hand. But Yuri had been the one whose whole life was completely hijacked when he was enslaved by a nasty piece of Spellcraft. For an entire year, Yuri had been directly under Mr. Flint's thumb...and it had left a pretty big thumbprint behind.

Drew took in our stunned silence and said, "Is this another one of those Spellcrafter *faux pas* no one's deigned to inform me about?"

I said, "We're all, ah, familiar with Emery Flint."

"Too familiar," my cousin added bitterly.

Drew tossed his paintbrush in a can of thinner and dusted off his hands. "Well, you're about to get to know him in a whole new light—as the Pinyin Bay's first new mayor in decades—unless you can come up with someone better to oppose him."

With that, he bid his goodbyes and headed back home, but I could barely dredge up the effort to wave goodbye. I was too busy reeling in horror at the thought of Emery Flint taking over the whole of Pinyin Bay!

10

"Think, Yuri!" I said desperately. "There's gotta be someone we know who'd make a good Mayor. Especially when literally anyone else in the city would be better than Emery Flint."

We sat at our kitchen card table, facing each other over an ice cream carton that contained nothing but some sticky chocolate residue and two used spoons. It was well past midnight, and our conversation was punctuated by the occasional annoyed grumble from beneath the blanket covering Meringue's cage.

Yuri glared so hard at the tablecloth I'm surprised he didn't burn a smoking hole into the plastic. "The moment that man's name came up, everything was driven from my mind but the thought of tracking him down and making him sorry he even thought of running for mayor."

"And I share your righteous indignation one hundred percent! Not just on your behalf, either. If Mr. Flint was in power, our whole circuit would be in jeopardy. Right now, the laws and statutes on the books in Pinyin Bay are slanted in the favor of Spellcrafters—thanks to years of persuasion, plus the fact that Mayor Dunce was never one to revise so much as a stray comma. But if Emery Flint had his say, then any advantages Spellcrafters might have would go up in smoke."

"It is even worse than that," Yuri said firmly. "Emery Flint is the prime example of what happens when a Handless becomes obsessed with the *volshebstvo*. He went mad trying to take the power for himself—and he did not care who suffered because of his ambition. He would not just eradicate the laws which favor Spellcrafters. He would ensure we were actively persecuted!"

"We need a candidate. Someone who isn't a freegan...and who doesn't overthink every little thing. But who?"

"The Pinyin Bay Perch?" Yuri suggested.

"Could you imagine him on a billboard? People would love it. Unfortunately, it's hardly ever the same person twice inside the costume." I scratched my chin. "How about Crouch?"

"From the boardwalk?"

I nodded. "He's got a pretty unique look, what with the grease-paint and all. And I've never seen him eat from the garbage."

"But he would insist on giving his campaign speech in gestures—and we both know he is a terrible mime."

Not only were we running out of time, we were running out of options. We dealt with lots of different people on a daily basis, though. Maybe there was someone we'd simply overlooked. "I know! Let's go through our camera rolls. I'll bet we find someone who's perfect for the job."

It was a great idea...in theory. Until I realized that most of my shots featured either Meringue or Yuri. He glanced at my phone as I flipped through and narrowed his eyes. "Must you take a picture of me every time I bend over?"

"What can I say? I'm smitten with your badonkadonk." I turned my attention to Yuri's phone...which was currently showing a photo of a cinderblock wall. "Whereas you, apparently, have a thing for masonry."

Yuri scowled. "It is for my painting. I was making note of the way the light hit the texture."

Turned out that for every shot of Yuri's backside I'd taken, he'd snapped a photo of some random inanimate object. And neither a rusty farm implement nor Yuri's sexy butt stood much chance of running against Emery Flint.

We both continued flipping, growing increasingly more desperate. And we both paused on a shot of the same event.

Last winter, Practical Penn had celebrated twenty-five years at its current location. It was a pretty big to-do, not only with music and munchies, but plenty of coupons, games and raffles designed to keep our clientele coming back for more. Handless don't usually spend more time in the shop than they absolutely have to, but the silver anniversary shindig had drawn a pretty sizable mob.

"I have never seen the shop so crowded," Yuri said.

"Me neither. No doubt one of these Handless can give Emery Flint a run for his money."

"And if they are one of your family's customers, then they will be sympathetic to Spellcraft."

It was a great plan...until we zoomed in on the photos and took a good look at who those customers actually were. Mr. Miller, who was always trying to Craft away his bald spot. Mrs. Geist, who used Spellcraft in lieu of actual dentistry—with mixed results. And the shady guy who gave us a different assumed name every time he bought a Crafting—without so much as a halfhearted disguise to try and fool us.

Yuri pushed his phone away in disgust. "The only person in these photos with half a brain is your father. And no Spellcrafter would dream of taking the position."

"Not to mention the fact that Dad can barely stay awake for a campaign commercial, let alone a political debate." And the only position he truly wanted was that of the family's Hand. I thumbed through my own photos of the event, admiring the way my dad worked the room. "He sure is popular with the Handless, though."

"If he cannot run, then maybe he knows someone who can."

The next morning, we fortified ourselves with cold pizza and headed over to my folks' house hoping to catch them before work so we could pick my father's brain. Unfortunately, the Monte Carlo was gone and the house was quiet. We were just about to head over to the shop when we heard something tapping just under our feet... and a distant voice calling out, "Hello? Is somebody up there?"

"Dad? Is that you?"

"Dixon! What a relief! Come help me—I'm stuck!"

I pried the spare key out from under the dried-up birdbath, and Yuri and I hurried down to the basement to see what had happened.

The basement is the home of my father's stash. If you need something, anything at all, chances are he can find one he's trash-picked somewhere within its piles. That something might be dusty, outdated, and missing a few key parts—but it sure beats paying cash money.

A visit to the stash can be a pretty serious expedition. I personally don't venture in without a few granola bars and a spare bottle of water. But somehow Dad had ended up way on the far side of the stash—and it was barely 8am!

We found my father trapped behind a big pile of whatnot, with nothing but his legs sticking out. Rubber and metal, plastic and wood. No single thing was particularly awkward or heavy. But together, the mass had fallen in on itself just so, and Dad had no leverage to push himself free.

"Be sure never to introduce him to Sherman," Yuri said softly as my father flailed around in the pile. "He does not need to learn any new tricks."

"Don't worry. Dad's a picky eater. No freeganistic tendencies whatsoever...aside from the take-and-bake pizza." I hurried over to my father's feet and began the process of excavation. "Dad, I haven't seen you delve this deep in years. Good thing you landed near the front porch, otherwise we never would've heard you calling. But what're you doing this far into the stash?"

"Oh, just rooting around for a spare pair of galoshes...you never know when it might rain."

"He is looking for the kee-poo," Yuri said.

I nudged aside a set of bongo drums and gingerly lifted off a tarnished chandelier. "Is that true, Dad? Why not just say so?"

My father sighed, sending some yellowed fragments of sheet

music aflutter. "Because your mother was the one who insisted the kee-poo could be right under our very noses...and I don't want to give her the satisfaction of knowing that I think she might be onto something. You know how she loves to gloat."

"Don't worry," I told him. "What happens in the stash, stays in the stash."

A hand thrust up from the slide of random household objects like a toddler breaking the surface of a ball pit. Yuri leaned in, grabbed my dad by the forearm, and gave him a solid tug. He popped free with a great clatter of fishing lures and ping pong balls.

"Phew!" Dad shook a few flecks of sawdust from his hair. "Now that I'm on my feet again, we can get down to business. Whaddaya suppose this kee-poo looks like? Is it shaped like a key?"

I hated saying no to my dad, but fair is fair. "Dad, we can't—"

"Or is it shaped like—?"

"Forget it," Yuri announced. "We did not help Florica and we will not help you."

"Welp. You can't blame a guy for trying." My father picked up a clothes hanger and poked at a nearby stack of picnic baskets, which creaked alarmingly. "But I will say this: you two would do well to remember that the Hand represents both of you, too. And your mother is pretty sharp. Not just her mind—but her tongue. I know enough to give her the benefit of the doubt, but she's the love of my life. Casual acquaintances, though? I wouldn't count on it. Schmoozing is a big part of the Hand-job." Oh, come on. Him too? "Can we really afford to alienate the other families in the circuit by having such a blunt and outspoken member as our Hand?"

Dad had a point. I couldn't count the number of random people who'd come away from an encounter with my mother in tears. Though, to be fair, you'd expect a bouncer to be made of much sterner stuff.

My father tried his best to win us over to his side—and I had to admit, he really was a persuasive guy—but thanks to Yuri, I held my ground and left the choosing of the Hand to the kee-poo...which meant dusting my dad off, driving him to the shop and making a quick getaway.

Unfortunately, my neutrality had come with a cost. Without my dad's suggestions, we were still at a loss as to finding a decent mayoral candidate. Vano had been sending periodic messages to find out when his Nana could expect our candidate...and those texts were starting to get a little desperate.

Yuri said, "Either Sherman or Glenda would be better than Emery Flint, and we are running out of time. We must simply get on with it: pick one, throw our support behind them and hope for the best."

"Okay, let's think this through." I pulled out my phone and did a quick search. "According to the hospital's website, Dr. Slaughter was awarded the Bumpus Award for Emergency Room Excellence, and a special acknowledgement for the hospital's neatest sutures. According to her online reviews, people find her to be smart, attentive and thorough. Maybe with enough coaching she could make it through a debate."

"With Emery Flint?" Yuri demanded. "He would clean the floor with her. Glenda is too concerned with fairness and facts, while Flint would say or do anything to gain power. Even you and I fell for his lies. How could we expect the public to be any the wiser?"

"Unfortunately," I admitted, "you do have a point. Sherman, on the other hand, is super confident and outspoken, and he seems like he could actually stand up to Mr. Flint." I pulled up Sherman's Blig-Blog channel. "Maybe his dumpster diving isn't anywhere near as queasy-making if you can't actually smell the rotting fruit."

I tapped his profile picture and immediately my phone was filled with a horrifying closeup of a gnawed pineapple core framed by a lush beard, punctuated by moist chewing sounds.

Nope. Pretty queasy, even without the smell.

As I rolled down the passenger window to let in a little fresh air, the next video scrolled up and began to play.

Did you know that each and every day, Pinyin Bay throws out enough bananas to fill three shopping carts?

I was not aware of that fact! You'd think that with the telephone mimicking capabilities, fewer bananas would go to waste.

The camera zoomed in on a grocer putting down a crate of brown bananas in the alley. As he set out a few slip-hazard signs around it, a second voice joined Sherman's. "The problem is, bananas all ripen at once, but most folks only eat one or two at a time. The first few in the bunch are always too green, and the last few are too brown."

"That voice is awfully familiar," I said.

The shot cut to a little kiosk on main street that used to sell umbrellas. They did pretty good business until the owner started cutting corners and getting umbrellas that flipped inside out at the first touch of an errant breeze. As Sherman approached the kiosk, which was now painted a cheerful yellow, he said, "Only the in-between bananas are just right...which is why we realized that what this city needs is a banana exchange!"

Sherman panned his shot across a scattering of bananas—green, yellow and brown. "Take A Banana, Leave A Banana is a nonprofit community effort to minimize food waste and enhance the overall banana experience of Pinyin Bay. The concept is simple: exchange your over- and under-ripe bananas for the ripeness of your choosing. From planning your lunches for the week to making a huge batch of banana bread, the perfect bananas are right at your fingertips at TabLab! And best of all, this service is free, thanks to our generous donor: my good friend Beauregard Irving Fitzgerald."

The camera swung around to the sponsor. And the cheerful, handsome smiling guy in the banana T-shirt was none other than my fellow competitive hot dog eater, Biff. He beamed proudly. "You know me, Sherman, I love nothing better than solving problems! I'm just glad for the opportunity give back to the community."

Blig-Blog played on—more cringeworthy shots of Sherman pawing through refuse—but I was too busy reveling in the sensation of a bold new idea taking hold to be icked out by the spectacle. "Yuri...are you thinking what I'm thinking?"

"That only a fool would dream of touching a banana abandoned by a random stranger?"

"Upstanding. Decisive. Likable. And, most importantly, someone who gets along really well with Spellcrafters. He may not be the sharpest cheese in the deli case, but from where I sit, it looks like our best candidate is...Biff."

Hopefully, Biff would agree.

YURI

I was not entirely convinced we should throw our support behind such a simple-minded man. But in light of the other candidate—far too clever for my comfort—it felt much safer to back someone incapable of manipulation and treachery.

Dixon ran through the video yet again, then said, "The time stamp on this clip is pretty recent. Maybe we can still find Biff over by his banana exchange making sure everything's running smoothly. Or should that be...smoothie?"

That pun did not even merit a roll of the eyes.

We mapped the banana stand's location. "TabLab" was on a quiet corner near an aging car wash which was a notorious spot for extramarital flings. Apparently the cycle was so slow it wore down the paint finish...but it gave you ample time to rearrange your clothing before your car rolled out the other side.

"Do not get your hopes up," I told Dixon. "There is only so much oversight this ridiculous venture of his might need. We're likely to find nothing more than a sticky table scattered with a few half-rotten...."

I trailed off as I turned the corner and spotted the banana

stand—engulfed in a cheerful mob. The kiosk was so crowded, we had to park nearly two blocks away, unheard of in Pinyin Bay. The closer we drew to the banana exchange, the more animated the crowd became. A diverse bunch of people, Handless and Spellcrafter alike, lined up with bananas clutched to their breasts, eager to make a trade.

Dixon said, "Looks like TabLab is a pretty big hit! Just goes to show, never underestimate the power of *free*."

I scanned the crowd with a growing sense of unease. "Why did those people bring folding chairs? And what are they doing with that grill?"

"Tailgating!" Dixon answered my doubtful scowl with a reassuring nod. "I might not be much for sports, but I can graze my way through a parking lot with the best of 'em."

Indeed. It appeared that people had settled in for the long haul. By the time we reached the stand, hints of grilled banana perfumed the air. These people must be reserving their front row seats at a debacle, I decided. Crowds love nothing more than to see someone fail.

The throng was thickest directly around the stand, several bodies deep. I was sure that any moment now, things would turn ugly. Except that even amid the clamor and chaos, everyone looked unaccountably happy.

"Can I take a larger banana than I leave?" someone asked.

Another called out, "A ripeness chart, from green to brown, would really help us make up our minds."

"Is it possible to end up with my original banana if I come back tomorrow?" wondered a third.

How on earth such a simple concept generated so many questions was beyond me. And in the midst of the hubbub stood Biff, looking inexplicably cheerful and impossibly patient.

"Take what you need and leave what you can spare," he told them. "I replenish the bananas every morning if our selection needs a little bolster. The chart is a great idea—I'll tap an expert in PBU's agriculture department and see what they come up with. And does anyone really own a banana, or is it just passing through?"

I waited for the mob to realize Biff was an idiot. A personable idiot, no doubt...but an idiot nonetheless. And yet, the crowd showed no signs of turning on him.

It must be the novelty, I decided. Once the shine wore off, people would not be so enthusiastic. No doubt the car wash owner would agree.

We had worked our way toward the front when a woman clutching an armload of brown bananas bounced off my chest. A banana pinwheeled into the air, but I managed to catch it without squashing the thing. As Dixon made an appreciative murmur about my ninja reflexes, I handed the banana back to the woman. Our eyes locked, and we realized we'd met before.

Joan had been our competition when we were hoping to infiltrate Bruno's Brownerie—and she'd also been the only applicant who could actually bake. "I'm not surprised to run into a fellow baking aficionado here!" she said. "You must've had a sudden urge for banana bread. Isn't it wonderful to be able to find a properly ripe banana at such short notice? I can't imagine going back to the old way of doing things...the strategizing, the planning, the possibility that your bananas will all get eaten as they're ripening on the counter...."

The chance of bananas becoming banana bread in our home without divine intervention was practically zero. But before I could say as much, an uneasy murmur swept through the mob as a police car rolled past...then turned on its flashing lights and pulled over.

Pinyin Bay law enforcement is nothing like Russia. Old habits are hard to break, though, and I saw no reason to abandon a lifetime of caution. In my homeland, corruption is so widespread that bribes are the norm. Here, extortion is much less overt... though it does still exist. Everyone has their price, though it may be intangible, even instinctive. Pinyin Bay officers took their payment in deferential treatment and admiration. They expected to be addressed in a tone of respect—whether they had earned it or not. So, with the right currency—the currency of flattery—they could all be bought. All but the policeman who emerged from the flashing vehicle.

Officer Hotti looked more like a propaganda rendition of a police officer than an actual human being. His jaw was square, his shoulders broad, his gaze alight with intelligence. Even the single curl of dark hair at his forehead looked too perfect to be real.

The crowd parted for Officer Hotti as he strode up to the banana exchange, purposeful and confident. Only once he had passed completely by did people dare to check out his posterior. By the time he reached the banana kiosk, a hush of anticipation had fallen over the crowd. Indeed, even Joan (who could prattle on about baking-related matters forever) had gone silent.

"Who is in charge of this establishment?" Hotti asked in a clear and confident voice.

His tone might have intimidated a smarter man...but Biff apparently saw nothing to be concerned about. "That would be me!"

"This event is taking place in a no-gather zone. I'll have to ask you to break it up before anyone gets hurt."

Undaunted, Biff pulled out a certificate and handed it over to the cop. "Actually, that *would* be a problem—if this particular corner weren't zoned for moderate to heavy foot traffic, which it is. My lawyers worked it all out. So long as we don't add live music, we're good to go."

In Russia, such a reply would be taken as a challenge—one which the challenger had no chance of winning. But Hotti simply read through the paperwork, nodded once, and returned it to Biff.

"And is there any Spellcraft on the premises?"

"I'm not sure," Biff said. "Lots of folks carry around Craftings for luck."

The policeman strode over to a helpful set of instructions posted on the side of the kiosk and lifted the paper gingerly with one finger. "But nothing attached to the stand? People do seem unusually taken with it. There'd better not be any coercion taking place, not on my watch."

Biff was unperturbed. "Never underestimate the drawing power of a good piece of fruit."

"Well, then. Everything seems to be in order." Hotti let the poster flutter back into place, then held out a hand, which Biff shook vigorously. "Welcome to the neighborhood."

The crowd let out a collective sigh of relief as Hotti turned and strode back to his squad car. He paused only once, to tell the tailgaters to move their grill another two feet from the closest building, but that was all.

Dixon surveyed the happy crowd, and his face fell. "It's no use, Yuri. Who would give up something as awesome as this banana exchange to sequester themselves in that stuffy old mayor's office? We'll just have to go with Dr. Slaughter and hope we can talk her out of saving lives."

Normally I would agree—not that a ridiculous banana stand was preferable to City Hall, but that Biff was a terrible choice to begin with. However...something in the way he'd handled the stoic policeman gave me pause.

I said, "I may wonder about Glenda's medical recommendations, but it seems she is able to make clear decisions where doctoring is concerned. However, I suspect running a city would be too far outside her comfort zone. Whereas Biff..." we spied him replenishing the bananas with a smile on his face while the crowd around him scrambled to make their exchanges. I sighed. "Biff is calm under pressure. Probably because he does not know any better—but he is calm nonetheless. He is friendly. Enthusiastic. Popular. But your uncle has never cared for him. Let us hope Fonzo can see past that, for all our sakes."

DIXON

12

Three potential candidates. Each one had a teensy little flaw—okay...a big, honkin' flaw—but they each had their good qualities, too. And wouldn't any one of them be preferable to Emery Flint?

I could only hope the voting public would see it that way.

There was no way I could possibly deal with making that call. Uncle Fonzo would need to choose.

We headed back to the house to tell my uncle what we'd discovered. I'd been hoping to find him in a receptive frame of mind, doing something contemplative like sipping a cup of green tea while he raked designs in a little zen garden...never mind that he doesn't own a zen garden and the only tea-drinker in the house is Yuri. Instead, I came home to a chaos that was nearly at banana-stand levels. The living room was in a tizzy. Uncle Fonzo was yelling out orders. Sabina was yelling even louder orders. And Vano was standing in the corner holding a TV antenna in the air.

"To the right," Sabina snapped. "No, not the upper right, the right-right. Geez, Vano, get with the program!"

"No, no, no, you're making it worse," Uncle Fonzo insisted.

"Obviously it's the davenport blocking the signal! Hold it straight overhead and just tilt it toward the recliner, gently, like you're decanting a fine wine."

"Not this again," Yuri muttered.

Every time it rained, the antenna seemed to drop a channel or two. Never the silly shopping channels or news reports, either, but only the game show and sitcom ones that anyone actually wanted to watch.

"Give me that." Yuri snatched the antenna from Vano's unresisting hands. He jabbed it in various directions while Uncle Fonzo and Sabina called out contradictory suggestions.

"Toward the window," said my uncle.

Sabina countered, "Up high."

"What's so important you can't just stream it later?" I wondered.

"It's that dumb election," my cousin told me. "Thanks to some weird rule they just discovered where it has to be on a Tuesday, they're moving it up nearly a week."

A rule...or a loophole? No self-respecting Spellcrafter in the Pinyin Bay circuit would Craft for Mr. Flint, but he could very well have sweet-talked an out-of-towner into doing his dirty work.

Vano rubbed a shoulder. The antenna does get pretty heavy after a while. "Candidates are being announced on the local news channel as they get on the ballot. At least, that's the idea. But so far, no one's stepped up to challenge Flint."

"About that," I said. "We did have a few options—"

"Higher, Yuri!" Sabina demanded. "C'mon, put your back into it."

Uncle Fonzo mopped his brow. He was using the little yellow onesie from Venus Monger, but he was so frazzled, no one dared call him on it. "So long as it's not Flint, I'm game."

"They are most definitely not Emery Flint," I said. "In fact, we've found three candidates with lots of, er, *potential*. I'm sure that one of them—"

A burst of static came from the TV, and my cousin barked, "Higher, darn it—higher!" When Yuri couldn't figure out a way to extend his arm any further without dislocating his shoulder joint,

Sabina hopped up on a footstool, grabbed the antenna from his hand, and thrust it into the air like the Statue of Liberty. "Like this!"

And with that enthusiastic gesture...we discovered that amniotic fluid truly was nothing at all like peppermint tea.

Vano rushed to Sabina's side so fast his motions were a blur, and he managed to catch her before her knees buckled. "Get hold of the midwife!" he gasped.

Uncle Fonzo scrambled for his phone and made the call. Apparently the midwife was out on parole, since she answered. Unfortunately, part of that parole involved an ankle bracelet and an absurdly steep penalty for leaving the house.

"You two go pack a bag," my uncle told Vano and Sabina. "I'll start the car." And then he turned to me and clapped a hand on my shoulder. "Dixon, my boy—can I count on you?"

"Absolutely!"

I was so eager to find out which baby-duty I'd been picked for, I was nearly beside myself with anticipation...and so it took me a moment to absorb what Uncle Fonzo was actually asking. He said, "I can't be in two places at once—and right now, my little girl needs me. Which means you'll need to handle this whole mayor business yourself."

"You, erm, uh.... Wow. Me?"

"If Flint takes this election, I'll be up a creek without a paddle. Don't you see—the Head needs to keep an eye on the local government, make sure the community is a safe place for the members of the circuit. I'm a flexible guy, but if there's one man on the planet I can never in a million years deal with, it's Flint. What's worse, I'm sure he hasn't given up trying to steal the ability to Scribe for himself. Just think how risky it would be for every last one of our people if he ever came to power."

Geez. No pressure.

"I know you'll choose well." Uncle Fonzo gave my shoulder a reassuring squeeze. "Just do whatever it takes to make sure your candidate wins."

"You are telling him to Craft," Yuri said. "Even in America, I imagine the law would not take kindly to such a thing."

"It goes without saying you should be discreet," my uncle said as Sabina and Vano hustled themselves out the door. He grabbed his keys and hurried out right behind them, but paused in the doorway to add, "But just to be safe, don't name any names."

Normally, I'd point out that I would never dream of penning a proper name on a Crafting, even one commissioned by the subject. It was simply not done. But I suppose desperate times call for desperate measures. And when the antenna rolled to a stop half-under the TV tray that holds all of the remotes (plus a couple of spares that don't actually control anything), the screen flickered, then filled with the smug face of Emery Flint.

My blood ran cold at the sight of him, and the fateful night at Precious Greetings came rushing back, from the tarantula trap to my uncle's mutilated quill. But worst of all was the memory of Yuri enslaved, straining against the bonds of a particularly pernicious Crafting.

"Your uncle is right," Yuri said—and I half-expected a bolt of lightning to knock down the house. "Flint cannot win. At any cost."

"But each of our candidates has pros and cons—how will I pick the right one?"

"Maybe the decision does not rest with you...but with the *volshebstvo*."

These past several months, Uncle Fonzo had been training Drew Draws in the art of the Seer. Not the actual artwork part—everything my uncle tries to draw ends up looking like a rotten potato, or maybe a confused sheep. But that was fine—Drew could actually draw. What he needed to learn was harnessing the elusive energy of Spellcraft. And Uncle Fonzo knew plenty about that.

Lately, the dining room (normally a spot for card games and TV dinners) looked more like a makeshift art studio. Papers, pens, paints. Anything a Seer could want. Scriveners can't do their thing without their magical quill, but Seers can work with whatever was capable of making a mark. Yuri grabbed a paintbrush at random and snagged the nearest set of watercolors. It wasn't the tool that mattered—it was the *will* he was trying to channel.

Watching Yuri paint never gets old. He hunches over the paper and encircles it with his right arm as if he's protecting it from an impending storm. His brow furrows fiercely, and his focus narrows to the paper as if it's the only thing in the world that matters. Maybe, for that moment when he's calling down the Spellcraft, it truly is.

Is there anything in the physical world with more pure potential than a blank piece of paper? It's the canvas of a Seer, poised to receive the power of Spellcraft. It's the page of the Scrivener, waiting to be focused to the desired outcome. It's practically nothing... but that nothing is on the thrilling cusp of becoming *something.*

Yuri stared at that paper until I started to squirm. While he's never been one to dash off any old thing, this time he was concentrating particularly hard. There was just too much at stake to get it wrong.

He dampened the paper first, then laid down a few strokes of watercolor pigment, wet on wet. It wasn't the way he typically worked with his opaque gouaches, in which the colors stayed exactly where he put them. I couldn't quite make out what he was painting since his arm was in the way, but I had every confidence that whatever Yuri put on the page, I'd be able to Scribe.

By the time he set down the brush, a sheen of sweat had settled over his brow. But instead of sitting back in his chair and maybe letting his vertebrae settle in with a nice, satisfying crack, he remained hunched protectively over the work.

"Don't keep me in suspense," I finally exclaimed when I couldn't take it anymore. "Let's see what you Saw!"

With something between a grimace and a wince, Yuri drew away from the painting.

A single gray blob.

I might not be so brazen as to suggest he'd taken a play out of Rufus Clahd's playbook (mainly because I don't really understand sports analogies) but I'd never seen Yuri paint anything quite so... nonrepresentational.

I could've said it was subtle. Maybe even interesting. But Yuri really didn't appreciate it when you sugar-coated the truth. "I could run upstairs and get your usual paints," I finally said.

He scrubbed a hand over his weary face. "It would do us no good. The *volshebstvo* felt wild today, difficult to control. Any new attempts I made without resting first would only be twice as bad."

But I'd been counting on the Seen to help me figure out what I should be Scribing! *Look at that blob—who's the best man for the job?* Not only was the meter appalling, but the right man might well be a woman. I hate to think what kind of loopholes *that* would poke through the voljibby-jab.

I defocused my eyes and waited for the telltale tingle in my writing hand, but all that did was send the blob out of focus...which looked pretty much the same as it did in focus, being that it was still a blob.

Yuri gave it a poke. "It is still wet. Maybe once it dries...."

From the living room, a snippet of news broadcast pushed through all the static. "—if no one comes forth before City Hall closes today, Emery Flint will run uncontested—"

Frantically, I said, "Even if this was the best Seen in the world, there's no time to wait for it to dry."

Yuri jumped to his feet and strode out of the room. Before I could figure out whether or not I should run after him, he charged right back in with Sabina's blowdryer. "Stand aside," he said as he jammed the plug into a nearby socket. "I do not like to rush the *volshebstvo*...but it has left me no choice."

I froze in place as the blowdryer roared to life. Yuri may be the Seer, but I'd been trained my whole life to treat a Seen like it was worth its weight in gold—which it literally was, depending on the size of the paper and the current state of the futures market. I might power-dry a soggy Crafting to see if it was still active. But never an unscribed Seen, sizzling with nascent potential.

The suspense was too much to bear. By the time the blowdryer fell silent, I'd clenched every clenchable part of my body and squinched my eyes shut tight. I must have been waiting for an affirmation from Yuri. But seconds ticked by, and the all-clear never came.

Cautiously, I pried open just one eye...and found Yuri staring down at the Seen with an unreadable expression. Okay, it was a scowl. Yuri's scowls can mean any number of things: concentration, frustration, even constipation. In this particular case, though, when I saw the dried and finished Seen, I realized it was a scowl of confirmation.

Watercolor acts a lot less like gouache than you might think, especially if it's been diluted. As the water is forced out, the pigments move and blend, break and bloom. Here, what had once been a simple gray blob was now transformed into a fragile, delicate, subtly colored vista. And there could be no mistaking the contour of the bluish-gray shape in the center...because it looked exactly like an aerial shot of Pinyin Bay.

13

In our time together, Yuri has painted some incredibly stunning Seens—but this one was a real masterpiece! The delicacy of the line, the subtlety of the color, the serendipity of the pigments repelling or mixing to create waves and rocks and even a little stripe that couldn't have been anything other than a tiny little wolverine fence.

It was almost too pretty to Scribe. But not only was the whole city in danger of being taken over by Emery Flint—my Scribing arm was all a-tingle. By the time I'd inked my quill, the words came to me as clearly as the lyrics to a favorite lullaby.

Pinyin Bay deserves a mayor
who's honest, principled and fair

It sounded a lot better than *Anyone but Flint!*

My calligraphy was plain and measured. It was a sober occasion, and even the most restrained flourish would take away from the intricacy of the Seen behind it. As I dotted the final letter-i, the Spellcraft-tingles rushed down my arm, through my Quill and onto the page. But instead of feeling drained, I found myself energized. It was like a runner's high! Minus the sweaty gym socks. Plus a cockatoo quill.

Yuri, unfortunately, was still scowling. "You have done what your uncle asked of you, not naming names, and even the most vindictive judge could not fault this Crafting. But these words can apply to each of our three choices. None of them are liars. Each of them has strong principles and beliefs. And all of them, in their own way, are working to make the world a more balanced and equitable place."

And any one of them would be a way better mayor than Mr. Flint. As I searched for a good sheet of paper to start listing our pros and cons, another snatch of news broadcast sounded from the living room. "—candidates require two hundred signatures to get on the ballot."

Yuri's eyes went wide. "We only have half an hour to collect these signatures. Even if your whole family gets to forging them right this moment—"

"Actually," I realized, "that won't be necessary. There's a place where a bunch of people are just milling around, and I think they'd be happy to lend a hand."

The banana exchange was still in full swing by time we jogged up to the stand. While Yuri circulated the clipboards (and forcefully entreated people to sign *fast*), I pitched the whole mayor idea to our chosen candidate.

Luckily, it was pretty easy to convince Biff he was the right guy for the job. All I had to do was mention how much good he could do for the community—and the fact that he'd get to wield a big pair of novelty scissors at any ribbon-cutting ceremony—and he was totally on board.

As the clock ticked down, we bounded up the block, through the scraggly dog park, and across Main Street—taking care to use the crosswalk so as not to incur the world's most inopportune jaywalking ticket. I heaved myself up the City Hall steps two at a time with the signatures clutched to my chest, and just as the octogenarian clerk was tottering toward the entrance to lock up for the night, Yuri flung himself at the door. As he held it open, I skidded across the threshold and thrust the signatures into the clerk's wrinkled hands.

He was none too thrilled to stick around and count them. But according to the letter of the law, our signatures only needed to be submitted by closing time. Not counted. (Plus, there were fifty lines per page, so it didn't take long after all to see we'd met the requirement with a few names to spare.)

"Done and done." I dusted my hands together. "Now let's head over to the midwife's and greet our new little niece...nephew...first cousin once removed."

Yuri's eyes softened. "Agreed—let us greet the baby."

We climbed into the truck, and I relayed the address Uncle Fonzo had texted me. "It was really nice of the midwife to see Sabina in her own home."

"Nice, or pragmatic?" Yuri said. "With the ankle bracelet, she had no other choice."

"Anyway, I'm sure that's a good thing. Could you imagine poor Sabina having her baby on the davenport with Drew Draws scribbling away in the dining room and Uncle Fonzo's poker buddies smoking cigars on the porch?"

Yuri shuddered.

As we made our way over, I tried to picture what sort of environment a midwife would call home. "I'll bet her house is an oasis of calm. Clean lines, soothing colors, boring artwork, that sort of thing."

Yuri steered the truck around the corner and nearly snapped an axle as we careened off a massive pothole.

Welcome to Scrivener Village.

We drove a few more crooked blocks, and turned a blind corner... and there, between a mustache groomer and a second-hand flip-flop outlet, was a squat brick bungalow owned by the circuit's midwife, Bessie Hackles.

While the buildings all around had the typical ramshackle look so common in this part of town, Bessie's home was neat, quiet, even sedate. The lawn was trimmed, the pavement was swept, and the welcome mat was perfectly centered at the front door. "You see, Yuri?" I said. "Everything has a way of working out for the—"

A burst of gunfire sounded from the other side of the door, followed by the wail of a police siren. *Inside* the house.

"It's the TV," Yuri said, then proceeded to knock. Loudly.

Uncle Fonzo shoved open the door and pulled me into a rough hug as the massive cloud of sound enveloped us. Helicopters, and a distant explosion. "Great work getting Biff on the ballot! I knew I could count on you."

"So you're not upset I chose Biff?"

"He wasn't son-in-law material, that's for sure. But he'll make a nice, pliant Mayor!"

Uncle Fonzo really did get along with just about everyone.

He ushered us into the midwife's house and closed the door behind us. Once we'd crowded into the tiny entryway, I saw the source of all the sirens and explosions. The hallway opened into an orderly living room. The couch, coffee table and love seat were at perpendicular angles and the knickknacks on the book shelves had been aligned with great precision. The focus of the room was an ancient console TV that could double as a Winnebago. As I took in the massive tube in all its Technicolor glory, a helicopter in a rain of gunfire exploded...followed by a thin cackle from the opposite side of the room.

I turned to behold an old crone of a Scrivener ensconced in a floral-upholstered swivel rocker. She had an afghan across her lap and a bowl of cheese puffs on her knee. Her hair was steel gray, caught in a severe bun, and her eyes were pale with cataracts. Something else blew up on the TV, and she howled with delight. She may have had only one tooth—but at least it was a big one.

Yuri made the little kowabunga surfer gesture he does when he's feeling particularly superstitious, but the old woman didn't seem to notice.

"That's Mother Felicity," Uncle Fonzo said. "Bessie's mom. Happy as a clam so long as she can watch her shows."

"It's an honor to meet you," I told her.

"And she's pretty much deaf," Uncle Fonzo said.

"It's an honor to meet you!" I said, several decibels louder. "I'm Dixon Penn, and this is my grown man friend, Yuri!" Mother Felicity was pretty wrapped up in her shoot-em-up helicopter siren car chase and I couldn't quite say if she'd heard me or not, so I decided to leave her to it.

More gunfire, followed by a scream. Except the scream had come not from the TV...but the next room. "Sabina's in labor for real this time," Uncle Fonzo said. "But according to Bessie, it will take a while."

While my uncle went on ahead, Yuri bent to my ear and said, "Enough time to get her to a real hospital."

I wrapped my hand around his (casually suppressing the "horn" sign) and said, "You mean a Handless hospital. Look, Yuri, I've spent more time be-bopping around the world of the Handless than any other Scrivener I know, and so I totally get how some of our traditions come across a little convoluted and backward. But seeing our ways with fresh eyes, I've actually come to appreciate how we stick to our own values. Sabina wanted the midwife. We need to respect her decision."

Though when another strangled wail punctuated my argument, I could tell it wouldn't be easy.

The dining room held both the dining and kitchen tables, with the chairs all stacked up to leave a clear path through the room. And where the kitchen table would normally be, a hospital bed was set up. I averted my eyes from the stirrups...but unfortunately, I couldn't un-see them.

Thankfully, my cousin wasn't currently using said stirrups. She was waddling a slow lap around the room, with Vano supporting her on one side, and a drill sergeant of a middle-aged woman on the other.

Bessie Hackles had short-cropped hair, no-nonsense glasses, and plain clothes covered by a disposable plastic smock. Her sleeves were rolled up, and her forearms were just as ropy as Yuri's, though not quite as hairy. No doubt she was periodically addressed as "sir" by many a confused store clerk. When we came in, she glanced at us and barked, "Leave any Craftings you're carrying at the door. It's bad luck to Craft for a child until the head's all the way out."

"See, Yuri?" I squeezed his hand. "She's totally done this before."

Yuri was not reassured. "Should Sabina be walking around?"

With great authority, Bessie replied, "This is her first labor, and the contractions are still fifteen minutes apart. We could be here for several hours."

"We'd better be!" my cousin insisted. "I've always wanted to name a kid Wednesday." This was news to me, but I didn't contradict her. "I can't have it on a Monday."

The baby appeared to be onboard with Sabina's timetable and was in no hurry to greet us. Mother Felicity tottered off to bed, and midnight came and went. By the time the wee hours of Tuesday morning rolled around, the baby was still firmly ensconced...and I saw the logic in all the walking. Worn out, Sabina rolled onto the hospital bed to catnap between contractions while an exhausted Vano collapsed in a hammock on the back porch and my uncle snoozed on the couch.

Bessie said Yuri and I might as well go home and sleep in our own bed—but since she knew how Spellcrafters could be, she wasn't surprised we insisted on sticking around. We curled up together on the rug under the dining room table to be sure we'd be nearby if my cousin needed anything...though after the third or fourth wakeup to Sabina's grunting and panting, I just started incorporating the noises into some vivid dreams of being chased by an out-of-breath wolverine.

I woke to the sound of early-morning cartoons. Really violent ones, with more explosions, followed by "boing" sounds and sad trombones, all of it punctuated by the wheezy cackles of Mother Felicity. As I crawled out from under the table and brushed myself off, my stomach growled and I realized just how long it had been since I'd last eaten. "I'll go make a breakfast run," I announced to the house at large.

"No need," Bessie said. "Whatever's outside is fair game."

Yuri cut his eyes to me...but it was way too early to pretend I knew what *that* was supposed to mean. Luckily Uncle Fonzo did. He pried himself off the couch and said, "C'mon, kiddo, I'll need the extra pair of hands." To the cheerful sound of cartoon violence, I followed him out the front door...and found myself knee-deep in bins, bowls and baskets. Uncle Fonzo surveyed the bounty. "Not a bad porching, if I do say so myself."

"Porching," I repeated, trying on the word for size. "I had no idea that was even a thing."

"Why would you? When Sabina was born, you were only a toddler. You had no reason to think food didn't just appear on the doorstep every day of the year."

There were cookies and casseroles, sandwiches and stews—everything decorated with festive ribbons and bows, with cards tucked inside wishing the new baby a lifetime of happiness and luck. All of it in flawless calligraphy. Some thoughtful soul had even left us a big urn of coffee.

We carted the haul inside and arranged it on the dining room table I'd spent the night underneath. It was a far cry from cold, dried out take-and-bake pizza. Unfortunately, Sabina was too preoccupied to enjoy the goodies. As I picked a stray ribbon from my sleeve, she gave a strangled cry and told Vano a good dozen ways in which she'd like to kill him.

By the time our bellies were so full we all bore a striking resemblance to Sabina, it became clear that the baby still wasn't quite imminent, and our thoughts turned to the election. Good thing Mother Felicity hobbled off to the bathroom every half hour. (No pelvic floor, according to Bessie...which neither Yuri nor I really wanted to know.) Wifi was patchy and cell service no better, so her periodic pee breaks were the only time we could switch to the local news and see how Biff's mayoral bid was faring.

In the exit polls, a few folks did admit to voting for Emery Flint—not that they particularly wanted a felon for a mayor, but they just weren't a big fan of bananas. Nonetheless, Biff was something of a local celebrity, and most voters were eager to have him installed at City Hall.

In between election updates and contractions, Bessie saw to it that we didn't just lounge around. She put us all to work, my uncle washing windows, Yuri beating the carpets, me mopping the floor—and Vano sitting around looking carelessly fetching. He was also getting his non-Scribing hand squeezed nearly off by my cousin, though, so I supposed I wouldn't have wanted to trade places.

"Anytime now," Bessie finally said around nightfall—and she wasn't talking about the election results.

"Not yet!" Sabina insisted. "Tuesday is a ridiculous name for a kid!" In fact, she was so determined to hold that baby in until the clock struck midnight, the rest of us started to worry. My parents had shown up by that time for moral support—or to avail themselves of the porching—and they even stopped taunting each other for the time being about who would find the kee-poo.

My father said, "Just tell Sabina her contractions are farther apart then they really are until she thinks it's midnight."

"You've never been in labor," my mother informed the menfolk. "Sabina's not gonna stop and do calculus." Especially since she wasn't capable of it even without a baby pushing out of her swimsuit area.

Bessie agreed. "She must think it's at least Friday by now. I'll put 12:01 on the birth certificate and no one need be the wiser."

That might have worked, had it not been for the news now breaking through Mother Felicity's blaring programs to periodically reassure Pinyin Bay that they expected the votes to be counted by midnight. "I can make her a hot toddy," Uncle Fonzo offered. "Send her off to bed."

Bessie shook her head. "Don't get Mother started—you think the shows are loud? Just wait until she gets a drink in her and starts to sing. You don't appreciate how disturbing sea shanties are until you hear them at the top of her lungs."

A strangled scream from the kitchen—followed by a volley of

particularly colorful cursing—cut through the motorcycle chase raging through the living room TV screen.

"I'll just ask her nicely to go to bed," I decided, and headed over to try and reason with Mother Felicity.

The old woman had her cloudy eyes glued to the screen, where a motorcycle hung in mid-air for a moment, and then careened over a cliff, hit a ravine, and landed with a loud crunch. She let out a joyous cackle.

"Say, would you look at the time," I hollered over the noise. "Sure is getting late. I'll bet your snug, cozy bed is sounding really appealing right about now."

Mother Felicity's bluish cataract gaze fell on me—wow, I was actually making progress!—but instead of agreeing with me, she just pointed at me and let out another hearty cackle.

Startled, I fell back a step or two...and Uncle Fonzo gestured at a stray mop-string clinging to my shoulder. "How'd that get there?" I wondered. It wasn't as if I'd been mopping all that vigorously. "Random things have been sticking to me so much lately, you'd swear I was wearing a velcro jacket."

The soundtrack on the action show went low and dramatic as the motorcyclist clawed his way out from the wreckage in the ravine. To the sound of the tense violins—in the first time I'd actually heard her speak—old Mother Felicity declared,

"He who has this has the way to
Take the family well in Hand
Others must not countermand
Or doubt the wisdom of the kee-poo."

There was a moment of stunned silence...and then the TV motorcycle exploded.

YURI

14

Dixon's eyes went wide in wonder, and then guilt, as he tried to brush the string from his shoulder—a string which was clearly in the shape of a hand.

As had been the strand of garbage clinging to him from Bolter's dumpster, I realized. And the bit of yarn from the Buick's afghan. While Dixon's mother and father turned their little corner of Pinyin Bay inside out searching for the kee-poo, it had been stuck on him all along.

His parents were currently in the kitchen with Sabina, whose cursing had drowned out the old woman's singsong proclamation. But Fonzo and I both knew she was right. Dixon had been chosen. Not his mother. Not his father. Dixon.

"Obviously, Mother Felicity is mixed up," he said nervously. "Either one of my parents is infinitely more qualified than I am to be the next Hand."

"Hold on now, kiddo," Fonzo said. "I was only a few years older than you when your grandfather decided he'd had enough and named me the next Hand. I have every confidence you can do it. But...if you're truly not up for the job, I'll go stick the kee-poo on one of your folks. It'll be our little secret."

Not only was he offering to relieve Dixon of the responsibility of taking up his mantle. Fonzo was also willing to bear the burden of choosing the next Hand himself.

Judging by the look of concern on Dixon's face, he might very well take his uncle up on the offer.

But I could not let him do that just because he was overwhelmed. I caught his hand and gave it a squeeze. "Dixon, before you second-guess the *volshebstvo*, think about the arguments each of your parents made against the other. Your father is not creative...but you are. Your mother is not personable. But you are. You have the important traits they lack."

Dixon winced. "That's pretty harsh...."

"Think," I insisted. "Remember everything you and I considered when we were choosing our candidate for mayor. Sherman was filled with enthusiasm, even passion, for his beliefs. That is you. Glenda was intelligent and capable. That is also you. And Biff was friendly, outgoing, and dedicated to making Pinyin Bay a better place. All of these things describe you. I may not always see eye to eye with the *volshebstvo*, but in this case, I am in agreement. There is no one better to lead the family."

The old woman chortled and said, "You passed the test...the kee-poo knows best."

I released Dixon's hand and surreptitiously warded her away with the sign of the *koza*.

In the kitchen, Sabina gave a strangled cry—and this time, Bessie barked out, "It's time to push! Just like we practiced: four, three, two, one—push! Four, three, two, one...."

It was a wonder Pinyin Bay's Scrivener children didn't come out ready to march in a parade. But apparently the woman knew what she was doing. Sabina stopped complaining about the tardiness of midnight and went about the business of having her child.

I am none too fond of the word *miracle*, but considering the sense of elation I felt at the prospect of this child coming into the world, I could think of no better description. I stopped worrying about the election—after all, our Crafting would ensure a just mayor—and crept into the kitchen with the rest of the family.

Vano bent over Sabina, squeezing her hand and stroking her sweaty brow. "You got this, Sabina—just a few more pushes! You're gonna be the best mom ever."

Even I knew *that* was a stretch...but the way Vano gazed at her with total adoration, I suspected he believed it.

Dixon was the last Penn to slip into the room, studiously avoiding a glance between the stirrups. It must have been a challenge, given how eager he was to see the baby. But there were some things that should remain a mystery. He slipped an arm through mine and pressed up against my side. "They called the election," he said quietly. "Beauregard Irving Fitzgerald is Pinyin Bay's new mayor."

A great victory for the city's Spellcrafters, no doubt. But at the moment, the news paled in comparison to the arrival of the new baby.

It was just past eleven when Bessie Hackles stopped shouting marching orders, cracked her knuckles, and had Sabina give a great, final push.

And then...the newest member of the family greeted the world.

As the midwife cleaned the baby with a warm, wet towel, a tiny cry could be heard, even above the sirens and gunfire ringing through the living room. "It's a girl," Bessie said brusquely. "A healthy baby girl."

I looked eagerly toward the baby...and caught sight of the umbilical cord instead. My vision went gray around the edges and my ears began to ring. When my sight cleared, I was seated in the dining room with Dixon chafing my wrist. "Oh good, you're with us again! I felt a little faint myself for a minute there."

"I did not faint."

"And the placenta—who knew?—like something out of Sherman Bolter's dumpster diving excursions."

My vision grayed again. When I shook it off, Dixon was saying, "...but thanks to the TV constantly butting in with the election countdown, there's no way we can convince my cousin she made it past midnight. Maybe you can make her feel better."

Something no one has ever suggested to me. "How?"

"By imparting some comforting Russian wisdom, of course."

Perhaps I was still unconscious. But no. My mind could never have invented the exuberant uproar of the situation—Dixon's parents bickering, the TV blaring, the old crone cackling, and Sabina complaining. As I made my way back to the kitchen steadying myself on Dixon's shoulder, my eyes went right to the new baby cradled in Sabina's arms—pink and healthy, with chubby cheeks and a shock of Scrivener-black hair. Somehow, in the midst of all the hubbub, the little one slept the sleep of pure contentment.

Maybe she'd experienced so much commotion, even in the womb, she was inured to it all. Or maybe Spellcrafters have an inborn knack for thriving in the face of chaos.

Vano gazed at the baby with the same rapt adoration he gave her mother. "It's Wednesday in Australia," he offered.

"Does she *look* Australian to you?" Sabina demanded, though without any real ire. "Wednesday's a stupid name anyhow. Clearly, this baby is a Tuesday."

At least she didn't name the baby after Biff. That would have been awkward.

Dixon came up on tiptoe and pressed his lips to my ear. "We'll tell them about the kee-poo later. I wouldn't want to upstage little Tuesday's arrival."

So, he had decided to take on the duties of the Hand after all. I had meant what I told him before: he truly was the best one for the job. And knowing his parents, they would get over the sting of not being the next Hand soon enough. They were proud of Dixon already, and as the Hand, he'd give them even more reason to be pleased with all he'd accomplished. One could even argue that by choosing Dixon, the kee-poo chose them both.

But for now, all the family really cared about was the new baby.

An overjoyed Fonzo shoved a cigar into my hand, though thankfully, he didn't expect me to actually light it. I watched him head out to the backyard with Johnny to smoke the foul things, and wondered what it would mean for him to head the Pinyin Bay circuit. The Penn family had always been somewhere in the middle of the pack—respectable enough, though no great success. Joining with the Shirques was bound to be interesting, to say the least.

"While I call Nana, did you want to hold the baby?" Vano asked Dixon—and if that didn't soften Dixon's disposition toward him, nothing would. Dixon's face was alight with wonder as Sabina placed Tuesday in his arms. He snuggled up against me so that while he held the baby, I could wrap my arms around them both. Tuesday let out a contented snuffle and Dixon trembled with joy. And as for me...I had often thought my heart was already impossibly full. But again, I was reminded that there was always room for more.

A short while later, the baby woke up hungry, and we handed her back and hurried out of the kitchen so as not to gawk at Sabina's body parts. Mother Felicity was still in the living room—would the old woman never go to sleep? "Gee, it's late," Dixon called out over the TV. "Do you want me to help you upstairs?"

Onscreen, a dump truck careened off a bridge, spraying a load of fireworks, which exploded with an elaborate light show...but then the music swelled and the credits rolled. As the old woman reached for the remote, she said, "The Hand, the Head, the mayor elect, nothing quite like you'd expect."

Even Dixon looked disturbed. And he loves rhymes.

"Time for bed," I said firmly. Felicity's rheumy eyes locked on mine, and with a cryptic smile, she jabbed at the remote...not to turn off the set, but to change the channel.

A news desk filled the screen. "—sources say the last-minute change of the election date is to blame for the oversight. Counters are hard at work logging in the newly discovered avalanche of mail-in ballots, and we expect to reconfirm the election of Mr. Fitzgerald shortly."

Was it my imagination, or did I feel the tingle of the *volshebstvo* playing across the back of my neck?

The news anchor paused to listen to his earpiece and his eyes went wide. "In an unprecedented turn of events, a write-in candidate has overtaken *both* candidates on the ballot."

I chafed away the prickle on my scalp, calling to mind exactly what Dixon and I had Crafted. On my part, a perfect representation of the city. On his, a public official who was principled, fair and just. As long as Emery Flint was not elected, I told myself, surely there would be no problem...though I was clenching Dixon's shoulder hard enough to make him wince.

The anchor said, "A total recount is scheduled for tomorrow—as well as another *really good* look at the mailroom—but preliminary figures indicate that Pinyin Bay's next mayor is long-time Pinyin Bay resident and respected police officer, Herschel Hotti."

A file photo of Officer Hotti filled the screen, giving a stern solute as the police chief handed him some sort of silly award. The anchor began listing all of Hotti's various achievements and qualifications. While Hotti did seem to be qualified—and was most definitely a better choice than Emery Flint—concepts like fairness and justice mean something entirely different to a Spellcrafter than they do to the general public.

Hotti's brand of fairness couldn't possibly jibe with that of a Scrivener. And yet, for whatever reason, the *volshebstvo* had chosen to side with the masses.

"You win some, you lose some," Dixon's mother declared as she bustled out of the kitchen with a huge bag of porching food. "Just make sure no one catches you when you cheat."

Once Dixon's parents headed home and Mother Felicity tottered off to bed, Dixon and I found ourselves alone in the midwife's fastidiously neat and strangely quiet living room. He craned his neck to peer into the kitchen and make sure everyone else was occupied, then retrieved his messenger bag and pulled out the Crafting. "I know my mother was just saying one of her Mom-isms...but I really would hate to be caught trying to influence an election. Especially if, after the recount, stick-in-the-mud Officer Hotti does turn out to be the new mayor."

On one hand, I had no love of a man as besotted with rules as seem more vigilant about Spellcraft than your ess. But on the other, I suspected he would be dif- impossible, to corrupt.

es, if Biff ever were to take office, it was only a matter of oefore he got stuck in the revolving doors at City Hall and ever found his way out again.

"I could make an argument for or against the policeman," I told Dixon, "But in every way that matters, I am a part of the Penn family—and you are the family's Hand. It is your opinion that counts. Whatever you decide, I am behind you."

Dixon gave me a long, assessing look—for him, a very serious look, indeed. And then he smiled, eyes twinkling, and said lightly, "Except when I'm the big spoon, Yuri—and then *I'm* behind *you*."

If there was any concern that Dixon was not ready to be the Hand, those worries were groundless. He took only a moment to consider the Crafting before he tore it in half to set it, and tucked it back into his bag to dispose of later. He shivered and chafed away some goosebumps...and then he leaned in, nestled his head against my shoulder, and said, "Just when I think I'm the happiest guy in the world, you say or do something that makes me even happier."

I covered Dixon's hand with mine, enjoying the faint tingle of the *volshebstvo* dissipating between us. Various replies occurred to me, but none of them held a candle to how I felt...and in the end, the best response I could give was to turn and press my lips to his.

ABOUT THE AUTHOR

When Jordan Castillo Price finds something stuck to her, it is invariably cat hair, and never a kee-poo.
She would love to attend a competitive eating event someday.

www.jordancastilloprice.com

www.ingramcontent.com/pod-product-compliance
Lightning Source LLC
LaVergne TN
LVHW041109080826
845145LV00007B/1740